THE BROTHERHOOD OF LIGHT AND DARKNESS

A∴ T∴

R∴

THE BROTHERHOOD OF LIGHT AND DARKNESS

AN ALEXANDER SEBASTIAN NOVEL

A∴   T∴

R∴

BY JASON AUGUSTUS NEWCOMB

The New Hermetics Press

Sarasota, FL

First published in 2007 by
The New Hermetics Press
P. O. Box 18111
Sarasota, FL 34276
www.newhermetics.com

Cover Design and typesetting by Fr∴ E. I. A. E.

ISBN: 978-0-6151-5683-5

14 13 12 11 10 09 08 07
8 7 6 5 4 3 2 1

Special thanks to the many wonderful readers who cast a critical eye on the early draft of this book, including Bob, Mike, Joel, Leila, Carlos and any others who I am shamefully neglecting.

OTHER BOOKS BY JASON AUGUSTUS NEWCOMB

Nonfiction:

21ˢᵗ Century Mage (Weiser Books, 2002)
The New Hermetics (Weiser Books, 2004)
Sexual Sorcery (Weiser Books, 2005)
The Book of Magick Power (New Hermetics Press, 2007)
Practical Enochian Magick (forthcoming)
The Advanced Adept Manual and Workbook (forthcoming)

Dedicated to my Mom

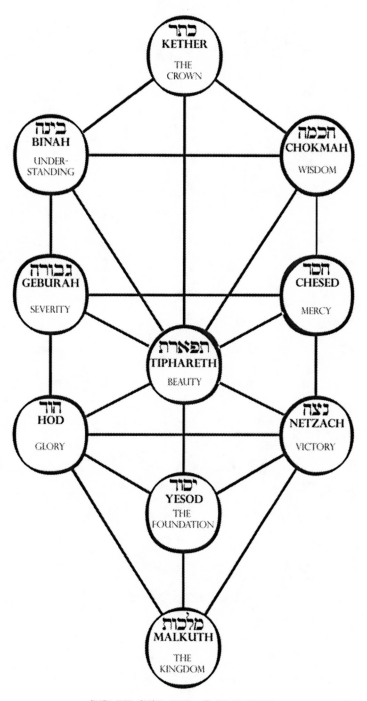

THE TREE OF LIFE

ONE

☿ Wednesday, September 18, 1996

5:45 PM

I sat on the edge of my bed, finished the last few hits from a joint, and began to escape into one of my usual flights of fancy. If memory serves, my favorite daydream at the time was that I was a rock star who became a sort of messiah with fans who were disciples of my doctrine of mystical realization through special brainwave-enhancing frequencies of distortion guitar. I know, it's embarrassing, but all too true.

I think at a certain point in life, most people realize they are probably not going to be a Mozart or an Einstein, or even a one-hit wonder pop star, and settle into some form of middle-class mediocrity. But at twenty-four years old, I was still entertaining pretty grandiose fantasies about myself. Despite the fact that in all honesty I'd never achieved anything of significance in any endeavor, I still felt sure that my true destiny was just waiting to knock on my door. I spent my days waiting for this call to greatness, occupying my time smoking pot and fantasizing about my illustrious future.

But today's reverie was shattered by the sound of the front door opening. Shit! I'd completely forgotten that my sister and her stupid cop husband were coming over for dinner. I could hear them walking through the front hall, and my mom's ridiculous cooing.

"Don't you two look lovely! Such a pleasure to have such beautiful visitors..." Then she shouted up to me, quite loudly, "Alex, get down here and greet your sister and Peter!"

1

This didn't sit very well with me. I considered myself a grown man, however ludicrous that sounds looking back at the situation. I was still living in my mother's house, with no real plans for my future. I was hardly a grown up. But the thought of my 'mommy' calling me down to say 'hello' to visitors was what seemed ridiculous to me at the time. And family time was always a total buzz killer. Still, I stumbled down and greeted them as politely as possible while I avoided looking them directly in the eyes. I always had a serious case of red-eye when I smoked that Visine never really helped.

With my view angled toward the floor I noticed that my sister and her husband were dressed up more than usual. Peter was wearing a cheap-looking gray suit with a red shirt and matching tie, while Therese was wearing a sort of burgundy evening dress thing with little fake pearls around her neck. Their outfits were totally incongruous in my mom's ragged living room, with its mismatched chairs and completely worn out wooden floors. They almost looked like missionaries, Jehovah's Witnesses or something, trying to save my mother and I from our pathetic lives of suburban decay.

A confusing feeling of guilt crept up my spine. Had I forgotten some important event? Was I hopelessly underdressed? My t-shirt had rather questionable stains and numerous holes. I'd been wearing the same jeans for at least three days. Yes, I was really a disaster.

But I couldn't think of any reason why they would be dressed up either. There was no special occasion. I was sure of it. If these two wanted to play dress-up that didn't mean I had to. After all, my mom was just wearing her usual faded house-dress in an indeterminate shade of pastel.

6:05 PM

We all sat in near silence, eating my mom's dinner- fish sticks I believe. I felt vindicated. Therese and Peter were official-ly over-dressed. My attire was perfectly appropriate for fish sticks.

Suddenly, Peter broke the silence with a very strange question. "So Alex," he said, clearly trying to sound nonchalant.

"Your sister tells me you know a little bit about witchcraft and Satanism. That true?"

"Uh, yeah, sort of," I muttered with a mouthful of fish stick.

"Do you know anything about five-pointed stars and maybe, I don't know, black magic curses?" He said it with a noticeable eagerness that crept through his attempt to sound casual.

"Um, well, sure, I guess," I said, hoping this wasn't going to be a drawn out discussion. I was far too stoned to have this kind of conversation with Peter Ippolito the cop.

To tell the truth, I'd been modestly collecting occult books since I was about thirteen. The subject deeply interested me in a sort of impractical philosophical way, and I had about thirty or forty occult books in my room. But I really didn't know much about "black magic" or "Satanism" other than some reading. Although I fantasized about occultism quite a bit, I'd never had any kind of real experience in the subject.

But before Peter could discover how little I really knew, my mother cleared her throat in irritation. "Let's not talk about this at the dinner table," she said with just the slightest bit of force under her tone, and Peter quickly changed the subject, engaging in a long monologue about the recent warm weather.

7:45 PM

Later, while we all sat in my mom's shabby living room chairs drinking after-dinner beers, Peter brought up the subject of the occult once more. He asked me again what I knew about five-pointed stars. My mom cleared her throat again, but there was no stopping Peter this time.

I told him pretty much everything I knew about pentagrams in just a few sentences. "From what I know, in modern ritual magick pentagrams, er, five-pointed stars, are basically symbols of, well, protection and power. The five points represent the four ancient elements and the fifth element of spirit. I think they're used to command invisible entities and spirits."

"What, like ghosts?" Peter asked.

"More like angels or demons, or elementals."

"I told you he knew all about this creepy shit," said my sister, sneering. She almost always sneered when she talked about me.

Peter ignored my sister and gave me a bright smile. "So tell me more," he said. "I'm fascinated."

"I guess it all depends on the way you trace them. They banish or command different spirits when you trace them in different ways," I said, waving my finger around like a wand.

"Hmmm. And what about if they're drawn on surfaces like walls or paper or... skin?"

"Uh, I guess that would be talismans, or amulets, or sigils or something," I mumbled. I really had no idea what I was talking about, but Peter seemed impressed.

He stared at me intensely for several seconds, really stared right through me, then smiled again and said, "Do you think you might be willing to come down to the station tomorrow and look at a few photographs from a crime scene?"

My mom seemed quite troubled by the proposition, but it sounded extremely interesting to me. I'd never seen photographs from a real crime scene, and I found myself incredibly curious to see photographs of a crime scene that somehow involved pentagrams, witchcraft and Satanism. Was it some sort of ritual killing, right here in Arlington, Massachusetts?

I had no idea how much trouble my curiosity was about to get me into. He told me I needed to come to the station early the next morning. Early morning wasn't generally the best time for me, but I assured him I'd do my best.

Two

4 Thursday, September 19, 1996

11:45 AM

Despite my best intentions, I didn't manage to wake up very early at all. I believe it was shortly after eleven. But as soon as I was coherent enough to operate my car, I started to make my way down to the Arlington center police station. I stopped briefly at my favorite Dunkin Donuts for a little coffee to go along with my first cigarette, struggled to quickly gulp down the burning hot beverage, and made my way up Mass. Ave to my appointment.

As I stepped inside the station I began to feel an escalating queasiness. I had no idea what was actually going to be expected of me, and there's something really quite creepy about the inside of a police station.

A large, overweight man in a police uniform sat behind a metal reinforced glass screen right at the entrance to the station. He had an expressionless face that sat uneasily on his bulbous head, all held in place by a greasy comb over. I nervously identified myself as "Alexander Sebastian," and asked him for Detective Peter Ippolito. He pointed toward a gray metal door with a grunt. I approached the door and heard the loud 'click' of a lock opening. As I pushed the heavy door open I noticed that there seemed to be an inch of grayish filth coating everything in the building. The whole place smelled like thirty years of stale cigarette smoke mingled with a layer of Windex, creating a dull, bitter foulness. The inner labyrinth of desks and offices was a thoroughly unaesthetic mass of cement, industrial metal, plastic, and paper, too bleak to even fully register on my consciousness.

Peter seemed a bit perturbed when he saw me, grumbling something about missing lunch. As uniformed police officers walked past they stared at me narrowly with dull eyes, like I was some sort of derelict under arrest. I quickly found myself wanting to get out of there as fast as possible.

I slumped into a chair at Peter's desk and stared down at his name placard: "Det. Peter Ippolito." It was a cheap looking plastic thing. The whole police station seemed cheap, dingy and unkempt.

Peter ceremoniously opened his desk drawer and took out a fairly thick file folder. He pulled out a stack of photos from the top of the file, but didn't hand them to me. As he glanced down at them he visibly cringed and quickly shoved them under the fold of his armpit. He looked at me gravely. "These photographs are quite graphic," he said. "They might be a bit disturbing to look at."

Nothing could have really prepared me for what was in store. He hesitantly pushed the photographs into my hands and the gore nearly leaped off the pages. I'd never seen anything so incredibly disgusting in my life. The pictures were of a man disemboweled. The majority of his insides were on the outside. It was like he'd been torn to pieces by a bloodthirsty wild animal. It was putrid, insane. I'd seen some things like this in movies, but somehow knowing it was real, I just felt like vomiting.

Peter told me that the victim's name was Edward Bailey, but I could barely even recognize the slumped and mangled mass of gore as a human being. I knew I had to avert my eyes soon or I was going to be sick all over that smelly, dirty, police station.

I began to wonder why Peter was even showing me this when I noticed that there were strange, occult symbols everywhere amidst carnage. The body seemed to be lying in the remnants of some sort of magical circle, and all through the pictures, on the walls, floors, and on what was left of his skin, there were dozens of pentagrams, other magical looking symbols and what looked like numerous different arcane scripts. There were concentric circles of bizarre symbols, as well as more randomly scrawled glyphs on pieces of blood-soaked paper scattered throughout the room.

"I really have no idea what the hell I'm looking at," I said immediately. I felt like I was just barely holding back from throwing up. I told him that whatever this was, it way beyond my knowledge level.

He proceeded to explain that they discovered this insanity two days earlier in a townhouse on Grant Avenue, in the wealthiest part of town. "I've never had a case like this, Alex," said Peter, suddenly looking a bit vulnerable. He actually glanced around the large open room to make sure that no one else was paying attention. Apparently no one was. "I've never even heard of a case like this in Arlington- ever. It's really important that I close this."

"Sure," I said shakily. "I'll try to help if there's any way I can." I felt completely overwhelmed and totally under-qualified. What could I possibly know about something like this? But I found myself looking through the pictures over and over, despite my queasiness. There was a horrible, gruesome sort of sublimity in those photographs. The blackening gore smeared across the spidery lines of occult diagrams. It was fascinating and sickening all at once.

"That'd mean so much to me, Alex, to me and your sister. This case could mean big things for me. Therese and I could really use a better pay grade, you know?"

I'd hardly ever seen this more human side of Peter. I felt unsure how to respond. I really didn't want to fully like him, because I instinctively disliked cops, but he was suddenly starting to grow on me. I still didn't know how I could possibly be of any help.

Peter told me they found drugs and drug paraphernalia all over the apartment, and near toxic levels of heroin and cocaine, as well as THC, in his bloodstream. It seemed he was attacked and brutally killed right in the middle of a massive overdose. He asked me a bunch of repetitive questions about the occult symbols visible in the pictures, despite my inability to answer any of them. He said that anything I recognized might be helpful, handing me a piece of paper with a number of symbols crudely rendered on it.

"These are a few of the symbols we found at the scene," he said. "We found them repeated several times. Maybe you can at least tell me what these are?"

I took the sheet, but I could barely even look at it. I felt guilty that I was being so unhelpful, but all I could think about was that poor, pathetic guy, disemboweled on the floor of his apartment. I really had to get the hell out of there. I needed a cigarette, and a lot of pot. I told him I'd see what I could find out about the symbols on the sheet, and stumbled queasily out of the station.

THREE

2:00 PM (approx.)

When I got home I immediately rushed up to my room and smoked a huge amount of pot. I really wanted to get those pictures out of my head. But they wouldn't go. And I soon found myself starting to get curious again. There's really no stopping my curiosity once it gets started. This was definitely, by far, the most interesting thing I'd ever seen in my life. The mutilated corpse, those occult symbols all over the place, it all seemed like some kind of supernatural nightmare- like the poor guy had been torn to shreds by a monster or a demon- something right out of a horror movie or an H. P. Lovecraft novel.

Peter had told me he was sure it was some kind of ritualistic cult activity- some sort of Satanic cult. I'd dutifully informed him that as far as I knew Satanists don't really even exist except in the form of zitty, teen-aged losers wearing upside down pentagram necklaces and reading those silly Anton LaVey "Church of Satan" books. He didn't seem impressed. It was all about the pentagrams for Peter. Pentagrams at the crime scene- pentagrams around the Satanists necks- it all added up. I told him that I really couldn't help him with that theory, and he was very disappointed.

Sitting there in my room, smoking, I found myself drawn back into the murder scene, running the pictures through my mind over and over in agonizing detail. I started thinking that maybe somehow this murder was my destiny finally calling on me. Something was stirring inside me, something I'd never experienced before. I found myself feeling an unfamiliar sense- that I really needed investigate, to understand what was actually going on in that bloody townhouse. I'd seen a hidden

9

realm of dreams and nightmares open up to me in those forensic photos. There was real black magick going on right under my nose. And maybe, just maybe, I could have some role to play in discovering this occult killer. I was certainly no expert on the occult, but I had read a good deal about it. Was there an outside chance that I could really help Peter? The symbols I'd seen looked familiar. I thought they might be in one or more of my books somewhere. But even if I knew what the symbols were, could that even tell me anything about this murder? The more important issue was certainly discovering who these people were, really practicing black magick right here in Arlington, Massachusetts. I needed to discover this world. I needed to find out what was really going on.

I started thinking about this girl I knew from high school, Kerrydwen. She used to call herself Kerrie, but her name was Kerrydwen. I'd always had a little crush on her, but I'd never had the courage to try to make anything happen between us. She was a very pretty girl, sweet and funny. She'd had blonde hair that was matted in those grubby Caucasian dreadlocks, but somehow they worked for her. I think it was because she was just so damned beautiful. But the reason she popped into my mind wasn't because she was beautiful.

It was because her parents were witches. Not 'Sabrina the Teenage...' or 'Harry Potter...' They were neo-pagans. They had a 'coven' and danced around bonfires on the full moon and all that. And they owned a pagan bookstore.

It pretty much made her a total outcast in school. I always liked to talk with her, and she seemed to like me too. I even talked with her about magick and the occult pretty regularly. She invited me to a few of her parents' full moon ceremonies and some pagan festivals, but I was always too nervous to really go. We were pretty good friends at school, you know, ate lunch together sometimes. I think we went to a few parties together too. That whole high school period of my life is a bit of a blur. I hadn't talked to her in years.

I certainly wasn't thinking that her family or their 'coven' had anything to do with any kind of crime, let alone a grisly murder. I knew about modern witchcraft, that it was basically just a Goddess-worshipping, Earth-friendly, tree-hugger type religion and that no witch (or 'Wiccan' as they usually call them-selves) would ever consider doing anything like what I saw in those photographs.

But I did think they might know something that could be helpful. They were tuned in to the whole underground magical community. They might know if there really were any black ma-gick occult groups around in the local area. And maybe I was just looking for an excuse to catch up with Kerrie after all. I went downstairs and dug out the town phone book.

No luck. Her family's number wasn't listed. I thought that was going to be the end of it, but then something very strange happened.

As I was shoving the phone book back into place in the pan-try, a slim yellow booklet fell onto the floor from the back of the shelf. When I picked it up, I realized that it was my old high school phone directory. It must have been just sitting back there for years. Not only that, but it opened as it fell- right to the page that listed "Kerrydwen Thornapple."

A creeping numbness instantly chilled my spine. Somehow this seemed like more than a mere coincidence. It may not be that strange for a book to fall open to the exact page you need, but it really felt very odd at that moment. Perhaps it was just the marijuana, but I felt that something extremely significant was happening. I stumbled over to the phone and dialed before I had a chance to think.

"Hello?" said a deep voice on the other end of the line.

"Uh, hi, um, is this Kerrydwen Thornapple's house?"

"Who is this?" asked the deep, gruff voice.

"I'm, well, a friend of hers from high school? Alex Sebastian. I think she'd remember me."

"Hold on."

I waited for a very long time. At least it seemed like forever. I was still pretty stoned. After a million years or so I heard the phone being picked up.

"Hello?" said a soft, sweet voice that I immediately recog-nized as Kerrie's.

"Hi Kerrie, it's Alex Sebastian. How are you?"

"I'm good Alex. It's nice to hear from you," said Kerrie in a friendly but hesitant tone. "How did you know I was here?"

I wasn't sure how to respond. "Don't you live there?"

"No, I haven't lived here in years. I'm just visiting," said Kerrie.

I started to feel disoriented, like I was dreaming. It was a strange floating sensation that began in my stomach and threatened to carry me up out of the top of my head. I was suddenly completely embarrassed calling this poor girl out of the blue. There really was no way I could ask her if she knew anything about an occult murder. I barely knew her anymore.

So I just acted like it was a perfectly normal social call. We'd always had a great time talking to each other, and it really was nice to speak to her again. We spent a couple of minutes catching up. She was living in New York City, doing something in computers and banking. I was working at a video store. Michael Sweet from third period Pre-calculus dropped out of college to go to India. Sarah Barrows was working at NBC. Others were doing other things, and so on and so on.

"So, if you don't mind me asking, to what do I owe the pleasure of this call, Alex?" she asked as the banter finally began to fizzle.

"Um, well..." I really didn't have a good answer.

"Because the thing is, I'd really love to talk to you more, but my parents and I are packing right now. We're going to a festival tomorrow."

"A pagan festival?" I asked.

"Yep. Oh, that's right. I forgot. You were always obsessed with 'the Pagans' weren't you?" I could almost see her smirking through the phone.

"I wouldn't say obsessed, exactly," I said coyly, trying to remain charming. "Just interested."

"Well, you know what Alex?" She said. "I've invited you many times before, but you could actually come with us this time if you want. There's room in the car. I'm sure my parents wouldn't care."

I was shocked. Here was yet another coincidence, inviting me down a path that surely led into the mysterious unknown.

"Uh, when is it? Where is it?" I managed to get out.

"It's all weekend. Out in the Berkshires. We leave tomorrow morning."

THE BROTHERHOOD OF LIGHT AND DARKNESS

It sounded tempting on many levels. The Berkshires are a range of rolling green hills and mountains on the western edge of Massachusetts. It's the kind of place where cool mists float through the low valleys, and the rich smell of fertile earth pervades the air. Perfect setting for a pagan festival. I was hooked. If I went to this festival I could certainly try to dig up some useful information for Peter, and go a long way towards appeasing my own personal curiosity about magick. I'd always wanted to go to a pagan festival with Kerrie, but I was always too shy and introverted. Now it was being laid right out for me once again. And I wasn't feeling shy anymore. This was all just too fascinating to resist. Perhaps I really could help Peter solve this murder.

I told her I'd love to go. As usual, I immediately began to drift into reverie, imagining myself becoming a great mystical detective, investigating occult crimes all over the world, and unearthing all manner of unholy secrets.

Kerrie quickly drew me back to reality. She told me I'd need $35 for registration plus some extra for food and drink, warm clothes, a sleeping bag and any snacks I liked. There was plenty of room in her tent for both of us. And just like that, I was on my way to a pagan festival. Little did I realize that my life really was about to change forever.

Four

♀ Friday, September 20, 1996

10:15 AM

I managed to wake up just before Kerrie and her parents arrived to pick me up. Luckily, I only had a sleeping bag and a small duffel, because their station wagon was really pretty tightly packed.

The drive out to the Berkshires seemed like it was going to last forever. We took route 2 west to 95 south, and merged onto the Massachusetts Turnpike. The leaves were just starting to get serious about changing colors, the way they do each year around this time. Once we were on the Pike the trip was just a sea of green, orange and red hills and Roy Rogers restaurants. The rolling landscape was so colorful and alive that I really felt like I was beginning some great adventure.

Kerrydwen hadn't changed much in the last few years. She was still as beautiful as ever. The dreadlocks were gone, replaced by shoulder length, silky blonde curls. Her taste in clothing seemed perhaps a bit more 'New York,' but not to the point of pretension. She still smelled the same, like wonderful oatmeal cookies.

We sat next to each other quietly in the back seat, and I felt slightly light-headed as her bare thigh continually rubbed against mine from beneath her short black skirt. She smiled at me frequently as we made our way across the state, a confusing smile that left me wondering if there might still be a possibility for something more than just friendship between us.

THE BROTHERHOOD OF LIGHT AND DARKNESS

Kerrie's parents were genial, unreformed, aging hippies, her father Arthyr sporting long curling blonde hair that was just beginning to gray and thin, wrapped up in a ponytail. He was fairly plump, but it seemed to suit him, giving him an air of joviality and warmth. Her mother Morven had long, dark, red hair, of a shade that seemed only possible to achieve in one of Boston's finer salons, and she wore a flowing purple dress that adequately hid any signs of aging in her figure. They didn't speak to me much, just the requisite 'hellos' and 'welcomes,' and of course a little chit chat about the weather, which is every New Englander's favorite subject. Still, they seemed friendly. But I just mostly stared out the window unless Kerrie spoke to me.

I had the piece of paper with the occult killer symbols all over it stuffed into the front right pocket of my jeans, but there was no way I was going to pull that thing out. I don't even know why I bothered to bring it. I hardly knew these people, and I didn't have any way of even beginning a conversation about magical murder.

2:50 P.M.

We finally reached our exit off the Pike and quickly turned onto a bumpy little road that seemed like it hadn't been serviced in thirty years or more. The trees somehow seemed older and more weathered here. Twisting, bony, wooden fingers reached up into a sky that was a darkening blue, streaked with spider webs of cloud, like a rare old piece of Native American turquoise.

For some reason I had purposely not brought any cigarettes or pot with me on the trip. I guess maybe it was because I knew Kerrie didn't smoke or something. That and I sometimes just wanted to test my will power. I never liked to feel that I was enslaved to anything, so back then I would sometimes try to deprive myself of my favorite vices, just to stay in control. I was really starting to regret it as I could feel my body crying out for a nicotine fix. I felt grouchy and bored, a frequent emotion for me back then. But my boredom would soon be over for good, without any sign of ever coming back.

The ride started getting bumpy, and this seemed to perk up my travel companions. They began to talk with me animatedly about what was in store for us. According to Arthyr Thornapple, there would be a huge bonfire, dancing, nudity, people having crazy, often traumatic, mystical experiences, and magical energy vibrations coursing through the whole festival grounds. After about a mile, colorful ribbons were visible, tied to the tired and bent old trees. The pavement ended and we started travelling over rough ground. Dirt, rocks and large tree roots splayed haphazardly across our path.

Morven, Kerrie's mom, explained that this land was purchased by the Bloodmoons, a coven of very successful witches, back in the seventies, and that it had been used for ritual magick for more than twenty years. "If you look carefully by the side of the road as we drive by, you might just see an earth spirit checking us out to make sure we really belong here. 'Faerie' is very powerful out in these woods," she said eerily.

I wasn't sure whether she was making a joke or being serious. She broke into a wicked smile, raising her eyebrows, and I was even more confused. Kerrie and her dad were straight-faced so I didn't really know what to think. As I gazed out the window, I did see several shadows looming in the darkness of the trees, but I was pretty sure they were just deer. Looking back now, I'm not so certain anymore.

As we neared the festival grounds, more and more trees were adorned with multi-colored ribbons, and Kerrie's family got more and more excited. We reached a turn off and a long-haired man in his late twenties stood up from a rusty metal folding chair and signaled us to stop. He was wearing colorful hippie gear that was rumpled and worn. He walked officiously up to the driver's window and Kerrie's mother rolled it down. As I saw him up close, I wasn't at all sure how old he was anymore. Significant creases marked his face, like he'd been living outdoors for years. Yet he had a childlike quality to his movements. His walk, though carrying the weight of authority, seemed playful, as if everything was just a game. He stood like a dancer waiting for the downbeat to send him dancing merrily away, as if he really was some sort of woodland spirit.

"Greetings, what brings you into the forest today?" He chanted it sonorously, ritually, as if he'd been saying it over and over.

"Fox! It's just us! Blessed be!" said Kerrie's mom in a friendly but mildly scolding tone. Fox's face lit up immediately as he recognized her.

"Morven! I can't believe I didn't realize it was you. My radar must be down today or something. Blessed be!" His voice was now all giggles, nearly flamboyant.

"Kerrie's with us again this year, and her friend Alexander," said Morven cheerfully. Fox smiled and waved at Kerrie, then noticed me. He looked me over quickly, out of the corner of his eye, like he was trying to subtly inspect me. It wasn't very subtle. He finally turned and smiled at me. I guess I somehow passed his little test. Something about him instantly irritated me, but it might have just been because I really wanted a cigarette.

"Welcome to Alban Elfed 1996, Sisters and Brothers! If you hurry you'll still make the opening ritual!" He bowed deeply and foppishly like a court jester, prancing away from the car.

As we pulled past him Kerrie's dad muttered that we had plenty of time to get to the opening ritual because this festival ran on 'pagan standard time' which meant at the very least forty-five minutes past the scheduled start. We rounded a bend past a cluster of fir trees and I saw row upon row of parked cars. I hadn't realized how many people there were going to be.

Kerrie's mother pulled into a nearby space and we swiftly unloaded the station wagon. Her parents bickered over who should be carrying what so I volunteered to carry as much of the heavy gear as I could manage. I won big points there. They couldn't stop thanking me and commenting on how strong I was.

As I looked around from beneath my burden I saw throngs of hippies giving each other long, soulful hugs of welcome amidst a vast forest of oaks and maple trees. The signs of autumn were more numerous here, leaves were changing color and falling right before my eyes. But between the trees, obese, nearly naked women ran toward each other breathlessly, their pendulous appendages flapping heavily as they bounded. Long haired, bearded men sang to each other in ancient, unrecognizable bardic tunes. I saw capes and cloaks and princesses and wizards in all directions. I'd arrived in a strange, alien, fairy kingdom. Many of the denizens were really quite dirty looking, but they seemed so genuinely happy to see and embrace one another that I couldn't help but feel a little lonely and left out.

Then I smelled the faint but familiar scent of marijuana on the breeze, and I felt things might somehow work out all right. Kerrydwen, perhaps sensing my nervous state, slid her arm under mine and pulled me off toward the camping area. It felt very nice, her arm in mine. My load was so heavy that it was hard to move with her arm there, but I managed the whole walk without complaint. Seemingly hundreds of tents were pitched in all directions. The tents were of all varieties, from the most modern colorful polyester to quite ancient canvas draped pre-cariously from trees. Many different odors of incense and herb mingled seductively in the air, as the wind maneuvered bet-ween the trees and the wildly colored banners and tapestries hung by the festival goers to decorate their sites. Kerrie turned to me, still clinging to my arm. She smiled.

"I haven't been to one of these things in years. It's good to be home." As I gratefully dropped my load, I smiled back at her with a sigh. I could see that she really did feel like she was home, and looking around I had to admit, strange as it was, it might be a pleasant home.

Then, as I looked at the cheerful pagans all around me I suddenly realized that one of these people might well be a very grisly murderer. A chilling thought since I was now trapped in the woods with them. We set up camp quickly once Arthyr and Morven caught up with us, placing our tents far enough apart that I knew Kerrie and I would be able to get some privacy if we needed it.

We then went to a large, ancient looking log cabin to register and finally join the pagan festivities.

Five

4:25 PM

I found myself seriously thinking about cigarettes and pot again as Kerrydwen led me back through the rag tag tent village toward the opening ceremony. I longingly wondered if there might be something to be had in one of these tents. The lack of nicotine in particular was starting to make me feel ill.

I also began to notice that there were quite a lot of attractive women all around. All shapes, sizes and ages of beauty surrounded me, from budding teens to radiant matrons in their fifties and sixties, all bubbling with palpable sexual energy. Many of them smiled as we passed. A few seemed to recognize Kerrydwen vaguely, but not enough to start a real conversation.

I followed Kerrie onto a well-worn path through dense forest, with a few other festival patrons straggling along behind us. There seemed to be dirt paths leading off in several directions through the forest, and I noticed a number of wooden cabins along the way. Kerrie explained to me that all of this belonged to the Bloodmoons, that they'd designed this property specifically for hosting pagan festivals. We reached the edge of the path we'd been following. An archway constructed entirely of interlocking deer antlers stood between us and the sounds of drums, laughter and boisterous chatter. The antlered gate was quite beautifully constructed, over eight feet tall, its splaying jagged edges bringing me instantly into a prehistoric state of mind. Two slender men in their mid-twenties stood on either side of the gate. They were both sporting ponytails and woolen South American robes. Their robes did not particularly match in style or color, and it seemed more like coincidence than plan that they both happened to be wearing them.

"Blessed be," said the one on the right. "We need to smudge you before you enter the sacred circle." Kerrie stepped forward eagerly, which gave me the brief opportunity to see what 'smudging' was exactly. The man plucked a small bundle of smoldering gray leaves out of a large, iridescent seashell, and began waving it near Kerrie's body, all the while fanning the smoke toward her with a Chinese fan. The other robed hippie started looking at me expectantly, and I realized that he wanted to 'smudge' me. I acquiesced. The smoke smelled fairly awful, but in an herbal sort of way. Kerrie told me that the burning leafy bundles were sage. I'd actually seen those bundles of sage around at New Age stores a few times, and now I finally knew what they were for.

After we'd been thoroughly smudged with the stinky sage smoke we were given deep hugs by the two men, and led under the antlers into a large cleared field with an unlit bonfire in the center. A huge mound of wood was stacked ten feet high in a crude pyramid shape. People turned and cheered ecstatically as we entered, and I really felt very welcome for the first time. I was hugged and greeted by more people of all shapes and sizes than I could possibly describe or remember. There was a general cacophony of laughter, talking and yelling, syncopated by some uncoordinated drumming for quite a while as more and more people were smudged and brought into the circle.

Then, in an instant, all sound ceased. I turned toward the antlered arch, and there, with his arms raised dramatically, was Ariathmus Bloodmoon. He was a handsome older man with long, curling, reddish hair prominently streaked gray, a thin beard covering what might otherwise be a somewhat weak chin. He was tall, muscular and barrel-chested, almost like an old-time circus strong man. There was something very charismatic about him, almost hypnotic. But he also somehow seemed rather cold, almost reptilian. In his right hand he held aloft an elaborately gnarled wooden staff which held a very large quartz crystal gripped within its gnarls. He wore a gray robe, some sort of rough linen, with a brownish animal hide tied around his waist.

A silvery wolf pelt clung about his shoulders. You could easily see how this man instantly silenced a crowd.

Kerrie later told me that "Dr." Ariathmus Bloodmoon was the head and mystical leader of Spiritmount Circle, a pagan outreach community organization that runs several festivals and events throughout the year including this one. But apparently he was also the high priest of the previously mentioned Bloodmoon Coven. And she further revealed to me under the strictest oath of secrecy that this Bloodmoon Coven was actually a bizarre sort of mini-cult which practiced group marriage, polyamory, communal living and that all the members took the last name "Bloodmoon," which she could not explain any further.

Just moments after the silence gripped the crowd, a single drum began to hammer out a driving beat. Ariathmus opened his jaws dramatically, as if about to devour us all.

"Earth I am," he chanted powerfully in time with the drum. "Water I am, Air and Fire and Spirit I am." He had a deep, melodious, baritone voice. Soon everyone took up the chant, repeating it over and over, "Earth I am, Water I am, Air and Fire and Spirit I am," clapping and stamping as more drums joined the rhythm, and Ariathmus took a small step forward. I was amazed at the easy control he seemed to have over the very large crowd. The chant did not strike me as particularly profound, but from the way everyone was bellowing, it seemed like I was alone in that opinion.

From behind Ariathmus two women appeared, bearing horn shaped cornucopia filled with fruit, grains and other harvest bounty. They danced and whirled into the center of the giant crowd, people cheering and making room for them as they danced. They were two of Ariathmus's wives, two of the priestesses of the Bloodmoon Coven. They were in their forties or fifties, very beautiful, with lithe, athletic bodies beneath loosely hanging colorful silk togas. Kerrie told me the names of all of the Bloodmoon women, but I never learned which one was which. There were seven of them, Lilias, Morgana, Callie, Dana, Terra, Kath and Lida Bloodmoon.

Two more of them appeared. Again, I couldn't say exactly which ones, but these two were holding large wineskins in their hands. They too danced into the crowd, seducing the throng with swaying sensual undulations and turns. I noticed that the first two were now circling the unlit bonfire, emptying the contents of their cornucopia around the edges.

Soon, two men appeared, waving long, silky scarves as they too danced into the crowd. These were two of the Bloodmoon men. The men were equally as indistinguishable as the women, all seeming to be slightly duller versions of Ariathmus. Kerrie told me that the names of the men were Pyramus, Taliesin, Orion and Running Bear Bloodmoon.

Two more men appeared through the deer antler gate, coming from behind Ariathmus. They bore two flaming torches. The crowd really started yelling and hollering as the chant continued and the drumming sped up.

"Earth I am, Water I am, Air and Fire and Spirit I am!"

Everyone began dancing clockwise around the circle as the Bloodmoon women threw wine and fruit onto the pile of wood and sticks in the center, and the Bloodmoon men twirled their scarves and torches. Then Ariathmus raised his staff again and everyone froze.

"We have come to celebrate the turning of the wheel of the year!" he bellowed as he approached the center, with the two torchbearing men quickly flanking him on either side. The crowd cheered deafeningly. "Welcome spirits of the elements! Welcome Gods and Goddesses of this and every land!" More cheers. "Let us kindle the sacred bonfire that will light our path as we move toward the darkness of winter!"

From beneath their tunics, the two men who'd been dancing with scarves produced hollowed animal horns, and blew a mighty blast of sound through them. With that, the torches were lowered to the flames. The crowd stepped back.

There was clearly something stronger than wine in those skins because the bonfire burst into flame with the ferocity of an explosion. Drums and cheering filled the air along with more joyful hornblasts as the crowd began to dance wildly around the fire once again. I sort of half-heartedly joined the circling, but I was a bit too self-conscious to really get into the spirit of it all. The ceremony seemed pretty short, without much content. It was very impressive how they worked the crowd. But I'd yet to see anything that resembled my definition of magick.

The Brotherhood of Light and Darkness

5:45 PM

After a short time, the crowd began to disperse. Kerrie's parents excused themselves to set up their booth down at the merchant's area. But the drumming continued, along with a small group of dedicated dancers. Kerrie grabbed my arm once again.

"Come on, let's go get some dinner before the line gets too long," she said with an adorable smile. "This'll be going on all night. We can come back later."

"What'll be going on all night?" I asked, unsure exactly what she was talking about.

"The fire circle. They're going to keep drumming and dancing all weekend long."

"These same people?" I was having trouble focusing. I felt dizzy and disoriented. I'm not sure what the main cause was, but I was definitely experiencing complete nicotine withdrawal, as well as culture shock. Kerrie smirked at me.

"Of course not these same people. Some will leave. Others will come, you know."

"Yeah," I muttered vaguely.

"Come on, let's go get some food, you're looking pale," she ordered, and proceeded to drag me through the antler gate back to the path.

Six

6:25 PM

Dinner was fairly uneventful, other than our reunion with Kerrie's parents. The rations were a fairly meager collection of camp foods for sale at what seemed to me rather inflated prices in the main building. The building was a large, crude, open cabin, big enough to seat over a hundred people at wooden picnic tables. One pleasant discovery that I made was mead, a sweet, honey wine that Kerrie's parents brought up from the merchant's area for dinner. A couple of bottles later I discovered that it was quite intoxicating and I was really losing any sense of clarity. We all had a great time throughout dinner, laughing constantly.

Kerrie insisted that we go back down the path to the fire circle for just a little while before going to bed. As we made our way out through the antlered gate into the clearing, I discovered that in the darkness the bonfire had an entirely different character. Of course, I was pretty drunk by then. But still, the flames were much more dramatic, with flumes of sparks spinning up into the night sky like fairy dust.

The dancers were very different too. Many of them had put on streaks of black face paint; some wore masks, animal horns or other atavistic ornamentation. The drum groove seemed more primal and raw. Many dancers swayed wildly, or shuffled unconsciously, as if in trance. Something different was clearly going on. Kerrie leaped eagerly into the midst of them and began dancing happily around the fire. I moved in closer, and felt the searing warmth of the fire on my face and limbs. I

24

danced a little, but I was feeling so strange and intoxicated that I soon wandered over toward the area of the drummers. There, to my great delight, I saw a shirtless young man in his late teens rolling an American Spirit 'roll your own' cigarette. He had a sharp, angular face, too serious for his age, and normally I would have found him intimidating. But my addiction called out more loudly. I stumbled toward him.

"Do you suppose I could bum one of those off you?" I pleaded pathetically.

"Not a prob," said the young drummer with a half-smile as he sealed the cigarette. "Take this one. I'll roll another." I was surprised by his quiet friendliness, quickly snatched up the cigarette and let him light it for me, gratefully sucking in those wonderful carcinogenic toxins. I exhaled, feeling an immediate dizzying head rush.

"Ah," I exclaimed, "Now that's what I needed. Thanks a lot. My name's Alex." I extended a friendly hand.

"Karl," said the young man as he briefly shook my hand with a smile and went back to rolling his own cigarette. "I know what you mean." We smoked our cigarettes together in silence, listening to the beat, and watching the flailing dancers as they bounced past the flames.

The cigarette built up my courage, and after thanking Karl once again I moved toward the fire and began to dance along with the crowd. As I danced, I noticed that many of the people dancing near the fire were naked. This would normally have made me feel both a little embarrassed and titillated, but instead I found myself just feeling very self-conscious as I moved around the circle. Each of my attempts at dance movements seemed awkward and ill coordinated. I started to actually feel bad about myself, bad about my dancing. Then I looked around and saw that nobody was paying any attention to me so there was really no reason to be self-conscious at all. Still, I couldn't stop thinking about myself, and I was very uncomfortable. I told myself that I shouldn't care what any of these people thought of me. They were just a bunch of weirdoes, fat naked weirdoes, and I could do whatever the hell I wanted.

I tried ignoring everyone else, just moving, being, and exploring the feelings of my body. I soon felt very light, like my limbs were moving on their own. The alcohol in the mead and the heat of the fire were making me quite disoriented. The fire seemed further and further away as I drifted, drifted. Everything was soft and out of focus like I was disintegrating into the night itself. I seemed to almost be dreaming, shadowy animal-like figures were coming in and out of view. I was floating in a sea of shapes and there were treasures, a jeweled princess, she danced just out of my reach and I floated forward to her.

And then I fell forward hard onto my knees, snapping me roughly back into reality. Kerrie and several others were quickly at my side, helping me up, giving me water, asking me if I was okay. I was completely incoherent, and Kerrie insisted that we go back to the tent right then, even though I really wanted to find my new friend Karl to see if he might have another smoke for me.

9:15 PM

Inside our little tent Kerrie helped me to unroll my sleeping bag and get into it. She smiled at me warmly as she started to zip it up. She looked truly beautiful, even in the darkness. I pulled her toward me, and kissed her on the mouth. It was very impetuous, but I was tired and a bit drunk. I knew that if I didn't do it right then I was going to just fall asleep and lose my chance. At first she seemed a little tense, and I almost pulled away, but then I felt her mouth softly opening, and she began to return my passion. She let her body mingle with mine in the folds of the sleeping bag, and I passionately ran my hands over her back and her behind. I could feel the seams of her undergarments and my penis swelling in the confines of my boxers. She kissed me hard, running her hands down my chest and just for a fleeting moment over my throbbing genitals. I was in ecstasy. Then she suddenly stopped and turned her head away, lowering her eyes.

"No," she whispered. "I'm sorry. I can't." I pulled her head back toward me and kissed her gently on the brow.

"What? What's wrong?" I asked as understandingly as possible. I felt a little anxious and irritated. It bothered me when girls did this sort of thing. Kissing you passionately one moment, then stopping cold. It was so confusing to me. Was it a game? Was it serious? I never knew how I was supposed to respond. But I really did like her, so I didn't want to spoil things by not being understanding.

"I can't do this," she said, her forehead leaning against mine, eyes staring down. An uncomfortable pause followed. I knew I was supposed to say something, but I really didn't know what that was.

"Why?" I eventually asked, although that wasn't at all what I really wanted to say.

"It's just..."

"Don't tell me you don't want to spoil our friendship because I know that line," I said sarcastically.

"Don't be mad at me," she said, and as she looked at me I could see that her eyes were glassy. "It's just. I'm very attracted to you Alex. I used to have a huge crush on you in high school." She did? Wow. That was news to me. I wish I'd known that then. "But, I'm kind of seeing someone in New York."

"Oh." Now here it was, the boyfriend somewhere else. I involuntarily shook my head.

"I mean it's not really serious or anything," she said, as if to communicate that she was not technically cheating by kissing me. "But I think it could be and, you know, this wouldn't be fair to him."

"Sure," I said. "I understand." But I didn't understand, and I didn't care about being fair to him. I felt cold and suddenly very alone. I wrapped myself up tighter in my sleeping bag.

"I really don't want this to spoil the fun we've been having. I really like you Alex," she said, smiling at me in that consolation prize sort of way. "Let's not spoil it."

I forced a smile. "Of course not." But neither of us believed me.

She put her arm around me, and kissed me on the top of my head. "I really wish things were different. The timings just off, you know?" she asked hopefully. I don't think she realized how wounded and vulnerable I felt. Maybe she did.

"Yeah, of course," I said quietly.

"You gonna be all right?"

"I am all right."

"Good."

"How 'bout you?" I asked, after a long while.

"I'm okay," she said quietly, and turned away. As I lay there trying to fall asleep I really felt like an idiot. I was alone in the midst of a bunch of strange pagans. Who did I think I was? Pretending to be a detective or something? Was I really expecting to solve that horrible murder? What an idiot I was. I didn't know what I was doing. I couldn't even get the girl. How was I going to get through the rest of this horrible weekend?

Seven

I walked through some deep forest, noticing that it was quite thick and tangled, and I hoped I'd be able to find my way back. There was no path. I was just scrambling through bushes, brambles and tall grasses. I'd done this sort of thing when I was younger, wandering in the woods. I don't know what I was looking for. I sure didn't seem to be getting anywhere. I was looking for something. Of course, there was a murderer somewhere in these woods, and I had to find him. I saw a figure, and froze. Could it be him? No, it was a very small person. It seemed to be some sort of an elf or a fairy! I'd never seen anything like it. It glowed softly, in a silky, gossamer tunic. I couldn't move or breathe. Then it dashed off.

I ran after the creature, and found myself no longer in the woods, but rather in what seemed to be a school campus. Brick buildings in rows with groups of students walking between. I looked around for the little fairy creature, and I saw a door closing in a distant building. I quickly moved toward the building. I ran through the door, but inside I only saw another group of students. One of them attracted my attention. She had alabaster skin, straight jet-black hair, mesmerizing ice blue eyes, and she was staring right at me. She wore a tight black top that scooped down to reveal a lot of cleavage, and a pair of faded blue jeans that showed off her sensuous curves. She walked toward me, and I couldn't take my eyes off her. She smiled as she got to me and rested her hands on my chest. Shiny red nails dug softly into my skin.

"I can see that we're going to be nothing but trouble for each other," she said, her moist, red lips curling into an inviting pout.

"I like trouble," I said, feeling very aroused, smirking confidently.

"What brings you here?" she asked as she slipped her arm around my waist and started leading me through the building.

"I'm looking for a fairy, or a murderer. I know I have to find someone or other."

"Who cares about any of that?" she said forcefully. "We're young. Let's go fuck."

That sure sounded a hell of a lot better than what I was doing. I don't know what I'd been thinking. "Okay, but we need a bed," I said helpfully.

"Come in here." She pushed a door open and we stepped into a room with soft, yielding floors, softer than warm bread dough.

"What is this place?" I asked.

"This is where we learn to fly, so the floors have to be soft," she said, shaking her head like I was a bit stupid.

"In case you fall?"

"Now you're getting it." And with that she took off her top. She had a shiny black push up bra on underneath and I really found myself getting aroused. "Let's fuck," she repeated, so I took hold of her and kissed her passionately. We dropped down to the soft yielding floor and our clothes were soon peeled away. This was so much better than what I was doing before. But for some reason I started to feel a bit guilty. I couldn't for the life of me remember why.

Then, just as she took hold of my swollen penis I started feeling like I had to urinate. Damn it. This was terrible timing. Peeing was the last thing I wanted to do. But I felt such a compelling need that it was totally distracting.

The beautiful girl asked me what was wrong. "Don't you find me attractive?"

I assured her that I did, but she stood up, looking ruffled.

"Honestly, it's just that I really have to pee," I said, hoping that would make her feel better.

She smiled at me darkly. "You could just pee on me."

THE BROTHERHOOD OF LIGHT AND DARKNESS

ħ Saturday, September 21, 1996

7:45 AM (approx.)

I sat bolt upright in my sleeping bag. What a bizarre dream. I looked over at Kerrie in her sleeping bag and I remembered the events of last night. Ugh. But she looked so cute curled up there with her eyes closed that I couldn't feel too resentful.

It was far too early for me to be awake, but I did really have to pee. So, I pulled on my shoes quietly and went outside. There were a lot of tents around, but I saw what looked like some good bushes on the other side of a small clearing. I started through the small gray field when I heard the telltale crackling of leaves behind me. As I turned to see who it was I spotted a dark-haired girl wearing a skin-tight black dress and combat boots. She looked up at me as she passed and when I saw those blue eyes I immediately recognized her. It was the girl from my dream. She gazed at me blankly and passed with none of the friendliness that she'd had in my dream.

The impossibility of this situation stunned me. How could I have just dreamed of someone I'd never met before and then seen her only moments after I'd dreamed of her? It was like the dream had created her- brought her into manifestation. But then again, perhaps I'd seen her out of the corner of my eye at the fire circle or something, and the dream was just a meaningless fantasy. I couldn't be sure. Not at the moment anyway.

As she stepped away down the path I saw her reach down into a small black purse hanging at her side. She pulled out a pack of cigarettes. Winstons. My brand. I had to find out more about her. This was too fascinating. She lit up a cigarette, and the sinfully inviting smell wafted back toward me.

"Excuse me?" I called out involuntarily, picking up my pace toward her. She stopped and turned back to me, staring blankly. "Could I bum a cigarette off of you?"

"Un-huh," she said, without smiling. She reached into her little purse and produced a cigarette. She looked me right in the eyes as she held the cigarette out toward me. I was instantly spellbound by those cold blue irises of hers. I found myself unable to move or speak or even think. She dropped it into my

31

frozen, outstretched hand. "Don't mention it," she muttered, and with a twist of her heel in the place of a goodbye she was off.

"Thank you," I said, freed from my stupor, stumbling after her. "I appreciate it, and, well, I'm sorry, and I hate to be a bother, but do you have a light too?" She was still holding her lighter, a silver Zippo, and she lit it dramatically, swinging it toward me violently as she stopped again. I leaned forward and lit my cigarette casually on the flame she'd thrust at me. I tried to be as cool as possible. "Thanks a lot," I said with an attempt at a wry smile. She snorted and started away again.

But as she turned, an older man was walking toward us swiftly, robustly, right out of the forest, and she stopped short.

"Good morning. Who is your friend?" said the old man, gesturing toward me amiably. He was a kind looking man who had to be in his seventies at least. He had a mop of white hair atop his head, and a large, patriarchal, white beard. He was slim and clearly limber for his age, but he did seem somehow breakable. He was like an aging reed of bamboo, still stronger than most plants, but just now becoming brittle and gray. He wore a tweed coat over a white cotton shirt. Neither seemed washed or pressed in quite some time, yet they were still somehow relatively clean looking. Dangling from his mouth was a blackened old pipe from which small puffs of an aromatic spicy tobacco smoke issued in rhythmic succession. He pointed two crooked, slender fingers right at me. The pretty girl turned and looked at me again.

"Is there something else that you want?" She practically spat. Now that I heard her speak a few more words, I detected just a touch of a Boston accent, well concealed, but definitely there.

"No, I uh... no," I mumbled. I was feeling more and more confused by the second. The girl rolled her eyes and strutted off. She had a definite grace to her step, even if her manners were coarse when she stopped to converse. I didn't usually have much interest in unfriendly girls, but the fact that she'd been in my dreams before I'd even seen her had me completely intrigued. The old man and I stared after her until she disappeared behind some trees.

Then the white haired man turned his gaze back to me, continuing to puff at his pipe slowly. There was something about him that I instantly liked. He just seemed to know something. Something we'd all like to know.

"Who are you, boy?" said the old man, smirking.

"Alexander Sebastian. Alex," I said, feeling very awkward.

"And what are you doing here, Alex?" asked the old man. But his tone was unnerving. He wasn't asking me what I was doing on that trail at 7:45 in the morning. He sounded like he wanted me to explain my whole purpose in life or something. I couldn't think of anything at all to reply.

"Who was that girl?" I asked, finally, still feeling stunned from her presence.

"Very pretty, hmm?" said the old man, making the understatement of the century. "Her name is Jessica Burnham. I'll introduce you, if we all ever happen to be in the same place at the same time. My name's Adin Stone, by the way, but you can call me Adin, or Stone, whatever suits you. It doesn't make a difference to me either way." He smiled again. That smile. There was something about his smile that made me want to be near this man forever. There was a quiet power behind his eyes, and also a sense of total harmlessness. He had no visible agenda whatsoever. "But you know, you never answered my question, Alex."

I suddenly remembered the reason I'd come outside in the first place was to go to the bathroom.

"I was trying to find a place to pee," I mumbled.

Adin Stone laughed long and heartily. "Well, I won't keep you from it," he said with another smile, and started off.

"Yeah, uh, okay," I stammered. "You will really introduce me to that girl?" I had to know more about her, why she was in my dreams, why I was unable to speak coherently when I even looked at her.

"It would be my great pleasure!"

"Thank you Mr. Stone."

"No, no!" he said in mock horror. "Mr. Stone was my father. I'm just Stone, or Adin. Either one."

"Sure," I said. "See you around Adin."

"Or Stone. Either one," he said with a smile, turned, and was off, moving swiftly down the trail. I couldn't really imagine myself calling anybody 'Stone.'

As I tried to finally find a private place to relieve my bladder I discovered that there now seemed to be people everywhere I went. It took me quite a while to find anyplace to be by myself. By the time I finally went to the bathroom quite a long time had elapsed.

I went back to the tent, but Kerrie was already up and off. A note on my sleeping bag read:

> So sorry about last night. Let's talk please.
>
> -K

I felt bad that I'd created this awkwardness. But kissing her was wonderful, and I was glad I'd done it. It was time for me to start taking action in my life, even if it caused me some little troubles along the way. Thinking about it, I really just wanted to mend fences with Kerrie and enjoy our reunited friendship. Who knows what could happen from there? I hoped that I hadn't completely screwed things up.

Eight

I looked all over for Kerrie, but she was nowhere to be found. Hopefully she was having fun, and not feeling guilty or anything. When I got to the main building and still couldn't find her I wasn't sure what to do. They were still serving breakfast, but it seemed to be the same sort of food as dinner, at the same prices. I decided to conserve the little money I had left. I noticed a bunch of copies of the schedule of workshops and events sitting on a table next to some free apples and peanut butter. I helped myself to all three. The first workshops were starting at 9:30 AM. I had several choices.

HISTORICAL DRUIDISM IN ROMAN HISTORY AND ARTH-URIAN LEGEND, as taught by Dr. Margaret Clutterbuck, EdD, PhD, Author of the book of the same title. Brighid House.

CIRCLECRAFT FOR THE SOLITARY WITCH, as taught by Reverend Doctor Lilias Bloodmoon, educational director, Spirit-mount Circle, a non-profit community outreach organization for all pagans. Juno House.

THE QABALISTIC MIDDLE PILLAR RITE, as explained and taught as a practical exercise by Dr. Matthew Wiley, Adeptus Minor of the A∴R∴T∴. Hekate House.

The first two sounded like a yawn, but that third one caught my eye. I'd heard of the A∴R∴T∴, but I didn't think it really existed- at least not any more. The A∴R∴T∴ was a near legendary occult fraternity. Some people say that "A∴R∴T∴" stands for "Ancient Rosicrucian Temple," but quite a lot of others say that the true name is a secret only revealed to its highest initiates. Either way, the A∴R∴T∴ was one of the secret magical societies that boasted the infamous Victorian poet magician Aleister Crowley as a member, and it shared his very mixed reputation.

Most people still think of Aleister Crowley as some sort of Satanic black magician, but I'd read his book, 'Magick in Theory and Practice' and it seemed to me that Mr. Crowley was probably just misunderstood by his contemporaries. He was definitely involved with homosexual sex and used drugs, but he was not necessarily evil. I wondered if something similar was true for the A∴R∴T∴.

But if the A∴R∴T∴ really was the hotbed of evil black magick that I'd read about, perhaps I'd found the right place to look for an occult murderer. Perhaps there was still hope for my career as an amateur mystical detective. Either way, the workshop sounded like a good way to kill some time until I could find Kerrie.

The flyer said that the workshop was taking place in Hekate House, one of several small cabins around the property built for housing workshops. Hekate house was probably the farthest from the main building, so I knew I'd better get walking if I wanted to get there on time. I grabbed a couple of apples for the road.

9:47 AM

It was a beautiful morning as I walked down the tree-lined path through the woods, maples interspersed with pines and oaks. The bolder trees had truly begun to put on their autumn colors in earnest. It was so invigorating to be out in nature that I started to feel glad that I'd come out to this festival after all.

I finally got to Hekate House, after walking too far into the forest and having to work my way back breathlessly. The 'house' was a crude, rough-hewn wooden cabin, unpainted and very rustic looking. Luckily, when I walked in, they were just getting started and closing up the doors. A good looking guy in his early to mid thirties ushered me in, closing and locking the door behind me. He shook my hand with a charming smile. He had dirty blonde hair, a strong jaw, and he was wearing what looked like yoga pants and a tight Grey sweatshirt over lean muscles. He seemed confident, the kind of guy who's everybody's pal.

"I'm Matthew Wiley. Welcome," he said with what seemed like well-practiced sincerity. "Everyone has already introduced themselves, so maybe you can just go ahead and introduce yourself, and tell us all a little about why you decided to come to the workshop today." I turned to the rest of the group and discovered that I was facing about thirty strangers, staring at me expectantly. My mouth went dry instantly.

"Uh, I'm Alexander Sebastian," I said shakily, my voice sounding awful, scratchy. I felt like an idiot. "And this is my first pagan festival and my first workshop, so I'm just going to go sit in the corner." That got a big laugh from the crowd, which gave me ample opportunity to actually skulk off into the corner.

"Well Alexander," said Matthew Wiley with a friendly grin, "we've already gone through a basic description of the Qabalistic Tree of Life." he pointed to a colorful poster depicting the Tree of Life glyph. "I don't really want to have to go through it all again. Are you at all familiar with the Tree of Life?"

"Yeah," I said as I sat down. In fact, I was familiar with it. The Tree of Life is a glyph with ten circles laid out in a pattern on three vertical rows or 'pillars.'

The glyph is used in the Qabala to represent the creation of the universe through ten emanations of godhead. Each of the emanations, called 'sephiroth' in Hebrew, is a quality or aspect of God. They are named: Kether 'The Crown,' Chokmah 'Wisdom,' Binah 'Understanding,' Chesed 'Mercy,' Geburah 'Justice,' Tiphareth 'Beauty,' Netzach 'Victory,' Hod 'Splendor,' Yesod 'The Foundation' and Malkuth 'The Kingdom.' I was even familiar with the Middle Pillar exercise which basically involves placing the middle sephiroth of the 'Tree' into your body with your imagination, along the spine, and chanting appropriate special names of God, as if you were building the Tree of Life inside yourself. I'd never tried it myself, but I'd seen it in a couple of different books. Of course, I didn't mention any of this. I just sat there with my mouth shut.

"Okay, that's great," he said. "So, we can finally go ahead and get started with the exercise."

As I looked around the room, I noticed that Jessica Burnham was there, sitting fairly close to me. She looked bored, and didn't seem to notice me at all.

"Let's all go ahead and stand up," Matthew instructed, raising his hands dramatically. Everyone obeyed with a few groans. "Let's stretch our bodies out a little bit, just to wake them up," He began bending and shaking out his arms. "I know a lot of us were up late dancing at the fire circle last night, and we need to be alive and refreshed for this." We all stretched and bent and rolled our shoulders and shook our arms and legs. "Okay, great," he said after a few minutes. "Let's all go ahead and get into position. Now, you can sit if you can feel like you can be comfortable, or you can lie down flat, or you can just stand up straight."

The whole group either sat or lay down. Clearly none of us were up to standing for a half-hour or longer, at least not for this exercise. I chose to sit, because I didn't want to fall asleep. My instincts were right. Within five minutes, at least two people were snoring. Matthew had us relax our whole bodies starting with our feet, releasing each body part slowly and soothingly until we reached the top of our head. I started to wonder if this was going to be the normal middle pillar exercise, or if the A∴R∴T∴ had some sort of 'evil' version that I was about to be exposed to. Oh well, I was already there, so I'd just have to see.

"Now, I'd like you to imagine that the top of your head is gently opening up, like a hatch door on the crown of your head is swinging open," instructed Matthew.

It seemed an odd instruction, but I did my best to imagine it. It was fairly easy. I imagined two trap doors swinging upward.

"And I'd like you to imagine that you are breathing through this opening at the top of your head," continued Matthew. "Imagining the breath entering you body through this opening. Now, this might seem somewhat tenuous at first, but don't worry about that for now. Continuing to breathe through your crown, visualize a sphere or globe of brilliant light shining just above your head, about the size of a grapefruit. See the light from this globe shining down onto you."

This was harder for me to imagine, but I managed a sort of hazy light, amorphous and weak. I was very relaxed, and didn't really mind either way.

"And now I'd like you to inhale deeply, imagining your breath filling up the globe above your head, and as you exhale, chant the sacred word 'eh-hay-ee-ay.' Watch and feel the globe growing in brilliance."

We all did as instructed, and the room was filled with the sonorous drone of 'eh-hay-ee-ay.' We repeated the breathing and chanting several times, and my visualization of the globe above my head became much clearer. I concentrated on the globe as I chanted, and it became brighter and more vivid.

The word we were chanting was 'Eheieh,' a traditional Hebrew name for God which translates to 'I am.' It is the name God called himself with Moses in the Old Testament when he gave him the Ten Commandments from the burning bush. This was clearly just going to be the regular middle pillar exercise, not an evil version. I must admit I was ever so slightly disappointed.

The exercise continued as Matthew had us visualize a shaft of light moving down through our heads from the globe above to our throats. When the light reached our throats we began imagining a globe of indigo light in our throats, and chanting 'Yay-ho-vaoh Ay-lo-heem' several times. We repeated the same process of moving light down into our hearts, imagining a golden globe and chanting 'Yay-ho-vaoh Ay-lo-ah Vay-dah-awth.' Then we moved our imaginary light energy down to our sexual organs, imagining a globe of purple light and chanting 'Shaw-d-eye El Ch-eye.'

After we finished with each globe, Matthew said, "Relax and observe your body, noticing any changes, and feel the pulsation of the energy." My body was definitely pulsing.

Finally, we moved the light all the way down from our heads through our throats, chest, genitals, and down to our feet, visualizing a fifth sphere or star around our feet, chanting, 'Ad-on-eye Ha Ar-ets.'

By the time we did this, I felt extremely relaxed, tingling with strong pleasurable vibrations all over my body. Matthew continued to direct the group in moving the energy in other ways, but I became lost in reverie about my own vibrations. It was a very ecstatic experience. I must have blacked out, because the next thing I clearly remember was Matthew saying, "And you can relax as long as you want or open your eyes whenever you are ready."

I was a little confused, so I opened my eyes immediately. Everybody else still seemed to have his or her eyes closed, including Matthew. He was sitting, peaceful as a Buddha. I looked at the group. It was much like a cross section of the rest of the festival, although some of these people seemed perhaps a little more shadowy. There was a little more hairspray and dark make-up in the room, but was there a murderer here?

I glanced over at Jessica. She was looking at me. She smiled a naughty, secret smirk at me with the corner of her mouth. We were the bad ones together. I smiled back and blushed what must have been a very deep red. Soon everyone was wiggling and getting up and telling Matthew how great the exercise had been for them. It was a good exercise, when I thought about it. I was still tingling.

I stood up, feeling a bit shaky, my legs slightly asleep. Jessica somehow slipped out stealthily. I didn't even see her go. Everyone quickly crowded around Matthew to praise him over and over for a while, so I used the opportunity to slip off too. I would have liked to talk to Matthew Wiley for a few minutes, but I didn't feel like fighting for it. It was almost lunchtime, and I still had to find Kerrie.

Nine

11:50 AM

When I got to the main building the kitchen staff was just starting to put out lunch, so I went back outside to look around a bit more at the festival. There wasn't much going on, but I managed to bum a cigarette off of a short, cute, chubby girl wearing a tight white t-shirt. The shirt was a deep cut v-neck, and her extremely large breasts were heaving out of it. I couldn't help but stare at them. She had short dark hair, a round, pretty face and bright red lips, freshly painted. Her name was Cat, and she told me that she'd just gotten up five minutes ago.

"I was at the fire circle all night. That's the real festival as far as I'm concerned," she said passionately, punctuating the statement with a deep drag of her cigarette that inflated her chest even bigger. "I mean, I'm sure the workshop you just went to was good and all, but that's not my scene. I'd rather be naked and dancing, you know?"

"Yeah. I was there last night," I said, trying to stop staring down at her bosoms. She smiled.

"I didn't see you there," she said, another drag, another heave of her elephantine breasts.

"I had to leave early," I said, taking a slow drag of my own cigarette as the events of the last twenty-four hours swirled through my brain. I found I had nothing more to add, so I just smiled.

She nodded. "But see, the circle doesn't really get started until one or two in the morning," she said very earnestly, clearly trying to help me, to inform me. "That's when the energy comes up. Once it's just the people who are serious about the circle. That's the transformation time. You know, the time between the worlds."

I had absolutely no idea what she was talking about, but it sounded a little nutty, and I didn't know quite what to say. I merely nodded in what I hope seemed like a meaningful way. But there was something relaxed and ingratiating about her that made me feel bold, so I asked her the question that had been on my mind since I'd arrived yesterday.

"Is there anywhere to get a little pot around here? I'd really like to smoke a bowl."

Cat looked around, clearly nervous, then smiled mischievously when she saw that we were alone.

"You can't just say that here!" she said in a confidential tone. She smirked again. "I wouldn't mind a little chronic myself, but there's no drugs at these festivals. The Bloodmoons are fanatical about it. Legal liability issues or something."

I nodded. But my nose told me otherwise yesterday. Someone had some pot around here. Oh well.

She stubbed her cigarette out on the side of the building and tossed it into a large green metal trash barrel. "Well, I hope to see you there tonight," she said, smiling, and it sounded like she really meant it. She leaned in and gave me a hard hug, pressing those huge breasts into the area around my solar plexus. I was aroused almost against my will. "Great to meet you Alex. Let me know if you find any chronic." She smiled.

"Sure. Great to meet you too," I said. "Thanks for the cigarette." She waved my thank you off and blew me a kiss as she wandered into the main building for lunch.

I took a few last drags off my cigarette, sucking it right down to the filter. I didn't know when I'd be getting another so I made it count. I stubbed it out next to Cat's and chucked it into the barrel. I was trying to decide whether to go in or not, when I felt a tap on my back. I leaped nervously away. As I turned, I saw Kerrie laughing at me.

"Jumpy huh?" she said, giggling at my gasping breaths.

"You can't just go around tapping people around here!" I said with a smile. "There are heathens in these woods!"

"Scary," she said, and she wrapped her arm around my waist in playful horror, crouching against my chest. "I'm allergic to heathens." She poked her head up around my shoulder, as if looking for any heathens that might be hiding behind me.

She laughed again, and dragged me into the main building. There was none of the tension that I expected. I wasn't sure whether we were supposed to pretend that last night never happened or what. It wasn't a conversation that I really wanted to have, so that was fine with me if that was her plan.

But that would have been too easy. As soon as we sat down with our plates full of crappy camp food she started it. "So, where were you this morning?" she asked, looking at me meaningfully with a mouthful of stale cornbread.

"Oh," I said, hesitating, taking a bite of macaroni salad. "I uh, had to go to the bathroom and I couldn't find anywhere that was private and I guess it just took a long time, you know?"

"Oh," she said, looking mildly confused. "Well, I wanted to talk with you, about what happened last night." she looked at me shyly, then turned her attention to her small green salad.

"It's okay. Honest," I said, looking down at my own plate. I wanted to end it quickly. I really didn't like having difficult emotional conversations. I really was fine with it all. I just wanted things to be back the way they were yesterday. "Last night, I was just... I don't know, lonely or something. I didn't mean to put you in an awkward position. It's not a big deal."

Kerrie looked injured. I must have said something wrong. She began eating her food without saying anything else.

"I, I mean, I really, our friendship is what's important to me Kerrie. I like you and you like me and that makes us friends, right? And last night, that was just you know?" I sounded like an idiot, but she wasn't saying anything so I kept going. "But we're still friends. That's the important thing. I don't want to spoil our friendship with any weirdness, right? I mean, we haven't been together, you know, as friends, in so long, but we're already really good friends again, right? And I'm just really so sorry for everything."

Kerrie looked up and smiled at me. I must have looked like a complete babbling fool. I could tell that my cheeks were going red. She patted me on the shoulder. "Okay, there, slow down," she said. "I'm the one that owes you an apology."

"No," I said. "No you don't."

"I wanted you to kiss me all day," she said meaningfully.

"You did?"

"Yes, and I didn't too, at the same time. And I was really throwing you mixed signals, I don't know. I have a crush on you, Alex. I won't lie," she said, looking quickly downward. "But I'm just not free right now, and I'm so sorry." She put her hand on my cheek and looked up at me, deep into my eyes. I really had no idea what to say. I felt confused and off balance. Thankfully, I didn't have to figure anything out.

"Alexander Sebastian!" came a voice from behind. I turned to see Adin Stone ambling toward our table with an outstretched finger and a beaming smile. "I was hoping to run into you again. Do you have a moment?"

"Uh, sure" I said, then turned back to Kerrie. "Can you excuse me for a sec?"

Kerrie nodded, looking confused.

"I'll be right back. Sorry." I got up and followed Adin Stone to a lonely corner of the mess hall.

"I'm amazed to see you sitting with the lovely young Kerrydwen Thornapple. You seem to have quite a knack for surrounding yourself with beautiful women." I looked back at Kerrie, now sitting by herself. She really did look beautiful. She was wearing small, colorful beads, a black tank top and jeans that somehow seemed a perfect blend of chic and pagan. "Why on Earth were you so interested in having me introduce you to Jessica Burnham when you've got such a lovely and charming young woman right there?"

"Oh, I, well... it's a bit complicated." I said.

"It's always complicated when it involves beautiful women. And I wouldn't have it any other way!" He laughed very loudly.

I looked back at Kerrie again, and saw her glance up at me, then turn away quickly.

"I guess this isn't the best time for us to talk, Alex," said Adin in a kindly tone. "You get back to your lady friend. I need to get some food before it's all eaten up! Some of these earth goddesses don't leave seconds! We'll talk soon!" And with that he shuffled off.

"What was that all about?" asked Kerrie as I got back to the table.

"Sorry, I don't know what that was all about. That guy, do you know him?"

"What guy?"

"Adin Stone. He seemed to know you."

"Adin Stone? Hmm? Sounds familiar, but I'm not sure. When you've been coming to these things as long as I have, the names start to blur together," she said mildly.

"Huh," I said, wondering what it was about Adin Stone that was fascinating me so much. Kerrie decided to change the subject.

"So, what have you been doing all morning, I mean after you went to pee?"

"Oh, that's right! I haven't told you, I went to a workshop. It was taught by someone from... The A∴R∴T∴," I said, emphasizing it darkly and dramatically, feeling rather brave for getting involved with something so dangerous.

"The A∴R∴T∴, huh?" said Kerrie, blandly.

"Yeah, I didn't even realize that it existed anymore," I said with unconcealed excitement.

"Oh it exists all right," she said, sounding like perhaps she wished it didn't exist.

"What?" I asked. "Do you know something bad about the the A∴R∴T∴ that I should be aware of?"

"I really don't know anything," she said, shaking her head. "You sure seem to be attracted to the strange elements around here. But I really shouldn't say anything, because, you know, 'cause I really don't know." She sounded strangely nervous.

"What's up?" I asked. Now she had me really curious. "What have you heard?"

"It's just, you know. It's just innuendo."

"Tell me."

"The thing is, I've met perfectly nice people in The A∴R∴T∴, I have some good friends who are in The A∴R∴T∴ so..."

"Tell me."

45

"I heard that they're evil," she said bashfully.

"And?"

"And that they sacrifice animals, and drink blood and..." she looked quite embarrassed.

"What?"

"It's just, it sounds stupid now. It's probably just bullshit." She was blushing. "I just heard that they have drug-induced orgies and practice black magick, you know, harmful magick. Worship devils. Conjure demons. To hurt people. It all sounds like the same silly stuff that Christians say about my parents so it's probably not true. But who knows."

12:40 PM

When we finished eating Kerrie told me that she had to do two hours of volunteer work down at the healing hall, then help her dad for the afternoon in the merchant's area, so I was going to be on my own again. I asked her what the 'healing hall' was. She explained that it was a cabin where they had band-aids, massage therapists, and Reiki energy healers to assist any festival goers that were hurt or having any kind of a rough time spiritually or just feeling too much festival energy. She, however, was just going to be helping with the band-aid aspect of things.

As I wandered through the festival grounds by myself once again, I thought about what Kerrie said about The A∴R∴T∴. I'd heard the same exact things. Evil. Blood. Demons. Orgies. It didn't seem to match with the pleasant man who taught the peaceful meditation workshop to me a couple of hours ago. But who knows what people do behind closed doors?

I was really getting curious. I wondered how a person could go about getting involved in The A∴R∴T∴. Did they choose you by invitation only? Or could anybody join? If I somehow could get involved with The A∴R∴T∴ it would make it much easier for me to find out if one or more of them were responsible for that murder.

Ten

It was really an amazing afternoon. The sun was shining in a sky with just a few puffy white clouds, and it was very warm, unseasonably warm for Massachusetts at this time of year. I continued to wander aimlessly around the forest paths for quite a while, silently watching the festival-goers laughing and prancing in their renaissance costumes and medieval peasant gear. A group of overweight young women sat in a circle in a field of clover, massaging each other, murmuring in delight. Further down the rocky path I saw a woman with a smoothly shaved head, standing on a small boulder, wearing puffy pantaloons and tights. She noisily serenaded a captive audience of ten or so with a tuneless song, accompanying herself on a small mandolin-like instrument. The cheerful audience contented itself by passing around several bottles of mead, and hooting along at the choruses. I smiled as I approached the group, and even bashfully danced a little as I passed by them- I received a lot of cheers. But I got away quickly. I felt the strong need for another cigarette soon.

I was really starting to get antsy when I spotted Matthew Wiley in the distance, in conversation with a small group of people. They were all standing under the shadows of some tall pine trees, smoking cigarettes. Matthew was talking to an older man, mid-fifties, short and slight of build. The man had jet-black hair with a shock of white at the temples, a goatee, and sunglasses. He wore a leather biker jacket that seemed a bit too clean for a biker.

47

Jessica Burnham was there, still looking beautiful, and still looking rather bored and irritated with existence. There was a young man in his mid-twenties with long stringy hair and a frizzy beard. He was dressed in colorful hippie clothes. On either side of him were two girls in their twenties. On his left was a girl with many piercings in her face, the left half of her head shaved bald. An angular tribal tattoo was there in place of hair. On the right side of her head her hair was dyed poorly, bright red, which actually complemented her deep green eyes. Somehow she managed to seem rather pretty. On the other side of the young man stood a slender, attractive Asian girl with a small perky body, and long, shapely legs accentuated in a black denim outfit. She seemed almost a little too clean cut and innocent for the rest of the group. They seemed a strange group in general, and I knew that I just had to walk up and talk to them. Since they were all smoking, I broke the ice with my usual cigarette bumming routine.

"You should really consider buying a pack," said Jessica Burnham with a dark smile. Perhaps I was growing on her.

Matthew was more than happy to share his cigarettes. He even remembered who I was. "You're the guy who came in late to our workshop this morning, right?" he asked pleasantly. He lit my cigarette for me.

"Yeah. I'm sorry about that. I got lost," I mumbled, savoring the cigarette.

"No worries, man," he said. "What was your name again? Allen?"

"No. Alex. Alexander Sebastian," I said, correcting him with a smile. He clearly didn't care either way. "I really enjoyed that workshop," I continued. "It was..." I couldn't think of anything interesting to say, and they all stared at me expectantly. "...really good." I felt stupid.

"Thanks, man." said Matthew. "So, um, let me introduce you to everybody." He pointed to the short, leather-clad man in his fifties, "Alex, this is our fearless leader, Damian Webster."

Damian Webster waved at me slightly, not really even pretending to be interested in meeting me. He clearly had something else on his mind. He had hard, piercing, green eyes, but they looked troubled, far away. "Alex," he muttered absently.

"Nice to meet you," I said. "What do you mean, fearless leader?"

The young hippie chimed in. "The A∴R∴T∴. We're all initiates of the A∴R∴T∴," his tone was a strange mix of pride and apology, as if he thought The A∴R∴T∴ was very cool, but was sure I wouldn't. "Damian is our Chief Adept." The sound of his title seemed to awaken Damian, and he bowed slightly, with a mock aristocracy.

I was quite excited. The A∴R∴T∴! And it was now clear to me that Jessica Burnham was a member of The A∴R∴T∴ too. Very interesting. Matthew introduced me to the rest of them, and with the exception of Jessica they were all quite friendly.

The young hippie was named Jeremy McClosky. He was a musician, keyboards, with a band named "Mount Abiegnus." The girl with all the piercings was named Lucy Grinder, and she was a professional body piercer. Not exactly a shock. The Asian girl was Catherine Chen, a massage therapist. They were all quite warm and welcoming. I quickly felt very comfortable with them.

"So, how does someone go about joining The A∴R∴T∴?" I asked, once I worked up the courage. They all instantly seemed even friendlier. Damian Webster even appeared to warm a bit, allowing a trace of smile to crack across his face.

"All you have to do is ask," said Matthew. "You've just taken the first step. We have fairly regular initiations. Of course there's a waiting period." He reached into his pocket and gave me a card. "Here. Give me a call if you ever want to talk about it more. My home number's the hand-written one. Don't call me at work."

I looked down at the card which read, "Burlington Chiropractic Care, Dr. Matthew Wiley, Your Wellness is Our Number One Concern," and then addresses and numbers.

"You're a chiropractor?" I asked.

"That's what my office assistants keep on telling me," said Matthew, sounding pleasantly sarcastic. I must admit I was a little impressed. He didn't seem very much older than I was, really, and he had his own office and assistants. But I guess it wasn't that hard to impress me.

"Uh oh," murmured Catherine Chen, tapping Matthew and pointing up the path. I looked up to see what she was pointing at.

An extremely overweight man in his late forties to early fifties was laboring slowly toward us up the path. He had to weigh 350 pounds or more, all of those pounds wrapped in an immense black velvet robe. He was very bald, but with a lonely patch of long, blondish hair growing on the back of his head. It was rather sadly confined by an elastic into a limp little pony-tail. He had bright red, mottled cheeks, and a swollen nose. He was sweating profusely. The effort of walking seemed to be almost too much for him. Luckily, he was trailed by three scrawny, pasty, bespectacled acolytes in matching robes, who steadied him as he approached.

My new group of friends tensed up as a unit, as if all subconsciously preparing for battle.

"Ninety-three and hello, fellow brothers and sisters of the A∴R∴T∴," said the fat man breathlessly. Something in the way he intoned 'A∴R∴T∴' did not sound quite right. I noticed that he had clots of cheesy matter lodged in the corners of his mouth that danced and jiggled as he spoke.

"Hello, Mackey. What can we do for you?" said Damian Webster without any pleasantness.

"I need to ask a tremendous favor of you," said the fat man in a wheezy, syrupy sweet tone. The cheesy globs continued to wiggle with his words. He paused and pulled a pack of cigarettes out, putting one in his mouth. One of his followers lit it for him instantly. He was still gasping for breaths as he smoked, which made him seem even more bizarre. I wondered if he was about to die.

"What?" snapped Webster, clearly irritated at the man's posturing.

"I need all of you members of the A∴R∴T∴ to make sure you are putting your cigarettes into proper receptacles," said the fat man pedantically.

"We're already doing that, man!" blurted the hippie Jeremy McClosky, leaping into an instantly aggressive posture.

"Well, I really don't know what to say then," said the fat man calmly, raising his hands in resignation. "Because there have apparently been a lot of complaints about cigarette butts getting left around, and the Bloodmoons are trying to blame it on me. Of course that's ridiculous. I know me and I know my people. We're very conscientious."

"We'll be careful," said Matthew, clearly trying to be conciliatory so that the man would leave.

"I hope so," said Mackey. "Ninety-three." He then looked at me for the first time. His eyes were gray, but somehow quite fiery, almost like opals. He seemed to take me in, but he said nothing, and quickly turned away. He lumbered off without another word. I watched him. After about ten steps he dropped his cigarette on the path and stamped it out, leaving it in the middle of the road. What a total asshole.

They told me his name was Paul Mackey. He was an active member of the A∴R∴T∴ for years, but he was eventually suspended for apparently, to put it bluntly, being a total asshole. He couldn't get along with Damian Webster, and they fought like cats and dogs for several years. That was his first mistake in the A∴R∴T∴. Eventually Mackey went out and started his own magical group, using mostly the A∴R∴T∴ materials, a group which he called the "Black Pullet Lodge." I guess that wasn't too popular with The A∴R∴T∴'s international office. That was his second mistake. Then he tried staging a sort of coup to steal away the local membership of the A∴R∴T∴, and that was his final mistake. But apparently no one was really very interested in Mackey's group, so he just looked like an ungrateful fool at the time he left. However, over the intervening few years he'd managed to grow his own small following.

"He's a Black Brother," said Jeremy.

"A what?" I asked.

"An evil adept," said Matthew, rolling his eyes. He didn't look like he was buying it. "A member of the Black Brotherhood. The Black Lodge."

"That fat fuck wishes he was a Black Brother," spat Damian Webster. "Even being a Black Brother takes some work. That lazy slob just runs off his mouth. I don't think I've ever seen him doing any magick, black or white. He and his pathetic 'followers' are just a bunch of ridiculous losers."

"I wouldn't be so hasty, Damian. Each of us have different ways of working magick," said Matthew. He seemed to want to at least be polite.

"What about the magical murder?" asked Catherine Chen, shyly. That got my attention.

"That was no murder," said Damian Webster. "That was a coincidence. It wasn't like..." then he fell silent.

"Yeah, Mackey had nothing to do with that," said Matthew.

"The only way that fat asshole could kill anybody would be to fall on them," spat Webster vehemently.

But I was intrigued- a magical murder. Were they talking about the murder I was looking into? Or was it another one? Was this a magical murder spree that I was uncovering? Could Mackey somehow be involved?

"What was this magical murder?" I asked finally.

"Let's not talk about this again," groaned Lucy Grinder. I was a little surprised to hear her voice. She had hardly spoken a word since I was introduced to her. She slumped to the ground and lit a cigarette.

"Yeah, this is a pretty done topic," said Matthew. "Its just a big mucky-muck in The A∴R∴T∴ who died a few years ago."

"He was an old man!" said Damian. "He had a heart attack. It's not unheard of."

I was a bit disappointed. This didn't sound like it was going to be at all related to my murder.

"So, how was Paul Mackey supposed to be involved?" I asked.

"Okay, I'll tell you the fast version, since these guys are apparently unable to," said Jessica Burnham with a scowl and a roll of her eyes. "This guy, Frater Merlin, he was a Magister Templi at the A∴R∴T∴ international office out in Los Angeles. He wouldn't advance Mackey, because, well, you met Mackey, I'm sure you can see why. So, Mackey calls and tells him he's gonna put a curse on him and the next day the old guy dies."

"I heard he was a really nice old guy, too," said Catherine.

"Abe Crane and he were friends going way back," said Matthew to Catherine. She nodded. I couldn't place the name 'Abe Crane.'

"Well," inserted Damian. "I met him on several occasions, and he seemed like an old wind bag to me."

"But you think everybody's a wind bag, Damian," said Jeremy McClosky with a smirk.

"Like who?" demanded Damian, indignant.

"Jacob Pilsner," said Jeremy.

"Abe Crane," suggested Lucy Grinder.

"And don't forget me," smirked Jeremy.

"I guess you're right. I do," said Damian Webster with a laugh.

"Can I ask another question?" I said, not really following the current train of their conversation.

"Sure," said Matthew.

"What does 'ninety-three' mean exactly?" I asked. "I heard Mackey say it a couple of times. I know it has something to do with Aleister Crowley."

"Oh, dude," said Jeremy McClosky. "That's like the traditional Thelemic greeting. It's the numeration of both the words 'thelema' and 'agape' in the Greek qabala. You say it kind of as a shorthand, because Thelemites are supposed to greet each other with the phrase 'Do what thou wilt shall be the whole of the Law,' and say goodbye to each other with the phrase 'Love is the law, love under will.' It's kind of like a fast way of saying all that, because 'thelema' is Greek for 'will,' and 'agape' is Greek for 'love.' Get it?"

I nodded, though I really wasn't quite sure what he was talking about.

"Most people don't say it much around non-initiates," said Matthew Wiley. "Because it makes you sound a bit odd. But I think Mackey likes being a bit odd."

Their talk started to veer off into subjects that I didn't know or care about so I politely said my good-byes with a hesitant "Ninety-three," and slipped off.

I could hardly take this all in. I really wasn't sure what to make of the last fifteen minutes or so. The A∴R∴T∴ people all seemed very cool, and funny. They certainly didn't seem particularly evil. But maybe I'm not such a good judge of good and evil. After all, I smoked an awful lot of pot. Maybe the truth was that nobody was evil, or everybody. I didn't know what to think. I'd met a lot of strange and interesting people, but I really hadn't found out a thing about the murder. Or maybe I had. I wondered if it would ever come together into any kind of meaningful picture, or if I was just wasting my time. I really just wanted to find Kerrie and relax for a while.

Eleven

I made my way down to the merchant's area, hoping to see Kerrie there. She seemed like the only possible relief from everything that I'd just seen and heard, a soothing balm. Sadly, she was nowhere around. The merchant's area consisted of dozens upon dozens of tents, canopied booths and tables full of jewelry, herbs, incense, renaissance costumes, stones, books, and all sorts of other strange and magical items. There were even three separate tents belonging to people selling mead and ale.

There was a young woman with dark, curly hair pulled into a tight bun sitting behind a large stack of books; all of which bore the same title, 'Wicca in the Age of Aquarius.' I think she was having a book signing, but no one seemed to be paying much attention to her. She looked quite young, maybe only a couple of years older than me. I wondered how she got a book published. She looked bored, sitting there, and I certainly could have struck up a conversation, but I really didn't want to have to buy her book so I moved quickly past her.

Eventually I spotted Arthyr Thornapple, Kerrie's dad, sitting at his booth. It was slightly more professional looking than a lot of the other booths. The Thornapple's booth had a wide selection of different kinds of occult knick-knacks from pentagram pendants to wind-chimes shaped like goddesses and an endless array of other odds and ends, all displayed on wooden pegs or within plastic cases. Kerrie's parents owned a very successful pagan business called 'The Five Sacred Trees.' They had three stores, and a mail order catalog, both retail and wholesale; and their booth was marked by a large vinyl sign with the symbol of their business, five trees winding together into a Celtic knot. Arthyr looked almost as bored as the young author, sitting there at his booth without any customers. There weren't many people in the merchant's area, and the few that were there seemed most interested in trying on renaissance costumes and giggling.

"Fancy seeing you down here!" called out Arthyr when he spotted me. He stood up and came out from behind his booth to greet me as I approached.

"Hi there," I said. "Seems a little slow around here."

Arthyr looked around vaguely. He didn't really seem very concerned. "Yeah," he said, nodding. "I used to do a lot of business at these festivals. But that was years ago. There wasn't so much competition for space, and people were a lot more excited just to be at a pagan event. Now, everyone's jaded. I used bring a whole U-Haul trailer and I'd still run out of product. I'll probably be bringing most of this stuff home again," he said, waving his hands over his merchandise. "And it all fits in the back of the station wagon. At this point I'm really more interested in handing out my wholesale catalogs to the other merchants. I make more money, and I don't have to haul it all around! UPS does it for me!" He laughed heartily.

That made a lot of sense. "Sounds like you've got it all figured out," I said, not really having anything bright or interesting to add.

"I hope so," he said with a smile. "I've been coming to these things for nearly twenty years." He patted me affectionately on the shoulder and sat back down behind his booth. He smiled wearily. "I guess I'm a little jaded too." He stared off for a moment, then turned his focus back to me. "You haven't seen Kerrie or her mom around anywhere, have you?" he asked.

"No," I said. "I was kind of hoping to find Kerrie myself."

"Well, she's not really due here for a little while yet..." He tapped the edge of his table rhythmically, staring off again. "That's too bad you don't know where they are, 'cause I really need to visit the john."

I told him I'd be glad to watch the booth for a few minutes. He was extremely grateful, leaping to his feet instantly and thanking me profusely. He excused himself quickly, telling me that if any customers came along I should grab hold of them and not let go for any reason.

But no customers came. I looked around at the other vendors, and they all looked about as bored as Arthyr Thornapple. I wondered how many of them had to use the bathroom, and if anyone was coming along to relieve them.

Arthyr returned after what seemed quite a long while, thanking me again, telling me that he owed me big. I assured him that it was really nothing. We chatted for a little while about the weather and what I'd been up to at the festival. I didn't mention the A∴R∴T∴, fearing that I'd just hear the same lecture Kerrie already gave me. I wished I could ask a few questions about the murder, but I couldn't find a comfortable way to steer things in that direction.

After a while our conversation naturally petered out, and I was about to excuse myself to look around for Kerrie when I saw Paul Mackey waddling in our direction. Since Mackey was the only person I'd met so far who seemed like he could be connected in any way with murder, I thought I'd stick around and see what he wanted with Arthyr Thornapple or me.

"Blessed be, Arthyr," said Mackey in a friendly but rather sanctimonious tone. He was wheezing of course, trying to catch his breath. He seemed to ignore me. "How is the afternoon treating you? It's a beautiful day today, isn't it?" He smiled and opened his arms expectantly as he reached the booth breathlessly. "Come over here you..." I noticed he still had that cheese in the corners of his mouth.

"Afternoon, Paul. It's so beautiful today that all the festival goers are off hiking or swimming in the lake," sighed Arthyr as he came out and gave Mackey a brief hug. "How are you, old friend?"

Mackey slowly shook his head. "It's a bunch of dilettantes at these festivals nowadays," he blustered. "They can't appreciate the quality of a merchant like yourself- a man of character- a man who has stood the test of time." Mackey then looked over at me, and stared. I instantly felt uncomfortable. "Ninety-three. I've been seeing you around everywhere today," he said pointedly. "You're not following me are you?" He laughed very loud. I wasn't sure if he was laughing at some joke in his head or if he was laughing at me, but I really wasn't liking him at all.

"Uh, no," I said stupidly. I felt nervous, and my mind never worked properly when I was nervous.

"My name is Paul Mackey," he said with a smile. He extended his hand, and I shook it cautiously. "But I'm sure your A∴R∴T∴ pals already told you all about me."

"Nice to meet you," I replied, "I'm Alexander Sebastian." I decided to ignore the second half of his statement.

"When I saw you with those A∴R∴T∴ shitheads, I was sure that you were not to be trusted, but any friend of Thornapple can't be all bad," continued Mackey with a friendly pat on Arthyr's shoulder. "I'll be seeing you around," he said to me meaningfully, disturbingly. "See you Arthyr," he tossed off casually, in a much lighter tone, as he turned and labored away.

"You take care now, Paul," said Arthyr cheerily, then as Mackey was out of earshot, "Quite a character, that one." He laughed quietly.

"How do you know Paul Mackey so well?" I asked. I wasn't able to see them being friends at all. Arthyr Thornapple was polite and generous and clearly a good person. Mackey didn't seem to be any of those things.

"You know, we've all been coming to these things for years," he said noncommittally. It didn't sound like he was telling me everything.

"But it sounded like you guys have some history together," I prodded.

"Well, yes, we do," said Arthyr, leaning in toward me with a smirk, taking a mildly conspiratorial tone. He paused, looking at me meaningfully. Then he sighed and went on. "It was back during the bad old days. Morven and I, we just had one store back then, and we weren't making any money. Much like to-day," he inserted with a smirk. "We needed to make ends meet, so we dealt a little grass. Mid-level stuff mostly. Mackey was one of our suppliers. He was big into it back then. I'm not sure if he's still doing that. A lot of the people I knew in that are gone now. Got busted. Moved away. Died." He stared off for several seconds, lost in reminiscence.

So Mackey was a drug dealer. I wondered if that was the real reason he was thrown out of the A∴R∴T∴. I also couldn't help but wonder if he might have any pot for me. Almost as if on cue, I saw Paul Mackey lumbering back toward the Thornapple's booth. Arthyr noticed him too, and looked startled, like he wondered if Mackey had overheard us talking about him. We stared at him in silence as he approached.

"So sorry to disturb you again," said Mackey as he reached us. Then he turned and looked right at me. "But I was wondering if I might have a moment of your time." He took several long gasping breaths, then pulled out a cigarette and lit it.

I wasn't sure what he meant. I was happy to talk to him. I really wanted to question him on a number of subjects. I wasn't sure how I was going to bring up drugs or magical murder, but I knew that if I could get him alone I'd have a better chance. I was taller by several inches and certainly in better physical shape so I really wasn't afraid of him other than in a creepy, psychological way.

"I know you told me your name, but it's eluding me at the moment," said Mackey, trying to cover up the fact that he obviously wasn't listening when I introduced myself less than five minutes ago- typical narcissist.

"Alex," I said, being polite despite his lack of reciprocation. "Alex Sebastian."

"That's right," he said, pretending to remember. "Alex Sebastian. Well, I need to speak with you, Alex Sebastian. It's a matter of some importance," he said very gravely. I really didn't know what to make of him. He turned to Arthyr. "Is it okay if I borrow your young friend?"

Arthyr nodded his acquiescence and I found myself walking off with Mackey.

Twelve

I followed Mackey along a dirt path leading away from the merchant area. I bummed one of his cigarettes as we walked, and I discovered that even his cigarettes were distasteful. The cigarette he gave me was some sort of generic, and it tasted awful. We walked together in near silence for quite a while, and I wondered where exactly he was taking me and why. Eventually we reached a very large, old fashioned canvas tent, large enough to sleep ten or more, which he identified as his home. Someone had scrawled numerous unrecognizable magical glyphs all over the sides of it. The crime scene photographs instantly came to mind. I heard what sounded like the monotonous whining of a small child from within.

Mackey pulled back the front flap, and I could see that the whining indeed belonged to a small homely girl running circles around a heavy woman sitting cross-legged in the center of the tent. The woman stared off into space, a cigarette dangling from her mouth, trying to ignore the shrieks of the child. Mackey introduced the woman as his wife Jackie, and the little girl as his daughter Hypatia, Hyppie for short. Mackey's wife was a woman who would've seemed overweight on any other occasion, but next to Mackey she seemed relatively fit. Both mother and daughter were quite hairy and dumpy in appearance. He introduced me as 'Sebastian.' I wasn't sure if he now thought that was my first name, but I wasn't going to correct him. In the dark recesses of the tent sat the three black-robed young followers I'd seen with Mackey before. He didn't introduce me

60

to them, nor did they speak to me even once. They barely seemed conscious. The whole tent was thick with a cloud of cigarette smoke. It made me feel dizzy just being in that atmosphere. I wondered what horrible health effects it was having on that ugly little child.

Paul Mackey slumped down onto a bed of dirty pillows, quickly reclining onto his side, then laying all the way down. He looked much more comfortable lying down, as if this was his customary pose. He bade me join him. I sat as close to the entrance as possible, to receive at least a trickle of oxygen. His wife Jackie asked me if I wanted anything, but I was sure I didn't want anything she could possibly offer. She got up and dug out some grapes and sliced oranges, placing them in front of Mackey. He helped himself to some of the grapes, looking like an absurd parody of a Caesar. The little girl sat in front of the plate of fruit and began to quickly devour it. No one would ever have thought of stopping her because for the first time she stopped making noise. I was wondering if Mackey would ever get to what he wanted to talk to me about. Mackey turned to his wife and pointed at me.

"Sebastian here is in the A∴R∴T∴," he said, like I was a laboratory specimen.

"Really," she said, not even pretending to be interested.

"No," I said, shaking my head. "Actually no, I'm not. I was just talking to them."

Paul Mackey looked very surprised. "You're not?" he repeated. "Then maybe there really is some hope for you!" He smiled, the cheesy slime around his mouth spreading toward his ears.

"I just met them for the first time today," I said.

"You'd better hope that's the last time, for your sake," said Mackey meaningfully. "Tell me then, what were you doing with them?"

"I was just chatting," I said, quite innocently. After all, that's all I was doing.

"Well, I saw you talking to that snake Damian Webster," spat Mackey.

"Uh, yeah, he was there."

"I've known that bastard for nearly thirty years. He's a real piece of work," said Mackey.

He was trying to get at something. His words were pointed, but surely there was something else he wanted from me. I hoped he was going to get to the point soon, because I was really starting to get a headache. It smelled so awful in there that I began to think about giving up cigarettes for good.

"You're not thinking about joining up with the A∴R∴T∴ are you?" asked Mackey accusatorily.

"No," I said, although that was a lie. I was certainly thinking about joining the A∴R∴T∴, at least in the back of my mind, and the idea of spiting Paul Mackey was making it even more appealing. But I wasn't about to tell him that. "I'm really pretty much a loner," I said. "I'm not a big joiner type. You know?" I shrugged, and Mackey nodded meaningfully.

"Well, good, at least you're not getting caught up in the A∴R∴T∴, that's a nasty web of deception and corruption," he grimaced. "But if you ever do want to join a real magical organization, the Black Pullet Lodge is the only real choice."

Shit. Had he dragged me all the way to his tent just to give me a weird sales pitch for his stupid magical group? His wife Jackie let loose a heavy sigh that indicated this was a routine she'd heard many times before.

"You see," he continued, unhindered by my total lack of interest or his wife's sigh. "With the A∴R∴T∴ you're going to get what I call 'McMagick.' It's made for the mass consumer. Psychic junk food. No real character or distinguishing qualities. The Black Pullet Lodge is the only true repository of the un-diluted ancient magick you're going to find. If you want McMagick, quick, easy crap, go with the A∴R∴T∴. If you want real, powerful magick, come see me and I'll try to get you into the Black Pullet Lodge. They only do initiations a couple of times a year."

I liked that. He was trying to make it look like the Black Pullet Lodge was something bigger than he was, and something exclusive. It was a clever tactic. But he didn't even know me and was quite obviously trying to get me to join. It didn't sound very exclusive to me. I began to wonder how I was going to wriggle my way out of that smoke-filled tent.

"I suppose Damian Webster has filled you with all kinds of misconceptions about me," said Mackey. "Don't listen to anything that man has to say. The man, and I use the term loosely, is a drug addict and a womanizer. All he ever wants to do is put his dick in whatever bitches get their cunts close enough for him to get it in, no offense honey," he said, turning vaguely toward his wife. "And I bet he's still accusing me of magically murdering that old dickhead out in L.A.?"

I shook my head vaguely. I didn't bother to tell him what Damian Webster actually thought of him.

"Well, that is a complete fabrication. I had nothing to do with any magical murder. The man just died. I do know he was afraid of me, afraid of what I had to offer, afraid of the contacts that I had made with the true and ancient order, the guiding forces behind the Lodge of the Black Pullet. That could have killed him. Fear is the great enemy. The whole order shook when I left, and it's been falling apart ever since."

This guy was unreal. I don't think I'd ever met anyone with such an inflated ego. He leaned in toward me, speaking to me slowly, meaningfully, looking deeply into my eyes.

"You can never know where anybody's loyalties really lie, Sebastian. Many people are coming to me because of what I have to offer, and some of them are still inside the A∴R∴T∴, letting me know exactly what's going on in there," and with that he smiled broadly, a bit crazily. He nodded his head meaningfully.

I wasn't sure what to think at all. Was he just nuts, or was he really letting me know something? He seemed like your standard megalomaniac. I guess I wasn't supposed to know anything for sure. Then I got an idea. I reached into my pocket, and pulled out the sheet of paper that Peter gave to me with the occult symbols on it.

"It sounds to me like you're a real expert on occultism," I said, watching him nod and smile broadly. "Well, I have these symbols here, and I don't know quite what they are. Do you recognize them?" I unfolded the piece of paper, and handed it to him, carefully noting his expression to see if he reacted suspiciously or guiltily. It was quite a brazen move, but I was starting to feel more confident.

He grabbed some black reading glasses out of a case and rested them on his nose. He looked down at the sheet and regarded the symbols coolly. If he had anything to do with them being at a crime scene he did not indicate it with his expression. I felt a bit disappointed. My only suspect now suddenly did not seem very guilty. He looked up at me.

"This a pretty eclectic group of symbols here," he said, then pointed down at a couple of the larger symbols. "These ones here are from the Lesser Key of Solomon. Here's the secret seal of Solomon, and that's the pentagram and the hexagram of Solomon." He pointed to more of the symbols. "And then these one's look like they're several Elder Futhark runes combined together, and those are some Enochian letters, and some Hebrew Letters, Yahweh, Eheieh, Adonai AGLA. It looks to me like it's probably a bunch of protective symbols." He handed the sheet back to me, and removed his glasses.

"Protective symbols?" I said curiously.

"Yes, like the sort of symbols you'd use if you wanted to keep something away, or out of your temple. It would seem to be a bit redundant to have so many. Where did you get them?" he asked, looking mildly intrigued.

"Oh, a friend of mine," I said in what I hoped sounded like nonchalance. "So, if you had those in your temple, it would be to protect you from something? To keep something out of your temple?"

"Yes," he said, frowning, like he was tiring of my questions.

But something important had just clicked into place for me. Peter thought the murderer put the symbols there, like it was some kind of sick, ritual hazing. But now it seemed obvious that it was the victim. Maybe the victim knew something was coming for him. Something dark and magical. And he was trying to protect himself so he drew those symbols everywhere. Could it really be that it was some sort of supernatural monster that killed him? Was that even possible?

"And would they work?" I asked. "Would they keep away unwanted evil spirits or whatever?"

Mackey shrugged.

"I think that would depend on a lot of different things," he said vaguely. "Spirits can be slippery little buggers." He

64

yawned. "Listen, I am feeling way too sober for this kind of conversation." He gave me a mischievous smile. "Do you want to smoke a joint?"

"Sure," I said. That wasn't an offer I was likely to refuse.

"Normally, I'd just spark up right here in the tent," he said, producing a fat joint from his pocket and slipping it behind his ear. "But the Bloodmoons are really getting fanatical about this no drugs at the festival garbage, so we'll have to step a little way into the woods." He smiled. And with that he began the long, arduous, struggle to his feet.

A brief argument commenced because his wife Jackie didn't want to be left out, but someone had to stay and watch Hyppie. It was eventually decided that one of the nameless minions would stay. Hyppie was pretty upset, but Jackie quickly shouted her into agreement.

When we eventually stepped out of the tent, it was starting to get dark. It made me feel suddenly nervous. I realized that Mackey and his cohorts were not trustworthy in my mind at all and now I was walking into the forest with them. I mean, I didn't think they were going to kill me or anything. But maybe, who knows? Maybe Mackey did recognize those symbols from the crime scene, and maybe he was taking me into the woods to do who knows what to me. But no, that was just silly. I didn't think he'd recognized them at all. We were all just going to smoke a little pot in the woods. Surely there was no harm in that. God I was stupid back then.

Thirteen

6:20 PM (approx.)

We all stumbled along for quite a way into the deep woods. I had no idea where we were anymore, and it was starting to get dark. Finally, Mackey stopped. A flash of light appeared in the air. Mackey had sparked a lighter. He pushed the unlit joint into my hand.

"You go ahead and take the green hit, brother Sebastian," said Mackey quietly.

I could see nothing but the joint, the lighter and Mackey's large, vague outline. He lit it for me and I drew in deeply. It had a thick, heavy, skunky flavor. I could tell it was some very strong pot. I took a second hit and then passed it to Mackey. He took a small hit, then passed it on to his wife. I kept the smoke in my lungs for a very long time, finally letting it go and coughing uncontrollably. It was very strong pot. I wasn't usually a cougher.

"What do you think?" he said. But I didn't have a chance to comment because the joint came back to me, significantly smaller. His little myrmidons clearly enjoyed pot as much as I did. I took two or three large hits because I didn't think I'd be seeing it again.

"You like it?" said Mackey, observing my fervor.

"Oh yeah, it's great," I said in a huge flume of smoke, as I let go of the last hit from my lungs. I coughed some more. I was already feeling an oncoming high.

"What do you think of the little something extra?" he asked. I couldn't see his face in the darkness, so I wasn't sure what he meant by that statement.

"Uh, what are you talking about?" I asked nervously.

"This pot is laced. A little of the good stuff."

"What?" I was shocked and confused.

"PCP? Angel Dust? It's good, right?" asked Mackey innocently. I heard his acolytes giggling in the darkness. Was he just playing with me?

"Are you kidding?" I demanded angrily.

"What do you mean?" asked Mackey.

"You didn't... I didn't... You have to tell someone before you do shit like that!" I shouted at him. I couldn't see him, or anything else, and I was really starting to feel buzzed. But was it a pot buzz coming on, or a PCP buzz? "Are you serious? Did you seriously give me PCP? That's fucking insane, man!" I was really pissed.

"I'm just kidding, playing with you a little, Sebastian," he said, and they all burst into raucous laughter. "I wouldn't do that to you, buddy." But he was starting to sound farther away. Was it my mind, or the drugs, or were they walking away from me? "I'm not that cruel. Especially in these woods. They can be dangerous at night. When you're by yourself. There are dark spirits in these woods. The festival stirs them up." He was definitely getting further away.

"Where the fuck are you going?" I demanded, stumbling toward the now distant sound of his voice. What was even worse, I was starting to hallucinate little spirits everywhere. I couldn't see the woods at all. Tiny, colorful angels and demons were flying all around me in geometric patterns. It was all I could see. I felt a buzzing in my ears and a creeping tension in the back of my neck, uncomfortable blue waves of tightness.

"You take care of yourself, Sebastian," said Mackey smugly. "Watch out for those spirits. They can be slippery little buggers. Walk a straight path through the darkness. Quit the night, and seek the day! Ninety-three!" And that was the last thing I heard him say.

I could hear them all laughing in the distance. But I couldn't even tell what direction it was coming from. My spatial perceptions were totally shot. Was I on PCP? I'd never done PCP before. I didn't even really know what it was supposed to be like other than those scare talks you get in school where every drug turns you into a raving lunatic. I was definitely seeing spirits everywhere. That much I can say for certain.

I was completely disoriented and terrified. Then I started feeling things touching me. I don't know if it was spirits or insects, but something kept touching my arms. I tried to swat whatever it was away, but I couldn't find anything. I started getting totally freaked out. I didn't know where I was or what was going on. I thought I heard something, a humming, like a sort of singing or maybe buzzing. Tears began to fill my eyes. I felt like things were touching me all over. I fell down onto the ground and I saw shadowy snakes and insects, crawling toward me. This was too much. I was filthy and cold and terrible things were everywhere around me. What was I thinking coming out into these woods with that asshole? I started crawling blindly. I don't know where I thought I was crawling.

I felt something poke at me. Was it a twig? No, it was poking me again and again, then more pokes from other directions. It slowly became more like scraping, and I was sure it was shadowy creatures, wild creatures, unearthly creatures. Was I going to die? I felt tearing. Tearing right through me. I was totally cracking up.

Then I heard a clear and loud female voice in the darkness.

"Apo Pantos Kakodaimonos!" It was close by. Somehow, the presence of another person cleared my mind a bit. But I still couldn't see a damn thing.

"Soi, O Kteis," I heard the female voice cry out in strange gibberish.

"Uh, hello?" I said sheepishly.

The female screamed in utter shock. "Holy fucking shit," she cried out. "Who the fuck is there?"

"Uh, I'm sorry to scare you. I'm kind of lost."

"Christ, you scared the shit out of me, I thought I'd be alone way out here. Fuck, you can't get any privacy around here," said the girl. A flashlight flipped on, blaring right in my face, forcing me to cover my eyes. "Hey, I know you," said the girl, struggling to place me. "Where do I know you from?"

"I don't know, I'm really very sorry" I said, I could feel dried tears on my cheeks and I was really embarrassed to have that light on me.

THE BROTHERHOOD OF LIGHT AND DARKNESS

"You're that guy. We were talking to you this afternoon," she said, and shined the flashlight briefly on herself. It was Jessica Burnham. I felt unbelievably humiliated. "You look like shit. What the fuck are you doing out here?"

I didn't feel like I had any choice but to explain exactly what had happened. I couldn't possibly think of any other plausible reason why I'd be crawling around in the dirt in the middle of the forest. The story came out rather disjointedly, but she seemed to follow it. She didn't seem at all surprised that Mackey would pull a stunt like that, and she couldn't understand what possibly would have provoked me to wander into the forest with him. She took pity on me and helped me up, saying she'd better take me to the healing hall. She gave me a couple of cigarettes along the way, which was very nice. The walk back still seemed to take forever. I was feeling completely out of it, hallucinating trees and rocks that weren't really there every few steps. I still didn't know if it was just really strong pot, a strange drug in the pot, or just my mind playing tricks with me.

Fourteen

Jessica dumped me off at the healing hall, wished me luck, and walked away. But she turned and smiled at me as she left. She had a really beautiful smile for someone who was generally so unpleasant. And then she was gone, leaving me standing alone at the entrance to the healing hall.

The healing hall was a large cabin, constructed from rough wood, but covered with a thick coating of light purple paint. I walked inside nervously, and was greeted with a smile from a weak-chinned skinny male in dirty clothes. I explained that I was just sort of feeling out of it, leaving out the potentially PCP-laced marijuana from my story. The weak-chinned man offered me a Reiki healing. I wasn't quite sure what that would consist of, but I agreed. I knew it was some sort hand waving type of energy healing. That was about all I knew.

He led me to a massage table, and I lay down. He then held his hands about three or four inches from my head. He closed his eyes and it looked to me like he was deeply concentrating. I don't know if he was supposed to be sending me energy or something, but I didn't really feel anything. However, I closed my eyes and within two minutes I was fast asleep.

Paul Mackey stood in front of me, laughing. I'm not sure where we were. Was it back in the woods, or just in another very dark place? Mackey's laughter was deep, echoing and haunting.

"Sebastian Alexander, your initiation has now begun!" cried Mackey as he laughed. I felt furious that he'd just tricked me, and that he still didn't seem to know my name.

"Why are you fucking with me like this?" I shouted at him furiously. I was still lying down, and for some reason I couldn't get up.

"It's not me," said Mackey innocently. "Talk to your buddy Adin Stone. This is his show." He pointed behind him. There I saw Adin Stone, softly glowing in phosphorescent white robes. He looked like a wizard from a storybook. On either side of him stood Jessica Burnham and Kerrie Thornapple. They were both completely naked, their shapely forms delicately highlighted by Adin's glowing atmosphere.

Adin raised his arms dramatically, sending whirling cascades of light into the air around him. The two young women approached me, and I realized that I was actually lying on a stone slab, completely naked myself. As they came to my sides, they both smiled at me, saying nothing. They put their hands on my chest, gently caressing me. I could feel my penis stiffening from the stimulation of their caresses, and I felt a little embarrassed. They didn't seem to mind.

Both of them began to sink they're fingernails into my skin, cutting into me, scraping tiny X's into my flesh, over my heart, on my shoulders, on my stomach. Jessica reached up and touched my forehead. Her fingers burned intensely. I sat bolt upright, shocked.

Fifteen

8:25 PM (approx.)

I sat right up on the massage table! I'd been dreaming! Another crazy dream! I noticed that my penis had actually gotten hard too. This night was all about embarrassment. The weak-chinned Reiki guy looked pretty shocked and embarrassed too.

"Are you okay, man?" he asked, still holding his hands out in front of him in his Reiki position.

"Oh yeah," I mumbled. "I was just having a weird dream is all."

"Sure, man," he replied, dropping his hands to his sides. "That happens sometimes. That's good. You want to lay down again?"

"No," I said as politely as possible, slipping off the table. "I'm actually feeling a lot better. Thank you. You helped me out a lot." I wasn't telling the truth. I still felt awful, but I really didn't want anymore Reiki. I shook his hand, and he pulled me into a hug.

"Sure, man, sure. I'm glad to help, man," he said softly. "If you need anything else, just come on back."

I thanked him again, and stumbled out of the cabin, wondering what the hell was going to happen to me next.

8:39 PM

I didn't know what to make of my dream. It was very short, but it had a really powerful impact. My unconscious mind was placing strange people together. Mackey and Adin Stone couldn't be working together! Could they? And what about Kerrie and Jessica? I made my way to the fire circle, hoping against hope that I could finally find Kerrie.

As I walked down the path toward the rhythmic pounding of the drums, I noticed that the glow of the fire was turning the arch of antlers into a truly eerie silhouette. No one guarded the gate tonight. We were all welcome. I wasn't sure how comforting that really was to me after my experience with Mackey. As soon as I stepped through the arch, I felt a powerful blast of heat. In my somewhat altered state I wasn't sure if it was really a physical heat, or something more subtle. It felt unnatural, supernatural. Whatever it was, I couldn't bring myself to go anywhere near the fire.

I sat on one of the large, overturned logs that served as crude benches on the outskirts of the dancing. There were at least a hundred people dancing, probably closer to two hundred. The crowd throbbed and undulated to the beat of the drummers. I hoped that I would be able to spot Kerrie, and that she'd take me back to our tent so I wouldn't have to fall asleep by myself. But I didn't see her anywhere.

I did spot Jessica Burnham. She spotted me too and smiled at me again. The smile lingered, and there was something really seductive in that smile. It almost made me feel like she knew I was now constantly dreaming about her. But that was just silly. I was just really stoned. Still, she stopped dancing and approached me from out of the throng of gyrating dancers.

"How are you doing?" she asked, actually sounding fairly friendly and caring.

"I've been better," I replied, noticing that I was starting to get a headache. Jessica leaned toward me and gave me a soft kiss on the forehead.

"Take care of yourself," she said with a smile. "I don't want to have to keep rescuing you." She laughed. But her kiss rushed through my body like a lightning bolt. I felt dizzy and giddy. I looked up at her, but she was already dancing away. As I watched her move back into the crowd I saw Kerrie push past her, moving toward me. Kerrie seemed annoyed.

"That was pretty fast," she said sharply.

"What?" I was totally confused.

"Yesterday you were kissing me, and today you're already hanging out with someone else?"

I hesitated to even speak, because I was surprised that Kerrie would think she had any right to care either way. Besides, she was sort of correct in her assessment of the situation. Still, I hadn't formed any kind of relationship with Jessica Burnham except in my strange dreams, so there really wasn't anything for Kerrie to even concern herself about. I was feeling too tired, stoned, and overwhelmed to go into why I was talking to Jessica. Besides, I wasn't going to tell Kerrie anything about my most recent experiences with the A∴R∴T∴ and Paul Mackey. I knew she'd just give me a lecture.

"No," I said eventually. "No, that girl was just helping me. I barely know her. I got lost in the woods. She found me and brought me to the healers hall."

"Oh, I'm sorry," she muttered, looking guiltily down at the ground. "I guess I don't really have any right to be jealous anyway." She looked at me thoughtfully. "Are you okay?"

"Yeah, but I kind of have a headache."

"Sure," she said, stroking my cheek. "I'm sorry I haven't seen you much today. I'll take you back to the tent soon. But I just got here to the fire circle, so I want to dance for a little while."

I nodded, and she was off. I wandered over to the drummers and found my cigarette buddy Karl. We rolled and smoked several American Spirits before Kerrie eventually found me and took me back to our tent.

Sixteen

I stood in front of a long and beautiful staircase. The stairs were made up of a checkerboard pattern of white and black square tiles. At the top of stairs I could see a large gateway made of intricately carved stone. The gateway opened into a vast field of stars, a starry abyss. I thought I heard a voice whispering to me that it was vitally important for me to get up through that gateway. Was the voice behind me? Or inside my head?

I stepped onto the stairs, and started to make my way up toward the gateway, but with each step I took, I got no closer to the gateway. It was like I was trying to walk up an escalator the wrong way. No matter how fast I walked I couldn't seem to get any closer to the top, to the gateway. Or perhaps my legs were not working correctly.

I began to sense an icy cold on the back of my neck, like something was breathing on me. I knew it was something unearthly. I felt a cold touch on my neck.

☉ Sunday, September 22, 1996

2 AM (approx.)

I woke up with a gasp. Feeling uneasy, I turned over onto my side, toward Kerrie. I wasn't sure if I liked all these strangely vivid dreams.

"What's up?" groaned Kerrie as she stirred. She leaned up on her elbow and smiled sleepily at me.

"Sorry, I didn't mean to wake you," I whispered.

"Is everything okay?" she asked.

"I've just been having these really strange, vivid dreams."

"Yeah, me too," she said, nodding reassuringly. "It always happens to me at these festivals. I was just dreaming that I was flying through a field of giant sunflowers. I was touching the petals and the leaves. It was so real." She smiled sleepily.

"What's causing it?"

"Don't ask me," she said with a shrug. "My mom would say the energies of the festival are magically stirring things up- that it's causing spontaneous projections out onto the astral plane."

"Is that what you think it is?" I asked.

"I don't know," she said, shrugging again. "I think it's just dreams. This festival activates your imagination." She softly tapped her forehead.

"Don't you believe in magick?" I asked, a little surprised.

"Well, yeah, in a way. I think it's really done a lot for my parents," she said. "But I'm really too sleepy for this conversation right now." And with that she gave me a kiss on the cheek, then rolled back away from me in her sleeping bag.

I closed my eyes, Kerrie's words and kiss swirling around in my mind. Thankfully, if I had any more dreams I didn't remember them. I awoke to Kerrie nudging my shoulder.

Seventeen

8:15 AM

"Alex, Wake up," Kerrie whispered in my ear as she jiggled me gently. My eyes crept open. "Your friend Adin Stone is here. He wants to talk to you."

I opened my eyes wide, very surprised. I slipped my clothes on quickly, Kerrie informed me she'd meet me at breakfast, and I crawled out of the tent. Adin Stone was waiting for me, leaning casually against a tree, puffing on his pipe.

"Good morning, Alex," he said with a smile. "You must forgive me for pulling you out of your slumber." He looked me up and down. "You look like you're waiting for me to say something important. Sadly, I don't have anything particularly important to say." He laughed heartily, looking at my obviously bedraggled appearance. "I wouldn't have disturbed you if I'd known. I just assumed you'd be up by now." He smiled again.

"Uh, that's really okay," I muttered. I wasn't yet alert enough to even know what was going on around me. Adin led me down the dirt path away from my tent. We were alone. It was strangely quiet as we meandered through the reddening forest. Only the soft twitter of birds filled the air. The sun shone kindly, still fairly near the treetops, warming me into wakefulness as we walked.

"So, what do you think of the festival so far?" he asked.

"Oh, it's good, really good," I said, mildly wondering what was going on. What did he want with me, important or not? I didn't particularly mind either way. Being in his presence was

77

soothing; his voice was relaxing. I felt very good every time I was around him.

"I sense something a bit odd about you, Alex," he said, making me instantly tense up. "What brings you to this festival? Is there some ulterior motive?" He looked at me meaningfully. I felt exposed, like he could see right through me.

"No," I assured him, but then I felt guilty because of course there was, and I couldn't lie to him. It seemed like he already knew. "Well, actually, there is a little." I paused, but he looked at me intently, encouraging me to continue. I felt like I had to tell him the truth. "I'm very interested in magick and the occult in general, but well, I'm here because I'm looking into a murder."

"Really?" said Adin, but he didn't actually look particularly surprised.

"Yes," I said. "A young man was murdered in Arlington, that's where I live, and, I was just trying to help my brother-in-law, who's a police detective, find out a little information about paganism because the murder seemed to have the feeling of an occult-related crime." I couldn't believe I was really telling him all this, but something in his eyes just compelled me. I implicitly trusted him.

"Edward Bailey," he said authoritatively, to my great surprise. "I knew him." He shook his head gravely. "Terrible tragedy. I can understand why you're here."

I was stunned. "You knew Edward Bailey?"

"Yes," he replied quietly. "He was at one time a young man brimming over with potential. But troubled. That's the sad fact about many of the most promising young magicians today. It's hard to make contact with the deeper truths in this fast-paced world."

"So he was a magician?"

"Of course. Why else would you be here at this festival?"

My question was foolish and I knew it. Of course Ed Bailey was heavily involved in the occult. After all, I was now fairly certain that he was the one who drew all those magical symbols in his room. "So, do you have any idea who might have done it? The, you know, the crime?" I asked.

"No. I can't imagine why anyone would even consider doing something like that. Not to Ed, or anybody. Not anyone that

78

I know." He shook his head again gravely, and took a few puffs of his pipe.

"He didn't have any enemies?"

He paused for a long while, looking concerned. It was the first time I'd seen what looked like true sadness in his eyes. The expression didn't seem to suit his face. "No, not that I know of."

"Well, what do you know about Paul Mackey?" I asked.

Adin smirked. "Paul Mackey?" he repeated, and suddenly he was practically laughing. "You don't think he had anything to do with Bailey's death, do you?" He looked like he thought that was the silliest thing he'd ever heard.

"Well, I just-" I stammered, feeling stung. "I, uh, heard that he might have been involved in a magical murder a few years ago, of, a Frater Merlin, I think? And..." But I stopped in mid-sentence because Adin scowled at me. Anger seemed to suit him even less than sadness.

"Nathan- Frater Merlin was a good man and a fine magician! Paul Mackey is a silly, fat fool!" said Adin Stone. "There is no way he could be connected with Merlin's death in any way!" Adin must have noticed the shocked expression on my face because he quickly softened. "I'm sorry. I didn't mean to raise my voice but it's simply such a ridiculous rumor and I don't know why it continues to this day."

"Mackey seems dangerous to me," I finally dared to say.

"What makes you say that?" asked Stone, sounding genuinely interested.

I explained the events of the previous evening and Adin Stone listened appreciatively. He still didn't believe that Mackey had anything to do with any murder, even after I told him about my experience in the woods. I showed him the sheet of paper with the occult symbols and his assessment matched Mackey's. They were protective symbols from a number of different sources. He agreed with me that Ed Bailey most likely put the symbols there himself.

But there was an important question that was bothering me again. It had been coming up in my mind over and over, but I kept trying to dismiss it as just plain silly. I didn't know exactly how to ask, but eventually my curiosity got the better of my shyness.

"So, do you think it was some kind of supernatural creature that killed him?"

He laughed. "That's a complicated question, and I feel the only way to answer it is rather convoluted."

"That's okay," I said. "I'm getting used to feeling confused most of the time." I was surprised that he was going to answer me seriously at all.

"To answer your question I will have to tell you a myth, which means that it is untrue," said Adin slowly and deliberately. "Except that it is true in the magical world, because the magical world is a myth itself. And sometimes myths are more true than the realities they describe."

"All right," I said. That was quite an opening. I was fascinated to hear what he would say next.

"There is one great and sacred brotherhood to which we all belong," said Adin. "And this brotherhood consists of all sentient beings, both in the physical world and the subtle, spiritual world beyond. In truth, we are all one, at our core each of us is the totality. The purpose of this brotherhood is to advance the evolution of consciousness in the universe into unity, perfected by the experience of differentiation. This brotherhood is largely secret, and most of its active agents do not exist on the physical plane at all. Some are humans who have, through countless lives, ripened their own consciousness, and are now assisting the rest of humanity from the higher planes.

"Others are subtle beings who have been called spirits, angels, gods and demons. These are merely human ideas and names for higher beings, but still these descriptions do convey something of their essence. As the universe descends into physical existence, these advanced beings appear to guide the progress forward, and also come into being as a result of that forward momentum. What humans call 'demonic beings' exist as a kind of residue in the process of creation, though they do participate in the evolutionary process, in their own peripheral spheres.

"As creation reaches its nadir, the majority of the units of consciousness descend into the mineral kingdom. Consciousness evolves slowly, over millions of years. Each individual unit of consciousness passes from the singularity of divinity down to mineral consciousness, and slowly evolves through the vegetable, animal, human, and then through several layers of spiritual existence before returning again to singularity, but enriched with the beautiful experiences of division and reunion. Humanity represents an intermediate stage of consciousness, between the spiritual and the physical, partaking of both qualities at once. Because of this, the brotherhood focuses most of its attention on the human consciousness. The brotherhood teaches humanity to become more, to achieve a more equilibrated consciousness, to awaken to the inherent divinity within each unit of life."

I was truly fascinated by his speech. He was so sure of this story, like he'd told it a thousand times. And I almost felt that I'd heard it all before too. His words were like dreams, and I felt myself floating off with them into fantastic realms. But I couldn't see how it had anything to do with Ed Bailey's death. "I don't think I understand," I said. "How does this relate to my question?"

"I told you it would be convoluted," said Adin with a smile. "If a demonic being was involved in this murder, it was most likely an issue of influence, and the meaning of this may be far more complex than it appears on the surface. Inner planes beings do not have physical bodies, so it would be highly unlikely that a demon could physically kill a human being. However, this doesn't mean that a demon wasn't involved. And if there was a demon involved, this murder may have much more serious implications than merely the death of a single human being."

"Like what?" I asked.

"The end of equilibrium."

"And what does that mean?" I asked.

"That is a subject that will have to wait for another conversation. I'm afraid I need to end our chat for today." He smiled at me warmly. He reached into his pocket and pulled out a card. "Here. Give me a call sometime if you'd like to talk about this more." He pressed the card into my hand. It had his name and a phone number. "I like you, Alex. I'd like to help you in any way I can. In the meantime, look after yourself. You're poking around into dangerous territory."

We said our brief good-byes and he was off. I stumbled back to my sleeping bag and lay down, but I couldn't fall asleep again. I felt uneasy, scared, and confused by Adin's story. His gentle warning chilled me most.

I wandered toward breakfast at the main cabin in a daze. I knew I was being sort of foolish looking into this murder, but his words somehow made me fully awake to the fact that I might be putting myself personally in real danger. The events of last night might just be the tip of the iceberg.

I then began to think darkly about Paul Mackey and Adin Stone as I walked. What if they were in fact working together? My whole conversation with Adin could have been purely for the purpose of throwing me off the trail. But no, that was just silly. Mackey and Stone were like oil and water. Stone was a good man, and clearly a wise man. I knew that instinctively. There's no way they were working with each other.

The main cabin was in sight when two older women with very serious faces quite unexpectedly stopped me. It took me several seconds to realize that they were two of the Bloodmoons. They told me that Ariathmus Bloodmoon wished to speak with me personally, and I could tell by their tone that something was very wrong.

Eighteen

The two Bloodmoon women led me off down a side path I hadn't noticed before. A cluster of large trees grew in front of the opening along the main path, so it was relatively invisible unless you knew to be looking for it. We walked in complete silence. I started feeling anxious, but I tried to appear as composed as possible. After a half-mile or so I saw a large red house in the distance. It looked like an old, colonial farmhouse with several visible additions. As we drew closer I saw that it even had a large, ridiculous looking swimming pool in the back. Several loose chickens clucked past us as we made our way across the dry grass of the yard.

The two women ushered me quickly through the front door of the farmhouse, through an opulently furnished front hall and into the lush velvety crimsons of their living room. There I saw a large centrally displayed rack of rifles, along with dozens of animal head trophies hung along the dark mahogany walls. Someone around here was obviously into shooting things. The two women directed me with a gesture toward a screen door at the far end of the room that led out of the house.

As we stepped out I saw the large crystal blue swimming pool, and Ariathmus Bloodmoon sitting under a canopy made from animal skins. The pool area was set up in what looked like a strange cross between a Greek temple and a Neolithic Celtic druid warrior camp. It seemed like two decorators were battling for aesthetic dominance. The pool itself hardly seemed to be a consideration. Ariathmus looked very smug and self-important sitting there, holding court. He took a sip from a mug of steaming beverage and stood up.

"Welcome. Please, sit down." He gestured toward a chair near his own. I looked around and noticed that the two women were suddenly gone. As I approached the chair he extended his right hand and shook mine. "I am Ariathmus Bloodmoon," he said as if I really might not have known. He looked even more imposing and frightening up close. "And you, I believe, are Alexander Sebastian?"

"Yes," I murmured as I nervously sat down.

"Please, don't be frightened," he said sweetly. "I don't bite." He smiled reassuringly. "Unless the lady gives me her permission," he said with a laugh. He looked at me expectantly so I dutifully tittered even though I didn't find it at all funny. "You're probably wondering why I asked you to visit..."

I hadn't felt particularly 'asked,' but I wasn't going to make a point of it. "That has crossed my mind," I replied.

"Well, I'm afraid it's not just for coffee," he said with a frown as he picked up his mug and took another sip. "Oh! Where are my manners? Can I offer you anything?" he asked with boyish wide eyes.

"No," I said. I really just wanted to know what this was all about so I could go have breakfast with Kerrie. "I'm fine."

"Well, okay then, here's the issue," said Ariathmus. "Now, I'm not going to get into any specifics here at the moment, but someone has brought it to my attention that you were under the influence of some illegal drugs here at the festival yesterday." He raised his hands, as if to calm me. "Now, I know that everyone likes to indulge in a little chemical exploration now and then. Heck, even I like a nice doobie every once in a while," he said with a smile. But then his face became very grave, frighteningly severe. "But we have rules at this festival. This is our home." His voice grew louder. "We've invited you to our home, and we have asked you not to bring drugs to our home. There are enemies of paganism out there. People who'd like to take all this away from me." He made a sweeping gesture encompassing the house, the pool, and the surrounding forest. "And your bringing illegal substances to a public event at my home creates all kinds of serious legal liability issues for me. Do you understand what I'm telling you?"

"Sure," I said quietly. I really felt pissed. Where was this coming from? How could he even know I'd been doing drugs? I didn't bring any drugs to his stupid festival. I really didn't appreciate being dragged off and lectured by this guy. His tone was so condescending, so belittling. I decided right then that I was going to be as unhelpful as possible. I was quite bull-headed back then, especially when pushed, even if it got me into trouble.

"So, I'd like to ask you to just turn over whatever illegal drugs you have, and I'll give them back to you at the end of the festival tomorrow."

"I don't have any drugs," I said. "I didn't bring any drugs to your festival. Honest."

He looked at me carefully, locking his glare onto my eyes forcefully. I felt like he was trying to read my thoughts. But I was telling the truth, after all, and he eventually nodded. "Then who gave you the drugs yesterday?"

"Nobody," I said. "I haven't been using drugs." I looked at him innocently, and he smiled at me knowingly.

"Come on Alexander. Be cool. Just let me know where the drugs are at my festival."

"I don't think there are any. I haven't seen any."

I watched a moment of dark rage sweep across his face. It was gone as fast as it appeared. He absolutely knew I was lying, but there wasn't really anything he could do. He smiled tightly and sent me on my way. Screw him, I thought to myself. I was being totally irrational, but I really didn't care.

I walked back toward the festival grounds as quickly as possible.

As I stepped out onto the main path I clearly saw Mackey's three pasty acolytes watching me, laughing with each other. I got the message. It was a total mindfuck. They'd set me up for a fall twice in a row now. But why were they so interested in messing with me? Did it have anything to do with Ed Bailey's murder or were they just total assholes? I shook my head and hoped there'd still be a little breakfast food left at the main cabin.

Nineteen

I spent the morning with Kerrie and her parents, giving them a highly edited version of events over the past twenty-four hours. They promptly insisted that I stay close to them for the rest of the festival, since I was 'clearly capable of causing myself a great deal of trouble.' So, we all sat at their booth, chatting about nothing of any real importance. At one point Kerrie's mother let slip that Ariathmus was 'a bit of a control freak,' but I'd already figured that one out.

We went to lunch without event, although the rations of food were now quite stale and tasteless. After lunch Kerrie and I attended a very boring lecture on pagans and paganism in the context of the wider middle-class American community. The event quickly devolved into a series of boring personal anecdotes and brief periods of arguing about nothing. I doodled all over the hand out, but this did little to alleviate my suffering.

3:45 PM

After the workshop finally came to its slow and excruciating conclusion, Kerrie and I walked to the fire circle for the final ritual, the official "Ritual of the Equinox." I was really beginning to feel exhausted, and looking forward to going home. I hadn't had a cigarette all day, and I was getting irritable again. As we made our way through the antlered gate, I saw the hundreds of festival goers talking animatedly with each other, excited about the upcoming ritual. Drums were beating in a loud, arhythmic drone. I must admit, I was a bit curious about what would happen next.

Ariathmus and his cohorts stood close around the fire, hands held taught at their sides. They faced the fire, which was smaller than usual, clearly so that they could stand so near without being cooked. They appeared to be concentrating intently, deeply engaged in silent thoughts which they clearly considered greatly important. I hoped they'd start soon.

Several minutes passed with no action. They just stood there, frozen. I looked around at the crowd. I didn't see Mackey or his band of goons anywhere. I eventually spotted a few of the A∴R∴T∴ people standing off on the far side. They were smoking, of course. I longed to go join them, but I didn't dare. I thought I saw Adin Stone coming through the antlered gate with a group of older women. Adin didn't see me and I quickly lost sight of him in the crowd. Perhaps I hadn't seen him at all.

After an eternity, Ariathmus turned from the fire. "We are now at the center of the balance between lightness and darkness," he bellowed in his rich voice.

I was standing directly in front of him, and he noticed me. I could swear I saw a dark glare sweep across his face. Oh well, you can't be everybody's friend, I thought to myself glibly.

"We stand at the fulcrum of the turning wheel of destiny," Ariathmus continued. "Tomorrow the darkness overtakes the light. But today, equilibrium." He spread his arms dramatically at shoulder height. "The circle is cast! Let us call forth the guardians of the four watchtowers of the universe."

The drums began to pound loudly, and all the Bloodmoons turned to the far end of the field. The whole crowd followed, turning along with them. The Bloodmoons chanted slowly and passionately in unison, "Guardians of the watchtowers of the east, guardians of the air, be with us. Blow through us and amongst us even as the breath that moves upon the face of the earth, and the breath that moves in and out of our bodies. Open our minds and let the clouds of thought clear as your rhythmic gusts of air fill us. Spirits of air, be here prompt and active amongst us. Even as we breathe, as the breath of life flows through us, spirits of air awake."

Almost in spite of myself, I became more aware of my breathing, and began a brief reverie about yoga breathing and air spirits and prana, and how they must all be pretty much the same thing.

But the whole crowd soon turned clockwise, a quarter of the way around the circle, to what was, I suppose, the south. The Bloodmoons chanted, "Guardians of the watchtowers of the south, guardians of fire, be with us. Burn through us and amongst even as the life force that drives us forward and whose life is the life of every star, and every cell in our bodies. Awaken our power, the driving force and will to life and love. Spirits of fire, be here energetic and strong amongst us. Even as the heat of our bodies rises in the fervor of our rite, spirits of fire awake."

The words seemed to have a sort of hypnotic effect on me. I could feel the heat from the bonfire on my face and hands, and I could feel the heat inside my body. I quickly felt an almost sexual sense of arousal.

The whole crowd turned clockwise another quarter turn, and the Bloodmoons again cried out in chorus, "Guardians of the watchtowers of the west, guardians of the water, be with us. Flow through us and amongst us even as the mighty oceans deep, and the watery blood that pulsates through our bodies in waves outward, and waves of return. Awaken our hearts to the feelings of love and bliss, and agony of ecstasy. Spirits of water, be here flexible and attentive amongst us. Even as the water of our bodies moves in rhythmic motion through the dance of life, spirits of water awake."

Another turn, and the Bloodmoons cried out again, "Guardians of the watchtowers of the north, guardians of the earth, be with us. Support and shape us even as the bones and sinews of our bodies, for through their rigidity we are sustained and renewed. Awaken our bodies, that we may move, and be still, in awareness of the fullness of our lives. Spirits of earth, be here laborious and patient amongst us. Even as our skin and bones contain and maintain us, spirits of earth awake."

The crowd turned again, to where they had started. Ariathmus stepped away from the fire, as the rest of the Bloodmoons began to slowly circle it, chanting something in an incomprehensible language in a low whisper. Ariathmus raised his big voice again, "We stand at the center of the four watchtowers of the elements, at the time of the balance of light and dark. Let us then seek balance within our selves, to sustain us on our journey into the darkness of winter. The elements are around us and within us." Many people closed their eyes and raised their hands in the air. "Let us establish equilibrium," and with that he closed his eyes, and raised his own hands. The circling Bloodmoons also stopped, and raised their hands, eyes closed. The drums stopped beating, as all the drummers raised their hands and closed their eyes.

I wasn't sure what I was supposed to do if I closed my eyes, so I just looked around. Most everybody was standing there with eyes closed and arms raised receptively in the air. A few people seemed to be crying. If it weren't for the renaissance costumes and the bonfire it almost looked like a tent revival. Then I saw Jessica, standing forty feet away, looking at me. Her eyes weren't closed either. She smiled a naughty little smile. We always seemed to be being the bad ones together. This silence went on for quite a while.

One of the Bloodmoon women, not one of the ones who had dragged me off, finally stepped out from the others. Eyes still closed, She called out in a husky voice, "Farewell, Father sun, glorious god, who shall return eternally, you now depart through the Gates of Death, you become the hidden god. Yet as you will be diminished before mankind, you will be found within the hidden seed, the newly harvested grain, and hidden within our mother earth, indwelling the seed of the stars. That which is unborn never dies. Therefore the wise do not weep, but instead rejoice."

Ariathmus opened his eyes and beamed, shouting, "I declare the Autumnal Equinox! The sun has entered the sign of the scales, and the year is now moving toward it's close! The dark days are at hand."

5:30 PM

Dancing, cheering and drumming recommenced with some fervor at the end of the ritual. But the numbers dwindled quickly, because it was time for the final feast of the festival, a free meal, at which we were promised there would be some actually edible food. I was quite excited.

The main cabin was decorated seasonally with colorful dried leaves, Indian corn, cornucopia, and orange and brown ribbons. A huge buffet was set out with roast beef, turkey, ham, several kinds of potatoes, all manner of vegetables, and many pies. I wondered if they had hired a caterer. This was light years ahead of what I'd been eating for the past two days.

Kerrie and I found her parents, discovering that they had obtained several bottles of mead for us all to enjoy. Looking around, I saw that most people had mead on their tables, and several people seemed already under the influence. I also noticed a performance stage set up toward the center of the room. I hoped that I wasn't going to have to watch some sort of gruelingly boring pagan song and dance show.

I took a couple of gulps of mead and then got up to join the insane struggle to get to the buffet tables. Large, hungry women loomed threateningly in all directions. There were long lines at everything but the salad, so I started with a nice helping of salad. It was a really good salad bar- little fancy greens, arti-choke hearts, they even had those crunchy chow mein noodles. I became convinced they'd hired a caterer.

When I got back to my table Kerrie and her family were still on line for food, so I ate my salad alone. It gave time to think a bit more, and to drink a couple of glasses of mead. The festival was coming to its end, and I wasn't really sure if I'd learned anything on this trip. I'd met a lot of strange people, but I couldn't see any of them brutally attacking someone. Maybe Paul Mackey, but I couldn't see him having the physical strength to do it. But then, perhaps it wasn't even a person that committed the murder at all. I mean, maybe it was some sort of evil magick demon or something. But I couldn't really bring myself to believe that. I certainly hadn't seen any evidence to suggest that anything like that even existed. Except when I was stoned, of course. Then I'd seen all kinds of horrible things. One thing I knew for sure, all of these pagans here at the festival were far too good-natured to have had anything to do with any kind of murder. I drank some more mead.

THE BROTHERHOOD OF LIGHT AND DARKNESS

Kerrie's family returned, and I finally got up and got some roast beef and ham, and some scalloped potatoes. But before I even got back to the table several of the Bloodmoons took to the stage with huge grins on their faces and began to torture us with what would become an endless barrage of corny songs and skits. I hurried back to the table and drank some more mead. Soon I was intoxicated enough that I don't even remember most of the show. Everyone seemed to enjoy it.

6:56 PM

This was the actual moment of the Autumnal equinox. Contrary to the statements of Ariathhmus Bloodmoon at his ritual, the Sun officially moved into 0°0′0″ Libra at 6:56 PM, and summer was over. The days would now continue to get shorter and shorter until the winter solstice. The autumn, the death of the year, had begun. The dark days were indeed at hand.

Twenty

Kerrie spent much of the feast trying to convince me to stay up all night at the fire circle so that we could 'greet the dawn.' Apparently it was something to experience. She was so relentless, and I was so drunk, that I finally agreed to stay up with her.

But as we walked back to the fire circle, I felt a chill in the air. It felt like the autumn really had begun, as if some invisible lever had been pulled, and dropped the temperature fifteen degrees. I made Kerrie stop at the tent to get my sleeping bag. If I was going to stay up all night, I didn't want to freeze to death.

As soon as we got to the bonfire, I immediately hunted down a cigarette. I was still tipsy from all the mead, and I spent a while dancing around the fire with Kerrie. There was quite a crowd. I guess a lot of people were trying to catch that last festival energy before returning to the world of the mundane.

After a few hours, the crowd died down, and I started to feel really sleepy. I moved a little way from the fire, wrapping myself in my sleeping bag and sitting on the ground. After a while, the drumming became slower, and people began singing folk songs and telling magical stories. There seemed to be a lot of laughter. Kerrie saw me sitting off by myself, and walked over to me.

"Are you okay?" she asked.

"Yeah. Of course," I replied sleepily.

"Are you still enjoying yourself?"

I really wasn't, but I didn't want to be rude. "Sure," I mumbled. "I'm just really tired."

"You gonna make it all night?" She looked dubious.

"Yeah, I'll just sit here for a while. I'll be fine."

I spent the rest of the night fitfully falling asleep sitting up, and being woken either by falling over into the dirt, or by some loud noise made by the small crowd at the circle.

☾ Monday, September 23, 1996

6 AM (approx.)

After an eternity the sky finally started to turn a dull gray in the east, and I knew that the night and the festival would soon be over. As the first point of light appeared over the top of the hills, all the dancing and drumming stopped.

Everyone raised their arms in the air, facing the light, and chanted loudly together, "Hail unto Thee who art Ra in Thy rising, even unto Thee who art Ra in Thy strength, who travellest over the Heavens in Thy bark at the Uprising of the Sun! Tahuti standeth in His splendor at the prow, And Ra Hoor abideth at the helm. Hail unto Thee from the Abodes of the Night!" Cheers and clapping became deafening.

It was now only a matter of packing up before we'd be heading out. As we drove home that afternoon, I couldn't help but wonder if and when I'd see Kerrie again. Things were a bit strange between us, but I certainly hoped this wasn't the end.

Twenty One

5:20 PM

As soon as I walked through the door my mother gave me a message that Peter wanted me to call him. I was exhausted, but I was also really excited. I was exhilarated in a way I'd never felt before, both from the experience of the festival itself, and because there was a chance I might have discovered something useful in solving the murder. I certainly hadn't been able to piece anything sensible together myself, but maybe some of it would turn out to be useful in the long run.

My mother was truly shocked when she saw me going directly to the phone after quickly grabbing a pack of cigarettes from the carton in the cabinet. They were my mom's cigarettes, but we smoked the same brand, and she didn't seem to care when I took them. I picked up the phone receiver, and my mother told me to call him at home. She recited the number, and stood there staring at me with her arms crossed.

"Do you mind, Mom?" I said, mildly irritated. My mom raised her hands in apology and scuttled off. She could be so irritating. It was nice to have a break from her for the weekend.

My sister picked up the phone on the fourth ring. "Hello?" she said breathlessly, as if she'd run to get to the phone.

"Hey, Therese, is Peter there?" I asked, lighting a cigarette and taking a grateful drag.

"Uh, yeah. Hi Alex. Why are you calling?" she said. She sounded almost as shocked to hear from me as my mom had been when I called.

"He asked me to call."

"Oh, hold on." I heard the thud of the phone against the kitchen counter. After a few unintelligible murmurs the phone was picked up.

"Alex!" Peter sounded happy to hear from me, certainly much happier than Therese. "What can I do for you?"

"You sound like you're in a good mood," I said.

"I think my partner just got a really good lead on that murder case today. You know, the one we were talking about?"

"Oh really," I said blandly. I felt a little disappointed. I wanted to be able to help. "What's that?" I asked, trying to sound cheerful.

"We found a Satanic cult, with members right here in town," said Peter enthusiastically. "Got a solid tip. It's the real deal. Haven't questioned any of them yet, but we're watching."

"That's great," I mumbled, wondering what he could possibly be talking about. I was pretty doubtful about that tip. There weren't any Satanic cults in Arlington. That much I was sure of.

"So, do you have anything for me?" Peter asked.

"Yeah, yeah I do. I went to a pagan festival this weekend."

"What's that?"

"A bunch of pagans, camping," I said glibly. "You know, with group rituals and stuff."

"What kind of rituals? Satanic rituals? Shit, why didn't you tell me about this?" He sounded hostile.

"I found out about it at the last minute."

"Holy... This is dangerous shit, Alex! What were you thinking? You actually met with these Satanists?" he demanded.

"They weren't Satanists, Peter. They were pagans," I said coolly.

"Same difference. They all worship the Devil, right?" He laughed hollowly. "So, did you find anything out?"

I felt really annoyed. How was this guy supposed to solve a case like this? He was obviously completely ignorant about the occult world. And now, after spending one whole weekend with them, I thought I knew pretty much everything. Looking back, I was just as big a fool as Peter. But I wouldn't figure that one out for quite a long time. I felt like a real expert at the moment. "Yes,

I found out something about those symbols you gave me," I said finally.

"Great, that's great. What did you find out?"

"They're protective symbols."

"Protective symbols, yeah. Go on."

"So, they weren't put there by the murderer. They were put there by the victim." I said, feeling proud of myself. I knew this was important.

"No, that doesn't fit. This was a cult thing. The perps left the symbols. Some kind of ritual killing. We know that much," said Peter, closing the book on my theory. "Maybe they put them there to protect themselves from getting caught or some shit like that. Or maybe someone just got their wires crossed on that protective shit. These Satanists did the symbols."

"How do you know that?" I demanded. "Why are you so sure it wasn't the victim?"

He paused for several seconds. I could tell he was trying to think. "It's what we're going with. It's what makes sense. Do you have anything else for me?" It had a dismissive finality.

I felt totally deflated. I'd gone through all the trouble of doing this research, and now he was totally disregarding my contribution. I quickly found myself growing furious. How could I help him if he wasn't even going to listen to me? I was in no mood to share any more with him today.

"Uh, a few things, I guess," I said. "But, I have to, uh, you know, sort things out. I just got home. I need to unpack."

"All right, sure." he said. "Call me if you think of anything more." He didn't seem to really care.

I think he was writing me off. Well, screw him. He wasn't going in the right direction at all. Satanic cults in Arlington... he was probably doing surveillance on a yoga class. We said our good-byes and hung up.

It was becoming very clear to me that, even though I knew nothing about solving crimes, I had as much of a chance at solving this as Detective Peter Ippolito. He was being ridiculous. I was going to have to keep an eye on Peter just to make sure he didn't harm any of my new friends. I decided I'd call him very soon and tell him about Paul Mackey and the Black Pullet

Lodge. But not today. I needed to follow up on the leads I'd discovered before I gave any more information to Peter.

I went up to my room and dug out my little stash of pot. I smoked a bowl, and threw my stuff from the festival onto my bed. It wasn't much. Just my dirty clothes, a hand out from the boring pagan discussion group- I'd give the handout to Peter. It contained an essay that clearly explained what paganism was all about. It probably wouldn't do any good, but I had to try helping him out of his ignorance.

I decided that I would call Matthew Wiley and Adin Stone immediately. They'd given me their phone numbers, and there was no reason to hesitate. I went back downstairs, and poked my head into the living room. My mom was staring at the television, transfixed, a cigarette dangling from her fingers. I was glad to see she was distracted by the T.V. for now.

I went back to the kitchen and dialed Matthew Wiley's home telephone number. I got an answering machine, so I left a message for him to give me a call back.

I started to feel very sleepy. I was really quite drained from the pagan festival. I went upstairs and lay down on my bed. I'd call Adin Stone in a little while. But as I lay there on my bed I kept thinking about him as I drifted in and out of slumber, so I eventually just got up and called him.

"Hello?" said his smooth voice across the line after a couple of rings.

"Hi, um, this is Alexander Sebastian," I stammered. "I met you at the festival this weekend?"

"Of course. I remember you," said Adin mildly. "I knew you would be calling, but that was fast. What can I do for you?"

"I, um, wanted to talk with you about the murder."

"Yes, of course," he said as if that was obvious. "Why don't we get together sometime this week?"

"Uh, sure," I said.

"How about Wednesday?" he asked.

"I'm working."

"Do you get a lunch hour?"

"Yeah, okay," I mumbled. "Sounds great."

"Where do you work?"

"I work near Alewife, by the T" I said. I suddenly felt a little embarrassed to admit that I was a shift manager at Videohut.

"Oh, well, how about Rosario's right there by the station?" he asked. Rosario's was a cheap Italian place that still managed to serve pretty decent family style food. It was built right next to the subway station, just a couple of blocks from the video store where I worked.

"Sure, sounds great."

"What time?"

"One thirty?"

"Great. See you then."

He hung up. I looked around the kitchen restlessly. I wasn't sure what to do next. I didn't have any more leads, and I was still so tired. Looking at the kitchen wasn't helping. The place seemed dingy. I felt like my world here in Arlington was black and white. Totally dull. The strange newness of the pagan festival made my whole life seem utterly prosaic and thoroughly mediocre. Even the buzz from my pot seemed boring. I went upstairs to smoke some more, and flopped onto my bed once again.

7:50 PM

"Alex, there's someone named Matthew Wiley on the phone for you," came my mother's voice up the staircase.

I opened my eyes. I think I may have fallen asleep. I wasn't sure. No time seemed to have passed. But I knew I didn't hear any ringing. I made my way down to the phone.

"Hello?" I said into the receiver, a little more groggily than I expected.

"Oh, I'm sorry," said Matthew. "Did I wake you?"

"No," I insisted. "I was just relaxing. I wasn't asleep."

"Well, I'm glad that you called," said Matthew.

"Great," I said, not really sure what else to say.

"So, you're interested in initiation I take it?"

"Uh," I said giving myself a couple of seconds to think. I wasn't quite sure how to respond. I was sort of interested in magical initiations, but I wasn't at all sure about the A∴R∴T∴. Still, I couldn't think of any other real reason to have called.

98

"Yes," I said, finally. "Yes I am." I immediately felt trapped. Did I really want to join the A∴R∴T∴?

"That's great," said Matthew cheerfully. "Listen, we're doing initiations this Thursday, so if we rush the paperwork we might be able to get you in."

Thursday! That was just a few days away! Matthew asked where I lived, so he could swing by with the application. I felt very uncomfortable with the idea of having him come over to my house. I told him it would be easier to meet me at work, because that's where I usually was. He agreed to meet me there tomorrow.

I got off the phone with him, and started feeling really scared. What was I getting myself into? My mother started asking me a bunch of questions about all my new friends, but I ignored her and went back upstairs.

Twenty Two

♂ Tuesday, September 24, 1996

1:32 PM

As usual, work was extremely boring. Videohut was not a particularly satisfying job. It was a locally owned store desperately struggling to compete with the new Blockbuster less than a mile away. Videohut liked to pretend that its claim to continued existence was based on its high quality selection including a large foreign and classic movie section, but really it was surviving almost exclusively because of pornography. Blockbuster had no porn. At least half our business was from men in their fifties grabbing a special little dirty treat for themselves on the way home from their soul-sucking corporate jobs.

I'd been working since ten in the morning, and we'd had exactly five customers. Actually, one of them was someone I'd seen at the festival. I'd never learned his name, but I knew he looked familiar over the weekend. I realized today that it was because he was a regular customer at Videohut. I smiled at him in recognition when he came in, but he didn't even make eye contact. I discovered why ten minutes later, when he came to the counter with a stack of porn. In fact, every customer so far that day had been a porn customer.

I was leaning against the counter, staring off into space and thinking about taking a cigarette break, when an extremely attractive woman with golden-blonde hair walked in. She had a very pretty face with full, sensual lips, and large, almost ridiculously round breasts. She looked like a stripper, wearing a low-cut dress that clung to her curves for dear life. My co-

100

worker Dave rushed to assist her, asking if he could help her find anything.

"Are you Alex Sebastian?" she asked in a soft, smoky voice. Dave shook his head and pointed to me dejectedly.

"Hi," I said, wondering what was going on. "I'm Alex."

"Ninety-three, Alex," she said, offering me a handshake. "Connie Drake. Matthew is parking the car. Is there somewhere we can talk?"

So she was from the A∴R∴T∴. Well, this A∴R∴T∴ was certainly getting more and more interesting. "Sure, we can go outside," I said, and turned to Dave. "I'm taking a cigarette break, Dave."

Dave nodded his head mutely as Connie and I stepped out of the store. I took out my cigarettes and pulled one out of the pack.

"Thanks," I said with a smile. "I was looking for an excuse for a little break." I offered the pack to Connie. "Want one?" I asked. I didn't usually offer cigarettes to strangers, but she looked like a smoker. She took one out of the pack and smiled. Those lips of hers were amazing as she smiled. They were soft and full, painted in a deep, shiny pink.

"Thanks. Don't mind if I do," she said as she put the cigarette between her smiling lips. I lit hers, then mine. I struggled for something to start a conversation, but my mind was totally blank. Luckily, Matthew appeared from the parking lot behind the store with a briefcase in his hands.

"Ninety-three, Alex," he said as he approached.

"Hi. Uh, Ninety-three."

"So, I've got an application here," he said, patting the briefcase. "But before we get started, are you completely sure you want to be initiated into the A∴R∴T∴?" He spoke very seriously. "I want to be sure this is really something you want." He looked at me meaningfully in the eyes.

Of course I wasn't sure. I didn't even know that the A∴R∴T∴ really existed a week ago. And everything I'd heard was that the A∴R∴T∴ was bad news. But I wasn't going to stop now. I was way too curious, and I'd been going along for the ride this far, so why not?

"Of course," I said nervously. "I'm ready." I didn't sound very convincing, but they didn't really seem to mind.

"Let's go back to the car," said Matthew, and he turned toward the lot. Connie and I followed silently. "The application requires two witnesses, which is why I asked Connie to come along. I assume you two introduced yourselves." We both nodded.

"So," I said hesitatingly. "Does this cost money? To get initiated?" I managed sheepishly after a short silence. We reached Matthew's car, and he turned to me.

"There's an initiation fee of sixty dollars of course, just to cover the cost of your robe and a few other items. Then there are also local and international dues. Those are twenty dollars each, due at the equinox. Lucky for you, you're joining right after the equinox, so you won't need to pay any dues until spring."

"Oh," I said. "That's really nice, but I actually only have about forty-five bucks on me at the moment."

Matthew smiled indulgently. "Well, I guess I can lend you the fifteen dollars, if you want, as long as you promise to pay me back."

"Sure, okay," I said. I was beginning to wonder why they were being so nice to me. It was almost a little creepy, like they were actually trying to drag me into their cult or something. I tried to dismiss the thought.

Matthew gave me the application and I sat in his car filling it out. It was just a standard sort of application. Name, address, phone number, place of work, and a few personal and philosophical questions.

Then it asked for a magical motto, a new name for within the order. I thought for a few seconds. The first thing that popped into my head was, 'Prometheus.' Somehow it seemed appropriate. I wrote it down.

I finished the application and brought it out of the car. Matthew and Connie looked it over very briefly.

"What do you think?" asked Matthew.

"Looks fine to me," said Connie. They both signed in the two empty spaces for witnesses and smiled at me.

"You're in," said Connie dryly. "For what it's worth." She smiled warmly and gave me a little hug. Her perfume smelled like peach blossoms, but its aroma competed with the scent of freshly smoked cigarettes. It was a strange but rather sexy fragrance.

"Thank you. You guys are being so helpful and nice, coming out here and everything. It's almost a little scary," I said, hoping it would come off as funny. They didn't seem to think it was.

"You are getting very special treatment, Alex," said Connie. "We don't ever do this. Come out to someone's fucking job." She didn't seem upset, just serious.

"There's usually a sixty day waiting period for any application to the A∴R∴T∴," added Matthew.

I shook my head in confusion. "Why are you doing this for me?"

"Someone in the order is your sponsor and benefactor, Alex," said Matthew mysteriously. "They are looking out for you."

We said our good-byes and I went back to work, wondering what the hell Matthew had been talking about. Who was looking out for me? Who in the A∴R∴T∴ even knew me? Could it be Jessica Burnham? That was the first thing that popped into my head, but that couldn't be true. She barely knew me. I wasn't even sure if she remembered my name. But who else could they be talking about?

Twenty Three

1:47 PM

When I walked into Rosario's Italian Restaurant, Adin Stone was already sitting at a table. He'd chosen a table in the back, in the smoking section. I didn't generally sit in the smoking section myself, because it's usually chokingly smoky, but I was willing to concede to Adin's taste because I was almost twenty minutes late after all. Adin's pipe dangled between his fingers as his hand leaned on the red and white checkered tablecloth. He stared vacantly off into space with a blissful grin as I stepped into the restaurant, but he quickly noticed me and stood up to greet me. I was surprised at his agility and seemingly endless energy, considering his obviously advanced age.

"Good to see you Alex," he said cheerily. "Please, sit down. I was so very pleased to hear from you."

"Hi, yeah," I muttered as I sat down. I looked around and noticed that the restaurant was fairly quiet, although the piles of plates and unset tables seemed to indicate that I was coming in just after the rush. I was glad of that, because I knew our conversation might seem quite strange to others. "Sorry I'm a little late, I couldn't get away."

"That's perfectly all right. I got to watch the end of the lunch rush. Now we won't be disturbed," he replied, as if reading my thoughts. I almost asked him if he was a mind reader.

The waiter appeared moments later, tossing a basket of bread onto the table, and blasted through a list of specials in a fast monotone. I noticed that Adin already had a plate of food in front of him, so the waiter focused on me. I just ordered what I usually do, the rigatoni with meat sauce lunch special and a Coke. The waiter disappeared as suddenly as he'd arrived.

"I'm very curious about Ed's death," said Adin, getting right to the point. "He was an interesting young man and I find the whole situation quite troubling."

"It is very troubling," I agreed.

"I'm glad they've managed to keep this out of the papers, although I'm sure Ed's mother was right on top of that. The family's quite well off, from what I understand. Old money out of Salem or some such place. No good having the family name dragged through the tabloids."

"I think my brother-in-law is trying to keep it all pretty quiet," I said.

"That's good. You say he's the detective assigned to this case?"

"Yes."

"He's a good man, then?"

But the waiter appeared again before I could reply, slinging my coke feverishly onto the table with a small amount of splashing. He wiped up the spilled soda with the edge of his apron, and bolted off without apology.

"I think our waiter is getting anxious to go home," I said, recognizing the familiar desire to be done with a shift.

Adin smirked indulgently. "Well, I don't think I'd want to be here any longer than I had to either." We both laughed. Then Adin's face took on a mild frown. "Do they have any leads? The police I mean?"

I shook my head. "I'm almost embarrassed to admit what their theory is," I said, looking down at the little bottles of cheese and red pepper at the edge of the table. I couldn't continue.

"Well?" prompted Adin.

"They think it's part of some kind of Satanic cult ritual."

"And you don't?" asked Adin, with what looked like a very serious expression on his face. It seemed odd because he didn't seem to be a person who would even treat something like that seriously. I wondered what he could be thinking.

"No," I said, eventually.

"So what do you have to do with the investigation?" he asked.

"Nothing really," I admitted. "But I feel, I don't know, I'm just interested, you know, in making sure that it all turns out all right. It sounds kind of stupid when I say it, but, I guess I just want to make sure this thing really gets solved."

"A personal quest!" suggested Adin. He sounded like he was poking fun at me.

"Yes," I said, "I guess so."

"Good, that's good. Don't get me wrong," said Adin. "I just wanted to know where we stood. I'd like to see this thing get solved properly too. Perhaps we can help each other to help your brother-in-law."

"I'd like that," I said.

Adin then told me some of what he knew about Ed Bailey's death, which seemed like less than I already knew, other than that Ed was living off of an extensive trust fund, apparently so that he could attend community college and write poetry. I then started recounting for him my conversation with Peter until the waiter appeared with my food. He plopped it onto the table and was gone too fast for me to even notice that he'd brought me the wrong dish. Oh well, rigatoni with broccoli and chicken would do just fine.

"The last time we were talking," I said between mouthfuls, "I asked you about supernatural creatures, and you said it was a complicated subject, and that it might have something to do with the end of equilibrium or something?"

"Yes, yes," said Adin, looking thoughtful. "Well, certainly, from what I've heard there seems to be a magical connection in this case, but..." He stopped in mid sentence, looking lost in thought.

"But what?" I ventured after a long silence.

"Something just doesn't quite fit. Demons, or unbalanced spiritual beings more properly, would most likely be acting through someone, motivating them to action. And this would only happen if the stakes were higher than a simple murder."

"What do you mean?"

Adin smiled. "Well, I'm afraid I must return to our myth in order to even begin to explain. You see, there are two major factions within the interior brotherhood that guides the evolution of consciousness. I call these the brotherhood of light and the brotherhood of darkness. The brotherhood of light believes that the best way to facilitate the evolution of consciousness is to remove all restriction, to allow complete freedom and expansion to every unit of consciousness. On the other hand, the brotherhood of darkness believes that the most effective way to facilitate this evolution is to direct all units of consciousness in an entirely structured and controlled manner, to make sure that no grave mistakes occur that might ultimately slow down or halt the process. By maintaining strict control over all units of consciousness as it slowly awakens, the brotherhood of darkness hopes to assure the success of every unit, even if this means a much slower progress.

"These two factions collide at every turn, and this collision actually assists in the advancement of consciousness. Brief interludes of imbalance help to keep the universe from periods of inert stasis. But if either of these factions every fully gained control of the brotherhood, the results could be disastrous. If the brotherhood of light were to overpower the brotherhood of darkness, the universe might collapse into utter chaos. If the brotherhood of darkness prevailed, the universe could freeze into complete stagnation. For the most part, the two factions exist in equilibrium. But there is always a danger that one will outstrip the other." Adin shuddered visibly. He looked troubled.

"And you think Ed Bailey's death may be a part of this?" I asked.

"Everything that happens in the universe is a part of this, at least when you look at the universe from the perspective of this myth. Every experience of each individual increases the consciousness of the all. Each of us has a unique role to play in the unfolding drama of universal evolution, even if we don't know what that role is."

"But what's the point of all this? What does this all have to do with Ed Bailey?" I asked. The whole story was starting to seem unwieldy and pointless.

"Alex, we are all of one nature, and that nature is expansive. It is a fiery nature. The necessity for this universal evolution comes from the natural tendency of consciousness to seek advancement and pleasure. From the highest to the lowest, each unit of consciousness seeks to increase its understanding, improve its position and to expand its pleasure. This is true of the all, the great one consciousness of the universe, who, beholding itself, expressed, and this expression became the universe.

"If, as I have asserted, Ed Bailey's death has something significant to do with this, I cannot understand the reasons for it. Sometimes even very small things have very large repercussions."

I wasn't entirely convinced. "So, you think somehow this brotherhood of darkness influenced someone to kill Ed Bailey, and that this is part of some sort of inner planes war or something?"

"Well, no," said Adin. "I don't know whether it was the brotherhood of darkness or the brotherhood of light. Either faction could have been a part of this. And I have no idea what the purpose of it could be. But I do know that if an inner planes being was involved in this, then the interior brotherhood was involved in some significant way."

"So both the brotherhood of light and the brotherhood of darkness have demons working for them?" I asked.

"There is only one brotherhood," said Adin. "And it has only one purpose. Darkness and Light are merely factions within the one interior order. They share everything, because they are one. They just work in opposite directions.

"Luckily, there is a third, much smaller faction within the great brotherhood. This group consists of the beings that might arguably possess the greatest wisdom within the whole brotherhood. For the most part, this faction does not act at all in the drama of evolution, but prefers merely to observe the interplay of forces and to passively instruct humanity with the timeless wisdom. But when equilibrium is too greatly threatened, when it appears that either darkness or light may overcome the other, on these occasions the third faction takes corrective measures."

This was all just too much for me. I decided to change the subject for a moment and told him that I'd decided to join the

A∴R∴T∴. He frowned when I told him that, and looked me right in the eye.

"Do you fully know what you're getting yourself involved with?" He asked in a heavy tone.

"I've heard that they're a black magick group, but I don't believe it," I said, matter-of-factly.

"They certainly aren't a black magick group," said Adin with a laugh. "They're simply a magical group. They work all sorts of magick, some of it good, some bad. Every magical group is basically the same. It's just a matter of perspective and customs. The A∴R∴T∴ curriculum is for the most part quite useful."

"So, then what's wrong with me joining the A∴R∴T∴?"

"Each step you take brings you deeper into things, Alex. The deeper you go, the more it becomes necessary to walk a path to its completion."

"Is there something in particular that you're warning me about?" His words were so cryptic. I wanted him to give me something clear to hold onto. I didn't realize that he was being as clear as he could be until much later. "Is there something I should know about the A∴R∴T∴?"

"These magical groups have many inherent dangers. Egos, in-fighting and the blurring of each other's wills, one into the other, and into the will of the group as a whole. You can lose yourself, your own personal journey when you become overly involved in the workings of a group. Each group has a collective destiny, and you link yourself to that when you join. The A∴R∴T∴ is a large, international organization. It has its own unique part to play in the universal drama. There is plenty of room to get lost in the agendas and intrigues of a group like the A∴R∴T∴."

"But I'm just really so curious," I said. "I mean, I want to know what it's like to be initiated, to be inside a magical group."

"Yes, yes of course," said Adin mildly. "But you must remember that you have already received initiation. Initiation on the inner planes." He gazed at me calmly, right in the eyes.

I felt stunned by his words and the intense look in his eyes. I felt he was communicating something of the greatest import-ance. Was he talking about those vivid dreams I'd had at the festival? They had seemed like an initiation. The whole pagan festival seemed like an initiation. Or was I just over-indulging my imagination? Maybe he was talking about something completely different? I looked into his eyes pleadingly, hoping for some sign of what he meant. "What are you talking about?"

Adin smiled warmly. "Your personal quest," he said. "An initiation is a beginning. You feel compelled to discover the truth behind Ed Bailey's death, you've been called to this quest, and this has moved a great deal into motion in your life. This is a true initiation that no ceremony could ever compare with."

I thought that over and sighed. I felt like I was becoming more and more confused with each word that Adin said. "Well, I've already signed up for the A∴R∴T∴," I said.

Adin laughed uproariously. "Well, then I guess you're really stuck!"

The ridiculousness of my statement wasn't lost on me, and I laughed too. "But I am really curious too. I want to join. I think I've always wanted to join the A∴R∴T∴."

"Then perhaps that is your destiny. Don't let my words dissuade you," he said. "I'm just a silly old man. You might even be able to find out some useful things for your quest. Ed was an initiate of the A∴R∴T∴, after all."

"He was?" I asked, surprised.

"Certainly!" Adin said, equally surprised. "I thought you knew."

Adin turned his attention down to his food as I tried to piece everything together. It seemed like every piece of information I learned shifted the puzzle around into a completely new direction.

"So," I said, after a fairly long silence, "if this interior brotherhood is overseeing everything, what's the point of all these magical groups at all, or even religions for that matter?"

"Oh boy," said Adin with a sigh. "That's a tough one. Maybe you'll be able to answer that one for yourself once you're inside the A∴R∴T∴. The easy answer is that they act as a gateway, an intermediary between the blind masses and the higher spiritual beings of the brotherhood. There have always been mystery schools, secret societies of learned men and women who teach mankind the way of return to a more universal consciousness. These schools exist to assist with the continuing evolution of the created universe. But this is highly imperfect at best.

"Some of these schools receive oversight from the brotherhood of light, and others from the brotherhood of darkness. However, they are almost always finally taken over by the brotherhood of darkness, because the freedom and non-restrictive characteristic of the brotherhood of light is not conducive to the structures required by an organized group. Great religious geniuses, Christs, Buddhas, Mahatmas and inspired leaders, these usually come into being under the tutelage of the brotherhood of light. The brotherhood of light is responsible for nearly all reforms, revolutions, inventions, new ideas and creative changes, but once the change has taken place, the outward form is often left to the brotherhood of darkness to run. So, within every generation new geniuses appear under the guidance of the brotherhood of light, and the whole process begins again."

I scratched my head. "So, are you trying to say that the A∴R∴T∴, all the other magical groups, and all organized religions are being run by this brotherhood of darkness?"

"I am just telling you a myth, Alex," said Adin. He chuckled. "Trying to apply it literally will only lead you to confusion. I am merely saying that where you see an organized structure encouraging rigid adherence to a specific belief or practice, you are seeing the influence of the brotherhood of darkness."

He was right. I was getting completely confused. "Nothing seems very clear at all to me anymore," I said. "Your myth, and this whole magical world isn't making any sense to me."

Adin looked at me meaningfully. "All of magick is a myth, in a mythical world of its own." He arched his eyebrows. "I'm afraid it's not possible to understand anything of any importance with the logical part of your mind. Magick is as much in the world of dreams as in the world of waking reality."

All of his words were making my head spin. "I've been having a lot of strange dreams," I muttered, almost to myself.

But Adin seemed very interested. "Yes?" He said excitedly. "Tell me about them." He looked at me with enthusiastic expectation.

"You know, they've just been strange," I said not quite feeling sure whether I wanted to share them, especially the one that actually involved Adin. I knew he would probably be able to help me sort through my dreams, and that I should probably tell him all about them, but I just felt uneasy about exposing my inner life so much. He didn't seem upset at all.

"Dreams are of paramount importance to your development. Dreams are windows into your soul, as well as times of learning. You will be receiving a good deal of magical home-work from the A∴R∴T∴, most likely including some dream work, and if you ever need any help with it, don't be afraid to ask. I am always at your service."

Adin soon left, and I spent the rest of the day equally anticipating and dreading my impending initiation into the A∴R∴T∴.

Twenty Four

✝ Thursday, September 26, 1996

6:47 PM

A large white van pulled up in front of my house. A horn
honked. As I made my way to the door my mother started
asking me her usual questions.

"Who's picking you up? Where are you going?"

I'd already told her I was going to be picked up by some
friends, so I just grunted my good-byes as I slipped out of the
house. I leaped off my porch steps directly into the unknown.

The passenger and driver's doors of the van opened, and two
males in dark clothing stepped out. I didn't recognize either of
them, but I could tell by their serious expressions that they must
be from the A∴R∴T∴, playing out roles in my initiation.

The older of the two opened the van's side door as I approached. The younger man pointed me toward the opening. As
I peered within, I saw two more young men blindfolded and
bound, sitting docilely in the shadows. Matthew Wiley sat
beside them, holding another blindfold in his hand. He beckoned me toward him. My heart started beating hard in my chest.
The reality of the situation and the serious expressions on the
faces of these men made me feel extremely anxious. As I stepped
up into the van, the door slammed behind me. I could hardly
breathe. Matthew leaned toward me swiftly, and drew his
mouth to my ear.

"Is it with your free will that you let me bind you and
hoodwink you, as is the ancient custom?"

113

"Yes." I could hardly speak. It was hard for me to force the air out of my lungs. With that, Matthew swiftly drew a hood-wink over my head. This made my breathing even more diffi-cult. My face grew instantly hot.

I knew that secret societies frequently blindfold candidates, but this was all so much more serious than I really imagined. I didn't know these people at all. Who knows where they were taking me and what they were planning to do with me? Even Paul Mackey thought the A∴R∴T∴ was bad news. What was I getting myself into?

I felt Matthew Wiley binding my wrists together with a strong rope. He tied them tightly, partially cutting off my circulation and causing my fingers to tingle. I wondered how long I was going to have to have my wrists tied up like this.

The doors of the van slammed shut, the engine started, and the van pulled away from the curb.

Plunged in darkness, it seemed like an eternity as the van bounced along. As we were jostled about, I discovered that I was actually tied to the other candidates in a chain gang. One of the other two young men started to ask a question but he was silenced with a guttural "no talking." No one spoke another word for the rest of the trip.

After an endless series of bumps, turns, bounces and near stops, we finally pulled to a halt. We were guided, tripping over each other, out of the van. Matthew spoke to us soothingly as we stumbled along through the darkness.

"Just move slowly. We're coming to a doorway now."

I put my elbow out and felt the door jam as I passed through. It seemed I was last in the procession. I felt myself pulled forward jerkily along by the ropes around my hands. As we came into the building I could hear a number of people whispering and moving around near me. I couldn't tell how many. The building smelled dusty. It was a heavy smell, like the basement of my grandfather's house.

I had no sense of space. I couldn't tell how large or small the room I stepped into was, or where I was going as I walked. It was more than a little alarming. I was turned this way and that. I got the sense that I was in some sort of maze or tunnel. I began to sweat underneath the hoodwink, and I hoped I would soon at least be able to sit down.

We were led up two flights of stairs, and then through a doorway into a space that smelled of moldering old tobacco and dead animals. I now felt my hands being untied. I heard more indecipherable soft muttering. Then Matthew's voice was right in my ear.

"There's a chair right in front of you. Reach for it."

I felt around in the air for the chair, but I couldn't find anything. Someone eventually grabbed hold of my hands and guided them to the back of the chair.

"Go ahead and sit down," said Matthew, still whispering.

I sat. Someone took hold of my hands and retied them together. There was more muttering, and several sets of footsteps walking away, then the sound of a door closing tight. I heard the click of the lock.

I was officially trapped. I could tell the other two were nearby, I heard them being placed into chairs at the same time I was. I sat in the silent darkness for quite some time, wondering what the hell I was doing there. Who were these two people I was sitting with? What was about to happen to us? Was there going to be some sort of test? Hazing? Torture? Were we being tested now? Was there a guard in the room with us, or were we alone? I sat there endlessly, wondering, dreading, and fantasizing.

My hands were only fairly loosely tied now. I could easily free them and remove the hoodwink. But I didn't dare move at all. I heard the other two breathing heavily. They seemed just as nervous as I was.

And why shouldn't we be nervous? The reputation of the A∴R∴T∴ was that of a dark order of evil magick. Who knows if we were even going to be initiated? Adin seemed to think the A∴R∴T∴ was harmless, but maybe they really were evil. I didn't know them very well at all. Maybe we were just going to be killed in some sort of human sacrifice. Could they really kill us? They certainly couldn't kill everyone that came along. Then there wouldn't be any new members. Perhaps I was going to have to answer a bunch of questions, and if I got them wrong I'd be sacrificed. I really worked myself into a frightened state.

Then the door opened.

"Joseph Molini?" said a gruff voice from the doorway.

"That's me," said one of the two tied up beside me. Footsteps approached him.

"Stand up slowly. That's it. Just let me guide you," said the gruff voice. I heard them slowly walk out of the room, and the door clanked closed behind them. Then silence once more.

"What's your name, dude?" said the other young man quietly as we each sat in our private darkness.

"Alex," I whispered. "But are we supposed to be talking?"

"I don't know," said the voice. "I doubt they want us to or nuthin', but I'm gettin' real bored. Oh, I'm Chris, by the way," he added.

"Are we alone in here, or is someone watching us?" I asked.

"I was thinkin' that too, but naw, I don't think so," said Chris.

"I guess if someone was in here they would have shut us up by now," I said.

"Yeah, right."

I didn't really want to keep talking to Chris. I got the sense that it wasn't worth potentially irritating our initiators by talking more to him, but now the silence was awkward.

"So, you nervous about this?" I asked.

"Naw," said Chris. "I've been initiated into tons of these things. They're all pretty much the same."

"But this is the A∴R∴T∴!" I said.

"Yeah," said Chris. He was clearly not as impressed as I was with the sinister reputation of the A∴R∴T∴. "But I'm in the T.O.S. and the O.T.O. and the C.O.S. and the T.O.T.O. and H.O.O.R. and the O.D.B. and the K.S.W. I'm tellin' you, it's all the same stuff. This bit of blindfolding us the whole way here—that was pretty cool I guess, but you know, whatever."

Any further conversation just seemed pointless. I wondered which one of us would be taken away next, and which of us was most likely to be sacrificed to the dark forces.

After what seemed like at least a half an hour, I heard the door open again. "Christopher Perkins?" said the gruff voice, and Chris was led away.

116

The Brotherhood of Light and Darkness

I was alone, left waiting in the darkness. And the wait was endless. I could have gotten up and walked out. There was a part of me that really wanted to leave, but I had no idea where I even was. Assuming I could get out of there in the first place, how would I get home? For all I knew I could be in the middle of a forest, a swamp, or inside a mountain.

But eventually the door opened, and it was time for my initiation.

Twenty Five

"Alexander Sebastian," said the now familiar gruff voice. As I heard him say my name, I suddenly realized that he had a fairly pronounced lisp. I'd been so nervous that I hadn't really noticed it before, but it had definitely been there when he'd said the names of the other two candidates as well. I heard him walk to my side. He whispered, "Stand up slowly and carefully." His lisp was so strong that I almost wanted to laugh now that I had noticed it. Still, I had no idea what was about to happen to me. Just because he had a lisp didn't mean he wasn't going to do something awful to me. I stood up, still in complete darkness.

We walked a short way together, the lisping man holding on to my shoulder to guide me. Eventually he stopped me and told me to remove all of my clothes. He briefly untied my hands so that I could remove my shirt, pants, underwear, socks and shoes. I felt very nervous that I was going to have to go through the whole initiation blindfolded and naked, but once I was out of my clothes the man handed me what seemed to be a robe and helped me slip it over my head. He then retied my hands, quite tightly this time.

The man with the lisp then stepped forward a few steps and knocked one time on a door in front of us.

"Who disturbs the seal of our holy vault?" came a booming voice from beyond the door. It sounded like Damian Webster, but the voice was so formal and melodramatic that I wasn't sure.

"An aspirant seeks entrance into our sacred fraternity," replied the lisping man, in an equally dramatic tone.

"Bring him to the Gateway," said the booming voice. I heard the door open, and felt the lisping man guiding me forward. "Thou who standeth at the gateway to our sacred vault, the entrance to the mountain of initiation– know that to enter this gateway is to invoke upon thyself a current of force that will transform thee forever! Is it thy true will to enter?"

I could now smell strong incense burning in the air around me. I could hardly breathe at all. My throat felt incredibly dry. My heart pounded heavily, so heavily that I almost felt it was audible. I could barely get my mouth to work. "Yes," I choked out.

"Let Alexander Sebastian pace the first steps into the darkness," said the booming voice that might be Damian Webster's. I heard the door close behind me as someone gently nudged me forward a step or two. "He now relinquishes this mortal name and will henceforth be known amongst us as Frater Prometheus. Very honored adepts of the A∴R∴T∴, assist in his reception." I felt two people take hold of my arms, on either side, and I started to powerfully shake with nervousness. "Son of Adam, you now enter the darkness."

The two people at my sides began to guide me forward, and the one on my right whispered in my ear, "Who art thou, Son of Adam?"

I wasn't sure what to say. Was I supposed to give my new magical name? Or my regular name? Or something else?

But before I could even open my mouth, the guide on my left whispered, "From whence didst thou come?" This voice sounded a lot like Matthew Wiley.

Then the first said, "Where dost thou intend to go?"

"What dost thou seek?" said the second.

Then two hands roughly barred any further forward progress. From behind me I heard the lisping man say, "Unpurified and Unconsecrated, thou art unworthy of our sacred vault."

I felt three splashes of water hit me. "I purify thee with Water," said the voice on my left, the voice that might have been Matthew Wiley's.

Then I felt something waved in front of me. The smell of incense became even more powerful and the voice on my right said, "I consecrate thee with fire."

"Bring the aspirant to the foot of the altar," said the first booming, melodramatic voice. Hands nudged me forward several more steps. "Son of Adam, Why dost thou seek to enter the mountain of Initiation?"

"He wanders in darkness and seeks the light of hidden knowledge. He believes that in this order knowledge of that light may be obtained," said the man with the lisp.

"Is this true?"

"Yes," I said, still hardly able to breathe.

"Thou hast signed a pledge to keep everything that relates to this order secret," said the booming voice. "I now ask thee, before this assembly, art thou willing to take a solemn oath to keep our secret mysteries inviolate? Art thou willing to take this supreme vow?"

"Yes, I am," I choked out.

"Then kneel before the sacred altar." Hands guided me down into a kneeling position, and bent me head forward. The booming voice continued, "Give me thy right hand. I place it upon the holy symbol of the Rose and Cross. Place thy left hand in mine, and say after me: I, Alexander Sebastian, in the presence of the Lord of the Aeon and of this sacred assembly do of my own free will and accord hereby and hereon most solemnly pledge myself to keep secret this order, its name, the name of its members, and the proceedings which take place at its meetings, from all and every person in the whole world who is outside the pale of the Order, and I will never divulge anything concerning this Order to the outside world even if I resign or should I be expelled." He paused every few words to let me repeat the words as he said them.

He continued, "I will not copy or lend to any other person to be copied, any ritual or lecture, unless I hold the written permission of the Supreme Magus to do so, lest our secret knowledge be revealed through my neglect or error. Furthermore, I undertake to deeply study the Occult Sciences, because this Order is not established for amusement, but a serious body of initiates. And I will never use my Occult powers for any evil purpose. I swear upon this sacred symbol to observe all of these points; under no less a penalty of submitting myself to a deadly and hostile current of will set in motion by the chiefs of the order, by which I should fall slain and paralyzed without visible weapon as if struck by the lightning flash."

As I uttered the last word I felt something cold and metallic strike me on the back of my neck. It felt like a knife or a sword. It sent a powerful chill through my body. I was stunned. Someone helped me to my feet, but I felt like I was floating. I was dizzy. I thought I might soon pass out.

Then the booming voice cried out, "Let the aspirant proceed through the four outer gates of knowledge."

"You now step into the Mountain of Initiation," said the lisping man, still behind me. "This path leads into the darkness, but fear not, there is a light to guide thy steps, a hidden lamp of knowledge."

Someone started pushing me forward, while another took hold of my right arm, guiding me off to my right. We walked for quite a way, turning several times. I was then forcefully stopped.

"Unpurified and Unconsecrated, thou canst not enter the gateway of the East," said the man with the lisp. Just as before I was splashed with water and incense was waved over me.

"I purify thee with water."

"I consecrate thee with Fire."

"Twice purified and twice consecrated," said the booming voice, "thou mayest approach the gateway of the East. To enter the gate of the East requires a password, and this password is 'FLATUS.' Give this password, and be admitted to the gate of the East."

At first I didn't know what I was supposed to do, but someone whispered in my ear, "Just go ahead and say 'Flatus.'"

I was really in a daze. I was losing track of where I was or exactly what was going on. But I somehow managed to say "Flatus."

As soon as I said it someone took hold of the hoodwink on my head and lifted it a few inches. A yellow rose was being held right in front of my eyes, in the hand of someone wearing a golden mask. The mask looked somewhat like a Greek god. The hoodwink was quickly pulled back over my eyes.

From behind me, the booming voice said, "The air of knowledge is the first element to which thou art exposed along this path. It symbolizes not only the air that thou breathest, but also the airy ether into which thy magical journey will take thee. It further symbolizes your intellectual development, for you must develop your mind into a beautiful, finely tuned instrument, discerning the truth from within the falseness of appearances. Be guided by this knowledge in your further pursuit of the light."

I was then led through the darkness for a long time again. I wondered how large this temple was. It might have been a large circle, but it was hard to tell. Eventually my way was roughly blocked, just as before.

"Unpurified and unconsecrated, thou canst not enter the gateway of the South!" said the lisping man. The two others purified and consecrated me, just as before.

"Thrice purified and consecrated, thou mayest approach the gateway of the South," said the booming voice. "To enter the gate of the South requires a password, and this password is 'IGNIS.' Give this password, and be admitted to the gate of the South."

This time I said it right away, "Ignis."

With that my hoodwink was lifted, revealing a red candle, right before my eyes, held in the hand of another person wearing a mask. This time the mask seemed to be made of copper, in the shape of a lion's head. I was quickly blindfolded again.

"The fire of will signifies the innate fire that is at the core of every natural body, concealed by the grossness of the surrounding matter," said the booming voice. "This fire is the very light of the soul, the nourishing divine light of the highest, hidden at the core of every being. This fire is thy will to life and love, and thou wilt need this power of will to get through the challenges of the path to the light."

I was led forward again, and eventually stopped again.

"Unpurified and unconsecrated, thou canst not enter the gateway of the West!"

"I purify thee with water."

"I consecrate thee with Fire."

The repetition was sending me ever deeper into disorientation and confusion. I wondered how far I was walking, and how many more purifications and consecrations I was going to experience. But my mind was fairly numb. I wasn't even sure how long this initiation had even been going on.

"Four times purified and consecrated, thou mayest approach the Gateway of the West. To enter the gate of the West requires a password, and this password is 'AQUA.' Give this password, and be admitted to the gate of the West."

"Aqua."

This time, as the hoodwink lifted for a moment, I saw a silver chalice before my eyes, held in the hands of someone wearing a silver bird mask.

"The water of courage signifies the water that is the menstruum of the world," said the booming voice. "Without water life would cease to exist. It further symbolizes thy heart and thy aspiration, that pursuit for the living water of eternal life that is at the center of thy quest. Drink of this water and thy burdens are released, thou art cleansed and purified. Make noble thine heart, and the path will become clear and easy."

I was pushed forward, once again. I felt myself stumbling, like I might soon fall right over. Someone on my left seemed to notice, and took hold of my arm. I was eventually stopped roughly again, but the person who stopped me also seemed to hold me up.

"Unpurified and unconsecrated, thou canst not enter the gateway of the North!"

"I purify thee with water."

"I consecrate thee with Fire."

"Five times purified and five times consecrated, thou mayest approach the Gateway of the North. To enter the gate of the North requires a password, and this password is 'TERRA.' Give this password, and be admitted to the gate of the North."

"Terra."

The hood was removed again for a moment, revealing a platter with small round bread wafers on it, held by someone wearing the mask of a bull.

"The earth is silent, dry and cold. It is passive and fixed, the final crystallization of all natural bodies. We are all formed of dust, and to dust will our bodies return, when this journey of life has come to its conclusion. Keep silent and still as the earth and thou wilt come to know the secrets of eternity. Thou hast known the four gateways of the outer temple, pass thou on to the cubical altar of the universe."

I was beginning to think that I wasn't going to end up getting ritually sacrificed at all. I was led a short distance, and once again guided to my knees.

"Do what thou wilt shall be the whole of the Law," said the booming voice.

A crowd of voices responded, "Love is the law, love under will."

"The initials of the four passwords thou hath just received form the word FIAT," continued the booming voice. "Fiat LUX! Let there be light! I come in the Power of the Light; I come in the Light of Wisdom; I come in the Mercy of the Light; The Light hath Healing in its Wings. O Nuit! Continuous one of Heaven, let it be ever thus that men speak not of Thee as One but as None; and let them speak not of thee at all, since thou art continuous!"

"Child of Darkness, we call thee to Life," said another voice.

"Wanderer in Chaos, we call thee to the Light," said a third voice.

The hoodwink was quickly and suddenly removed from my head entirely. Damian Webster stood directly in front of me, wearing a scarlet robe. On either side of him stood Matthew Wiley and a much older man, both wearing bright white robes. All three held multi-colored rods, crossing them over each other above my head. I noticed that I was in an elaborate temple room, furnished in dark red velvet. A small crowd of robed initiates sat on either side of the hall, on long wooden benches. I recognized many of them.

"Frater Prometheus, we receive thee into the light, as a neophyte in the order of the A∴R∴T∴," said Damian Webster with a broad smile. The three men lowered their rods. "Let the Neophyte be led to the East of the Altar."

The three men stepped back a few steps. In front of me was an altar made of two large black cubes, one set atop of the other. On the center of the altar was an equal armed cross with a five petaled rose in the center. Around this cross were placed the yellow rose, red candle, silver chalice, and platter of bread that I'd seen in flashes throughout the initiation.

Then I saw the man with the lisp clearly for the first time as he helped me to my feet. He was a man in his early fifties with a visible potbelly, hanging over the cord tied around his black robe. He guided me around the altar, closer to Damian and the others. I noticed that they were standing between two pillars, one painted white, the other black.

"I will now communicate to you the secrets of our order in this grade," said Damian. "They consist of a step, a sign, a grip and a word. The step consists of advancing your left foot a short pace, as if stepping through a doorway." Damian stepped forward, indicating with his head that I should do the same. "This symbolizes that you have taken the first step on the path to Rosicrucian Adepthood. Then follows the sign, which consists of thrusting both your hands forward, palms down, hands level with your eyes." He demonstrated, and I followed again. "It signifies reaching out from the darkness toward the Light, and equally for sending the power of your own Light out from the darkness. You then step back firmly so that the left heel touches the right, and place the tip of your right finger to your lips." We both put our hands to our lips. "It alludes to hermetically sealing your energy back within yourself, and to the solemn oath of secrecy that you have taken."

I nodded, feeling suddenly overwhelmed with unexplainable emotions. For some strange reason I wanted to cry.

"The Grip or Token consists of taking the hand of your brother or sister like this," said Damian. He took hold of my hand folding his thumb over my fingers. "By gripping all four fingers thus, you signify that you have understood and mastered the four elements, and the four powers of the sphinx. The grip demands a word. That word is 'FIAT,' symbolizing the beginning of your journey to the light." Damian turned and walked back through the temple, taking a seat on Red velvet throne at the back of the hall.

The man with the lisp took hold of my shoulders and guided me forward. "With this knowledge, I now place you between the two pillars of initiation," he said, and nudged me directly into the center between the white and black pillars.

"Let the final consecration take place," said Damian from his throne.

The older man approached me with a small basin of water, sprinkling me three times, saying "I purify thee with water."

Matthew Wiley then approached me with an elaborate incense burner, waving it over me three times, saying "I consecrate thee with fire." When they finished purifying and consecrating me, the two men went to Damian and sat on either side of him.

"Let the rope of binding be removed," said Damian. "The last remaining symbol of darkness." The man with the lisp untied the rope from my wrists. I noticed for the first time that my hands had fallen asleep. They felt swollen and painful, and I found myself rubbing them for the rest of the ceremony.

"Welcome my brother," said Damian cheerfully. Everyone in the temple applauded and cheered. "Please announce the joyful arrival of our brother within the mountain of initiation," said Damian.

"With pleasure, wise Chief Adept," said the man with the lisp. He looked around at everyone in the temple. "Do what thou wilt shall be the whole of the law. In the name of the Lord of Initiation, I proclaim that Alexander Sebastian, who will henceforth be known among us by the motto Prometheus, has been duly admitted to the Neophyte grade of the A∴R∴T∴."

The entire crowd cried out loudly, "Love is the law, love under will."

The man with the lisp guided me to take a seat on the side of the hall next to the other two new initiates.

"Let us seal the vault of the Neophytes," said Damian Webster. "What is our first responsibility in this temple?"

"To assure ourselves that the temple is properly guarded," replied Matthew Wiley.

"See that this is so," said Damian Webster.

Standing by the door I entered through, the lisping man said, "The temple is secure."

"What is our second responsibility?" asked Damian.

"To see that all present are initiates of our sacred fraternity," said the older man at Damian's side.

"See that this is so," said Damian.

The older man stood up, and said, "It is the wise Chief Adept's request that you prove yourselves true initiates."

Everyone stood up, took a step forward with the left foot, and thrust their arms forward at eye level. The two other new initiates and I followed along as well. We all drew our feet back and pressed our fingers to our lips.

"Wise Chief Adept," said the older man, "All present are true initiates."

"Let the temple be purified and consecrated," said Damian. Matthew and the older man stood up, circling the room, sprinkling water and waving incense.

"I purify the temple with water."

"I consecrate the temple with Fire."

When they finished a complete circle of the temple they returned to their seats beside Damian Webster.

"Nothing now remains but to partake together in silence of the Mystical Eucharist, composed of the symbols of the Four Elements," said Damian Webster. He got up from his throne and walked to the altar, attended by Matthew Wiley and the older man at either side of him. He walked around the altar to the side where I'd been standing, and projected his hands forward, right over the altar. Then he took up the yellow rose and said, "I invite you to inhale with me the perfume of this rose, to feel with me the warmth of this sacred fire, to eat with me this bread and to drink with me this wine." He placed his hand over the flame, ate a wafer of bread and drank a sip from the silver chalice, then finally put his finger to his lips. He then returned to his throne.

One by one, every single person in the temple went to the altar and imitated Damian's gestures exactly. Finally the two other new initiates and I went up to the altar and participated as well.

Damian smiled as I finished the last of the wine. "May what we have partaken in bring us to the Quintessence, the accomplishment of our true wills, the Great Work, the Summum Bonum, True Wisdom and Perfect Happiness."

Twenty Six

10:15 P.M.

As I emerged from the temple, a newly made neophyte of the A∴R∴T∴, Damian Webster handed me a small red book. Its cover read, "The Book of the Law."

"This is the key to it all, Alex," he said. "It contains the highest and most important magical philosophy within its pages. I can say nothing further."

Moments later, Matthew Wiley approached me and gave me a hug, handing me my street clothes. "Welcome, brother," he said warmly. He then politely reminded me that I still owed him fifteen dollars. I dug through my clothes and found my wallet, giving him the money gratefully. What I had just experienced was well worth the sixty dollars it cost.

Matthew then handed me a workbook with various practices, exercises and occult information for the Neophyte grade of the A∴R∴T∴, and led me toward the bathroom to change back into the clothes I'd arrived in.

Now that I was no longer blindfolded, I realized that I was in a Freemason Lodge Hall. The walls were covered with arcane emblems, swords and antique costumes of masonry, along with pictures of old men spanning more than a hundred years of Masonic membership. I asked Matthew Wiley if the A∴R∴T∴ was somehow associated with the masons, but he told me that the A∴R∴T∴ merely rented the hall from them once or twice a month. Apparently a lot of the old masons had died off, and the ones that were left needed the rent money.

THE BROTHERHOOD OF LIGHT AND DARKNESS

When I came out of the bathroom in my street clothes, Matthew led me downstairs to a hall with tables and chairs, where wine and snacks were laid out. I was formally introduced to my fellow new initiates, Joey and Chris. We shook hands and exchanged a few meaningless pleasantries. Soon the other attending initiates and initiation officers trickled down into the refreshment area. Everyone was extremely friendly and full of 'congratulations' and 'welcomes.' Even Jessica Burnham gave me a smile and a hug. I was introduced to the older man who had acted as an officer in the ritual. His name was Abraham Crane. He was a fairly ancient looking man with a large white moustache, quite yellowed at the tips. Apparently he had been a member of the A∴R∴T∴ for over thirty years. He was unofficially Damian's second in command, and officially the treasurer of the temple.

The man with the lisp was introduced to me as Jacob Bartholomew Pilsner III. "I feel right at home here in the Masonic hall," he told me proudly. There was that lisp again. If it weren't for his baritone voice, he would have sounded like a child. "I've been a mason since 1974- Scottish Rite 32°. I've only been in the A∴R∴T∴ for a couple of years, but I'm moving along very swiftly through the degrees. I'm already a Philosophus."

He struck me as rather pompous and ridiculous, but I wanted to be polite. I wasn't sure what to say. Luckily, an attractive redheaded woman in her mid-forties came right between us, and shoved a glass of burgundy colored wine into my hand.

"Don't hog up our new initiates Jake! We have to make a toast," she said, smiling at me warmly.

"Alex," said Jacob Pilsner. "I'd like you to meet my girlfriend, Mary Culling. She's an Adeptus Minor."

"Oh please, Jake. Stop telling everybody that I'm an adept. It's embarrassing."

"I'm just proud of you, baby."

"And Alex," said Mary, looking at me with a smirk. "Jacob and I are not in an exclusive relationship." She winked at me meaningfully. I noticed that Jacob's face reddened slightly, and his eyes narrowed.

Damian started clinking his wineglass with a fork, and everyone came to attention. "Do what thou wilt shall be the whole of the Law!" he proclaimed loudly.

"Love is the law, love under will!" replied everyone else.

"To our newest initiates," said Damian, raising his glass. Glasses clinked and we all drank. Once I finished the wine I slipped off through the exit door to see about having a cigarette.

Twenty Seven

As I stepped outside I discovered that the hippie Jeremy McClosky and another young man were already out there, smoking cigarettes too. They seemed to be having a serious discussion, which I was clearly interrupting. They stopped talking and stared at me as I opened the door. I felt a bit awkward, but I really wanted a cigarette, so I stepped out purposefully.

"Mind if I join you?" I asked.

"Not at all, brother," said Jeremy. He smiled warmly, dropping his previous serious demeanor instantly. "Tonight is your night, and right here is definitely the place to be. You'll see pretty much everybody if you hang in the smoking area long enough."

"Cool," I said. Jeremy raised his hand in the air and insisted on giving me a friendly high five. I couldn't help but wonder, in the back of my mind, why all these supposedly spiritual people were smokers. But it was hypocritical for me to think about that too much.

"So, how'd you like your initiation?" asked Jeremy.

"It was amazing," I said.

"Yeah," said the other young man. "These guys really know how to do it up right." He smiled.

"Have you met Steve?" said Jeremy.

"No, not yet."

"Well, then let me introduce you. Steve, this is Alex. Alex, this is Steve Curtin."

131

"Great to meet you, Alex," said Steve extending a friendly hand. Then he pulled me into a hug. "Welcome brother!" Jeremy hugged me too, repeating the same. None of this was the scary behavior you'd expect in a den of iniquity and evil.

"Hey," said Jeremy. "Do you two want to get high?"

"Sure," I said, and Steve agreed. I momentarily flashed back to the situation with Mackey in the woods, but I didn't think these guys would do that to me. Still, no one had been ritually sacrificed yet, and the night was still young.

We slipped behind the Masonic building and Jeremy produced a fat joint filled with extremely strong sinsemilla. We got very high, very fast, as we passed the joint around.

"You should really try to make it to some of the classes," said Jeremy. "'Cause that will really help you out with all the magical work that you need to do."

"Great, that sounds great," I said. "When's the next class?" A class sounded like it might be good opportunity to find out more about everything.

"Oh, dude, they're generally every Wednesday, right?" said Jeremy, seeming a little confused from the pot.

"Right," said Steve.

"Cool," I said. "I'll definitely be there if I'm not working."

"If you ever have any questions about anything," said Steve. "You should feel free to give me a call. I'm pretty new to the A∴R∴T∴ too. I know what it's like to be confused by it all. I'd be happy to go over anything with you."

"Thanks," I said.

"And if you ever need any more of this 'chronic,' feel free to give me a call," said Jeremy with a grin, as he sucked down the remnants of the joint.

We all laughed and exchanged phone numbers with each other.

"I have a question," I said, once I got up the courage. It was burning in my mind, and I just had to ask it.

"Shoot," said Jeremy.

"Why does the A∴R∴T∴ have such a bad reputation? I mean, everyone's been so nice, the initiation was very spiritual and uplifting. Why does everyone seem to think that you're a bunch of black magicians?"

They both smiled knowingly at each other, as if they'd been expecting these words.

"Ah, the dread question!" said Jeremy.

"I think we all want to know the answer to that one," said Steve.

"Well," said Jeremy. "I think that one of the biggest problems is that anything associated with Aleister Crowley gets automatically branded as 'evil.'"

"Yeah, but all the sex and drugs we do don't help," said Steve. We laughed.

"I think it's really like in the Qabala," said Jeremy, looking thoughtful. "When you're in Netzach, it seems like the only way to get to Hod is through the Blasted Tower. But it's the same from Hod to Netzach. Ultimately, it's all the same path, know what I mean?"

I nodded, even though I had absolutely no idea what he was talking about.

"Oh, and don't forget all the evil stuff you have to do in the next grade, once you're a Zelator," said Steve. "Right, Jeremy?" He and Jeremy both smiled devilishly.

"Right. You're going to have to get your hands on an unbaptised baby pretty soon."

I laughed, but I couldn't help wondering if the jokes concealed some other, perhaps even more disturbing truth.

A few minutes later, we went back inside, and made our way back to the reception room. Things had changed in the time we were gone. The lights had been turned down, and the music had been turned up. Several people were making out with each other, while others were lying on large cushions, in writhing piles of cuddling bodies. I quickly lost sight of Steve and Jeremy. Everyone suddenly seemed to be involved in some sort of orgiastic behavior.

At first I saw no sign of either of the other two new initiates. Then I noticed that Joey was sitting in the corner of the room, engaged in quiet conversation with Jacob Bartholomew Pilsner III and Mary Culling. Jacob looked like he was lecturing Joey on some subject, and rarely seemed to be taking a breath.

The other new initiate Chris was gone. For some reason I felt sure I'd never see him again.

I wasn't in the mood to jump into somebody else's orgy, and I certainly didn't feel like listening to a lecture from Jacob Bartholomew Pilsner III. I grabbed a glass of wine and wandered out of the reception room to take a look at the Masonic regalia that filled the walls in the rest of the building.

As I stepped out into the hall, I saw the pretty blonde girl, Connie Drake, sitting on a large velvet bench. Her head was buried in her hands. I walked over to her cautiously, and sat down.

"Hi," I said. "Are you okay?"

"Yeah, great," she said, not even looking up at me.

"Is there anything I can do?"

She looked up at me. Her mascara ran down her cheeks, but she still looked quite beautiful. She smiled at me, her eyes filled with tears.

"Thank you. No. I don't... I'm just feeling a little sad."

"I can tell," I said. I wasn't sure what to say or do. I was pretty useless in emotionally intense situations. I didn't have much talent for consoling people, and I was feeling pretty stoned. So, I just sat there next to her, staring at the floor. After a long silence, she spoke.

"I don't know if anyone told you, but my boyfriend- well, he wasn't really my boyfriend, I guess, but we fucked a lot and lived together..." She stopped talking, and picked up a glass of wine from beside her. She drank it all down in one gulp. "He died a couple of weeks ago," she said. "I mean, I was okay, you know? It's not like we were married or anything. But he really loved the A∴R∴T∴. Being here tonight, I don't know, somehow it's just bringing stuff up. You know?"

I nodded in what I hoped seemed a meaningful way. I really had nothing I could say to console her. But I felt sure that this 'boyfriend' was Ed Bailey. I realized as I sat there that she was probably one of the most important leads in Peter's case. I wondered if he even knew about her. He hadn't mentioned a girlfriend. But I was too stoned and stupid to know what to do with her. I noticed that she was eyeing my wine, so I handed it to her. She drained it.

"Do you have a cigarette?" she said.

"Sure, of course," I said reaching into my pockets. She put her hand on my shoulder and stood up, gesturing with her head toward the door.

We went outside and I lit us each a cigarette, trying to come up with a way to ask her some questions about Ed Bailey's death without seeming like a jerk.

"So, um, what was your boyfriend's name?" I asked.

"Ed," she said, exhaling a cloud of smoke.

"Wow," I said, trying to seem nonchalant. "How'd he um..."

"He was murdered. Let's not talk about this anymore."

"Sure," I said. That was the end of that. She turned away from me, staring off into the night. I had to be the worst amateur detective ever. I watched her pretty lips quivering, sucking on the cigarette I gave her. I wondered what she knew, what she could tell me if I knew how to get her to open up. I really wished I knew what I was doing as an investigator. She suddenly turned back to me and smiled.

"So, what did you think of your initiation?" she asked. I guess she really was ready to change the subject. She moved closer to me, and looked me right in the eyes. I felt myself blushing under the pressure of her stare.

"It was great," I said. "Totally blew my mind."

She laughed a little. "It looked like your mind was being blown." She laughed more loudly. "Listen, I didn't mean to be rude about Ed," she said. "I'm just, you know, it's all still such a shock. I don't mind talking about it if you have a question. You must be really wondering about us. I know the A∴R∴T∴ has a crazy reputation, but people don't usually die. Honestly."

"Oh, sure, no, I was just curious," I said. "I didn't, it didn't even occur to me that the A∴R∴T∴ would have had anything to do with it.

"Well it didn't," she said, her face hardening again. "I can't even imagine how it happened. He was doing some sort of ritual, I guess. That had something to do with it. He was always doing dark stuff. I don't know why he was so obsessed with the dark stuff."

"The darkness can be tempting, I guess," I said, not sure what else to say. I wasn't really even sure what she meant.

Demons I guess, black magick. Hell, I'd seen the crime scene photos.

"You don't look like you'd be into the dark stuff," she said.

"No?"

"No, you look like a nice boy," she smirked and took hold of the collar of my shirt, straightening it. I suddenly got the sense that she was flirting with me. One second we're talking about her dead boyfriend, the next she's touching me.

"Well, I'm not always that nice," I said, flirting back a little. "Sometimes I can get a little naughty."

"I'll bet you do. I'd like to see that." Now she was definitely flirting with me.

"I'm available anytime," I said.

She leaned forward and kissed me hard on the mouth. That was easily the biggest surprise of the whole evening. We made out for quite some time, until we both became conscious of the fact that we were kissing under the lights in front of the Cambridge Masonic Hall. People were staring. She dragged me inside.

She pulled me into the men's bathroom, locking the door behind us. Then she silently unbuckled my belt and dropped my pants to the floor. I had no idea what she was thinking. She went to her knees and grabbed a hold of my swelling penis. I was stunned. I am sure this is not the way a proper investigator would interview his number one witness, but I really wasn't going to stop her.

She put my penis into her mouth and pleasured me to a degree that I can't even describe. The whole situation was insane, but incredibly erotic. Moments ago, she'd been crying, and now she was sucking my penis. I'd never experienced anything like this before. After a few minutes I came right between her lips, and she swallowed every drop of my semen. She pulled herself to her feet and started kissing me again. I could taste my own semen in her kiss. So this was what being in the A∴R∴T∴ was all about.

Then there was a knock at the door.

"Hello?" came a voice from outside. It was Matthew Wiley. "I don't know who's in there, but we were supposed to be out of here by eleven, and it's after midnight. We're all packing it in."

Connie smiled at me sexily. I bent over and pulled my pants up. My wallet spilled out onto the floor, and I had to get down on all fours to scoop up all of my belongings.

"Listen," said Connie. "You can't just get an orgasm, and not give me one."

"Okay," I said, still on my knees. I wasn't sure what she meant. Did she want me to go down on her right then, with Matthew outside the door?

"Since you didn't return the favor, you owe me." She pulled me up to my feet.

"Sure," I said. "Anytime."

"I look forward to it, but I have something else in mind too."

"Anything," I said.

"You have a car?"

"Yes."

"Good," said Connie. "I need someone to drive me to see Ed's mom this Saturday, and I'm picking you." She pressed a polished fingernail into my chest, with a coy smile.

"Okay, sure," I said, feeling incredibly lucky. Perhaps I was a better investigator than I thought. Not only did I get a blowjob, I also got a new lead. She made me write my phone number on the back of her hand, and told me she'd call on Saturday morning.

Connie left the bathroom first, and exchanged a few words with Matthew that I couldn't quite hear. I felt embarrassed to come out with Matthew still standing there, so I waited a minute or two. When I finally came out, Connie was gone, but Matthew was still standing right there. He asked if I needed a ride, or if I could take the train. I couldn't look him in the eyes, much less get into his car. The Porter Square T station was only a block or so away, so I just took the train.

Twenty Eight

2 P.M.

I slept in late the next day. Even though I was supposed to be at work by four, I don't know if I would have gotten up during the daylight hours at all except that my mom knocked on my door, saying that Peter was on the phone. She told me it was the third time he'd called. I could see by the tight creases in her forehead that she wanted me to explain why Peter was calling so much, but I didn't bother. If I took the time to explain it all to her she'd just get upset.

When I picked up the phone I found myself on hold, listening to a tinny recording of Barry Manilow singing Copacabana. Eventually Peter came back on the line. He asked me why I hadn't been in touch lately, and I told him I just didn't have anything new to tell him. He started by asking me a bunch of meaningless questions about my mother, life, and the weather. I really started to get bored. Then he finally got to the point, and my hair stood up on end.

"Have you ever heard of something called the A∴R∴T∴?"

I had no idea what to say. The last thing I wanted was for Peter to start investigating the A∴R∴T∴, at least not before I was done checking things out myself. I knew he couldn't possibly understand the A∴R∴T∴.

"Huh?" I muttered, eventually.

138

"The A∴R∴T∴, Alex. The A∴R∴T∴. We know for a fact that Ed Bailey was deeply involved in a Satanic organization called the A∴R∴T∴."

"How do you know that?" I asked. Great. He was already connecting the A∴R∴T∴ with his stupid Satanic theory.

"We received a tip, and we've thoroughly investigated it." Peter paused. I wasn't sure if he was waiting for me to say something. "But you know what, Alex? The most interesting thing is that you have been seen in the company of several members of the A∴R∴T∴ in the last few days." He said this pointedly, with more than a little bit of accusation.

"You've been following me?" I was shocked.

"No, Alex," said Peter. "We've been conducting surveillance on the A∴R∴T∴. Why am I holding pictures of you talking to these people?"

"All right," I said. I'd been caught. No point trying to avoid it any longer. After all, I didn't have anything to hide. "I've joined the A∴R∴T∴."

"What?" shouted Peter. He sounded horrified. "Why on earth would you do that?"

"I was curious, you know, and to help you with this case."

"Why the hell would you do that without checking with me? This is some kind of Satanic cult, Alex! Not a quilting club! These people are dangerous! There's drugs and... at least one of them is a killer!"

"It is not a Satanic cult, Peter." I sighed. "They're perfectly nice people."

"They are not nice people! I can guarantee you that!"

"You don't know what you're talking about!" I said, nearly shouting into the phone.

"Look," said Peter, taking a breath. "I'm afraid you're the one who doesn't know what he's talking about. This is a totally fucked up case. These are fucked up people. There's things I didn't tell you about the crime scene. Things from the autopsy. I wanted to leave you out of it."

"What?" I asked.

"We found a large amount of semen, Alex. Semen in both the rectum and the mouth of the victim. We think it may be from as many as three or four separate individuals. This crime is an abomination. These people are fucking nuts!"

Despite Peter's melodramatics, that was a troubling piece of information. But it still didn't seem to fit with my experiences of members of the A∴R∴T∴, and I told him that as clearly as I could. He didn't seem to care.

"It doesn't matter what you believe, Alex," said Peter. "The facts are the facts."

"Well, I'll keep my eyes open. I promise," I said, hoping to appease him so I could get off the phone.

"You're not still planning to associate with these people, are you?"

"Why not?"

"My God!" shouted Peter. "They're assfucking murderers!"

"So you say."

Peter took a huge gulp of air, and I knew that he was about to start yelling again.

"Listen," I said. "How do you know it was member of the A∴R∴T∴ who did this? There are many other magical groups, even groups that have a grudge against the A∴R∴T∴. I met a group at the pagan festival called the Black Pullet Lodge. It's headed by a guy named Paul Mackey. This whole thing sounds a lot more like their style. They were total assholes. Why don't you look into that!"

"I will," he said, and I believed him, because I heard him scrawling something with a pen.

"The Black Pullet Lodge," I repeated. "Paul Mackey."

"Mackey," said Peter. "That name sounds familiar. He might already be in my notes."

For a moment I actually felt triumphant. Peter soon started questioning me again. He wanted every detail of my experiences with all of these people.

I probably shouldn't have opened up my mouth about anything, but I told him all I could remember about Paul Mackey, and the Bloodmoon coven, and the fire circle, and the pagan rituals I'd seen at the festival. Peter ate it all up with a spoon. Every time I finished describing something, he seemed to want ten things more. I finally forced myself off the phone with him, after over an hour.

THE BROTHERHOOD OF LIGHT AND DARKNESS

I felt a little guilty telling him so much about the pagan festival, almost like I was selling people down the river just to get the A∴R∴T∴ off Peter's shit list. But I knew that the A∴R∴T∴ couldn't be directly involved in the death of Ed Bailey. Could it? And some of these other people really might be involved.

I put them all out of my head as I began to recall the mind-blowing oral sex I'd received last night in the men's bathroom of the Masonic Hall. I wondered what on earth I was going to do about Connie Drake. Was I going to return the favor? Was I going to have sex with her? And I wondered if Connie or perhaps Ed Bailey's mother would be able to lead me any closer to solving this murder. It was time to get ready for my shift at Videohut.

Twenty Nine

10:45 AM

I picked Connie up at her parents' home in Waltham. When I came to her door, she gave me a very chaste kiss on the cheek, and commented that I might be a little underdressed. I noticed that Connie was looking quite beautifully put together in a silk blouse and slacks, high-heeled sandals, and French manicures on both her fingers and feet.

But my t-shirt was clean, and she hadn't mentioned anything about a dress code. Oh well. I felt like a sloppy loser. That was nothing new to me. We were soon off on our way in my beat-up, tan Chevy Caprice Classic. Usually I enjoyed my car's quirky, dented appearance, but today it just reminded me how run-down my whole existence had become. But things were beginning to move forward. I felt certain that my life was finally starting to take shape. I was doing something, and that was a huge step in the right direction.

Along the way, Connie filled me in on a lot of details of her life, and her life with Ed Bailey. Apparently, she and Ed had basically been living together for about a year. Connie still kept the bulk of her things at her parents, but spent most nights with Ed- until recently. But they really weren't that serious, and still slept with other people when they felt like it. Connie always had the sense that Ed was just settling for her rather than settling down with her.

I told her that surprised me since she was such an exceptional and beautiful woman. She smiled when I told her that, but there was an unspoken sadness in her eyes, and that sadness

142

was there the whole time I was with her. She told me that she hadn't been back to her apartment since his death, and she was now staying with her folks full time until she figured out her next step.

Apparently we were actually going to visit Ed's stepmother. Ed's biological mother died in childbirth, and his father remarried about ten years later. Ed's father had passed away in 1995, leaving the house and most of his money to Ed. Ed hadn't wanted to live in the house, so he'd let his stepmother keep it. But he'd left a lot of his stuff there.

We were going to pick up some of that stuff. The house was in Newton. It really seemed more like a mansion to me. I'm not sure what the legal definition of a mansion is, but this house was very big. As we drove through the residential area, I noticed that all of the nearby houses were gigantic.

The Bailey house had a wide colonial façade, with several pillars at the entrance that almost seemed an afterthought. I half-expected a butler to greet us when we got there, but it was Ed's stepmother who came to the door. She was an attractive woman in her late forties with frosted blonde hair and a tailored steel-gray pantsuit. She smiled courteously as she opened the door, but it was only with her mouth. Her eyes remained cool, dispassionate, almost bored. I could tell immediately that she didn't particularly care for Connie. Luckily, she hardly seemed to notice my t-shirt or me at all.

"Good morning Constance," said Ed's stepmother with little inflection. "So nice to see you."

"Good morning Mrs. Bailey, this is my friend Alex. He's going to help me with Ed's things."

"Hello, Alex," said Ed's stepmother without even looking at me. She'd already turned back inside.

The house was as opulent on the inside as it was gigantic on the outside. Expensive looking vases filled with fresh-cut orchids sat on Edwardian tables, and original oil paintings adorned the walls of the front hall. Ed's stepmother led us into a large living room or den where there were fifteen or more boxes on the floor. The boxes were filled with books, notebooks, loose papers and other odds and ends.

"These are the items the police weren't interested in," she said, emphasizing 'police' as if it was a dirty word. She left us there, closing the door somewhat loudly behind her.

We both stared at the boxes for quite some time, transfixed. "Wow," said Connie. "I thought Ed had a lot of books at our apartment, but now I see that was just the tip of the iceberg. This is nuts."

"Are we going to have to move all this?" I asked. I hoped that I sounded at least nominally pleasant, though the idea of moving all these boxes seemed very unpleasant to me.

"I'm afraid so. You didn't think that blowjob was going to be free, did you?" She smiled charmingly. Her smile was totally enthralling. I think I probably would have jumped off a bridge if she asked me to. She looked amazingly beautiful.

Just then Ed's stepmother came in with a tray bearing three glasses of lemonade. I sincerely hoped she didn't hear that blowjob comment. She didn't seem to notice. She put the tray down on one of her antique hardwood tables, and picked up one of the glasses herself.

"I thought you might like some refreshment before you get started," she said pleasantly.

The gesture actually made me almost like her. I smiled and thanked her, picking up my lemonade. I knew just the type of person she was. She was from that peculiar set in New England who are so incredibly Caucasian that they are entirely unable to express any kind of genuine emotion whatsoever. I was quite familiar with her type; half of my family was that way. I wasn't really so very different myself. We all sipped our lemonades in silence for quite some time.

"Oh yes," said Ed's stepmother finally. There was such a rehearsed tone in her voice that I felt sure she'd just been silently waiting for dramatic effect. "Don't let me forget to give you these." She held up a set of car keys and Connie stared at them dumbfounded.

"The Z3?" said Connie, sputtering. Her lower lip quivered.

"Yes. He left it to you, in his will," said the stepmother with a cool smirk. "Did you know he had a will?"

Connie shook her head, clearly in shock.

"Neither did I," said Ed's stepmother, shaking her head too. "I didn't even realize that he knew where his own investment accounts were. He's also left you some money and some stocks, bonds and such, but I'll let the lawyers contact you about that. I hope you don't mind I've given them your parents' number."

Connie seemed utterly stunned. Ed's stepmother pressed the car keys into Connie's shaking hands.

"The lawyers will talk to you about the title transfer and such. It's all so shocking, isn't it? The dear boy left me quite a lot too. This house, his father's collections, some money- I was so surprised," said Ed's stepmother. Her eyes suddenly began to mist up, and her hands went reflexively to her eyes as she gulped back tears. "I never realized he even liked me." Tears began to roll freely down her cheeks. "Excuse me," she said, sobbing, and she quickly left the room again.

Connie stared blankly at the car keys in her hand. I felt very uncomfortable, like I'd witnessed a moment, private and personal, that was not meant for me. This had nothing to do with my little investigation, and I felt like a peeping Tom. I watched Connie for some time. She wouldn't take her eyes off those keys.

"So, you have a car now," I said finally, unable to bear the awkward silence.

"A BMW," she muttered, still in shock.

"That's pretty cool."

Then Connie started crying, bawling loudly. She dropped the car keys to the floor and flopped down beside them. I really didn't know what to do.

I started to stare at the boxes of books. I recognized quite a lot of the occult books in the boxes from my own bookshelves. It seemed that everyone who was interested in the occult collected certain books. The Sacred Magic of Abramelin the Mage, The Key of Solomon, Agrippa's Three Books of Occult Philosophy, The Witches Bible, Cunningham's Encyclopedia of Magical Herbs and many, many others filled the boxes. He certainly had a lot more books than I had. I felt like I was in a strange psychic loop. It was because of my own interest in occult books that I was standing here. If I hadn't been so interested in these books myself I would never have ended up standing in this extremely large house, sipping lemonade while disturbing the privacy of two weeping women. Connie must have seen me staring at the books.

"You know, there are way too many books here for me to deal with, I've got my own books too, so feel free to take any that you want."

Looking at all those interesting books, a part of me wanted to take her up on the offer, but I felt too strange about it. I mean, I was supposed to be looking into this poor guy's murder. I'd already gotten a blowjob from his girlfriend, and a lemonade from his mom. Now I was going to pick through his books?

No, I decided, not now. If the offer still stood later, then perhaps. I told Connie that I'd wait until later to think about it, and she nodded. She was no longer crying, but her reddened eyes still stared off blankly. I felt incredibly uncomfortable. I stood there for quite a while, trying not to think about taking the books, not really sure what to do. Connie eventually seemed to snap back to reality.

"Well, I guess I won't need a ride home," she said, matter-of-fact. She almost sounded cheery. Her mood swings were dizzying. "We're not going to be able to fit all this in the Z3, so would you mind following me with some of them?"

"No, of course not," said."

She stared at the boxes fixedly, ruminating. "You know," said Connie, "my parents aren't going to be too happy about all these boxes." She gave a hollow chuckle.

We spent the next twenty minutes or so moving Ed's possessions into my car. Ed's stepmother made another brief appearance about halfway through the process. She still looked like she'd been crying, but she'd clearly applied a new layer of make up.

When all the boxes were loaded into my car, Connie approached me with a sheepish smile, taking hold of my T-shirt sleeve flirtatiously.

"Listen," she said. "I'm realizing my parents are really going to go nuts if I try to bring all this stuff into their house. They're neat freaks. I really don't have anywhere to keep all this." She paused and smiled at me expectantly." I don't suppose I can persuade you to keep them here in your car or something for a few days until I can find someplace for them? I'll make it worth your while." She smiled again and stroked my arm affectionately.

She obviously knew how to play men very well. How could I resist an offer like that? Besides, I really wanted to look through the boxes anyway. Who knows what kind of information I could find in them? They could hold the keys to murder, for all I knew. But I still let Connie believe that I was letting her put a great imposition on me. After all, I wanted her to make it worth my while.

We said our very stiff good-byes to Ed's stepmother and left the house. Once Mrs. Bailey was out of sight Connie kissed me lightly on the lips and disappeared toward the garage. Moments later she emerged behind the wheel of the BMW Z3 and drove off fast with a smile and a wave. She didn't even say goodbye.

I have to admit I was a bit disappointed that I wasn't going to get my reward immediately, but I was also really looking forward to digging through those boxes. I could hardly wait to see what kind of clues I could uncover.

Thirty

I didn't want to bring all the boxes into the house when I got home. My mother wouldn't have been much more pleased than Connie's parents. I grabbed the most promising box that I could find. It seemed full of personal notebooks.

I went upstairs with it, and luckily my mom didn't even see me. I sat on the floor of my room and began pulling out the loose papers and notebooks. It was mostly just scrawled poetry and meandering doodles that reminded me of the sort of thing made by a person who was very high on drugs.

I started thinking about smoking a little pot myself. But I knew from just looking at the disconnected thoughts and imagery on these pages that it would be impossible to concentrate if I got high. So I just kept looking through the papers.

Amidst the poems and drawings, I found quite a few essays and papers for classes at Middlesex Community College. They were dated as early as 1988 and as recently as 1996- this year. Ed was clearly taking a long and circuitous route to a two-year degree.

Then I found something that really caught my eye. It was another essay, but clearly not one for school. It was titled "Principles and Practices of Aleister Crowley's Sex Magick." I began to read it eagerly.

> In order to understand Aleister Crowley's magick at all, one must understand that it all relates to sex and sex energy. Using sex energy is

> in fact the whole key to practical magick of every sort. Aleister Crowley was first introduced to sex magick through Theodore Reuss and the Ordo Templi Orientis, a sex-magical Masonic fraternity. Aleister Crowley soon devoted nearly all his energy to the exploration and practice of sexual magick..."

I heard the phone start ringing in the distance, but I ignored it, continuing to read.

> In essence, the secret of sex magick is incredibly simple, a sort of wish fulfillment. One simply has to think of what one desires at the moment of orgasm, and that desire will manifest. However, in practice, this is harder than it seems. An understanding of the metaphysical nature of the sex energy, and particularly the incredible magical virtues of semen, will be of great benefit to the interested practitioner..."

This must be the explanation for that semen they found in Ed Bailey. He was practicing some kind of sex magick. Maybe this was the 'dark stuff' that Connie had been talking about. Who knows?

I'd never even heard of such a thing, and yet it all seemed to make so much sense. Magick energy is sex energy. Sex energy is the energy that operates the universe. Or rather, perhaps the energy that manifests the universe exists in us most powerfully in our sexual parts- the parts that continue and expand the species- and the universe! After all, a single teaspoon of sperm has millions of cells in it, so it contains millions of potential people. That's a pretty powerful teaspoon!

There was a knock on my door. It was my mother.

"Alex. You've got a phone call."

"Who is it?" I said, reflexively burying the sex magick essay back into the box.

"Someone named Steve Curtin. He says he's a friend of yours?"

It took me a moment. Then I remembered he was one of the guys I got stoned with after my initiation. I wondered why he'd be calling.

"Yeah, okay," I said.

I followed my mom downstairs and picked up the phone off the kitchen counter.

"Hello?"

"Ninety-three, Alex, how are you?" said Steve in a cheery tone.

"Good," I said. I was about to say 'ninety-three,' but I noticed that my mom was still in the room. I couldn't bring myself to say that in front of her.

"How are you recovering from your initiation?"

I looked over at my mom, who was watching me like I was in a fish tank. I waved her away with my head. As I turned my attention back to the phone I realized that I hadn't really thought about my initiation much at all since that night. But I actually was feeling a bit different. I felt somehow more focused, more purposeful. I also noticed that I had a subtle tingling over my whole body. I hadn't really consciously noticed it until that moment, but it was there, especially around my stomach and groin. I was sure I'd been feeling it since the night of the initiation, but I guess I'd been so stoned and distracted by other things that I hadn't really registered the sensation fully.

"You know," I said, "I guess I'm feeling pretty good, really. Sort of energized."

"Yeah," said Steve. "Are you finding the study guide confusing?"

Then I realized that I hadn't opened or even looked at the study guide at all. I felt too ashamed to admit this, so I fibbed.

"Uh, no," I said. "It all seems to make sense."

"Even the rituals?"

Rituals? What sort of rituals? I really wished I'd taken a look at that stupid booklet. What was I supposed to say? "Well, yeah," I said, finally. "Those rituals are a bit, um, confusing, I guess."

"I figured," said Steve amiably. "They all seem simple until you actually try to do them. Then it's suddenly a whole different story."

"Yep," I said. I felt more and more guilty by the second for being such a liar.

"Well, I'll be glad to go over them with you sometime soon, if you like," he said.

"Oh, okay." I wondered why he was being so friendly. I guess that's what happens when you're all in the same secret cult. But I wasn't used to people going out of their way to be nice to me.

"What's your schedule like this weekend," he asked.

Wow, all that was left of the weekend was the rest of today and tomorrow. That was awfully soon. I really wasn't sure if I even wanted to get together with him. But perhaps he'd be able to give me some more useful information about the A∴R∴T∴ and its members. I wanted to follow every possible lead that I could. We agreed to get together the next day at his apartment.

When I got off the phone with Steve, I felt guilty about lying to him and not even looking at the A∴R∴T∴ workbook. I decided to leave off studying Ed Bailey's writings for the moment. I went back upstairs and turned my attention to the workbook that the A∴R∴T∴ gave me instead.

The workbook began with an explanation of the grades of the order, which were ten in number corresponding to the ten sephiroth of the qabalistic tree of life.

> 1=10   Neophyte
> 2=9   Zelator
> 3=8 Practicus
> 4=7 Philosophus (portal)
> 5=6 Adeptus Minor
> 6=5 Adeptus Major
> 7=4 Adeptus Exemptus
> 8=3 Magister Templi
> 9=2 Magus
> 10=1   Ipsissimus

Then the workbook went on to an explanation of the "astral light," describing it as a medium through which spiritual energies move and transform our perceptions. The workbook explained the importance of setting up goals and that the astral light was quick to respond to a singular and focused goal, when one directs all of one's attention to its accomplishment. When your attention was focused in this way, the astral would bend toward you, and you had the whole weight of the universe propelling you toward your goal. That was easy enough for me: My goal at the moment was to find Ed Bailey's killer.

After that there was a lengthy section describing the four elements, with meditations on each element. The workbook explained that our personal character traits can be analyzed through the four elements, and by balancing the elements in our personalities we can begin to master the four elements of nature. By doing so we become masters of ourselves and the physical world around us.

The workbook instructed that every initiate of the A∴R∴T∴ was to keep a journal of all magical work conducted, and a record of dream experience, particularly emphasizing dreams that seem to have a magical character.

I was beginning to wonder if I'd ever find any rituals in this workbook, until I came upon the next section. It was detailed instructions for performing a ritual called the "Lesser Ritual of the Pentagram." It contained complex visualization exercises for a ritual largely working with the four elements. As I pored over the elaborate instructions I was glad that I was going to get to work on this with Steve the next day.

Then followed even more complicated instructions on the "Lesser Ritual of the Hexagram," the "Greater Ritual of the Pentagram," and the "Greater Ritual of the Hexagram." These rituals were apparently intended for invoking specific elements and planetary forces. I really didn't know where to begin. I had seen these rituals in books, but I'd never seen such detailed explanations. It was all very strange and exciting.

The next section contained instructions for astral projection. This really caught my attention. I had always been interested in astral projection, and these instructions made the matter seem quite easy. I read through the simple instructions twice, because they almost seemed too easy.

THE BROTHERHOOD OF LIGHT AND DARKNESS

1. Sit or lie down in a comfortable place; it is probably a good idea to begin in a darkened room.

2. Begin to imagine a figure resembling yourself, standing directly in front of you.

3. Move your consciousness into this figure, so that you look back at your physical body sitting or lying, now before you.

4. Once you feel comfortable in your imaginary body, let your consciousness rise in this body, very high up into the sky.

5. When you have risen to a great height above your earthly and physical body you may stop and look around.

6. You may begin to see and experience any number of different images, creatures or scenes, depending on your own nature and the power of your will to hold on to the experiences. You may experience both pleasant and horrific visions with this technique.

7. When you have seen enough, let your 'body of light' return to your physical body and completely reunite with it.

8. It will take some practice to achieve a sense of success with this, but it may be dangerous even from the beginning. It is probably a good idea to begin and end all experiments with the 'Lesser Ritual of the Pentagram.'

I lay down on my bed and tried to follow the directions as well as I could, but I couldn't seem to get any sense of separation from my body. After about ten frustrating minutes I sat up and re-read the directions. I couldn't figure out what I was doing wrong. I wasn't using the 'Lesser Ritual of the Pentagram,' but this seemed quite optional in the directions. The instructions couldn't just be nonsense. There were quite a few members in the A∴R∴T∴ and surely someone would have complained by now if these instructions were inadequate.

I decided that maybe I needed a little pot. That would help loosen me up and relax me. I smoked a couple of bowls, and lay back down in order to try again. I closed my eyes and relaxed. I sank deeper and deeper into relaxation. I felt myself sinking.

Thirty One

⊙ Sunday, September 29, 1996

11:54 am

I didn't wake up again until the next morning. I guess it was really more nearly afternoon. I felt a little irritated that my astral experiments had been such a failure, but I had to get ready quickly and leave in order to get to Steve's house anywhere near the time we agreed on for our appointment.

Steve lived in Brighton, up Route 2, and then through an innumerable series of one way streets and difficult left turns. Luckily, Steve had given me fairly comprehensive directions over the phone.

12:56 PM

I arrived at his house, a puke green duplex with a wide cement stoop. He greeted me eagerly when I got to the door, leading me past his sleepy female roommate who was drinking Coke straight out of a two liter bottle with half-closed eyes. She was wearing a pair of men's boxers and a large T-shirt, last night's dark eye make up smeared down to her cheeks. She still looked fairly attractive, even in this state.

"Hi," she said, as we passed her. It was really more of a grunt. I greeted her back, but Steve pulled me into his tidy, sparse bedroom before we could interact anymore. I asked him if she was his girlfriend, but he said she was just a roommate.

"She's cute," I said.

155

"I'll introduce you if you want," said Steve. "She's a total slut. You'd have no problem getting in there." He smiled wryly.

"Uh," I stammered, not really sure what to say.

Steve started laughing loudly. "I'm just messing with you," he said, continuing to laugh. "Well, no, I mean, she is a total slut." This time I couldn't help but laugh along with him.

"I do like sluts," I said, laughing.

"Don't I know it," said Steve. "I heard Matthew caught you and Connie Drake in the bathroom. That's classy."

I was taken aback by this statement, and it must have been written all over my face because he looked at me reassuringly.

"Don't worry. There's no secrets between your brothers and sisters in the A∴R∴T∴. Everyone knows everything about everybody, sooner or later. Don't get scared. We all love each other."

"So you think Connie Drake is a slut?" I asked.

Steve cocked his head to the side and eyed me with a smile. "Alex, let me tell you something. Pretty much everyone in the A∴R∴T∴ is a slut."

"Really?"

"Oh yeah," he said with a smirk. "Okay, remember Jeremy? Smoked us out at the initiation? Well, he's been sleeping with Lucy Grinder, Catherine Chen, and of course Mary Culling." Steve counted the names out on his fingers. "Mary Culling sleeps with just about everybody. You'll definitely get to fuck her if you want. Just watch out for Jake Pilsner. He thinks he owns her, just because she lets him fuck her all the time. Poor guy. She'll fuck anyone, anytime. Apparently he's hung like a French bread or something, though. That's really why she puts up with him. But anyway, Jeremy lives with Catherine, but I don't even know if they're really together anymore. Jeremy fucks anyone he can get his hands on. I don't know if Jeremy's fucked Connie Drake. But Connie's old boyfriend Ed, he was fucking everybody too."

That caught my attention, but I didn't want to appear too interested in Ed. I nodded in what I hoped looked like in-difference. A dark look of sadness crossed Steve's face moment-arily, clearly he was recalling that Ed had just died, but the sadness quickly disappeared as he returned to his gossip. I pretended that I hadn't even noticed.

"And Lucy Grinder, you know, the girl with all the piercings?" said Steve, making sure I knew exactly who he was talking about. "That girl is crazy. She lives in a little apartment on the top floor at Abe Crane's house. Every time I'm over there she's fucking somebody else. It's like a revolving door at her place."

"Well, what about you?" I asked. "Who are you sleeping with?"

"Oh, I don't kiss and tell, Alex," said Steve with a wry smile. "Let's just say I have slightly more discerning tastes than most."

"What about that brunette girl, Jessica Burnham?" I asked. "What's her story?"

Steve looked at me with a deeply inquisitive expression. "Jessica Burnham?" he asked, squeezing my arm playfully. "Have you got a little crush on her?" He smiled broadly, and I could feel myself blushing. "It's okay. Everybody does."

"I don't know," I said. "I was just asking."

"Don't try to snow me, Alex," scolded Steve. "I'm very psychic."

"Okay, sure." I said. "She's cute."

"That's too bad, 'cause you're definitely not her type." He must have seen me look a little crestfallen, because he started cackling wildly. "I'm just teasing," he said, still laughing. "I'll bet she's got her hands between her legs right now, thinking about you." I laughed with him against my will. Steve was very funny in a sick sort of way. I was really starting to like him. "She's a bit of a tough nut to crack, but as far as I know, a few have cracked her." Steve laughed again.

"That's good to know, I guess," I said, chuckling.

"Well, I'll stop gossiping away," said Steve, "so we can get down to what you came out here for, huh?"

"Yeah, okay, sure," I said. I really would have been just as happy to gossip for a while longer, but I didn't want to make Steve suspicious of my motives. So I shifted gears to the subject of my own occult studies. "I was trying to do some astral projection last night, but I fell asleep."

"That'll happen," said Steve. "Probably shouldn't do astral traveling at night in bed. You'll pretty much always fall right asleep."

I nodded. It was amazing how quickly he shifted from saucy jokester to magical professor.

"Did you start off with the Lesser Banishing Ritual of the Pentagram?" he asked.

"No," I said. " I just pretty much, you know, tried to do it."

"Well, I don't know if there's really any reason behind this or not, but most people say that you should start off any magical work with the L.B.R.P."

"Oh."

"I mean it's probably just tradition, but I don't know. Maybe it could even be dangerous if you don't."

"Dangerous?"

"Well, astral critters could come and possess your body while you're out or something. It's probably just a bunch of hooey, but I'll teach you the L.B.R.P. anyway."

"Sounds like a good idea," I said. I wasn't really sure if he was being serious or not, or even if he knew what he was talking about.

I'd read the ritual yesterday, and several times before that too, in various books, though I'd never tried actually doing it. I looked forward to seeing it live in the flesh.

"So, okay, well. Let's get started," said Steve. "You begin by facing East, that's this way in my apartment." Steve pointed to one of the walls in his room. "Go ahead."

I had hoped he was going to demonstrate it for me. The thought of acting out the ritual in front of him made me quite uneasy. But I was determined to not let those kinds of feelings dominate my life anymore, so I stood up and faced the wall.

"Good," said Steve. Now, you want to imagine a glowing ball of light above your head. That's basically like your crown chakra, or your higher self, or your Holy Guardian Angel- your personal Kether. It's the source of your magical inspiration. So, go ahead and close your eyes." He pointed to his head, then ran his fingers over his eyelids.

I closed my eyes and tried to follow along with what he was saying as best as I could.

"Now touch your forehead, imagining the light from above coming down into your head, and you say "Ateh.""

"Ateh," I repeated, touching my forehead.

"Right, now touch your heart, and say, 'Malkuth,' imagining that light shining down through your whole body, and forming another sphere of light at your feet." I followed his instructions. "Touch your right shoulder, imagining a ball of light there, and say 'Ve Geburah," and you're left shoulder, forming another light ball, "Ve Gedulah. Now put your hands together, like your praying, and say "Le-Olahm Amen.""

"Le-Olahm Amen."

Now, what you've just said basically translates from Hebrew to 'Thine is the Kingdom, the Power and the Glory forever, Amen.' Just like a good Christian boy," he added with a snort of laughter.

He then went through the rest of the ritual with me, which consisted of tracing pentagrams in the four directions, along with various Hebrew god names, and calling upon the four archangels, Raphael, Gabriel, Michael, and Auriel.

We went over the ritual several more times over the next forty-five minutes or so, until I had it completely memorized. He would stop me frequently to make sure I was concentrating on the various images and energies. I was impressed with his thorough knowledge and I eventually had to ask him how long he'd been in the A∴R∴T∴.

"Oh, just a few months," he said. "I've just become a Zelator.

"Wow," I said. "You sure seem to know an awful lot!"

"Well, to be honest, I used to be in the Black Pullet Lodge."

"Really?" I asked. I was shocked. I couldn't picture Steve amongst Paul Mackey and his pasty myrmidons.

"I know it seems crazy," said Steve, blushing visibly. "But I was young and stupid. I didn't know any better. They were the first real magical group I found."

"How long were you involved in the Black Pullet Lodge?"

"A few years. I'm an Adeptus Minor with them."

"What made you quit?"

"It really used to be a lot better than it is now. A lot of people left. Paul Mackey was just too much of an arrogant asshole. I was practically his right hand man, and he didn't treat me any better than a servant. The only people still in his group at this point are either really stupid, or just have some kind of beef with the A∴R∴T∴. The guy barely has his own life together and he tells everyone he comes in contact with how they should run their lives. And usually all he really wants to do is badmouth how horrible the A∴R∴T∴ is. So, eventually I just felt like I should check out the A∴R∴T∴ and see what it was like. You know?"

"How does it compare?"

"So far, much better," said Steve. "The people, the work, the parties. I mean, all of Mackey's magick is stolen right out of the A∴R∴T∴ materials. The only thing is, he skips stuff and changes stuff. He totally screws some stuff up too."

"Hmm," I said.

"Listen to me," said Steve, looking over at a clock radio on his bedside table. "I've just been talking your ear off. I'm sorry."

"Oh no, don't worry," I said. "I find it all fascinating."

But he didn't share anymore about Paul Mackey or the A∴R∴T∴. He told me that he had to end our get together, because he had plans that evening. I thanked him profusely, and he assured me that he'd be happy to talk more anytime.

On the way out, we bumped into his roommate once again.

"Bye-bye," she said to me with a smile.

"You see," said Steve. "She likes you. You're in. I told you she was a slut."

His roommate threw a couch pillow right at Steve, bouncing it roughly off his head.

"You fucking suck, Steve!" she shouted in what sounded like mock rage. Still, I hurried out, feeling a bit embarrassed by the scene. I decided that as soon as I got home I was going to try astral projection again. This time I'd start out with the Lesser Banishing Ritual of the Pentagram, to keep away those "astral critters."

Thirty Two

5:02 PM

Once I got home, I immediately went upstairs, and very quietly performed the LBRP. I didn't want my mother knowing how truly strange I was becoming. I then laid myself out on my bed and tried to leave my body. Again I fell asleep almost immediately.

☾ Monday, September 30, 1996

3:45 AM

I woke up. It was the middle of the night, but I found myself wide-awake. I couldn't remember my dreams at all, but I felt like I'd been with some people, learning something about magick. I was frustrated that I couldn't remember anything clearly.

I got up and went downstairs for a glass of water. I felt very dehydrated and achy. I decided that I really needed a cigarette.

I went out onto the front porch for a little fresh air and a smoke, and to my very great surprise there was a small white envelope with my name written on it neatly by hand sitting right in the middle of the porch.

I tore open the envelope, and at first it seemed to be empty. Then I discovered a small disk of parchment paper was wedged in, right against the bottom crease of the envelope. The disk of parchment had some kind of glyph or symbol inscribed on it in purple ink.

This small piece of paper disturbed me greatly. It was clearly some kind of magical object. The parchment was wrinkled and stained, as if it had gotten soaked and later been allowed to dry. It looked like it had been dipped into some kind of yellowish liquid. I reacted very badly to it immediately. I felt panicky, my heart started pounding in my chest. Who would put something like this on my porch? I had no idea what to do with it, so I put it back into the envelope, rushed inside, and threw it into the recesses of the front coat closet.

I went back out onto the porch, breathless, pins and needles rushing through me. I lit a cigarette and walked away from my house, down the street.

I felt somewhat relieved to be placing distance between myself and the strange talismanic parchment. I drew deeply from my cigarette, still wondering hopelessly who could possibly have put that thing on my porch. And what was it? Was it some kind of curse? Or a gift? I couldn't imagine. It wasn't mailed. Someone actually came to my porch and physically put it there.

Of course, Paul Mackey immediately came to mind, but he didn't have my address. But maybe he got it somehow. Who knows? The Bloodmoons took my name and address when I registered at their festival. Maybe it was even someone in the A∴R∴T∴. They had my address. I couldn't think why anyone would do that, but I couldn't rule anything out.

I turned off onto the bike path that ran through the woods behind my house. I somehow felt safe there. The trees and birds were familiar. I could see a faint patch of light in the distance, so I knew the sun would be coming up in an hour or two. Still, it was pretty dark. I walked down the bike path for quite some time, trying to figure out why this object had been given to me.

Then, just as I was starting to calm down, I began to get the distinct feeling that I was being watched. I looked all around me in the bushes and the trees, but I didn't see anyone, or anything.

But I was sure something was there. My heart started to race again. Then I saw something move, off to my right. It was something moving in the bushes. I was sure of it, but when I focused on the bushes there was nothing there.

I started walking faster, and that something moved along with me in my peripheral vision. But again when I looked directly it was gone. But no, there was something. Not a glow or a shadow, but instead just a sort of distortion. It was as if an amorphous blob was warping the surrounding shadow. It seemed somewhat rounded, five feet or more in diameter. It was almost imperceptible, but it was definitely there.

It lurched toward me about a foot, and I felt distinctly like I was going to vomit. My stomach churned violently, dropping and rising like a stormy sea. I could neither run nor scream nor even raise my arms. I was frozen like an animal. I'd never seen or felt anything like this before. It continued inching closer and closer, and I felt sure it was going to do something horrible to me.

The terrifying object stretched toward my abdomen, and I felt like I was spinning. It touched me, right on the side of my belly. I knew I had to do something, because the touch felt slightly painful, like it was scraping me from the inside. All I could think to do was the Lesser Banishing Ritual of the Pentagram that I'd just learned.

I screwed up my courage and touched my forehead.

"Ateh," I said, my voice shaking.

This seemed to agitate the strange thing. I felt it move, but it kept on touching me. I tried to get out the rest of the ritual, but my voice was too weak, I was shaking too violently. I quickly gave up and ran for it.

I ran and ran down the bike path, but I felt sure the strange thing was right behind me the whole way. I felt it near me, unpleasant shivers running up and down my spine. I ran back out onto the street, and once I got under the light of the street lamps, the thing seemed to be gone.

I sat down, leaning against a street lamp, breathless. I stayed under the light for quite some time. I couldn't think of anything else to do. I smoked another cigarette, constantly eyeing the darkness beyond the street lamp for any sign of the thing. But there was nothing. Eventually I decided to make a run for my house.

I made it inside without any sign of the thing, but I still turned on all the lights in the front half of my house, just to be sure. I smoked several cigarettes in the kitchen, trying to stay as far as possible away from the parchment talisman in my front closet.

6:03 AM

My mother came down into the kitchen, and was very surprised to see me awake.

"I'm going to turn off some of these lights, Alex," she said scolding me. "No need to waste all this electricity. The sun's coming up."

I didn't stop her, though I still felt pretty uncertain about the strange thing from the bike path. She seemed to notice that I was agitated, but she didn't ask me any questions. Instead, she just told me a funny story about how my Uncle Bob had accused the person next to him on a plane flight of stealing his glasses. It turned out they were sitting on top of his head the whole time, but the person felt so uncomfortable about embarrassing my uncle that he never mentioned a thing for the whole flight. Her silly story helped me relax about my experience for a little while, and I went upstairs and tried to get a little more sleep.

Although I closed my eyes, sleep wouldn't come. I kept seeing that strange thing in the shadows of my mind. I couldn't make it go away. I knew exactly what I had to do. I went down to the phone, and called Adin Stone.

Thirty Three

9:25 AM

When I finished describing my strange experience to Adin over the phone, he felt that the situation was urgent enough to warrant immediate attention. He came right over to my house.

"So, let's get to the details," said Adin as he came through the door. "Why would anyone be trying to attack you magically?"

"I don't know," I said. "I was thinking maybe it's because of the murder investigation."

"Hmm," said Adin thoughtfully. "Perhaps, but perhaps not. No, I doubt it."

"Why?" I asked.

"Well, me personally, if I was seriously trying to stop you from doing something, I think I'd probably just shoot you." He laughed cheerfully.

"Okay," I said, smirking against my will. "Sure, but maybe they're just trying to scare me off."

"Yes, maybe. And it looks like they've done a pretty good job of it! You're pale as the grave!"

"Something's out there! In the woods!" I said, feeling my heart jump to my throat. "I felt it touch me."

"Alex, this is really not something you need to worry about. Unless you make it something to worry about."

"Well, I'm pretty worried!"

"I can see that. So, let's take a look at the talisman in question."

"It's in the closet," I said, pointing to the closet door behind us.

"Well, go get it," he said, matter-of-fact. But I couldn't bring myself to move. "You really don't have any idea who would send something like this to you?" he asked again.

"The only name that keeps popping into my head is Paul Mackey."

"Hmm," said Adin. "Yes. This definitely sounds like the type of thing Paul Mackey might do. So, let's have a look at the talisman, Alex. Hurry up."

I very hesitantly opened the closet door and retrieved the envelope. I held it out to Adin. He shook his hand at the envelope and instructed me to open it. I plucked out the talisman and showed it to him. He looked at it very briefly.

"Demon," he said. "Goetic. Astaroth. See, you can read the name around the edge of the circle," he said, pointing to the letters on the talisman. "An odd choice."

"How bad is it?" I asked. "Is it trying to kill me? Am I in trouble?"

"No, no," said Adin with a chuckle. "As I've been trying to tell you, demons are magical beings, beings that dwell in the realm of dreams and fantasy. They are for the most part only as dangerous as you allow them to be."

"That thing on the bike path was not imaginary!"

"No, it was magical. But there's only a delicate difference, really. At least from a practical perspective. Your fear was feeding the demon, making it more and more powerful, more and more real. Magick is slippery stuff. Part of it depends on the magician, part depends on the target. You are an excellent target."

"So, what can I do?"

"Oh, I think this will be fairly easy to take care of," said Adin confidently. "You're really in an unfortunate place right now. You've entered the magical world, but you don't really have any knowledge or skills yet. But, don't worry, I'm here. And you won't be in this place for long. Soon you'll be much more capable than Mackey or any of his followers. For now, I'll help you diffuse this situation."

He had me drive him to a nearby New Age store, where I purchased some sea salt, some sulfur, several different herbs, a black cloth and a small glass jar.

Outside the store, Adin told me to throw the talisman into the jar, then put the rest of the herbs and salt in on top of it. He told me to wrap the jar up in the black cloth, then placed his hand over the jar.

"I hereby bind this magick," said Adin. He was very calm, displaying none of the bravado I'd seen from others at the pagan festival or my initiation. "Return to sender." He instructed me to tie the cloth up around the jar, and we got back into my car.

Adin directed me to drive up Mass. Ave. quite a long way, until we reached East Arlington. Once we were very close to the border of Cambridge, he told me to turn right into a residential area. He eventually directed me to stop in front of an ill-kept gray house. The paint was cracked and peeling. Fast food wrappers, garbage and several broken, rusty appliances were strewn across the lawn.

"Where are we?" I asked, though I had a funny feeling I knew where we were.

"This is Paul Mackey's house," said Adin. That was exactly where I was afraid we were. "I'll bet you didn't realize that the two of you lived in the same town." Adin smiled enthusiastically.

"What are we going to do?"

"We're going to give him back his talisman."

My heart slammed against my chest.

"But..."

"Go on," said Adin. "Run and put it on his porch."

"Uh..." I felt very uneasy. The idea of walking up to Mackey's house with the jar wrapped in black cloth did not sound like much fun.

"Do you want to put an end to this talisman or not?" he said with a frown. I sighed and grabbed the wrapped jar. I got out of the car and stepped cautiously toward the house. I strained my eyes looking into the windows, hoping no one was watching. All I could see was darkness and reflections from the street. My heart was really pounding as I reached the porch. I quietly

167

placed the jar down on the cement stairs. The quiet thud of the wrapped jar against cement made me shiver.

I ran back to the car as fast as I could. When I got back inside Adin was laughing uproariously.

"Good job," he said. I couldn't tell if he was teasing or serious. I began to wonder if the whole thing was some sort of elaborate game for him. I started to feel strangely angry as I drove back toward my own house. Adin seemed to notice.

"Your emotions really swing all over the place," he said. "That's not good. It makes you very susceptible to attack, and it won't be helpful in your own magical work, either."

I didn't really know what to say so I just nodded. We drove in silence for a minute or two.

"What sort of magical work are you conducting with the A∴R∴T∴?" asked Adin.

"Banishing rituals and astral projection," I said.

"Yes, very appropriate in terms of the Hermetic Qabala. Malkuth and the path of Tau."

"What?" I wasn't sure what he was talking about.

"Malkuth is the tenth and lowest sephirah on the tree of Life. It is the sphere of the four elements. So the Lesser Banishing Ritual of the Pentagram is exactly the sort of thing you ought to be working on. The path of Tau is the path leading from Malkuth to the ninth sephirah Yesod. This is where your astral travels take you."

"I haven't had much luck with astral travelling," I said.

"Oh no?" said Adin with a devilish smile. "It's hard to get very far with your emotions swinging all over the place. You don't even know where you are half the time. You need to calm down. Then you should find it quite easy. You have a knack for experiencing the astral plane."

Moments later, we got back to my house, and Adin said goodbye. He assured me that we could talk more about astral travelling again very soon. As he left I felt more confused than ever about everything.

I tried to stay calm for the rest of the day, hoping that the strange demonic thing was really gone, wondering why Adin thought I'd have a knack for astral projection.

Thirty Four

Once again, I found myself in front of a staircase checkered with black and white stairs. I tried to walk up the stairs, and still found myself completely unable to make my way up. My legs could hardly move, and with each step I found myself no closer to the top.

As I looked up, I saw Adin Stone emerging from the gateway of stars at the top of the stairs. He waved to me kindly, beckoning me upward. As he beckoned me, I found it even more difficult to move.

Then Kerrie and Jessica appeared at either side of Adin. I really wanted to get up those stairs, but I just couldn't move.

"You can come up anytime," said Adin, wrapping his arms around the waists of the two young women. "Then you will have conquered the astral plane."

I tried to respond, but I couldn't seem to talk. Jessica seemed to think it was very funny. She covered her mouth with her hand so I couldn't see her laughing at me.

As I continued to struggle, a shadowy figure emerged in front of me. All sight of the stairs was obscured, and I stepped backward nervously. The shadowy figure swelled before me, twisting into shifting demonic shapes full of razor points and crooked claws.

I turned and tried to run, but as I attempted to get away, my legs would still hardly move. Now I seemed to be in a forest. I knew immediately that it was the forest where Mackey had taken me to drug me. I could feel shadowy, demonic shapes

169

brushing against me as they swarmed through the woods around me. But the largest of these demonic creatures stood right in front of me, growing and twisting like an evil tree. No, he was hairy, like a beast, with greasy black teeth, and many arms, each clenching and unclenching long, sharp claws. Click clack. Click clack.

I could see a soft, bluish-violet light behind the demonic creature. I felt that if I could just get past the demon I'd be safe in that light. I couldn't tell you why I was convinced of this, but I was very certain.

But there was no way to get past this creature. It kept growing in every direction, until its breathing began to shake the whole ground around me. I was shaking too. I suddenly realized that the whole forest was the beast, and I was inside this demonic forest beast. I had no way out, and I felt my shaking legs being wrapped and drawn down into the mire.

♂ Tuesday, October 1, 1996

2:20 AM

I woke up, shaking. My body was covered with a cold sweat. I felt my insides churning, like my stomach and chest were swarming with snakes. My arms and legs were almost numb. I could barely move. It was all so real and terrifying.

I didn't want to call Adin again. I didn't want to keep disturbing him. But I knew this was somehow a very important dream. It had to have some significance. It was too strange, too vivid.

I reached for my pot pipe, which still had a little left in it. I didn't light it. I couldn't light it. My mind raced. What if Adin was underestimating the danger? If Mackey had sent a demon to kill Ed Bailey, then maybe the thing that attacked me was supposed to kill me. Perhaps I was supposed to be dead now. If Adin hadn't come to help me with the talisman, maybe I would have been dead. Maybe the danger still wasn't completely over.

I couldn't bring myself to smoke pot. I couldn't. I knew it would make me even more paranoid, and I wanted to follow

Adin's advice. I had to stay calm. I lay in bed and stared at the ceiling until morning.

3:00 P.M.

At work the next day I felt completely confused and exhausted. As usual things were very slow. I was alone in the store because my co-worker Sue was out on her lunch break. Three men in business suits were skulking through the aisles, picking through the porn tapes that ran along the top shelves of the store. I didn't bother to pay any attention to them. They were regulars.

I sat behind the counter lifelessly, my mind turning over everything that I'd learned so far about this murder. I was able to piece together next to nothing. Still, I felt more determined than ever that I was going to figure it out. I had to now. I was becoming more and more in the middle of it.

But I still couldn't even figure out why anyone would want Ed Bailey dead. And why would they send me a demonic talisman? Was it even the same person?

I hadn't met anyone other than Paul Mackey who seemed to have any problems with anybody. But could it be Mackey? Was he really capable of murder? He was far too fat and unhealthy to physically kill anyone. But what about magical murder? I didn't know what to think.

Connie certainly didn't have a problem with Ed, though she did seem to gain from his death. But I definitely don't think she was expecting that. Matthew Wiley didn't seem to have a problem with Ed. Neither did Steve or any of the others. Still, I didn't know any of them very well yet.

The A∴R∴T∴ magick class was on Wednesday. That would be my next opportunity to learn more about these people. I wondered if they would ever trust me enough to even mention Ed's murder around me. No one but Connie had even hinted at it.

Then in the midst my ruminations the front door of the video store creaked open, and I nearly fainted as Paul Mackey lumbered through, followed by his hairy wife and their fat little daughter. Mackey wore a billowy brownish shirt over immense jeans, his wife in a nearly identical outfit. The little girl was wearing a filthy little pink dress, covered with what I sincerely hoped were chocolate stains.

They looked around the video store momentarily. Then Mackey spotted me. As Mackey waddled up toward me at the counter, he had such an exaggerated expression of surprise on his face that even an imbecile would have known it was phony.

"My god," said Mackey. "Sebastian, right?"

"Uh, yeah," I said blankly.

"Ninety-three! I didn't realize you worked here. What a small world," said Mackey.

I couldn't imagine how he'd found out where I worked, but I was very sure he was only there to see me.

He turned to his wife. "Look, Honey. It's Sebastian from the festival." His wife looked up at me with total disinterest, then went back to chasing their daughter through the store. The plump little girl was plucking every video within a child's reach off the shelves. Mackey's wife was following behind, picking them up off the floor as they dropped out of her child's fat little hands. I noticed she was just putting the videos back haphazardly in all the wrong places, which I found very annoying. I knew I was the one who was going to have to put them back in order.

"Such a strange coincidence," continued Mackey. "I was just thinking about you the other day."

Of course he was. He was doing black magick on me. "Oh yeah?" I muttered, trying to look impassive, but I started feeling really nervous. The man was stalking me now. I was going to have to tell Peter about this. This was just too much.

"It's so nice," said Mackey. He was intentionally trying to make his voice sound sweet and angelic- it made me sick to my stomach. "I didn't know if I'd ever see you again." He leaned over onto the counter heavily. It creaked audibly under the strain of his immensity. "Such a nice surprise. We live close by, and we'd never been to this store. Thought we'd take a look around. And then lo and behold, here you are!" Mackey smiled at me, an ugly smile. "Listen, I've been feeling a bit guilty, Sebastian. I really must apologize for that little trick we played on you at the festival."

I looked at him coolly, in what I hoped was an unfriendly but not overly rude expression. He eyed me carefully, clearly trying to assess my expression. Then he continued, seemingly untroubled by my silence.

"We only meant it in fun. My disciples and I like you. You seem like a bright and promising young man."

"Thank you," I muttered, unsure what to think of this man at all. His casual use of the word 'disciples' really disturbed me. Who did he think he was? His utter self-involvement was practiced and comfortable, like no one ever questioned him in the slightest.

"I really hope that we can be friends, Sebastian," he continued with a smile. "The magical world is a small world. It's good to have friends."

"Sure," I muttered.

"Good, good, that's good." Said Mackey. "I hope you mean that. I'd hate to think you took our little joke the wrong way."

I thought about his other little joke- the demonic talisman. I felt a strong urge to mention something about it, but I couldn't bring myself to speak. Surely he knew that I'd put it on his doorstep, but would he bring it up himself? How could he? That would be admitting he put it on my doorstep in the first place.

He didn't seem at all disturbed by the fact that I'd hardly spoken a word to him. Mackey reached over the counter, and placed his thick hand on my shoulder. His hand was moist and hot, and I immediately felt twice as uncomfortable as I'd felt the moment before.

"I'm so glad we can be friends," said Mackey with another ugly grin. I desperately wished that he'd just go away. "Listen," he continued without removing his hand from my shoulder. "I want to warn you again."

Uh oh. Now I was really getting to the supreme stages of discomfort. He looked at me right in the eyes. His gray eyes smoldered.

"Okay," I said.

"You really must steer clear of the A∴R∴T∴. They are the blackest magicians you'll ever meet. If you want to taste the true filth of hell's reek, there's no better place than the A∴R∴T∴."

"What makes you say that?" I demanded. This was just too much.

He laughed a wheezy, phlegm-filled chuckle. "They're a pack of liars and drug addicts," he said, far too loudly.

A businessman in a blue suit looked uneasily toward us from the back of the store. He quietly put down the porn box he'd been looking at and headed toward the exit.

"Sure, they seem pleasant enough," continued Mackey. "With their pre-packaged McMagick formulas, and mechanically orchestrated rituals. But under the surface they have dark designs, Sebastian. Dark designs." Mackey took his hand off my shoulder, and rested it on the counter again. He leaned toward me, getting as close as he could with the counter between us. "They are an international organization, Sebastian. An international organization. That's something to think about." He glared at me meaningfully, trying to make sure that I'd taken in his innuendo.

"They seem perfectly nice to me," I said, unable to stop myself in the face of his silly assertions.

Mackey looked troubled. "Perhaps it's already too late for you," he said quietly, blinking and squinting at me eerily. "But I think not. I teach classes at the Black Pullet Lodge every Thursday evening at 7:30 PM. Feel free to come by anytime. He handed me a business card with magical emblems surrounding an address. I recognized it as the address where Adin and I discarded the talisman. I took the card and dropped it on the counter in front of me, holding it down with my fingers.

"Thanks, I'll see about that. I appreciate it."

"You ought to come by. It's more than just a class really. We open gateways to unseen worlds every week. Prepare to have your mind blown if you come to one of my classes. It's not like the A∴R∴T∴, where you'll just blow your wallet." He laughed again loudly, then shook his head slowly from side to side. "That A∴R∴T∴. Terrible bunch."

He was really trying so very hard to sell me on that. I did my best to remain expressionless and passive, hoping that he would soon go away. But he just kept staring at me, smiling creepily.

The door creaked open and my fellow video clerk Sue walked in, sipping from a Burger King soda cup. She looked at

Mackey warily. Anyone could see that he was a strange and unsavory character.

"Hi Sue," I said with a forced smile. "All done with lunch already?"

"Yeah," she said, still staring at Mackey, her mouth full of soda.

"Well, I really must be going," said Mackey. "It was wonderful running into you. I'm so glad we're going to be friends. Ninety-three." He turned to his wife, bellowing. "Come on, Honey!"

Mackey's wife took hold of their chubby little daughter and began dragging her toward the exit. The little girl cried out, wailing for a movie that she clung to with all her might. Mackey's wife wrenched it out of her fat little hands, saying they couldn't afford it. She tossed it randomly onto a high shelf.

The whole entourage then left the store without another word. Mackey hadn't even so much so much as glanced at a single video box the whole time he was in the store. I knew what I had to do. There was no choice now. I really had to get in touch with Adin Stone again immediately.

Thirty Five

6:25 PM

I went home after my shift at the videostore with every intention of calling Adin the second I got inside. But to my very great surprise he was already sitting on my front porch when I got there. Just seeing him gave me a sense of comfort, like everything was going to be okay. How had he known that I wanted to see him? I felt a little uneasy, like Adin was somehow reading my mind. I parked my car and rushed to him, asking him why he had come over. He told me that he just wanted to make sure that everything was okay since we'd gotten rid of the talisman. I described Mackey's visit, and Adin listened attentively. When I finished, he sighed.

"Well, Alex. It does seem like Mackey has taken an unhealthy interest in you."

"Yes," I said. "And if he's a murderer, who knows what he's capable of."

Adin chuckled. "Well, I don't think you need to worry about that."

"How do you know? He's definitely nuts!"

"Well, yes, he probably is, but--"

"But what? He's showing up at my store! He knows where I live!

"Alex," said Adin in a reassuring tone. "Mackey is really not as dangerous as you think. I've known him for many years. He's relatively harmless."

"I'd really like to believe you, but this is all so weird! It's insane! I feel like I'm going insane!"

176

"You chose to get involved in this world. You knew it was going to be weird. You wanted it to be weird. You've opened up the gate of the labyrinth. I'm afraid that the only way out is through."

He was right, and I knew it. I'd always been attracted to the strange and the unusual. Now I'd placed myself right in the midst of it. He smiled calmly.

"You're very brave, Alex."

"I don't feel very brave," I said.

"Are you kidding?" said Adin with a chuckle. "How many people would have done what you've done already? You've thrown yourself right into the most troubling thing that's happened to the magical community in years. There aren't murders every day you know."

"I know! I'm... scared. Scared of demons, scared of murder, scared of Mackey." I could feel tears threatening, and my throat clenching. I choked back the urge to cry. I had to stay in control. "Mackey isn't just coming to the store, he's also been in my dreams. So have you."

Adin looked at me silently for quite some time. "That's interesting," he said eventually, quite calmly. "I hope you're keeping track of your dreams."

"I'm trying to keep track of everything," I said. "It's the only thing that might keep me sane."

"Tell me more about your dreams."

What I really wanted at the moment was for him to embrace me, to hold me like a little boy and tell me everything was going to be okay. He made me feel safe. He was the only thing that made me feel safe right then. But I didn't know how to ask. I didn't even know how to fully form the thought. So I just broke down and told him about most of my recent dreams. He seemed quietly interested throughout, and didn't look for a moment like he was going to give me the hug that I really wanted.

"Listen carefully," he said when I'd finished. "These dreams you're having are highly important. Our dreams occupy a third or more of our lives, and dreams are one of the most important parts of our lives for magical development. Your progress as a magician depends on developing your dreams into encounters with magical realms, and you are well on your way to that already.

"There is a dream school, in which we are all enrolled. This school is run by the interior brotherhood. We attend these lessons in our dreams. Surely you can recall dreams that involve school, some of which seem very strange. These are dream lessons from the interior school of the brotherhood.

"But please keep in mind that your dreams combine many elements, both from the magical, the collective unconscious, as well as personal anxieties, fantasies and wish fulfillment. Be careful in applying meaning to your dreams right away. Record them, and let them percolate for a little while. Don't get lost in the details right away. Dream elements may appear to mean one thing, when they really mean something entirely contrary. You may discover that some seemingly significant experience from your dreams turns out to be just a small piece of a much larger puzzle."

"But what about Mackey? What is his significance?" I asked.

"Don't waste your time worrying about Mackey. I can't understand his part in this at all. But then, I don't have all the answers."

"I don't find that very comforting."

"Why don't you just go to one of Mackey's magical classes," said Adin, chuckling to himself. "He wants you to so badly. I think that would give you a very clear impression of the kind of magician Mackey really is."

I tried to feel comforted by Adin's words, but they fell on me hollowly. He hadn't given me what I wanted. He hadn't even given me any real answers to anything. I was still sure Mackey was dangerous. He had to somehow be involved in Ed Bailey's death. He had to.

Adin left me, telling me again to stay calm, stay focused, and keep up the good work.

I spent the rest of the day trying not to think about any of it. I drank some beer and smoked quite a lot of pot. Still, I couldn't help feeling chilled. I went to bed quite early again. As I drifted off to sleep, I had no idea that the most chilling experience yet was waiting for me in this evening's dreams.

Thirty Six

I was in a dark forest. It seemed familiar, though I had no idea where I was. Was I back at the pagan festival? I saw a bright orange light up ahead and I walked toward it. There was no path, so I had to push aside bushes and prickly vines to approach the orange light.

As I got closer I saw that it was a bonfire. I moved toward the fire, staying as concealed as possible behind some small shrubs. A large group was assembled holding hands and slowly circling the blazing fire. They were chanting, and I saw that the chanting was being led by Paul Mackey.

Everyone was wearing black robes. Mackey's wife and daughter were dancing at his sides. With them were many other people that I recognized. Kerrie and my mother were there, along with several members of the A∴R∴T∴. Adin stone was also dancing and chanting along with the rest. I tried to understand what they were chanting, but it was just gibberish to me. It sounded like:

"Untu la la ulula umuna tofa lama le li na ahr ima tahara elulu etfoma ununa arpeti ulu ulu ulu maraban ululu mahata ulu ulu lamastana..."

I looked at the bonfire because the flames were growing and contorting. In the midst of the flames, a huge fiery apparition began to take shape. The flames swelled and danced, swirling into the shape of a fiery demon. Its mouth opened and it let out a hideous shriek.

The fiery demon looked right at me fiercely, easily spotting me behind the little bushes. I tried to crouch lower, but the huge flames lit up the area so brightly that there was no place for me to hide.

The dancing and chanting stopped abruptly, and all eyes turned to me. The huge fiery demon lurched up into the sky above the bonfire and swept down toward me. I tried to run, but once again my legs failed me. The demon smashed into me, knocking all sense out of me. We began to tumble over and over together. I lost all sense of up or down or where I even was. I wrestled as fiercely as I could, but I felt nothing but spinning, falling and burning.

I felt my body thud against the ground, and the fiery demon was suddenly gone. My clothes were gone. I was completely naked.

I looked around. I recognized the place immediately. Magical symbols scrawled amidst bloody gore- it was the Ed Bailey crime scene. The smell of death was overwhelming. But that was the least of my worries.

In the center of the room I saw that a dozen or more small slimy demons were tearing fiercely at a gruesome carcass. The creatures were scaly and black, with haunting filmy white eyes. Razor claws extended from their spidery fingers as they tore at the rapidly disintegrating human body. Flesh and blood spattered everywhere. I stepped toward the beasts, and they looked up at me greedily. The demons began to crawl toward me like a hungry pack of animals. I discovered that I was holding a silver rod in my hand, and it suddenly occurred to me that I should trace a banishing pentagram.

I quickly traced the pentagram in the air. The star burned in the air before me, glowing like liquid neon, looming between the demons and me. They stopped in their tracks, covering their eyes and backing away from the glowing pentagram.

But to my horror the pentagram quickly melted away. It simply evaporated as if it were made of soap film, too flimsy to last for more than a few moments. The demons began to clatter toward me again.

I quickly traced another pentagram. Again the demons were held at bay, but the second pentagram soon disappeared too. I

180

didn't know what to do. Surely this couldn't go on forever. I traced a third pentagram, and a fourth, and a fifth. I kept wildly tracing pentagrams in the air, until all was obscured in their glow.

As the pentagrams dissolved one by one, I discovered that I was alone with the hideous corpse. The demons had disappeared. I walked over to look at Ed Bailey's shattered body, but I quickly discovered that it wasn't Ed Bailey at all. It was the hippie: Jeremy McClosky.

☿ Wednesday, October 2, 1996

9:30 AM

I woke up, drenched in sweat and shaken, once again. I heard the phone ringing in the distance. I quickly opened up my journal and began to record the bizarre dream.

But just as I was scrawling down as many details as I could recollect, my mother called to me. Peter was on the phone.

"Alex, something's come up," said Peter when I got to the phone.

"What?" I said, feeling a sense of dread that I knew exactly what he was about to tell me.

"There's been another death. I think it might be connected."

I was stunned.

"I want to talk to you about it," said Peter. "Since you seem to have an inside track on this A∴R∴T∴."

"It wasn't Jeremy McClosky, was it?" I asked.

Now it was Peter who was stunned. "I think you'd better get down to the station right away."

Thirty Seven

10:15 A.M.

"How the fuck did you know the name of the victim, Alex?" demanded Peter for the third time. His eyes grew more and more fierce with every word. On this visit to the station I wasn't sitting at Peter's desk. I was in a small glass-walled room, sitting on a dirty couch. Through the windows, I could see dozens of uniformed cops walking by. The room must have been sound-proof, because they didn't seem to notice Peter's yelling.

"Peter. I told you. I dreamed it last night. That's all I know. I swear."

Peter looked like he wanted to punch me in the face. "That's fucking ridiculous!" He shook visibly, like he was about to explode. "Is that really your fucking story? This Jeremy McClosky is a member of this fucking Satanic cult you joined! We've got him on the short list for Ed Bailey! I want to know what you know that would make you think he was about to get killed! Now!"

"I don't know anything!"

Peter paced back and forth, menacing me each time he passed me. "That's not gonna fucking do! You know something! You obviously knew he was about to get killed. And you didn't tell me! That could make you an accessory- maybe an accomplice. I might have to press charges against you. Help me out, Alex."

"I don't know anything, Peter. I swear to God."

"Can you Satanists even swear to God?"

"Peter!" I shouted.

Peter took a deep breath. "I'm sorry, Alex. I'm sorry. I'm just under a lot of stress here. I've never had a case like this before. None of us have. We have hardly any clear evidence, and now my little fucking brother-in-law suddenly seems to know more than I do. I don't want to have to press charges against you. I just want the perps. I want to believe you're not one of them."

"I'm not! God! I'm not," I said. "I don't know anything."

"Look, I believe you. You know I like you. But this thing is getting bigger than me. They're talking about the Feds around here right now. FBI-Violent Crimes. If this case gets out of my hands, I'm not going to be able to protect you, Alex."

"I'm not involved in this!"

"Okay, right, but I need something. Are there any other people that might be killed? Do you know anything else?"

"I really don't have any special knowledge. Honestly."

"Well, what do you know?" said Peter.

"Look," I said. "I just had a dream. That's all. I don't under-stand it either. I've been having a lot of strange experiences late-ly. I do know that Paul Mackey showed up at the video store yesterday, and said a bunch of fucked up things about the A∴R∴T∴. That's who I think you should be looking at!"

"Paul Mackey's not a suspect."

"Well, he should be."

"Mackey's an ex-cop. Right here in Arlington. Left the force six years ago for health reasons."

"You're kidding!" I could not picture Mackey as a cop. And wasn't he dealing drugs? I guess they're not mutually exclusive. I wondered why Arthyr Thornapple hadn't mentioned the fact that Mackey was a cop.

"No. I'm not. And besides, Mackey has an alibi for the first murder. He was teaching a class with seven other people in attendance."

"He was?" I said, genuinely surprised.

"Yes, so he's not currently a suspect. You're higher on the suspect list than Mackey."

"Me?" I suddenly felt naked and alone. I'd never felt more alone in my life. How could Peter even say that?

"You."

But I suddenly had a strange thought. "What was the class Mackey was teaching?" I asked hopefully.

"Why the fuck would that matter?"

"What if he was raising a demon in the class? Maybe he sent a demon to kill Ed Bailey! That's what I dreamt!"

Peter looked at me like I had five extra heads. "I don't know what the fuck you're involved in, but we are not currently pursuing the hocus-pocus and dreams angle on this thing."

I knew he would never listen to me. So I just sat there staring at the dirty cement floor. Could Mackey really have sent a demon to kill Ed Bailey? That would get rid of his alibi. His whole group could be involved whether they knew it or not. He'd sent a demon after me.

But it hadn't killed me. How could a demon like that kill someone who was so much more experienced at magick than me? And what was Mackey's real motive other than just disliking the A∴R∴T∴? Was that enough? And even if he did send a demon, was there even a law against something like that?

"Alex," said Peter eventually. "Look. I know you're not a part of this. I'm on your side. But I need your help. We have the names of many members of the A∴R∴T∴, but I know our list is very incomplete. This A∴R∴T∴ is much bigger than I ever imagined." Peter ran his hands through his slightly receding hair. "Get me some names, Alex. Addresses. Phone numbers. Anyone else who you think might be in danger, okay?"

I stared at him blankly.

"Two people are dead!" he shouted. "Who knows, you could be next! Get me some names, and then get out of this A∴R∴T∴. Stay away from these people. You have no idea how dangerous this could end up being. Do you hear me?"

I nodded. I was in danger. I knew that, but I didn't fully want to believe that it had anything to do with the A∴R∴T∴. Perhaps I'd get a more clear idea at the A∴R∴T∴ class tonight. Hopefully I'd be safe. Perhaps this thing really was too dangerous for me. But I remembered Adin's words, "The only way out is through."

Thirty Eight

Damian Webster lived in a very new-looking condo complex in Andover, MA- about a forty-five minute drive from my house. I followed the directions I found at the back of my neophyte package, parked in the visitor's area, and walked the short distance across manicured lawns to the entrance of his building. I dialed the number for Damian's condo at the intercom call box.

After a few moments Damian Webster's scratchy voice came through the intercom. He said, "Hello?" in what seemed a careful, hesitant tone.

"Hi there, Ninety-three?" I said with equal uncertainty. "This is Alexander Sebastian. I'm here for the class?"

"Oh," he said, across the line. "Ninety-three."

There was a very lengthy silence from his end. I began to wonder if he was going to come back at all.

"Come on in," he finally said. "It's up the stairs. First door on the left."

I climbed the stairs and found myself faced with a series of identical doors on either side of a long, cream-colored hallway. I knocked on the first door.

Matthew Wiley opened the door and ushered me in with a 'ninety-three' and a polite greeting. The condo was decorated tidily in burgundy tones but reeked of marijuana and wine, mingled with what smelled like a tropical air freshener of some sort. Matthew directed me to sit down on a plush reddish leather couch.

185

Damian Webster sat across from me on an identical leather couch, next to Abraham Crane. Crane smiled through his yellowing white moustache, but he looked quite troubled. Matthew sat down beside me. No one else seemed to be there yet, which surprised me, because I thought I was slightly late.

"I'm very sorry about this, Alex," said Damian Webster. "We had to cancel the class tonight. We're having an emergency officer's meeting."

"Oh, I'm sorry," I said. I shifted uncomfortably on the couch as they all looked at each other and then at me. I wasn't sure if I should just get up and leave.

"I guess we should just go ahead and tell him," said Damian with a sigh. "You'll find out soon enough for yourself. One of our members has just died."

Of course I was already well aware of Jeremy's death, but I tried my best to look surprised and shocked. I didn't know what I would be expected to say or do in a situation like this. I supposed that the best course of action would just be to keep my eyes wide open and my jaw slacked- ambiguous complete surprise.

"He's the second member of our local temple to die in the last few weeks. Both under rather suspicious circumstances," said Damian.

"They were murdered," said Matthew flatly.

"My god," I said, continuing to play the part of the surprised outsider. But this situation suddenly gave me the luxury of asking some very direct questions. I cautiously proceeded. "Do you... Do you have any idea who did it?" They looked to each other again warily.

"No, we don't," said Damian Webster. "But we're going to find out."

"I think that's really sort of why we're having this meeting," said Matthew.

"Yes, that's exactly why I called us together," said Damian. He sounded upset, but controlled.

I continued to feel extremely out of place. "I'm sorry that I disturbed you," I said. "I didn't know."

"It's perfectly understandable," said Damian. "Of course you didn't know. I'm sorry that you've been initiated at such an unfortunate moment." He paused, thinking. "But let me assure you of something. This isn't going to happen again." Damian then reached down between the couch cushions beside him, and pulled out a small snub-nosed pistol. "I'm going to make sure of it." He placed the pistol down on the table in front of him, next to an open bottle of red wine.

Matthew Wiley and Abraham Crane both looked extremely embarrassed.

"Damian, don't be silly," said Matthew. "What are you going to do with that?"

"I'm going to do whatever I have to," said Damian aggressively. I suddenly noticed that he sounded a bit drunk. "To keep this temple secure."

"Where did you even get that?" said Matthew.

"I've had it for years."

"Do you always keep it in your couch cushions?" asked Matthew.

"As long as I've known him," said Abraham Crane with a dry laugh.

"You could never use that," said Matthew. "You're too nice."

"Don't you be so sure about that, Matt," said Damian. He stroked the pistol, still sitting right in the middle of the table. "I killed a guy with this gun back in Philadelphia."

Matthew and Abraham looked even more embarrassed.

"No, you didn't," said Matthew, rolling his eyes.

"I most certainly fucking did!" said Damian. "I never told you about that? It was almost twenty years ago. I lived in a terrible neighborhood. Lots of blacks. So I got this gun from a buddy. One night this young kid jumped me. Tackled me right to the ground. I shot him in the neck."

"And you didn't get caught?" I asked in horror.

"No," said Damian dismissively. "He was just some drug addict thief. No one gave a shit about him."

Abraham Crane cleared his throat. "I'm not sure this is the sort of talk we should be having in front of brand new members." He bobbed his head in my direction. I'm sure I must have looked a bit white.

"I'm not worried about this kid," said Damian. "I can see he's a stand up guy. Besides, He's taken the oath of the neo-phyte. He's not going to break that oath. Are you, Alex?"

"Of course not," I said, my voice scratchy, but sincere. It felt nice for Damian to trust me so much, so easily. "I wouldn't say anything to anyone." I really hoped I'd be able to keep that promise. "I only want to help, any way I can," I said.

"That's very nice," said Abraham Crane, looking at me with a glint of suspicion still in his eyes. "But you know, you've driven all the way here for a magick class. Perhaps we should take a little break from our meeting and answer any questions you have about your initiation. That way you won't have come out for nothing." Abraham Crane then reached into his shirt pocket and removed a long white cigarette. He lit the cigarette, and the smoke plumed between the hairs of his yellowed moustache.

I really wanted to ask some more questions about the murders, but now it would seem a little odd. I looked down at the floor, trying to think of a question to ask about my initiation.

"I'm really sorry you didn't hear the class was cancelled," said Matthew guiltily. "We're usually very good about these things."

"That's okay," I assured him.

"No, it's no good," said Matthew. He reached for a briefcase, beside him on the floor. "We have a phone list, and a calling tree. I just haven't had time to add you to the list." He pulled out a stack of papers and began to look through them.

"Matthew is the best secretary we've ever had," said Damian. He reached for the wine bottle and refilled his glass. Wine clearly brought out Damian Webster's generous side.

He saw me eyeing the wine, and offered me a glass. I took it gratefully and gulped a lot of it down immediately, hoping it would make me feel a bit less awkward. Damian refilled the glass just as fast.

Matthew turned and handed me a few sheets of paper. "Here's a list of our local members." I couldn't believe it. This was exactly what Peter was looking for from me, and I didn't even have to ask for it. As if he was reading my mind, Matthew added, "Please don't give this out to anyone."

"Yes," said Damian Webster, quite gravely. "That list is under the oath and seal, under the pledge of secrecy you've made to this temple. Membership in this organization is private and confidential. Many of our members would not want their identities to be known outside of the temple."

"I'll keep it safe," I said, folding the sheets and placing them on the table, right next to Damian's little pistol.

"I'll be sure to add your number to the calling tree," said Matthew. "Do you have email?"

"No," I said. "Not yet. I'm working on it."

"We're moving more and more online these days," said Matthew. "Have you seen our website?"

"No," I said.

"It's a great little site," said Damian. "Jake Pilsner designed it. I have to admit it's pretty amazing even though he's generally an idiot." Everyone laughed and agreed.

"So, is there anything you'd like to know in regard to the neophyte grade, Alex?" asked Abraham Crane again. He continued to puff on his cigarette.

"I have a lot of questions, really," I said, still trying to think of one.

Matthew took out a cigarette and lit it. I finally broke down and asked him if I could have one. He handed one to me and lit it for me. As I took a few drags of the cigarette, I remembered my failed attempts at astral projection.

"I really want to understand astral projection," I said. "That's what I've been thinking about the most lately."

Abraham Crane grinned. "Excellent," he said. "One of my favorite subjects."

"Abe is a true master of the astral," said Damian. "You're asking the right guy."

"Oh, I don't know about that," said Crane, with a tone of great humility. "I'm just a student like the rest."

"Don't be falsely modest, Abe," said Damian. "You know you've taught just about all of us."

"Yes, well, I've just been at it a while," said Crane. "But how can I help you, Alex?"

"Every time I try to project I keep falling asleep."

"That is always a difficulty," said Crane. "But the first thing you must understand is that astral projection is just a vision, like any other vision or dream."

"So, then am I astrally projecting when I'm dreaming?" I asked.

"To an extent," said Crane. "At least partially. But you shouldn't view the astral in mechanical terms. It's not like going to visit another city. It's shifting your awareness to a different level. It's all very fluid. Simply imagining that you are having a projection is a projection to a certain extent, as long as you are imagining it vividly."

"So, is it all just imagination, then?

"There's a flaw in your question," said Crane. "'Just imagination' dismisses the great importance of imagination. Magick is the science of imagination. I am not talking about mere fantasy, but rather that great and important aspect of out inner consciousness that gives us access to what is normally unseen. The imagination is the key to the great treasure house of magick."

"But is astral projection real?"

"There's really no clear answer to that. The only way to get any distinction in your astral experiences is to ask yourself if you've learned anything new, anything of value from your visions."

"Oh," I said, not really understanding him at all.

"Ingo Swann, one of the most famous modern astral projectors- he was one of the developers of the U.S. government's remote viewing program back in the seventies- during his experiments at Stanford he was always aware of his body sitting there in the laboratory. So, was he just imagining things when he accurately described distant locations?" Crane looked at me seriously. "No. A part of his consciousness was aware of the distant location. Was that part of his consciousness actually leaving his body? Or was he receiving information from some sort of psychic storehouse that he tapped into? No one could say for certain.

"What we do know is that the mechanistic theory of the universe is highly suspect. The way that we perceive the physical world is a residue of perception. It does not exist in the way that we think of it at all. There is really only a quantum matrix of information and consciousness. There may not be anywhere 'to go' at all."

"Okay, sure," I said. I was just barely following him. I was taking in an awful lot of information- guns, murder, quantum matrices- it was all a bit too much.

"The best way to understand anything is to just do it," said Abraham Crane. "Would you like to do a little experiment, right now?"

"Sure," I said.

Matthew and Damian looked intrigued. "What do you have in mind?" asked Damian.

"We'll just do a bit of astral journeying, right here."

Thirty Nine

8:01 P.M.

"Do you have your temple room set up?" asked Crane.

"No," said Damian. "It's empty."

"Good," said Crane. "Damian, I want you to go find an object and put it on the middle of the floor in your empty temple."

"All right," said Damian.

Crane turned to me as Damian got to his feet and left the room. "Now, I don't want you to think about what Damian is doing at all."

"Okay," I said, beginning to wonder what I was getting myself into.

Abraham stubbed out his cigarette, and asked Matthew and I to put out ours. After a few moments, Damian returned.

"Done," he said.

"Fabulous," said Crane. "Matthew, you can participate in this too, if you like."

"That'd be great," said Matthew. "I can always use a little practice."

"Very well then. Both of you sit back and close your eyes on that couch and just start relaxing a bit."

I closed my eyes and found it very difficult to relax. My heart was pounding. I felt surprisingly nervous.

I heard Damian stand up. He began to perform the Lesser Banishing Ritual of the Pentagram, very sonorously and dramatically. The vibrating tones of his voice combined with my own

192

tension began to leave me feeling a bit mesmerized. As Damian finished the ritual, Abraham Crane cleared his throat.

"Please don't feel any pressure," said Crane. "This is just a little game. Just relax." I did my best to sink into the couch. "There's absolutely no pressure to get anything right. Don't try to guess anything, just simply let your body and mind relax.

"Now, move your attention down to your feet and begin to relax them, feeling a soothing tingling sensation moving up into your feet."

Crane then asked Matthew and I to relax each part of our bodies, guiding us to relax our calves, knees, thighs, buttocks, groin, belly- all the way up to the very tops of our heads. By the time he reached the neck, I starting finding myself so relaxed that I felt like I was on the verge of falling asleep. In fact, I may have momentarily blacked out a few times. I'm not absolutely sure. Then he began to instruct us in the actual projection.

He told us to imagine a shape resembling our own bodies floating above us, adding as much detail as we could. I did my best, though I could really only imagine a fairly dim and wobbly shape. He then instructed us to move our awareness into these imagined forms.

"Don't worry about whether it seems imaginary," he said. "Simply visualize the room around us from the perspective of your new body of light. When you are ready, simply move in your body of light into the temple room behind us and see what you can find there."

I did my best to imagine myself walking through the room toward the door that Damian had walked through. I didn't have any idea what was behind it at all. I'd never seen the room before, so I had no idea what to visualize as I imagined myself going right through the door.

At first my mind just went blank, and all I saw was darkness. I couldn't see anything, and I didn't know if I ever would. But I slowly began to see the contours of a room, about 10'x10', entirely empty, blank walls. No furniture, nothing. I didn't know if this was actually the room, or just a fantasy. It seemed very shaky and tenuous. I looked to the center of the room, but I couldn't focus on it very well. I felt like I could see some sort of object, but I definitely couldn't tell what it was. It seemed to be some sort of cylinder, grayish, maybe black. I thought of a top hat, but also perhaps a small drum or even a large boot—something hollow and cylindrical at any rate. It all seemed like it could just be pure fantasy.

I couldn't see any reason for continuing, since I couldn't see anything more clearly than this. So, I imagined myself returning to my body and opened up my eyes.

Damian smiled at me impishly, drawing his finger to his lips to keep me from speaking or moving. Abraham Crane continued to stare fixedly at Matthew.

Matthew just sat there silently, unmoving for a minute or so, then finally opened his eyes too. He smiled in embarrassment as he saw all of us staring at him.

"Well, I don't think that went very well," said Matthew, still grinning.

I guess he didn't do much better than I did.

"Don't say anymore," said Abraham Crane gravely, handing us each a sheet of paper and a pen. "Just go ahead and write down your thoughts and observations, in as much detail as you care to."

I took the sheet of paper and wrote just a few words:

Cylinder Shape? Top Hat?

Matthew seemed to write even less.

Once we'd both put down our pens, Crane looked at me expectantly.

"Okay. Describe your impressions."

"Well," I said, hesitating. "It wasn't too clear. I'm pretty sure I was just imagining things."

"But what did you imagine?" asked Damian.

"Well, a cylinder, I guess. Like a top hat or drum or something." I showed them my sheet of paper.

"And you?" said Abe, turning to Matthew.

Matthew showed us his sheet of paper:

GLASS JAR?

"I really didn't see anything," he said. "But the idea came to me- it's kind of interesting- just like Alex here- 'a cylinder,' and for some reason I thought- 'kitchen, something from the kitchen,' and then I started seeing a series of random images of glass jars."

"Interesting!" said Damian. "Very interesting!"

"They did well?" asked Crane.

"Neither of them got it quite, but... Well, let's just go take a look," said Damian. He hopped to his feet like a mischievous child.

We all went to the door, and Damian opened it dramatically. The room was actually a bit smaller than I'd seen it in my vision, but there in the middle of the empty floor sat a large cooking pot. I immediately felt a strange whooshing sensation in my stomach, like someone had removed the floor beneath me. Somehow I was sure that I actually had perceived this object. I looked over at Matthew and it looked like he was having the same feeling.

"This is very interesting," said Abraham Crane. "While neither of you quite correctly identified the object, both of you did correctly describe it, at least partially. Both of you perceived the shape, and Matthew correctly noted that it was a kitchen object."

"I'm usually fairly skeptical about these things," said Matthew. "But... somehow... I don't know, I feel that I did perceive this pot."

"Yes, definitely," I said. "When I saw that cooking pot, I felt a kind of 'pop,' like I was completing a perception that I could only nearly get to before."

"I felt that way too," said Matthew. "It's like the information wasn't fully sorted until you opened the door.

"Wonderful," said Crane. "That is exactly the way I see the nature of the astral plane. It is information, consciousness, ideas, and experience in a tenuous state of existence. When we find a way to observe this with the normal instruments of perception, the experience suddenly becomes real." He sat down and picked up his wine, sipping it. "Sometimes the experiences we have in the astral correspond more or less with the physical world, sometimes they don't. Perhaps this is because of the space/time illusion, perhaps something to do with quantum mechanics.

"But that question is rather beyond the limits of tonight's little digression. Suffice it to say it's very interesting that both of you seemed to have a fairly real experience."

Damian turned to me and smiled. "You seem to have some real potential as a magician, Alex." He almost sounded like a proud father. It felt good.

It was really impossible for me to imagine any of these people being responsible for multiple murders. Somehow, it had to be Mackey or someone connected to him.

We all chatted for a bit longer, but I quickly sensed that they all wanted to continue their meeting without me. So, I excused myself and left.

I sat in my car for quite a while, looking over the A∴R∴T∴ phone list. I knew Peter would love to get his hands on this. Perhaps he already had it. Ed Bailey must have had one of these. But then why would he want me to get him names?

I really couldn't see myself ratting out all of my new friends. But what if Peter was really serious about pressing charges against me. I didn't think he was really serious about that, but I needed to give him something or he'd never stop harassing me.

Chapter Forty

9:07 P.M.

I drove home, thinking very hard about astral projection, magical murders, and the A∴R∴T∴. I bought a pack of cigarettes at a gas station along the way. By the time I got home I'd smoked half the pack.

9:58 P.M.

I sat in my room, smoked some pot and several more cigarettes. I still wasn't sure what to do with the A∴R∴T∴ address list. I held it between my fingers. I could hardly bear to look at it.

Was there really any harm in giving Peter the list? He could probably get all the names anyway, through the courts and warrants and all those sorts of legal channels that I didn't really know much about. And surely none of these people had anything to do with the murders. I would just be making it easier for their names to be cleared.

I walked down to the kitchen with the list in my hand, and called Peter's house.

"Hello?" came Peter's gruff voice across the line.

I instantly felt a wave of regret that I'd dialed the phone at all. "Hi, it's Alex," I said.

"Alex," he said cheerfully. "It's good to hear from you. Listen, I'm sorry I was so tense the last time we talked. These homicides are really stretching me to the limit."

"I understand," I said, though I really didn't. I thought he'd been a rude bully. He couldn't possibly be as stressed as I felt. But, I suppose he probably was under a lot of pressure.

"So, I take it you've got some names for me?" he said, getting right to the point. He must have really known he'd hooked me with those threats. But I looked down at the long list of names, all of whom had gone through the same initiation ritual that I'd gone through, and to whom I'd sworn loyalty and secrecy. I couldn't bring myself to betray that trust. I couldn't break my oath.

"No," I said quietly. "They're very secretive about their members. I tried my best, but you know how it is."

Peter was silent for several seconds. I felt like I could sense his irritation right over the phone wires. "Well," he said slowly, "then just give me the names of all the members you've met so far."

"Oh." I was stuck. I knew I really couldn't refuse this request. After all, I'd gotten involved in all this specifically to help solve these murders. "Well, I don't know everyone's full names... and I, uh, a lot of people just go by assumed magical names they've made up... I don't know."

"Just give me everything that you have," he said. I was silent. "Listen," he added with a sigh, "I won't mention you or mistreat anyone in any way. I promise."

So I told him the names of almost everyone that I could remember meeting so far. I didn't mention either Jessica or Connie. Somehow it just seemed inappropriate for me to mention them. It still left me feeling terrible. He told me that he actually already had most of the names I mentioned, but I still felt like I'd broken my oath. I got off the phone with him immediately, and slumped up to my bed.

10:27 P.M.

As I lay there on my bed, I decided that I needed to try some more astral projection. My experience at Damian's left me feeling like I understood the concept much more clearly. I didn't attempt to start with the Lesser Banishing Ritual of the Pentagram. I was too tired to bother with that. I just began to relax my body, piece by piece, trying to get back into that loose and flowing state I'd gotten into at Damian's.

But I quickly started to feel a strange sense of dread that there would be some sort of magical backlash against me for giving away those names. Vibrations began to ripple across my chest, but I tried to ignore them and just kept on relaxing. I began to experience a sinking sensation, like I was falling through the bed. It was a bit disturbing, but I didn't fight it. I sank into a deep blackness.

Forty One

Thursday, October 3, 1996

9:20 A.M.

I awoke with a start. I knew that I'd just been doing something, something magical, something on the astral plane, but I couldn't for the life of me remember what it was. It was very frustrating. I felt sure it had something to do with the A∴R∴T∴ or the magical world in some way. But that was it, nothing specific.

I decided that I really wanted to call Adin Stone again. So much was happening and he seemed to be the only person I could talk to about it all.

I went down to the kitchen and my mother asked me if I wanted any breakfast. I felt famished, but I really just wanted to call Adin. I shooed her out of the room and picked up the phone.

Adin answered immediately, as if he'd been waiting for my call. "I heard about the second murder," he said. "I was wondering when you'd be in touch."

I described everything to him... my dream about the murder, my conversations with Peter, the A∴R∴T∴ class, and even Damian's gun, along with my astral travelling experience.

"Sounds like we have more to discuss," he said. "We should get together. Do you have any time today?"

I told him I was free all day and we decided to get together immediately.

10:15 A.M.

THE BROTHERHOOD OF LIGHT AND DARKNESS

I met Adin at a nearby park, where I found him sitting cross-legged in the grass, amongst the rapidly falling leaves of an oak tree. He smiled at me as I approached, but something about him seemed much more serious than ever before. His eyes, usually so joyful, now seemed reddish and tired. I sat down in front of him, but neither of us spoke.

Adin closed his eyes. He seemed to be meditating, as if he were a million miles away. I wasn't sure what to do, so I looked down at the grass for quite some time. It was dried out, yellowed, dying off for the season. The nearby trees creaked quietly in a light wind. Finally, Adin opened his eyes and looked at me gravely.

"I think that the murders are not over yet," he said quietly. "More people will die. There may have even been more murders already. Everyone in the magical community is in danger." He looked at me, his eyes intense and narrow. I didn't know what to say. "And I'm fairly certain that one individual is responsible for these murders so far, and that this individual is a member of the A∴R∴T∴."

"Who is it?" I asked, very surprised.

"That I don't know."

"Why do you think it's a member of the A∴R∴T∴?"

"You have your visions and I have mine," he said with a shrug, looking directly at me with penetrating eyes. "And as you must be coming to realize, visions don't always provide you with all the answers."

"So you just think it's an A∴R∴T∴ member because of some kind of psychic vision?" I asked. I felt a little annoyed that he was casting a cloud of darkness on all of my new friends, just because of some vague dream or something.

"No," he said, very seriously. "I know with every certainty that it is an A∴R∴T∴ member because of my own psychic vision."

"What did you see?" If he was going to make accusations, at least he had to give me some sort of evidence.

"That's irrelevant," said Adin, and that was it.

I could see that he wasn't going to go into any more detail. I felt frustrated that he wasn't sharing more with me, but I knew that I hadn't always shared everything with him either. We sat in silence. Finally, Adin cleared his throat.

"I'm also certain that the murderer is someone that you have met personally," he said. "Or someone that you are about to meet."

I really couldn't possibly believe that. I hadn't met a single person in the A∴R∴T∴ who seemed even vaguely capable of murder. But I was also aware that Adin Stone always seemed to know what he was talking about. I could tell, just from his presence, that he was the most capable magician that I would ever meet. There was a palpable aura of wisdom around him. And almost no sense of ego whatsoever. I wasn't sure what to think.

I still strongly suspected that Paul Mackey had something to do with the murders. He was the only suspect I could come up with and I tried to win Adin over to my theory, reminding him that Mackey was conjuring the demon in my dream. But he remained unconvinced.

"I'm really fairly sure that Mackey has nothing to do with this. Not directly." Adin's tone was very assured. "Your dream is certainly important, but you mustn't confuse the individual events of your dream with the overall message. What's clear to me is that you received a message that the two murders are connected. This is an important thing to recognize, because the murders were, after all, committed in entirely different ways."

I didn't follow him. "What?" I asked. "What do you mean?"

"Ed Bailey was viciously attacked, torn to pieces," said Adin. His eyes began to look sad again. "Jeremy McClosky was shot with a gun."

"He was?" I asked, shocked.

"Didn't you know that?"

"No," I said. I couldn't believe it. I had just assumed they were committed in the same way because of my dream. "Peter didn't mention anything about that."

"Interesting," said Adin. "But your brother-in-law still thought that the two murders were connected. I wonder why?"

"He knew that Jeremy was in the A∴R∴T∴."

"Ah, he figured that out," said Adin, smiling for the first time since I'd first gotten to the park. "He may not be as stupid as you think."

"But how did you know that Jeremy was shot?" I asked.

"I have many sources," he muttered cryptically, frowning once again. We sat in silence for some time again.

"I still can't help but feel that Mackey is involved in this, Adin," I said. I couldn't help it. Mackey just kept running through my mind. "Why else would he be bothering me so much?"

"Mackey is an odd character. He's angry and jealous of the A∴R∴T∴. That motivates his actions. You are just an easy target for him. Why don't you attend one of his magick classes. You'll see what kind of man he really is."

"I'm getting more and more scared, Adin," I said. I was vulnerable, and I couldn't hide it at all when I was around him.

"Well," said Adin, frowning. "You probably should be. But not of Mackey. There are monsters amongst us. Of that I'm certain."

Forty Two

1:00 P.M.

I returned home from my meeting with Adin Stone feeling just as confused as ever. He seemed to be getting less and less helpful. I wondered what was wrong. I lay down in my bed and tried to let my mind flow away from everything that was happening to me. But I felt too restless. I sat up, lit a cigarette, and decided to look through Ed Bailey's personal items some more. I wondered when, if ever, Connie was going to want them back. I hadn't heard from her since Saturday. But Ed's belongings were the only solid clues I had about anything, so I really didn't mind hanging on to them. I hadn't found anything monumentally important yet, but I hadn't looked through even a quarter of the materials. I rifled through the papers and notebooks, but nothing really caught my interest. My mind was moving too rapidly to really concentrate on anything.

Then I heard the phone ringing. My mother had gone out to visit with some friends, so I went downstairs and answered it. It was Kerrie Thornapple. She told me that she was in town for a friend's funeral.

I was instantly certain that this friend was Jeremy McClosky. She'd told me before that she had friends in the A∴R∴T∴. Of course one of those friends could be Jeremy McClosky. I was starting to grow accustomed to coincidences cropping up at every turn. Moments later she confirmed that it was indeed Jeremy that she was talking about, and I told her I'd be happy to go with her to the funeral since I'd met him.

THE BROTHERHOOD OF LIGHT AND DARKNESS

I didn't mention that I'd joined the A∴R∴T∴. Something made me feel hesitant, so I simply said that I'd talked with him at the pagan festival.

"I'd love for you to come with me," she said. She sounded grateful. "I've known Jeremy since we were teenagers, but I really don't know any of his friends or his family. My parents will be there of course, but I just... It'll be nice to have you along."

3:00 P.M.

The funeral was a rather odd affair. Apparently his family was Catholic, and the funeral mass was held in a huge, gymnasium-like church with large, colorful felt banners hanging from all the walls. There were no windows, and the air was thick with the smell of old women's perfume. The attendees were a mix of conservative-looking older people, clearly family, young hippies, and of course many members of the A∴R∴T∴. Catherine Chen sat with members of Jeremy's family, weeping constantly. I noticed Damian and Matthew sitting toward the back as I walked in, and they both seemed mildly surprised to see me.

As I sat down next to Kerrie, I felt very itchy in my dark gray wool suit. I never wore it, except to funerals, and I'd only been to two other funerals in my life. The suit had never even been cleaned, and it still had the uncomfortable stiffness of a brand new garment. I tried to avoid scratching, because I really didn't want to draw attention to myself.

I learned quite a few things about Jeremy in the course of the service, as his family members each stood up and said nice things about him. Apparently Jeremy's family was from Arlington, but I hadn't met him before because he'd attended Catholic school his whole childhood. He'd always had an interest in music, and had excelled at it since he was a small boy. His father was a firefighter, and his mother a homemaker. He had three brothers and one sister. Jeremy was somewhere in the middle. He'd been living with his girlfriend Catherine Chen for the past eight months in an apartment in Arlington, quite near my own. I couldn't help but shed a few tears as I thought about

205

the young hippie that I'd spent time with on the night my initiation.

Toward the end of the mass, communion was offered. Of course I didn't participate, not being catholic. Neither did Kerrie or her parents. To my great surprise, Damian Webster did take communion. I later asked him why and he explained to me, "I grew up catholic, and I enjoy god-eating, though I usually enjoy a much more tasty god." I couldn't imagine what he meant.

After the service several A∴R∴T∴ members said hello to me as we were walking out. Matthew took hold of my arm and politely pulled me away from Kerrie to a corner.

"Ninety-three, Alex," said Matthew, very quietly. "I'm so glad that I'm running into you. I wanted to tell you that we've rearranged the schedule."

"Oh yeah?" I said, glancing over his shoulder at Kerrie, who was looking at me with some confusion.

"We're going to actually have the class you tried to come to the other day tomorrow. I hope you'll be able to come."

"Sure, of course," I said.

"Good," said Matthew. "I was going to call you tonight, but I'm glad we took care of it now. We're all really troubled by these deaths, but we want to get things back to normal as quickly as possible."

I excused myself from Matthew, and made my way back to Kerrie.

Kerrie grabbed my shoulder and pulled me to her. "How do you know all these people," she said into my ear.

"Well," I said, hesitating. It was clear that I'd blown my cover with Kerrie. "I've joined the A∴R∴T∴."

"Really?" she said. She looked surprised. But it didn't seem to phase her very much. She smiled cheerfully. "How do you like it?" She sounded genuinely curious.

"It's pretty interesting so far," I said. But of course I didn't want to mention that I was really there mostly to investigate the murders that prompted the funeral that we were currently leaving. "I've really just been through the first initiation ceremony so far."

"How was the sex with the goat?" she asked with a mirthless smirk.

"Huh?" I asked.

"Oh nothing," she said. "It's just a dumb joke I've heard a lot. Guess you didn't hear that one."

"No," I said. "It was a pretty serious initiation."

"That's interesting."

"Why?"

"I just heard, you know, that the A∴R∴T∴ doesn't- that they don't take their initiations very seriously."

"No, I said. "No, it was very serious, very magical."

"Well," said Kerrie. "I'm glad for you." She smiled. "You're finally a part of the magical world. You've been wanting this as long as I've known you."

She was right. I had been waiting for this for a very long time. Now here I was in the middle of something that I couldn't fully explain to anybody. I didn't even understand it myself. We walked out of the church, Kerrie still gripping me tightly.

4:35 P.M.

Kerrie drove me home, and we sat in her car for quite some time in silence. There was a lot still unsaid between us, but today didn't seem like a good day for us to talk about any of it.

We both stared out of the windshield for a long time, though I don't think either of us were conscious of the world outside. Eventually the silence was too much.

"Well, I guess I should be going," I said.

"Okay, yeah," said Kerrie. "Thank you so much for being with me here today."

"Of course," I said. I felt an urge to hug her, maybe even kiss her, but I couldn't bring myself to do anything. I said a polite goodbye and slipped out into the street.

After a few steps toward my house I turned back to Kerrie's car, but she was already pulling away. I really wanted to say more to her, but I just didn't know exactly what I wanted to say.

Forty Three

6:00 P.M.

I sat in my room for a very long time, smoking marijuana and cigarettes, staring at the piles of Ed Bailey's documents. I couldn't see why anyone would want to kill both Ed and Jeremy. There seemed no other connection between them other than the A∴R∴T∴. Ed was from the upper class world of privilege, and Jeremy was the hippie child of working-class Catholics. Maybe Adin was right. It had to be the A∴R∴T∴. But all I could think of was Paul Mackey.

It suddenly dawned on me that Mackey's weekly magick class was tonight. It would be starting anytime now. I knew that if I were a real detective I would get up and burn rubber to that class.

But I was quite stoned and fairly exhausted from the funeral. There was no way that I was going to be able go deal with Mackey. He was hard enough to deal with when I was sober. But I thought of another idea. Maybe I could go to the class by doing astral projection. I hadn't had much success, but the experiment at Damian's house seemed to have been at least partially useful. Even if it didn't serve much purpose it would be an interesting experiment. It was better than doing nothing at all.

I lay down on my bed immediately, with the firm conviction that I was going to travel astrally to Mackey's house, and observe his class in whatever way I could. Unfortunately, I almost immediately fell asleep.

Once again, I stood alone in front of the black and white checkered staircase. I stared up at the gateway to the stars stretching out infinitely above the stairs. I knew that I had to get to the top of those stairs and through that gateway. It simply had to be done. But I couldn't move my legs at all.

"Just use your mind and your will power," said a voice beside me. I looked over and saw Adin Stone standing next to me. But he hadn't been there a moment before. How strange! And I still couldn't move a muscle. Why on earth couldn't I move?

"You can't move because you're dreaming," said Adin.

"I'm dreaming?" I asked, but even as I said it I knew that it was true. As soon as I realized this, I felt like I was swirling on the inside and starting to come to pieces. The staircase melted into a sea of dust and I felt myself falling backwards, toppling end over end. Adin was gone and I was falling through a black void, filled with momentary flashes of random indiscernible images.

Then I had the odd sensation that I could both feel myself falling and laying in my bed at the same time. It was like I was in two places at once. I knew that if I wanted to I could open my eyes, sit up in bed, and the falling would be over. But I didn't want to. The tumbling sensation was actually quite pleasant. The boundaries between my surroundings and myself were not clear. I couldn't feel much difference between the swirling sea of images and blackness and my sense of myself. I felt free and blissful, floating in a peaceful sea of consciousness.

But then I remembered that I wanted to go to Paul Mackey's class in my astral body. That had been my whole purpose in lying down. And just like that, I found myself looking straight at Mackey, as he slumped in a crumpled easy chair stroking his straggly little beard. The little globs of cheesy substance around his mouth still danced as he slowly talked.

"So we're going to be discussing attack magick tonight," he said. He smiled broadly. "One of my favorite subjects."

I looked around the room. Seated on the floor and on a dilapidated couch were the three pasty 'disciples' I'd seen at the pagan festival, along with two others, equally wormy and mind-less looking. All of them were dressed in black t-shirts with various hard core or heavy metal rock bands emblazoned on their chests. Most were smoking. The walls and furnishings of the room seemed permanently stained with an ugly yellowish nicotine film. A poster of the qabalistic tree of life hung promi-nently on the wall, along with several other mystical looking images, all curled and fraying at the edges, stuck up crudely with packing tape.

"But you must remember that attack magick is not a toy," continued Mackey. "The only time attack magick is ever appro-priate is when there is no other recourse. This is serious work, and you need to establish a protective barrier around your Ruach against any recoil or revenge from your target."

"But what about the Yechidah of your target?" asked one of the pasty disciples. "Isn't it impossible to place a barrier bet-ween your Yechidah and the Yechidah of your target?"

"Attack magick takes place totally in the plane of Yetzirah, with virtually no connection to Atziluth," said Mackey. All of the pasty disciples nodded mechanically. "You won't learn any-thing like that in the A∴R∴T∴." I really had no idea what any of them were talking about. I wondered if they even knew. "The key is to build up an image in Yetzirah, an attack image," said Mackey. "Then to charge it with the violent emotional feelings of the Nephesh. The higher portions of the soul are irrelevant to this form of magick."

More nodding. The conversation was so meaningless to me that I became distracted by simply looking around the room. It was all so vivid. I felt like I was right there. As Mackey conti-nued to pontificate, I noticed him tapping rhythmically on the arm of his chair- a nervous tic I suppose. But as I looked more closely I found it absolutely fascinating. His hand and the chair were both made up of thousands of tiny corpuscles of light. I looked down at my own hands and they too were made of dots of light. As I stared at these dots they started to separate and swirl. I turned my hands over and they seemed to melt, expand-ing and distorting. I thought about my real body, lying in my bed. I wondered what it was doing. And just like that Mackey's room fell apart into chaos once again, and I found myself in my bedroom.

8:45 P.M.

I opened my eyes, but I could hardly sit up. My stomach and chest were swarming inside. Cascades of oozing, vibrating sensations ran up and down my torso. My hands and feet tingled in and out of numbness. My whole body was alive with strange sensations.

Had those wild experiences I just had been merely dreams? I really couldn't tell. It all seemed so vivid. Had I really been to Paul Mackey's class? Or was it all just in my mind?

I grabbed my journal from beside my bed and quickly recorded the experience in as much detail as I could. I didn't know if I'd ever be able to verify the details of the inside of Mackey's house, but I wanted it written down just in case.

I lit a cigarette and sat on the edge of my bed. This magical world was so full of ambiguity. I was starting to wonder what was real and what was not. If I was really capable of seeing things from the astral plane, who knows what might be possible. Maybe it was possible for demons to possess or even kill people. And does that mean that the demons in my dream were real? I snubbed out my cigarette and lay back down in bed. I closed my eyes and sincerely hoped that I wouldn't find out anything more about demons tonight.

Forty Four

♀ Friday, October 4, 1996

10:30 A.M.

I woke up, covered in sweat, but I couldn't remember any more of my nocturnal adventures. I felt like more had happened. My sleep had been fitful, but I couldn't piece anything coherent together. I had to be at work by noon, so I took a shower and shaved, trying not to think about anything. I kept finding myself wishing I'd spent a little more time with Kerrie as I got ready for work.

12:45 P.M.

Working at the videostore brought me back some sense of mundane normality. The familiar smell of dusty plastic and popcorn made me feel like the real world still existed, exactly as always. Dreams and magick seemed a million miles away. But that didn't last long.

I was restocking videos to the shelves from the overnight drop bin when the phone rang. Melissa, the other clerk on duty answered the phone. She was a plump and generally unsociable girl. We almost never spoke during work.

"Alex," she said loudly across the store. "It's for you."

I immediately felt a profound sense of dread. The twenty foot walk to the phone seemed an eternity. No one ever called me at work. I knew that whoever was calling, it couldn't be good.

I forced the phone receiver to my ear. "Hello?"

"Alex, I'm so glad I found you." It was my brother-in-law Peter. I could tell instantly by his tone that my hunch was right. More bad news.

"Hi Peter," I said.

"I don't know exactly how to tell you this, Alex," he said, making me feel even more uncomfortable.

"What?"

"The FBI is investigating the homicides."

"They are?"

"Yes, but it gets worse."

"Worse?" I asked. "What's wrong with the FBI investigating?

"Alex, I think they're building a case against you."

"What?" I was absolutely stunned. "How could they possibly be building a case against me?" I dropped my voice to a whisper, but Melissa stared at me fixedly, her jaw slack.

"I feel terrible, honestly. It's really mostly my fault," said Peter. "They got a hold of my notes, and they just seem to be putting things together all out of whack."

"What the hell did you write in your notes?" I couldn't believe he was even saying this to me.

"Just our conversations- the connections between the murders, you and the A∴R∴T∴. Look, I know you don't have anything to do with these murders, but I had to keep records."

"Jesus fucking Christ!" I shouted.

"There's something else, too. I guess your mom let some agents into your room, and," his voice suddenly shifted into a scolding accusation, "they found a bunch of Ed Bailey's personal belongings in there?"

Oh yeah," I said. "I got those from his girlfriend. I was going to tell you about those."

"It probably would have been a good idea to give them to me right away," said Peter, with a very forceful sigh.

I started to feel trapped, claustrophobic. "This whole time I've just been trying to help you!" I was practically shouting.

"I know, Alex. I know," said Peter. "I'm really sorry Alex."

"Well that's not going to help me!" I shouted. "What the hell am I supposed to do?"

"This is all messed up. Once the Feds start building a case, things get really dicey. But there hasn't been a grand jury or anything yet."

"A grand jury?" I asked. "What the hell is that?"

"Listen," said Peter. "Try to stay calm. I'm still working on things. I've got a lot of ideas the Feds aren't even working on. I'm pretty sure there's a drug angle. Do you know anything about drug dealing in the A∴R∴T∴?"

"No, I don't know anything about that!"

"There were an awful lot of narcotics at both crime scenes," said Peter. "I think it's important. I just need more information."

"I don't know anything about drugs, Peter! What the hell am I supposed to do about the FBI?" I was really falling apart. I couldn't believe that Peter was still grilling me for information when I was about to be apprehended by the FBI. I just wanted to scream and hang up the phone, but I felt like Peter was my only lifeline. And I was suddenly hanging on by a very slim thread.

"Look," said Peter. "What I'm about to tell you is a crime for me to even say, but there isn't anywhere near enough evidence to bring an indictment against you. They know that. They're still sifting. You'll be cleared. I'm sure of it. But if I were you, if I were in your position, I'd try to stay scarce for a while. If the FBI can't question you, they really don't have much."

"You're telling me to run away?" I asked.

"No," he said. "Of course not. That would be crazy. I'm telling you to make yourself unavailable for questioning until this blows over. Is there anywhere you can go? Stay away from home for a few days? Do you have a girlfriend? I'll keep trying to work this case as much as I can."

My mind was reeling. I didn't know where the hell I could go. I didn't really have many friends anymore. I'd lost touch with nearly everyone from high school. I thought of Kerrie, but that seemed a stretch. She lived in New York.

"Oh, and you probably shouldn't drive your car," said Peter. "They've got your plates."

"Great," I said. "So I'm really a fugitive."

"Listen. I'm trying to help you. I could lose my job just for talking to you about this. I could get arrested. But you've got to make yourself scarce right away, or you could be in deep shit."

"Okay," I said. "I hear you. I just don't know what the fuck I'm going to do with myself."

"I'm real sorry about this Alex."

"Thanks." I hung the phone up and looked over at Melissa. "Listen. I think I've got to get out of here." She seemed to know that whatever I was involved in was way too big to question. She just raised her hands mutely and stared at me with bugged out eyes. I left the video store without looking back.

Forty Five

1:17 P.M.

I knew that the A∴R∴T∴ was having their make-up class tonight. All I had to do was kill some time and I could go there. That could be dangerous too, but I didn't have any other ideas. I abandoned my car at the Videohut parking lot and walked to the T-Station. Alewife station is the end of the red line, so there was only one way to go- inbound. I had nowhere particular in mind, so it really didn't matter. I got on the train, and sat down on a hard plastic seat. The train was about half full, and to me, everyone looked like a potential FBI agent. People travelling to and from work, teenagers, the homeless, the elderly, they were all equally nerve-wracking. Until that moment I never knew what it meant to have your blood run cold, but that's exactly how I felt. Paranoia ran through my veins like jagged icicles.

As the train began to move, I looked out the window into the murky darkness of the underground tunnel. Fluorescent lights flashed intermittently as the train car scuttled past them. I felt hypnotized.

I had a strong urge to call Adin Stone. He told me he would help me anytime, but perhaps harboring a fugitive was over the line. Still, I didn't have much hope at all, so why not? I reached into my wallet where I kept the business card he gave me. It wasn't there. I was sure I'd just had it. Had I left it at home? No, I was certain that I'd put it back after calling him. But it wasn't there. I was plunged into an even deeper darkness.

THE BROTHERHOOD OF LIGHT AND DARKNESS

I rode the train from Alewife station to Downtown Crossing and back again three times. I didn't know where to go. I wondered if I should go home, just really quickly. Just to grab a few things. Clothes, maybe my pot, and I could look for Adin's phone number. But that seemed like an unnecessary risk. I'd worn the same clothes for days many times. I would manage.

I eventually got off the train. It was just too intensely boring to go back and forth. I drank several Dunkin Donuts coffees and took a walk through the Public Gardens and the Boston Commons. The Commons had a spooky quality in the overcast autumn weather. The trees were growing more and more barren, and clusters of homeless people crowded the benches like tired ghosts. After an eternity of wandering I finally got on the green line to go toward Damian Webster's.

6:45 P.M.

The closest I could get to Damian's condo complex on public transportation was still at least a half-mile walk from his door. I had only worn my blue hooded sweatshirt today, and it was really getting quite cold. I clung tightly to my latest cup of coffee, wishing it was a blanket.

When I got to Damian's complex, Matthew Wiley stood outside on the cement stoop, talking animatedly with Steve Curtin as they both smoked cigarettes. They smiled and waved as they saw me approaching.

"Ninety-three! If it isn't the man of the hour," said Matthew with a grin. I must have looked confused.

"Everyone's talking about you," said Steve as if that explained something. He laughed pleasantly.

"We'd better get inside," said Matthew, stubbing out his cigarette against the black railing of the small cement staircase that led up the stoop to the door. A large gray ash stain and a pile of cigarette butts underneath showed me that this was the place where everyone was discarding their spent smokes. Steve followed suit, stubbing his cigarette in the exact same spot, and the three of us went inside.

There were quite a few more people here tonight than the last time I'd been to Damian Webster's. Nearly everyone I'd met

217

so far was in attendance. Jessica Burnham sat on one of the couches between Catherine Chen and Lucy Grinder, the girl with all the piercings. On the other couch sat the older man Abraham Crane sat next to the redhead Mary Culling and her glum-looking boyfriend Jacob Bartholomew Pilsner III. The other brand new initiate Joey sat on the floor next to Damian Webster, who sat in an overstuffed easy chair aimlessly plucking at the strings of an acoustic guitar. Connie Drake was not there, and neither was the new initiate Chris. I was now very sure I'd never see him again.

The moment I came through the door everyone stared at me fixedly. Damian put down his guitar and rose to greet me. "Ninety-three! We've been wondering if you'd show up here," said Damian. He took my hand firmly and looked me straight in the eyes. "Have you talked to the FBI yet?"

At first I was dumbstruck, but I eventually choked out a "No." How the hell did he know about the FBI? Was I the last person to know that the FBI was looking for me?

"Do you know that they want to talk with you?" he asked.

"Yes, but-"

"Several of us have had visits today," said Damian. "All asking questions about you."

I was so flabbergasted. I didn't know what to say. They all had to be wondering why the hell I was under investigation, me a total neophyte to their group, in every sense of the word. How could I explain this to them? I realized that there was really no other reasonable explanation except the truth. So I told them everything I could.

I told them about Peter, and I told them about my dream of Jeremy's murder, and how that had made me look like I knew something I shouldn't. I told them about some of my other dreams, and the sense that they were leading me toward the killer. I didn't mention anything about the fact that I'd joined the A∴R∴T∴ with an eye toward investigating the murders, or even anything about my dealings with Paul Mackey.

"Well," said Damian, once I'd finished my story, "We need to decide what to do about this." He turned to me. "Obviously you don't have anything to do with these unfortunate events.

You don't even know these people." I was relieved to hear that he still seemed to trust me, at least on some level.

"I really don't see what we can do," said Abraham Crane with a scowl. "I had a three hour talk with two FBI agents today. That's not something I'd like to repeat."

"I don't want the FBI coming to my house," said Jacob Pilsner with his ridiculous lisp. "This thing has nothing to do with me."

"Shouldn't Alex just talk to the FBI?" asked Catherine Chen. "After all, he hasn't done anything."

"No," I said firmly. "I can't do that. My brother-in-law told me that could be very bad."

Damian Webster agreed. He didn't seem to have much trust in the government at all. "They're all a bunch of mindless bureaucrats," he said.

"But this isn't our responsibility," said Abraham Crane as he pulled out one of his slim cigarettes and lit it.

"Of course this is our responsibility," said Damian. "And Mary specifically asked us not to smoke in the house tonight."

Abraham Crane snubbed out his cigarette with a sneer.

"Alex is an initiate of the A∴R∴T∴ in good standing," continued Damian. "Ed and Jeremy were initiates. Every part of this is our responsibility. This is a brotherhood, and we protect our brothers." Abraham and Damian locked eyes intensely for an uncomfortably long period of time.

"Well," said Crane, scowling. "You are the Chief Adept, master of this temple." It was very obvious from his tone that it was irksome for him to admit this. He cast his eyes toward the wall, practically burning holes in it.

"So what do you plan to do, Alex?" asked Damian, turning back to me with an inquisitive look. He hardly seemed to notice Abraham Crane's annoyance at all.

"I don't know," I said. "I don't think I can go home tonight."

"Then you'll have to stay with one of us," said Damian. He looked around the room meaningfully. There was a very long silence.

"I'd let you stay with me," said Steve, finally. "But I'd have to check with my roommate."

"He can stay with me," said Jessica Burnham, looking at me with a slight smirk. "The FBI hasn't talked to me. Maybe I'm not on they're list. Do you want to stay with me, Alex?"

"Sure," I said. It was unexpected. I really didn't think she even liked me very much.

"Then it's settled," said Damian. "Alex will stay with Jessica. Shall we talk a bit about the four elements now? That is why we're supposed to be here, after all." He smiled mischievously, and everyone laughed.

Damian lectured on the four elements for about an hour, mostly information I'd already read in the neophyte workbook. The four elements, fire, water, air and earth, first written about by the early Greek philosopher Empedocles, exemplify a number of qualities pertinent both to nature and the human psyche. They correspond to a number of issues in occultism including the four suits of the Tarot cards, the four traditional weapons of the magician, the four worlds of the qabala, as well as a number of character traits and natural phenomena. As initiates of the A∴R∴T∴ we were expected to balance the four elements in our personalities and in our lives.

Abraham Crane frequently interrupted Damian to interject his own thoughts. Damian seemed appreciative and good-natured about the constant digressions, but I found my mind frequently wandering when either of them spoke. I just couldn't get the FBI out of my mind. It seemed perfectly possible that they could burst in at any time.

I also found myself looking over at Jessica Burnham quite frequently during the lecture. I'd been harboring a little crush on her since I'd dreamed of her moments before actually meeting her. She was so strong and severe, unlike anyone I'd ever been attracted to before. I wondered what was going to happen when I stayed at her house. She would probably just give me a pillow and tell me to sleep on the floor.

Eventually Damian ran out of steam, and I slipped outside for a cigarette. Abraham Crane, Matthew Wiley and Steve Curtin followed right behind me. As I lit one up, Abraham Crane put his arm on my shoulder and smiled.

"Listen," he said. "I didn't mean to make you feel unwelcome, Alex."

"Abe can just get a little grumpy when someone disturbs his routine," said Steve Curtin, poking Abraham Crane playfully in the belly. Crane smiled even more broadly.

"I do like you, Alex," said Crane. "I just don't want to see the A∴R∴T∴ in any kind of danger. We don't need to be cast in a bad light. I'd be very happy if the FBI forgot all about us."

"But it looks like that's not going to happen anytime soon," said Matthew Wiley. "Whether or not we throw poor Alex here to the wolves."

"Yes, of course you're right," admitted Crane. "All of this is just so unsettling. The A∴R∴T∴ is supposed to be a mystical fraternity."

"Sometimes the mundane just gets in the way though, doesn't it Abe?" Matthew looked at Abraham Crane as he spoke. "We can't all be great adepts like you, capable of rising above everything but the highest."

"Yes, of course," said Crane. "Alex is a mere neophyte. We must enfold him under the protection of our wings."

"Until he's big enough for us to kick him out of the nest," said Steve with a laugh.

I felt uncomfortable with them talking as if I wasn't even there. "So," I said, "do any of you have any ideas why someone would want to kill Ed and Jeremy?" At this point there was no reason for subtlety.

"My but you are the amateur detective, aren't you Alex?" said Abraham Crane. He smiled again kindly, with a glint of sarcasm in his eyes.

"It seems like I have to be at this point, for self-preservation if nothing else."

"Ed had lots of people who didn't really like him," said Steve. "He was kind of an arrogant jerk. He lied. He manipulated. And he slept with everybody. I don't think he deserved to die for anything, though."

The door opened just then. Catherine Chen and Lucy Grinder joined us on the porch, lighting up cigarettes.

"I'm not sure at all about Jeremy though. Everybody liked him."

"Not Jake Pilsner," said Lucy Grinder. "He looked like he was going to kill him right there and then when he saw him fucking Mary in the temple last month."

Catherine Chen turned crimson. "I don't want to talk about this," she said, eyeing the ground. She was Jeremy's girlfriend, so I could understand her discomfort.

"I'm sorry Catherine," said Lucy Grinder.

"We're just trying to figure this all out," said Matthew in a conciliatory tone.

"Jacob hated both Ed and Jeremy," said Steve. "They both slept with Mary."

"If that's what it is, then Jacob's going to kill you all," said Lucy caustically. "Everyone's slept with Mary."

"I haven't," said Steve with a cheerful smile. "I guess I'll have to keep the A∴R∴T∴ going when you're all dead."

"This isn't a funny conversation!" spat Catherine. Tears instantly spilled forth freely from her eyes. She stormed off the porch into the parking lot with her head in her hands.

"I'll go talk to her," said Lucy as she followed Catherine toward the street. I could see that I wasn't likely to find out any useful new information.

"You really know how to say the wrong thing, Steve," said Matthew.

"I know. I'm awful," said Steve, but he continued to smile. He turned to Abraham Crane. "Oh great Adeptus, please absolve me of my sins!" Crane didn't smile. Instead, he turned to me.

"So, what are you planning to do with yourself?" asked Crane.

"I don't know yet. I guess I'm hoping that the FBI will find the real killer soon. Or else I'll figure this thing out- or my brother-in-law will."

"Does your brother-in-law have any leads?" asked Crane.

"Not really, other than me." I tried to smile, but couldn't quite manage it. "He thinks it has something to do with drugs."

"Is that so," said Abe, shaking his head disdainfully.

"Let's stop having this conversation," said Matthew. "We've already driven poor Catherine away."

"Very well," said Crane. He didn't seem to mind dropping the topic at all. The whole situation seemed to embarrass Abraham Crane very deeply. He obviously felt that it all reflected very poorly on the reputation of the A∴R∴T∴. I could imagine why. He'd been involved with the organization for over thirty years. Murder and drugs within the A∴R∴T∴ must have seemed quite humiliating.

The door opened and Jessica Burnham poked her head out. "Alex, I'm ready to go," she said. "If you're coming with me, you'd better get it together."

Moments later I found myself on the way home with Jessica Burnham.

Forty Six

9:25 P.M.

Jessica didn't seem to live far from Damian Webster's home. But it was hard to tell exactly how far it was because she drove around seventy MPH, even on back streets and, most surprisingly, through the parking lot of an elementary school. It was quite a sight to watch this gothic goddess at the wheel in her skin-tight black velvet dress and three-inch heels, gunning it past jungle gyms and swing sets. But her flawless features remained cool even when pulling a ninety-degree turn at sixty MPH. By the time we got to her house I was fairly convinced that she would forever be far too much woman for me.

She lived in the upper apartment of a two-story mid-century building. Her apartment was very sparse, but what little decoration she had seemed very dark, exotic, and expensive looking. There weren't even any chairs in the main room- just a stack of large, richly colored pillows with what looked like Indian or Tibetan embroidery in gold.

"Have a seat," she said with pleasant authority. She said it just forcefully enough that I found myself plopping down on a nearby pillow immediately.

"Can I get you anything?" she asked, as she walked toward what I assumed was the kitchen. It was a small alcove off to the right, just out of my line of sight.

"Uh," I stammered. I really didn't know what to say. I found her quite overwhelming.

"I'm having some wine," she said. "Do you want some?" She smiled, but placed her hand impatiently on her hip. I felt that I needed to be sure I answered correctly.

"I'll have a glass," I said. "Wine sounds great."

I seemed to have answered properly, because she smiled at me again. "It's red. I only drink red. Hope you don't mind." She didn't wait for my reply, instead just disappearing into the kitchen.

I looked around the room. The main feature was a large pair of brass sculptures. They were strange Eastern deities with many arms and ferocious looking faces, locked in sexual embraces with much smaller females. They stood on a pair of small, ornately carved dark wooden tables. Next to these were some intricate pieces of glassware and porcelain that also seemed Asian.

Jessica returned with two glasses and an open bottle of wine. She filled our glasses, quite full, and handed me one.

"To the Federal Bureau of Investigation," she said with a dark smile. I laughed nervously as I watched her drink deeply.

"You have a lot of interesting things around here," I said, desperately wishing I were better at small talk.

She shrugged. "I like to travel."

I started to put my glass down on the floor in front of me.

"You can't do that!" she cried out.

I froze, my glass mere centimeters above the hardwood floor. I glanced around, looking for a coaster.

She smirked. "You have to drink before you put your glass down or it's bad luck." I could tell she was kidding, she could barely keep herself from laughing. Still, I took a long sip from the glass, and didn't put it down at all. Disobeying this woman did not seem like an option.

"So, uh, how long have you been with the A∴R∴T∴?" I said, taking another stab at casual conversation.

"A long, long time," she said. "Almost five years."

"Wow."

"I'm an adept," she said blandly. "An Adeptus Minor. But really I've been an Adeptus Minor for a few years now. I've been taking a break for a while because I'm so busy with work."

"I'm impressed," I said, quite genuinely. This girl was my age, had obviously traveled the world collecting treasures, and still found the time to become a Rosicrucian Adept.

"A lot of people think I became an adept so quickly because I sucked Damian Webster's cock or something," she said, shaking her head in annoyance.

"Really?" I said. "People are so shallow sometimes."

"I know. I only sucked Damian Webster's cock because I felt like it."

We both laughed. I took another large gulp of wine. This girl was operating on a very different level than I was used to. All of the women in the A∴R∴T∴ seemed so unusual.

"And I only sucked his cock once," she continued. "You've got to suck his cock at least three times if you want to be rushed up to adept."

I practically spat out my wine laughing. Jessica Burnham was much funnier and wilder than I expected. I doubted that I could ever keep up with her. But I was beginning to feel the warmth of the wine, and I really felt a strong urge to lean over and kiss her. She seemed so far out of my league that all I could manage to do was say, "Wow."

"Wow what?" she asked.

"It's just," I said, but I didn't know what was going to come out of my mouth next. Luckily, the wine began to talk for me. "It's just that you're so beautiful, and you're so funny. You are just more and more impressive every second that I'm with you."

She smirked. "Well, well. It appears that Alexander Sebastian is being a little bit charming."

"Oh, I mean it," I said. "I'm just being honest."

"Aren't you sweet," she said. "But I think you're just hoping that I'll suck your cock too."

I wasn't at all sure what to say to that, and only managed to grunt incoherently.

"Don't even try to deny it. Connie told me all about you." She smiled broadly with a truly sinister glint in her eyes as she stared at me. I must have looked dumbfounded because she couldn't stop laughing.

"I know what we're missing," she said once she finally regained her composure. She got up and retrieved a small remote

226

control from behind one of the brass statues. She pressed a button, and some eerie electronic music began to throb in the background, coming from an unseen stereo system. "Music makes everything better," she said with a smile.

She then opened a drawer, and pulled out a small plastic zip-lock bag filled with clumps of chalky white powder.

"So does this. Interested?" she asked, shaking the bag at me.

"Is that coke?" I said.

"Colombia's finest."

"Uh, sure," I said.

"Good boy." She reached back into the drawer and got out a little silver tray with a razor blade already sitting on it. She put the tray onto the floor and began chopping up the cocaine into a fine powder.

I'd never done coke before, but I was almost always up for trying new drugs. This was proving to be a very interesting evening. I'd almost completely forgotten about the danger I was in. She pushed the tray toward me and handed me a small silver straw. She told me to go first. I looked down and saw that she'd separated the cocaine into four thick lines. I pressed the straw to my nose and snorted up one of the lines. It immediately burned all through my sinuses.

"Take another," she said encouragingly.

I snorted the next line up my other nostril. It burned again, and I still wasn't feeling any noticeable effects. Jessica took the tray from me and quickly vacuumed up the rest. She immediately dumped some more cocaine on the tray and proceeded to chop it up just as before.

A tingly numbness began to creep up my spine, spreading out in waves from my face as well. I felt slightly disoriented, but pleasantly energized as well. I felt myself grinding my teeth. Jessica silently stared at me with her intensely blue eyes as she continued chopping up the cocaine.

"Thank you so much for sharing," I said. "You really are being so nice to let me stay here. I mean, you hardly know me, and you're so incredibly beautiful and interesting, and it's really just so nice of you." I was starting to talk a mile a minute, but I couldn't seem to help myself. "Do you mind if I smoke?" I asked. "You smoke, right? I seem to remember you smoking, that's how I met you, right?"

"Yes, I smoke," said Jessica. She laughed. I could tell she was laughing about how fast and stupidly I was talking, but somehow it just didn't matter to me at that moment.

I dug out my cigarettes and offered her one. She nodded, but instead of taking it, she snorted up some more cocaine. I lit both of the cigarettes and handed her one.

"Man, I really needed a cigarette," I said. "I didn't even realize how much I needed a cigarette until right this second, but I really needed one. Thank you so much again for being such a wonderful, beautiful host." My lips seemed to be moving without any effort on my part.

Jessica poured some more wine for both of us. "It's my pleasure to help," she said. "You're the one dodging the FBI."

"Isn't that so weird?" I said. I was getting completely manic. A stupid grin forced itself across my face and I started waving my hands around wildly as I spoke. "I never could have possibly imagined that I'd be involved in anything like this. It's so crazy."

"It's a crazy world," said Jessica blandly.

"I've been trying to figure this whole thing out but I haven't been able to put anything together!"

Jessica smirked indulgently. "Well, what have you got so far?"

"Okay, well, as far as I can tell Ed Bailey was involved in some sort of homosexual sex magick."

"Excuse me?" she looked stunned.

"Yeah, apparently they found semen in his rectum and his mouth in the autopsy and I read an article about sex magick in his things." I probably shouldn't have been saying all this, but somehow I just couldn't stop talking.

"That freak! I never knew he went that way. Well, I guess nothing should surprise me. The guy was a sick fuck."

"He was? How so?"

"The fucking asshole raped me! That's one thing!" Jessica's eyes instantly flashed full of rage. "So you won't ever see me crying over his fucking corpse, I'll tell you that much!"

228

"I-I'm so sorry." I was floored. No one had ever told me they had been raped before. I really didn't know what else to say.

"Don't worry about it. It was more- I guess- more like a date rape or something." She looked down and I could see that her eyes were misting up. She quickly rubbed them and smiled. I still had no idea what I could possibly say. "I didn't mean to kill the buzz. I need some more coke," she said, and snorted two more lines from her silver tray. "So, anyway, here's the story. Ed and I were supposed to do this sex magick thing. Right in this fucking room, as a matter of fact. We started doing a ritual to begin with, and I just felt it was wrong, you know? I wasn't feeling it. But we were already kissing and he had his cock in his hand. I told him to stop and he said that wouldn't be 'magically appropriate.' I told him I didn't give a shit- he'd better start doing some god-damned banishing rituals and then he shoved me down and fucked me anyway. So yeah, he's a fucking asshole as far as I'm concerned. I told Connie to stay away from him but she just thought he was 'so adorable'- blech. He had bad breath and pimples on his back. The whole thing makes me want to puke."

"When did this happen?" I asked.

"Couple of years ago. Hey, I didn't murder him. If that's what you're thinking."

"No, of course not, I wasn't thinking that at all."

"I didn't like the guy, but I'm not that stupid."

"Of course, I'm so sorry."

"Fuck it," she spat. "I should've known better myself." She paused to take another snort of coke. "So, he wrote an article about sex magick? Did it include any tips about forcing yourself on women?" She laughed hollowly, but I couldn't bring myself to join her. My mind was racing and it seemed like my heart was beating a thousand times a minute. At the same time I felt somehow distant from my body, like nothing really mattered.

"No, I actually only read the beginning of it, really. Do you know a lot about sex magick?" I asked.

"I'm pretty familiar with the topic."

"Could you teach me anything more about it?"

"That's a pretty clumsy line, Alex."

"No, I'm really just curious, for you know, for information." I honestly hadn't intended my comment in any kind of lecherous way. But I certainly was attracted to her. Really I was so out of my mind that I didn't know why I was saying anything.

"Well," she said, pausing to look me over carefully, "I guess I could share a few basic things with you. They aren't specifically sexual, though. Don't get any ideas that I'm going to fuck you or anything."

"Not at all."

"Good, because I still haven't decided about that yet."

Forty Seven

Jessica led me into her bedroom and told me to take off my pants and lie down on my back on her bed. My heart pounded even more heavily in my chest, probably from both the cocaine and incredible nervousness I felt being in Jessica Burnham's bed. She sat down beside me.

"The first thing that I'm going to teach you is something from Tantric Yoga." She leaned over me, smiling like a delighted child. "It's called the Mulabandha. How should I explain this?" She scratched her head. "Okay, basically you want to find your perineum. This is the area between your balls and your anus."

She swiftly stuck two fingers between my legs, pressing lightly on a spot right above my sphincter. It tickled and I tensed it involuntarily. My whole sexual region started to tingle strangely.

"That's your perineum," she said, raising an eyebrow and smirking. "One of the central keys to sexual yoga lies right there. This is called the root lock, the Mulabhandha. By tensing this muscle, and directing your sexual energy, you will be able to control your orgasm and project magical energy."

"Okay, you have my attention," I said. "Tell me more."

"All right. Try breathing in, while pulling up on the perineal muscles, imagining that you are pulling your sex energy up into your body. When you breathe out, hold in the sexual energy.

I followed her directions. I felt a surge of pleasure rush up into my body. It was a ticklish feeling that reminded me of the sensations I experienced when waking up from one of my magical dreams.

"I feel something," I said. "I'm not sure what exactly."

"Good. Keep doing that for a couple of minutes."

I kept breathing, closing my eyes and feeling my sexual energy move around. I began to feel my penis hardening. Embarrassed, I opened my eyes.

"Keep going," she encouraged.

I sat up, blushing. "I'm starting to get an erection."

"Well, then I guess you have two choices." She reached behind her back and started unzipping her dress. "You can try to direct your sex energy up into your higher chakras and become enlightened or something..." She dropped her dress past her shoulders, exposing her bra. "Or you can fuck me."

My mind reeled. I suddenly felt like I was back in my dream from the pagan festival. This was all just so bizarre. But passion quickly overtook me and I pulled Jessica toward me, kissing her and pulling her dress down to her waist. I ran my hands over her smooth white skin, caressing her and becoming more and more aroused.

She pulled off my shirt and began brushing her lips over my chest, then biting my shoulders and neck. Moments later the rest of our clothes were scattered across her floor.

I kissed her breasts and her stomach, running my hands over her and caressing her neatly shaved vagina. She grabbed my penis roughly.

"Fuck me, Alex! Fuck me!" She shoved my penis inside her, and we started fucking wildly with her astride me. In less than a minute I felt an overwhelming urge to climax. She stopped moving. "Don't you dare come, Alex! Pull up on your perineum like I told you. Direct your energy toward understanding god or the mysteries of the universe or whatever the fuck you want to call it. Let yourself flow in the universal ecstasy or some shit like that. You're just not allowed to come."

I held myself back from orgasm, and an electric storm of energy surged through me. I felt like I was on fire.

"Now keep fucking me."

We continued having sex for I don't know how long. She seemed to have several orgasms, but every time I was about to come, she made me direct my energy inward and upward, 'to understand god or some shit.' Each time the burning ecstasy became more and more intense, until I found myself disintegrating into periods that I can't even remember. The ecstatic rush was too much. I would come back from these blackouts shaking all over. As soon as I was aware of what was going on again, Jessica would say, "Now keep fucking me." I lost all sense of time. It must have gone on for at least an hour, maybe much longer.

She finally told me that I could come, but just as I exploded, she pulled my penis out and I came all over her stomach.

She put three of her fingers into her vagina. A moment later she pulled them out, quite wet, and swirled them around in the semen on her belly. She scooped up some of the semen, smiling mischievously. "Here is the body of Christ, here is the Paschal Lamb for which they confess the passion of Christ."

Then she ate some of it. Before I even knew what she was doing she shoved the rest into my mouth. "Eat it," she said. "This is the most holy of sacraments."

This girl was so incredibly strange that I didn't even know what to do or think. I swallowed the semen. The room was spinning.

"You did pretty well for your first time, Alex. What do you think?"

"That was amazing." I was still shaking. I couldn't say anything more.

She patted me softly on the head. "Lay back and let your experience crystallize, while I go take a shower." With that, she stood up and walked to the bathroom.

I closed my eyes and instantly passed out.

Forty Eight

I walked down a dark alley, feeling uneasy. Something was definitely wrong. I felt like I was being watched. I turned to look behind me, and several shadowy figures instantly hid from my view, receding into the darkness. I was right. Someone was following me. I tried to hurry down the alley, but I found it was like wading through quicksand. I could hardly move.

I turned again and the shadowy figures were closer, but they again hid from view as soon as they saw me. I struggled forward, toward a dark metal door ahead of me. I could hardly lift my legs, but I knew I had to get to the door. I couldn't imagine who or what was following me.

I finally got hold of the handle. Thank god it was unlocked. But it was so heavy that I couldn't move it.

I saw the shadowy figures coming closer. They were becoming bolder. They didn't bother to hide anymore. I saw that they weren't strange creatures of the night, they were FBI agents in dark suits. I knew that I would be apprehended in seconds if I couldn't get through that door. I pulled with every bit of my strength and the door creaked open a few inches, just enough for me to squeeze through.

I pressed myself through to the other side and tried to pull the door shut behind me. But fearsome hands clawed their way into the opening, one after another, blocking me from shutting the door, and grasping at me viciously. I kicked and punched at them, pulling the door closed until they were finally forced back and the metal door slammed tight with a heavy groan. I fell back against the door, catching my breath.

Looking around, I discovered that I was now in what looked like a dark cave. Strange animals, unlike anything I'd ever seen before, scurried along the rocky ground through the darkness. I couldn't see them clearly, but what I did see made me quiver. I didn't really want to look any closer. My heart pounded. I made my way through the cave as quickly as possible.

But as I moved, I felt the strange creatures rubbing against my legs. I didn't dare look down at them. Some were slimy, others scratchy, and some of them felt hot, almost as if they were on fire.

I saw another door in the distance, and ran for it as quickly as I could, stumbling over the bizarre animals. They hardly seemed to notice me.

As I rushed through this door, I discovered something quite unexpected on the other side of it. I found myself standing in a small gourmet coffee shop. In one corner, a couple was laughing and talking animatedly as they sipped very large cappuccinos. At the counter a filthy looking homeless woman was paying for a coffee with a pile of change.

And then I saw Adin Stone, sitting by the window, sipping coffee from a lavender mug. As soon as I saw him, it all suddenly dawned on me. I ran over to him.

"I'm dreaming, aren't I?" I cried out loudly. Everyone in the shop stopped what they were doing and stared at me.

"Of course you are," said Adin. He smiled. "Sit down and have a coffee."

I sat beside him and shook my head. "No. I don't need one. I'm perfectly awake." In fact, I'd never felt so awake. The colors were vibrant. Everything seemed alive and shiny. "I have so many questions, but I need to talk to the real Adin Stone, not the dream Adin Stone. No offense."

He looked at me kindly. "What's the difference? What's the dream and what's the reality? Why don't you just pretend I'm the real Adin Stone and then there won't be a problem."

At the time, this somehow seemed reasonable, so I started to converse with him. "I'm being followed by the FBI," I said.

"I know."

"I've got to figure this all out or I'm going to be in real trouble. I need your help."

"I believe you'll figure it out." He took another sip of his coffee.

"Peter thinks the murders have something to do with drug dealing."

"Maybe Peter's right."

"But that just leads me back to Mackey," I said, completely confused and frustrated. "Kerrie's parents told me Mackey was a big drug dealer."

"Mackey's not the only drug dealer in the world."

"Why the hell are so many people in this magick scene involved with drugs?"

Adin sighed. He almost seemed bored. "Many people use mind-altering substances to awaken their magical awareness. It's been going on for thousands of years. Unfortunately, in our modern culture, this can also lead to all kinds of problems. It's really quite a shame. In this culture it's all too easy for the shaman to become a mere addict."

"But what do drugs have to do with these murders?"

"Well..."

"Alex!" I heard a familiar female voice. I felt someone shaking my shoulder. I opened my eyes.

ħ Saturday, October 5, 1996

7:40 AM

I was laying in Jessica's bed, amazed. I'd had another lucid dream. And what a strange dream it was. Jessica stood over me, wearing a black, fitted business suit. She looked just as sexy as ever, but now in a completely different way.

"I have to go to work. I know, it's Saturday, but duty calls." She sighed. "I just wanted to let you know I was going. Help yourself to anything in the fridge. Sorry that I don't have much. I don't cook. I think there's some leftover Thai food that's still good."

I couldn't get over her outfit. She looked like an entirely different person. Instead of the gothic sex goddess of last night, a businesswoman was now standing over me.

"What do you do?" I asked.

"I'm a programmer- well, I'm a manager now. We're developing internet telephony solutions for B to B- honestly, it's too boring to waste time describing."

"Wow," I said. "You are a very complex person."

"And here I am trying to simplify," she said with a sigh. "Oh well. I guess I'll just have to keep trying." She laughed, but her eyes were suddenly distant.

"I think you're great just the way you are."

"Oh, I know," she said with a smirk. "But I must ever strive on!" She raised her hand dramatically into the air. "Say, speaking of melodrama, that reminds me. There's a secret ritual tonight."

"A secret ritual?" I was intrigued.

"Yeah, it's not an official A∴R∴T∴ ritual, but some people are getting together over at Jake Pilsner's to invoke Astarte. Like somehow that's going to stop our troubles." She rolled her eyes. "If you haven't been arrested by the time I get home from work maybe you'd like to go?" She looked at me with a knowing smile.

"Of course."

"Thought so. Anyway, I gotta fly. Try to stay out of the clutches of the government goons." She blew a kiss and was out the bedroom door. A moment later I heard the front door being locked up and she was gone.

I turned over in bed wondering exactly where she and I stood. Was Jessica going to be my girlfriend? What about Kerrie? Or Connie for that matter? I still owed her an orgasm last time I checked. I soon slipped back into a very blissful sleep.

12:42 PM

I woke up again, startled. Had I just heard something? I could have sworn some sort of sound had woken me up. My heart started racing. Was the FBI about to come crashing through the door?

Forty Nine

12:43 P.M.

I got out of bed, still naked from last night's debauch, and poked my head cautiously out the bedroom door. The main room was empty, except for the glasses and the empty bottle of wine.

I stepped into the room, and there it was- a knock on the door. That's what had woken me. I wasn't sure what to do. This wasn't my house. Ignoring the knock might be the best course of action. But I walked to the front door and pressed my eye into the peephole. A short, dark-haired man in greenish cover-alls stood on the other side of the door, impatiently tapping a clipboard with dirty fingers. He didn't look at all like an FBI agent, and I decided it was safe to see what he wanted.

"Just a minute," I cried through the closed door. I retrieved my jeans and t-shirt from the floor of Jessica's bedroom. After quickly glancing through the apartment to make sure that nothing illegal was lying around I opened the door.

"Hi there, sorry to bother you," said the little man in a thick Boston accent. "Boston Edison. There's a problem with the gas lines in this area. I just need to check your lines. It'll only take a minute."

He sounded as if he'd said this hundreds of times and I felt sure that he was harmless. I let him into the apartment and he looked around curiously.

"Do you know where your water heater is?" he asked.

"Sorry, I'm just house sitting."

"Mind if I look around?"

"Not at all."

The small workman began to poke around the apartment. I quickly forgot about him and returned to Jessica's bed for a smoke. A few minutes later, the man called out "Okay, thank you." I got up and let him out.

After taking a shower, I spent the next several hours sitting in Jessica's bedroom, wondering what was going to happen to me. I felt more than ever like a complete washout as a detective. I hadn't found out anything definitive about the case, and now I was even a suspect- maybe the prime suspect. I wondered how long it would take for the FBI to find me. They could really come at any time.

I started to get a headache. I really wished Jessica had some pot, but I couldn't even find any more cocaine. So, I just sat waiting for hours.

6:30 PM

Jessica got home, and quickly changed out of her work clothes. She emerged from the bathroom in a short black skirt with a lacey red and black corset top. Her make up was darker, her lips a much more bold shade of red. The transformation was still amazing even though I'd seen it before.

She told me that Jacob Pilsner lived in Lowell, so we had to leave or we'd be late. After sitting on her floor all afternoon I was more than ready to go.

Fifty

7:45 P.M.

Jacob Bartholomew Pilsner III lived in a small crumbling house in a forgotten neighborhood comprised entirely of small crumbling houses. There were no streetlights on his street, but it was easy to see that everything was in the last stages of decay. The house smelled moldy both inside and out. Jacob greeted us at the door and seemed quite surprised to see me.

"Ninety-three, Jacob. Alex is my new sidekick- for the moment," said Jessica as we stepped inside. It was more a declaration than an explanation, and left little room for debate.

We walked through the kitchen into the rest of the house. Books, papers, and odd relics were piled three feet high against the walls in every room. The whole place had been paneled in wood, but that was clearly many years ago. It was buckling and falling off everywhere.

Jacob led us to the living room, where I found some familiar faces. Damian Webster, Abraham Crane, Matthew Wiley, Lucy Grinder and Mary Culling were all sitting, drinking wine and chatting. They all stopped talking immediately and looked up at me, as surprised as Jacob. I felt like a very unwelcome interloper.

"Hello all," said Jessica dryly. "I brought Alex along. Ninety-three." Her words seemed to shake them out of trance, and they all greeted us cordially.

"Please, do sit down," said Jacob, playing the host. "Both of you."

"Perhaps we should go ahead and get started," said Abraham Crane. "Since everyone's here."

"Don't be in such a rush, Abe," said Mary Culling. "They just arrived. Come here and sit next to me, Alex." She patted an empty spot next to her on a greenish couch. She seemed a bit drunk.

I looked over at Jessica, but she had an utterly blank expression, so I sat down next to Mary. Jessica took a seat in an orange easy chair on the other side of the room.

"I'm so glad that you're still with us, Alex," said Mary with a rather lascivious tone. She rested her hand on my arm, and leaned in toward me, pressing a breast into my shoulder. I could smell wine strongly on her breath. "We've all been thinking constantly about you and the FBI. There's something very sexy about a fugitive."

Jacob walked over to me swiftly with a nervous smile. He rubbed his hands vigorously and continuously against the sides of his shirt. It seemed to be some sort of nervous tic. "Is there anything I can get for you? A beverage? Everyone's drinking wine."

"Sure," I said.

"Okay, great," said Jacob, but he didn't move. "So, uh, you should feel really quite special, Alex. You and I are the only two people here who aren't at least Adeptus Minores. Of course, I'd be an Adeptus Major by now I'm sure, but I've only been in the A∴R∴T∴ a couple of years. I didn't realize the A∴R∴T∴ even still existed- until I met Mary of course- But I've been a freemason since 1974. If I'd known about the A∴R∴T∴ back then, who knows where I'd be?"

I couldn't believe he was telling me all this again.

"Why don't you go get Alex his wine," said Mary with a scowl.

"Oh yes, of course," said Jacob, but he still didn't go anywhere. His eyes remained fixated on Mary's hand, still on my arm, and her breast, still pressed against my shoulder.

Mary turned her attention back to me and smiled. "He'll talk your ear off until we all die of boredom if you don't make him shut up." She squeezed my arm.

I don't know if I'd ever felt so uncomfortable. Everyone watched the odd scene silently, a perverse pantomime. Jacob finally tore his eyes away from Mary and went to the kitchen for some more glasses.

"Perhaps we really should get started soon," said Damian Webster, his face twisting into an impish smirk. "Before poor Jacob has a heart attack."

"Let's robe up," said Abraham Crane eagerly, laboring to his feet. Everyone else stood up, and started moving toward putting on their ceremonial magick robes. Jacob returned with two empty glasses in his hands and looked around at everybody's movements in bewilderment.

"Are we ready to rock and roll?" he said with a silly grin. He put the glasses down on a coffee table and went to get on his own robes.

There was some confusion when everyone realized that of course I did not have a magical robe with me. Luckily, Jacob had his old black neophyte robe for me to wear.

I became much more conscious of Jacob's statement about rank once everyone was wearing robes. Nearly everybody wore bright white robes adorned with gold trim; a golden cross emblazoned on the breast. At the center of the cross was a colorful rose. Damian wore a mantle of crimson red above his robe, and Abraham Crane one of blue. Lucy, Mary, Jessica and Matthew simply wore their white robes unadorned. Jacob's robe was emerald green, and mine black. I definitely felt like a lesser creature in that plain black robe.

Once we were dressed for the ritual Damian gathered us all in front of a closed door. "Before we get started tonight I wanted to say a few words. There has been a tremendous amount of turmoil in our temple lately, and I would like to dedicate this ritual to establishing a greater sense of love and peace amongst our brethren. We have decided to invoke the goddess Astarte for this purpose, the Phoenician goddess of love. Soror Mishkala will be the high priestess for this rite, and I could think of no better embodiment for the goddess."

Mary Culling bowed slightly, and everyone applauded.

"Let us enter the temple and begin," said Damian.

Fifty One

8:00 P.M. (approx.)

A makeshift temple was erected in an empty room. Silk cloths hung from the walls, somewhat concealing the collapsing wood paneling underneath. On one side of the room, a large veil was draped a few feet in front of the wall, with a slight opening in the middle. I wondered if someone was hiding behind it. A large altar stood at the center of the room, with pink and green candles and a two-foot tall image of a plump goddess made of some sort of stone or plaster. She had a crescent moon on top of her head.

Matthew went to the altar, lit the candles, then turned to face us. He cracked a mischievous smile. "Since this is not an official A∴R∴T∴ event, I decided to bring along some party favors, or I should say sacraments, that may help to establish the proper mood." He poured a large handful of white pills onto the altar. Waving his hand over them, he added, "I consecrate thee, Ecstasy, in the name of Astarte."

All faces around me seemed to light up at once, followed by murmurs of approval. One by one, each of the congregants went up to the altar and took one or more pills.

I had taken ecstasy several times in the past, but I didn't really feel like tripping. I'd been using quite enough drugs lately, so I abstained. I noticed that both Jessica and Abraham Crane didn't take any either.

After everyone had swallowed their pills, Damian Webster, Matthew Wiley, Abraham Crane and Mary Culling moved to the center of the room. They stood at the four cardinal points, facing

243

the altar at the center. Matthew directed the rest of us with a hand gesture to sit down. Jacob Pilsner, Lucy Grinder, Jessica and I sat down in a semi-circle at the back of the room. The four standing around the altar joined hands and chanted the word 'AUM' slowly and melodically, three times in succession. When they completed the third 'AUM,' Mary Culling disappeared behind the veil at the front of the room.

After a moment of silence, Matthew began to perform the lesser banishing ritual of the pentagram. His smooth voice gave the ritual a delicate, flowing, poetic feeling. I found myself closing my eyes and visualizing the ritual along with him.

When Matthew finished the banishing ritual he returned to his place with the two other men and said, quite dramatically, "In the name of the Mighty and Terrible One, I proclaim that I have banished the shells unto their habitations."

Damian Webster picked up a basin of water from beside the altar and began to slowly circle the room, sprinkling water and chanting "I purify the temple with water."

When Damian completed his walk around the room, Abraham Crane picked up an incense burner from the other side of the altar. Crane circled the room saying, "I consecrate the temple with fire."

Matthew Wiley then moved to each of the cardinal points of the room, one after the other. In the east, south, west and then north he traced a large hexagram in the air, chanting, "Astarte... Ararita..." with each hexagram that he traced.

Then all three stood before the altar, raising their hands in the air. "I invoke Astarte," they cried out in unison. "Lady of Love and Generation, the Goddess that is the Veil of Creation itself. O fiery star of Byblos! O Thou of the crescent-crown. Thee, Thee I invoke. Astarte, lady of the beasts. Thee, Thee, I invoke. Astarte, lady of the sea. Thee, Thee I invoke! Astarte, mistress of horses and chariots. Thee, Thee, I invoke. Thou, whose priestesses bring earthly delight to every soul, and spiritual delight to all in the flesh. Thee, Thee I invoke. Thou whose eyes are as sapphires in the night sky, and whose skin is of ivory and of silver. Thee, Thee I invoke."

Mary Culling emerged from behind the veil. She had removed her robe, and was now entirely nude, other than a very sheer red scarf wrapped several times around her body. I couldn't help but admire the beauty of her naked form.

"Behold!" she cried out dramatically. "I am nature herself, all-powerful, creating, preserving, and destroying. All life springs forth from me, and to me all life returns!" She began to rub her body erotically.

I wasn't sure if it was the invocation she was taking or the Ecstasy, but she was definitely in an extremely altered state. I also felt that there seemed to be an almost imperceptible atmosphere around her. It reminded me of the shape I'd seen in the woods, a sort of distortion in the air around her. I felt a shiver in my spine, and found myself wishing to leave the room as quickly as possible.

"Mine is the invisible form, the matrix wherefrom even the Gods are sprung!" cried Mary, continuing to stroke herself sensually. "I give life and love unto every dweller of the watchtowers of the Universe. I am the mother of the sun, the moon, and mistress of the stars. The stars are my children, souls whose life eternal glows brightly in the night sky. Who worships me, worships me with joy and love and the sweetest delights! I am the heart filled with passion, love for the pleasure of life and fulfillment of earthly and heavenly bliss! I am fierce with my followers, and wade in the blood of my enemies! But to love me is better than all things! I am the lady of the lion, the horse, the sphinx, the dove, and the star. From Cyprus and Sicily to Sidon and Tyre my worshippers fall to their knees, crying out my love chant."

At this, Mary suddenly dropped to her knees and began chanting strange words. "Omari tessala marax, tessala dodi phornepax amri radara poliax armana piliuamri redara piliu son mari narya barbiton madara anaphax sarpedon andala hriliu..." She then fell onto her back and convulsed wildly as the sounds coming from her descended more and more into incomprehensible grunts and indecipherable gibberish. She writhed crazily for quite some time.

I saw Abraham Crane shoot Damian Webster a concerned glance, but Damian merely shrugged. It was clear that the ritual was not going to go any further as planned, since Mary was now just shaking and groaning. Crane bent over Mary, trying to hold her up in his arms. She stopped flailing and grabbed hold of Crane's head, kissing him hard on the mouth. He seemed to resist for a moment, but eventually just started making out with her. Mary pulled off the red scarf and pressed Abraham Crane's head into her breasts. He began to kiss and fondle them.

I looked over at Jacob Pilsner, but he was sitting docilely with eyes closed, like everyone else but me. When I turned back to Crane and Mary, she was holding her legs spread open on the floor. Crane hiked up his robes and I saw that he was sporting a large erection. I turned away in extreme discomfort as they began to copulate right there in the middle of the temple.

Mary began to make loud sexual noises and this finally roused the attention of Jacob Pilsner. He looked at Abraham Crane between Mary's legs with sheer horror in his eyes. This was clearly not something he was expecting to see in his house tonight. He struggled to his feet, tripping over his robe, and started toward the lovers with a very crazed look on his face.

Matthew Wiley stepped between Jacob and the couple, putting his arm on Jacob firmly. He whispered something in Jacob's ear, but Jacob still tried to push past him. Matthew took hold of Jacob more roughly, and whispered again in his ear. The two left the temple, Matthew nearly dragging Jacob out.

I looked back to the center of the temple and saw that Lucy Grinder had joined the orgy. She was making out with Mary while Abraham continued fucking her.

I got up and walked over to Damian, who stood over the writhing orgy, his own robe hiked up and his erect penis in his hand.

"Is this all right?" I asked, utterly shocked.

"She's a big girl," said Damian, stroking his penis. "She knows what she's doing."

I could hear Jacob yelling in the other room, but I couldn't make out exactly what he was saying.

Jessica sat a short distance away, leaning against a wall in the corner of the room. She watched the whole scene blankly. I had no idea what she was thinking.

I felt extremely ill in the hot, incense-filled room, looking at this bizarre orgy. Abraham Crane grunted continuously as he crudely thrust himself in and out from between Mary's thighs.

Damian leaned over and began fondling Lucy Grinder's breasts as she continued to lock tongues with Mary. It all seemed completely unsavory and totally unsexy to me. I decided that since the whole thing had clearly descended into utter chaos there would be no harm in leaving. I left the temple and went back into the living room.

Fifty Two

9:05 P.M.

"This is bullshit!" shouted Jacob Pilsner. "This is my house! This is disgusting!"

"Jacob, please calm down," said Matthew. His voice was tranquil, clearly modulated in an attempt to keep Jacob from losing his mind completely.

I stood as far away from them as possible, but this was rather hard. The living room wasn't very big. They didn't seem to notice me anyway.

"I'm not going to fucking calm down!"

"This is an Astarte ritual, this kind of thing can happen," said Matthew.

"I'll tell you what happened," said Jacob. "You fucking drugged my girlfriend! That's what happened. She's out of her fucking mind!"

"She took an invocation," said Matthew, suddenly struggling to keep himself from getting upset.

"She took a bunch of Ecstasy!"

The temple door opened and Jessica Burnham came out, quickly walking over to me.

"I understand that you're upset," said Matthew.

"Now Damian's fucking her," said Jessica quietly in my ear.

"Upset!" shouted Jacob. "Upset doesn't even begin to describe this!"

"Please calm down, Jacob. It's sex magick. Sex magick is a part of what we do," said Matthew.

"That's not sex magick," spat Jacob as he pointed toward the temple door. "That's magical rape!"

"Astarte is a sexual goddess. Astarte rituals often get sexual."

"Not at my house! Not with my girlfriend!"

"I totally understand how you feel," said Matthew.

"No you don't."

"Look." Matthew took a deep breath. "I'm sorry you're so upset Jacob, but you have to remember- Mary's made it clear to you a hundred times she's not going to be exclusive with you."

Jacob looked like he wanted to say something, or scream something, but instead his face dropped. He began to fume quietly, panting and wheezing. "I fucking hate ecstasy," he said softly. "It makes me feel crazy." Tears welled up in his eyes. "I just want her to love me, you know?" The tears rolled down his cheeks.

Matthew reached for Jacob and hugged him. "I know."

Jacob flopped his head onto Matthew's shoulder and sobbed.

Jessica turned to me with a frown. "I want to get the hell out of here."

I completely agreed. We threw on our clothes and ran for the door.

Fifty Three

9:45 P.M.

The ride back to Jessica's was incredibly long. Except for a few brief attempts at conversation, we mostly just sat in silence. The situation was almost too strange to even discuss, but Jessica did try to explain it all in some way.

"Things aren't always like this," she said quietly. "I hope you aren't getting too bad an impression. It's just been really crazy lately."

"I understand," I said, but I felt like I was beginning to get an idea why the A∴R∴T∴ had such an unsavory reputation. Still, everyone was so nice, individually. We drove along without talking anymore for quite some time, until Jessica eventually broke the silence again.

"Mary does like to fuck everybody, though."

"Does Jacob always freak out like that?" I asked, feeling quite sorry for him.

"He's not always right in the room."

"Do you think everything's going to be all right?"

Jessica didn't answer right away. She stared out at the coming traffic. "I don't know," she said. "I don't know."

I closed my eyes.

10:03 P.M.

I must have fallen asleep, because the next thing I remember was Jessica jabbing me with her elbow.

"Wake up," she said harshly. "Big Problem."

She pulled the car to the side of the road. We were less than a block away from her house. Jessica pointed ahead and I saw two black vans parked right in front of her house. Several men were milling in and out of her open front door.

"Fuck," I said.

"Fuck is right. It's a good thing I don't have anymore coke up there."

"What should I do?" I felt frozen in absolute panic.

"You better get out of here!"

"Where should I go?"

"How the hell should I know?" said Jessica with an irritated shrug.

I felt completely lost. I had nowhere left to go. If the FBI was here- how the hell did they find me so fast? Nothing was safe anymore.

"Listen," said Jessica. "Make yourself scarce for a while. I'll try to see exactly what's going on here, and then I'll meet you down at the Davis Square T-Station. You know where that is, right?"

"Yeah, just a few blocks away."

"Give me an hour or so."

"Okay." I tried to lean in and kiss her, but she retreated back.

"You better get going before someone notices us."

"Right."

"Don't be obvious when you get out."

"Right." I quickly opened and closed her door, and walked swiftly away from her house. I had no idea where to go at this hour. I had no idea what was about to happen to Jessica. Would she even be able to meet me? Maybe they would arrest her for harboring a fugitive or something. I walked as fast as I could. It was getting very cold.

 Fifty Four

10:17 P.M.

The Somerville area was pretty unfamiliar to me, and I really didn't want to get lost. At the same time I didn't want to just walk around in circles, so I made my way down to Davis Square directly.

The cobblestone streets were well populated with college students and young couples, laughing and enjoying the evening. No one took any particular notice of me. I was so disconnected, a ghost amongst the living. I felt invisible. I hoped I was also invisible to the FBI.

As I walked aimlessly through the crowds I suddenly noticed something that nearly made my head spin. Across the street there was a coffee shop. And sitting in that coffee shop was Adin Stone. I rushed through the traffic to the coffee shop and ran inside. There he was, sipping a drink from a lavender mug. A profound de ja vous took hold of me as I realized this was the exact coffee shop from my dream. The homeless woman buying coffee with change, the laughing couple, it was all exactly the same.

"Hello, Alex," said Adin with a warm smile.

"What the hell is going on?" I demanded.

"What do you mean?"

"This coffee shop! You! I was here, yesterday, in a dream!"

"Yes, I remember."

"What? What do you mean you remember?" I was utterly confused. "That was a dream!"

"Yes, yes, of course it was a dream," said Adin. "I'm really amazed that it's so hard for you to grasp all of this. You're such a natural magician."

"What? What am I supposed to understand?"

The happy couple stopped laughing and began to stare at me. I didn't care.

"Don't be upset, Alex," said Adin. "I'm here to help you."

"Well, you haven't been much help so far."

"Please sit."

I didn't sit. I couldn't sit. "Tell me what's going on! Am I going crazy?"

"No, of course not."

"Then what's happening?"

"You are learning magick. I am your guide, your teacher, from the brotherhood. Your guide on the inner planes."

"The inner planes?" I looked around and saw that everyone in the coffee shop was staring at me. "Am I the only one that can see you?"

"Yes, most likely."

I couldn't believe it. "No! That's not possible. I've called you on the phone. You gave me your number!"

"In dreams," said Adin calmly. "I've told you that our communications take place somewhere between the land of dreams and reality."

The bottom was completely dropping out of my world. "Then I'm going crazy! You're a hallucination!"

"No, no, no, Alex," said Adin in a pacifying tone. "I am an adept from the interior order. You are perfectly sane."

"What do you want from me?" I said, backing toward the door. I was sure that I was losing my mind.

"I want to help you. I'm here to help you."

"Why did you let me believe you were real?"

"I am real in the magical world."

Just then I noticed the guy behind the counter reaching for a phone- no doubt to call the police. I was loudly shouting at thin air, after all.

"I've got to get out of here," I said. I rushed out the door of the coffee shop. Adin followed right behind me.

"You're in terrible danger," said Adin, catching up to me.

"No shit," I said.

"You are about to be apprehended by the FBI if you don't listen to me," said Adin gravely.

I stopped walking and faced Adin directly. "If you're such a great adept why don't you just tell me who's responsible for these murders? That'd be a real help!"

"That's not possible," said Adin.

"Of course not," I shouted. "Because you're a fucking hallucination and I'm fucking insane! There probably weren't even any murders! I'm just a god-damned lunatic!" I started walking away fast, but Adin stayed right on my heels. My whole concept of reality was crashing down around me. I was falling into an abyss, and Adin was cheerfully following me into my ruin.

"I am neither omniscient nor omnipotent, Alex, though I have certainly experienced both at critical moments. But I am here to help you. You have to understand, Alex. There is more to this situation than just you and your problems," said Adin.

"I realize that, god damn it!" In the distance I saw the Davis square T-station, just across the street and about a block up on the left.

"Yes, Alex, get on the train, right now," said Adin forcefully.

I began to jog toward the station. I didn't know what else to do. Adin kept right up with me as I crossed at a light.

"Keep going, Alex. We can get through this," said Adin.

I saw Jessica, just beyond the station, looking around nervously. I stopped. She really looked terrified. I'd never seen her look like that before. What the hell was going on? Then she saw me. She looked at me fiercely with those cold blue eyes of hers. She shook her head, almost imperceptibly. I didn't know what she was trying to communicate, but I knew it couldn't be good.

"Get on the train, Alex!" said Adin, still right beside me. "Just go!"

I ran for the bright metal doors of the station and pushed my way inside. I reached into my pockets, searching for change. I didn't have enough quarters.

"There's no time for that," said Adin. He ran past me, vaulting over the subway turnstile as nimbly as an acrobat.

I held my breath and followed him, stumbling clumsily over the chrome spokes of the turnstile.

"Hey, wait!" shouted the elderly man behind the enclosed glass counter.

I kept running. Adin and I bolted down the tiled hallway to the trains. The doors were just starting to close on an inbound train. I threw myself against the left-hand door, squeezing myself inside before the doors closed all the way. I sat down breathlessly. Adin sat down beside me and silently pointed out the window.

Several men in FBI windbreakers spilled out onto the platform, just as the train was pulling away. I'd escaped, though barely, and for how long I didn't know.

Fifty Five

10:30 P.M.

I looked around the train car and discovered it was totally empty. Even Adin had disappeared. I sat breathlessly on the red padded seats of the train car, completely and utterly exhausted. My mind was numb. What the hell was I going to do now?

The train arrived at the next stop- Porter Square. A tinny robotic voice announced the station in an incomprehensible garble. The doors creaked open. My heart raced. Were FBI agents about to come on board, pulling me off to who knows where?

Instead, three teenage boys clomped onboard, followed by an elderly black woman. They all sat far away from me, the teenagers laughing loudly about some private joke. They sounded drunk. A pretty woman in her twenties got on just as the doors were closing. She sat just a few seats away from me and smiled at me as she sat. I couldn't even crack a smirk in return. My body felt dead.

As the train started moving again the teenage boys started talking to the pretty woman, harassing her with sexual innuendoes, but I wasn't able to even pay attention. My thoughts raced in meaningless circles.

Somewhere between Porter Square and Harvard Square, the train suddenly stopped. It just ground abruptly to a halt. The lights went out for a moment, causing the teenagers to shout raucously. I knew this couldn't be good. My heart raced. A few moments later the lights came back on and the teenage boys started to boo loudly. Then the train doors opened- opened into the darkness.

I felt like a trapped animal, about to be hunted down and killed. I thought for sure that it was just a matter of time before FBI agents stormed the train. But what the hell was I supposed to do now?

I gripped the armrest hard for comfort, and looked out the open doors, waiting. But then I saw Adin Stone, out in the darkness of the tracks.

"Alex! Come on! You've got to run!"

I knew it had to be madness, but everything else had gone mad, and there didn't seem to be any reason to hesitate now. So I listened. I got up from my seat, and leapt out of the train car onto the tracks.

"Dude, what the fuck are you doing?" I heard one of the teenagers shout.

I didn't bother to reply. Adin ran up ahead and I followed as fast as I could. The air was stale, like old smoke and tar. The tunnel was dimly lit by widely spaced fluorescent lamps. I quickly noticed that the tunnel was crawling with life. Rats, mice, and pigeons fled from me with nearly every step. It was hard to make progress. The thick wooden beams holding the tracks together were widely spaced. I stumbled constantly. I felt like I could hardly breathe, but I kept going.

I soon lost sight of Adin. He was running much faster than I could. I was really a fugitive now, alone in a dark tunnel. There was no way of getting around it. I was running for my life. I couldn't tell if there were FBI agents right behind me, but I knew they were somewhere in the distance. I didn't dare to stop. All I could hear was the clatter of my footsteps, and the flapping, skittering and squeals of the tunnel creatures. I ran for a very long time.

Then I saw a brighter light ahead. I could hear music- an acoustic guitar, played badly, and an echoing, gravelly voice. It was Harvard Square.

I reached the underground platform, and painfully pulled myself up from the tracks. A fairly large crowd of people stood waiting for the train. A scruffy street musician sat playing his guitar on a thick wooden bench. My heart thudded noisily in my chest and throat. Everyone looked at me curiously as I knelt breathless on the platform, but no one said a word.

I didn't have any idea where to go, but I knew I had to keep moving. I walked swiftly up the red brick inclined path to the main part of the station. I looked around wildly, hoping not to see any FBI agents or police. I saw none. Dozens of people milled through the station, none taking any notice of me. I was nobody. And I had nowhere to go.

Fifty Six

10:48 P.M.

I desperately wanted to just go home. I knew there was a bus out of Harvard Square that would take me right into Arlington. I'd taken that bus hundreds of times. I could be home in less than an hour. But there was no going home now. That was the last place I could go.

But I had nowhere else to go either. Perhaps it was lunacy, but I decided to get on that bus. Why not? I would go back to Arlington. Maybe they wouldn't expect that. I wouldn't go home. I'd just go near home. There wouldn't be any harm in that.

I walked up the turning slope to the bus terminal, and saw my bus, the 61, coming down the tunnel. That was a stroke of luck. I ran to the stop and got on board just in time. I threw the last of my change into the receptacle and sat down in utter exhaustion as the bus began to pull out of the station. Hopefully no one had noticed me.

As the bus toddled along down Mass. Ave. I took a good look at myself. The feverish run down the train tunnel had left me truly filthy. A dark gray coating of grime covered my whole body.

What the hell had I gotten myself into? I just wanted my old, boring life back. What could I possibly do now? It was just a matter of time before I'd be caught. I couldn't run forever. I didn't even have any money. Just a few dollars in my wallet. That was all.

I looked around at my fellow passengers. There were half a dozen other people riding the bus with me. They seemed as lost as I was. Gray, lifeless, none of us had anywhere to go.

I rode the bus all the way to the end of the line- Arlington Heights. My house, and most importantly my bed, were just a few blocks away. But that may as well have been a million miles. I might never see my bed again. I couldn't help but wonder what my poor mother was thinking. Hopefully Peter explained something to her. I'm sure she would never believe anything bad about me. She loved me unconditionally. I suddenly felt guilty that I rarely paid any attention to my mother. She was always there for me. I was a terrible son. Perhaps this whole thing was just a punishment for me being such a rotten person. If I were a better person I would have more friends. I'd have somewhere to go. My whole life seemed empty and meaningless. I got off the bus and looked around hopelessly. Where on earth could I go now?

Then it occurred to me. My old fort. There was a forested conservation area behind my house, and I'd built a wooden fort in there as a kid. It was a fairly small fort, just some plywood and two by fours crudely hammered together, but it was sort of a shelter. I used to go there sometimes as a teenager, to drink beer and smoke pot with friends- back when I had friends. It was probably still there. That might be just the place to go. I knew I could be safe there- at least for a little while.

I walked away from the bus depot to the bike path that runs parallel to Mass. Ave., the very path where I'd encountered the spirit. I hoped I wouldn't see anything like that again. I turned off the path into the woods, wondering if I could still remember how to find the old fort. Each step into the forest gave me a greater sense of dread. I felt watched, as if someone, or some-thing, was in the forest with me. I tried to put the idea out of my head, though I found myself looking all around me, hunting for a watcher in the darkness. But I saw no one. I didn't even see any strange shadows.

In just a short time I stumbled upon the fort. It had been pretty heavily covered with graffiti and broken in a few places. Clearly I wasn't the only person who knew about this fort, but at least it was still here. As long as it didn't rain, I could spend the night. I was truly exhausted, probably insane, and totally alone. I crawled into the fort, smoked a cigarette, and fell asleep instantly.

Fifty Seven

I stood before the stairway; its black and white checkered stairs leading up to the portal of stars. I tried to mount the stairs, but once again found myself unable to make any progress.

I realized that I was dreaming almost immediately. It was like a blast of fresh air when you've been stuck in a stuffy room. Suddenly everything seemed so clear and easy. I took a step onto the stairs. Then another. There was no resistance. I was actually getting closer to the portal of stars. It seemed like the answers to all my problems were just beyond that portal, no matter where it led.

"Alex!" came a fevered cry from somewhere behind me.

I tried to ignore it. I didn't recognize the voice, and I was just about to finally make it up those damned stairs.

"Please! Alex! Help me!" shrieked the voice again. I couldn't help but turn to look.

Matthew Wiley was at the bottom of the staircase, pinned to the ground by a large, black, dog-like creature with the wings of a raven. The creature's skin seemed iridescent, insect-like. Its clawed fingers held Matthew's arms down, as grayish drool poured freely onto Matthew's face from between the creature's large black teeth. It turned to me as I stared at it, and its twisted face seemed to smirk arrogantly.

I looked back at the portal. I was so close to getting through. Still, I couldn't just let Matthew be killed by that demonic creature. I turned away from the starry gateway and tried to climb back down toward Matthew. I found that I couldn't make any progress toward him. Now I couldn't seem to get down the stairs! But I still somewhat recognized that I was dreaming. This was my dream. There had to be some way to take control.

I leapt into the air and found myself able to stay aloft, though I felt myself sinking slowly. With an effort of will I managed to float slowly downward toward Matthew and the creature. There was a tight knot in my stomach, as if my flight was somehow maintained by an abdominal exertion.

Seeing me approach, the demonic creature casually tore off Matthew's right arm, tossing the arm into its mouth and crunching the bones effortlessly. Matthew shrieked in terror and pain. The creature reached a clawed hand into Matthew's stomach like it was a bowl of peanuts, pulling out intestines and devouring them.

"Help me! God, please," shrieked Matthew over and over again.

I flung myself onto the creature's back. I was tossed around by the flapping of its bristly wings. I couldn't even hold on, much less stop the beast. The creature turned and eyed me with its smug grin. Matthew's bodily fluids dribbled all over the creature's face.

"This hasn't happened yet," shrieked Matthew. "You can stop this!"

With that the demonic creature turned its attention back to Matthew and bit off his whole head in one bite.

Fifty Eight

⊙ Sunday, October 6, 1996

4 or 5 A.M.

I woke up in terror, the hard, dirty floor of the fort pressing against my face. I sat up immediately. It was still dark out. I didn't know how long I'd been asleep, but my limbs were already aching and I felt awful.

What the hell did that dream mean? Was Matthew really about to die? Jeremy had died when I dreamed about him dying. Could Matthew actually be in danger? Could I even prevent Matthew from getting killed if the danger was real? I certainly hadn't been able to stop anything in the dream. But if Matthew was truly about to die, and I could stop it somehow, surely I had to try.

I poked my head out of the fort and looked more carefully at the sky. It was definitely still fairly dark, but I could see the gray of dawn looming in the east. What was I supposed to do now? I was a fugitive. I had no car and no money. How could I even tell anybody?

I really wished that Adin Stone would come back. Hallucination or not, I felt incredibly alone, and Adin's company would at least have given me some sense of hope.

I knew that the bike path led straight to Arlington Center, and practically right to the police station where Peter worked. It would be a long walk, and I felt like I could barely even stand. Still, I could probably get there before the sun was completely up if I started walking right away. I could wait for Peter to come in, if he was even working today, and stop him before he got

264

into the station. Maybe he wouldn't have to arrest me. Maybe I could convince him to believe me. Maybe he could convince the FBI. It was a pretty shaky plan, a lot of maybes, but it was the best I could come up with under the circumstances. It was all I had. I struggled to my feet and set out toward the bike path immediately.

No one was on the path. It was still too early, even for joggers. Still, I pulled the hood of my sweatshirt tightly around my head, hoping that it might somehow make me invisible.

As I walked up the path I felt truly terrible. I was cold, exhausted and hungry. Each step was an agonizing test of everything that I was. I just wanted to lie down on the side of the path and pass out. But I couldn't stop now. I knew my life, and maybe Matthew Wiley's, depended upon this walk.

It took forever, but I finally reached Arlington Center. The sun still hadn't come up, and the streets were empty. I saw the police station in the distance, just a block away, and I didn't dare go any closer. For all I knew there was a life size 'wanted' poster of me right inside the door. I found a bench and sat down to wait.

Waiting was almost harder than walking. It was nearly impossible to keep my eyes open. There were no pedestrians anywhere in sight. Just a few trucks occasionally drove by. The wait was endless.

6:15 A.M. (approx.)

As the sun began to rise, it occurred to me that there might be some sort back parking lot for the police officers. From where I was sitting I might not even be able to see Peter come in. That could ruin everything. I had to spot Peter, even if it took me all day. I stood up and carefully made my way a little closer to the building, just to scope out the situation. As I neared the station, the door opened and two men emerged. My heart leapt into my throat, pounding so forcefully that I felt almost sure the two men might hear it. I backed away, leaning behind some bushes.

Then I realized that one of the two men was actually Peter. I was once again amazed by my luck. The hand of fate was certainly on my side, and I breathed a silent sigh of relief. Somehow

I was going to make this work. But they were heading away from me, talking and laughing. I didn't know what to do. I couldn't just go up to them. I had no idea who the other man was. Peter might be forced to arrest me, right then and there, to avoid getting into some sort of trouble.

They were quickly getting away from me, so I followed them, staying as far away as I could without losing sight of them. They turned a corner into an alley, and I momentarily lost sight of them.

I rushed to the alley and tentatively looked around the corner. A hot flush washed over my face. I almost felt faint. I couldn't see where they had gone. I'd lost them. Was fate now suddenly mocking me? I was terrified to walk through the open alleyway, totally exposed. They could appear from around the corner on the other side at any time. But I really had no choice now. I cautiously stepped forward into the alley and moved toward the back of the buildings. It was truly nerve-wracking. I knew that I could be spotted at any time. I felt I was in enemy territory, exposed and vulnerable.

When I reached the end of the alley I peered out from between the buildings and saw a large, mostly empty parking lot. Peter was standing at an open car door with his back turned to me. The other man sat in the driver's seat of the car, facing me directly. Luckily he was engrossed in talking to Peter and didn't seem to notice me at all.

I crept back into the alley, flopped down beside a dumpster and froze. My mind was completely numb. I couldn't think of anything to do. If Peter got into that car, I would lose him. But I couldn't move. I closed my eyes, took a few deep breaths, and tried to calm down.

"Alex," said a calm voice beside me. I nearly had a heart attack. It was Adin Stone.

"Where the hell have you been?" I demanded in a harsh whisper. "I thought you were supposed to help me."

"I'm trying to help," said Adin.

"I've got to talk to Peter. I think there's going to be another murder. He's right over there." I pointed toward the parking lot, and Adin's eyes followed my hand.

"Actually, he's coming right this way," he said with a smile.

Adin was right. I looked and saw that Peter was coming right toward me.

"Peter," I said, still whispering as he approached.

He looked completely shocked to see me. "Alex? Is that you?"

"I really need your help, Peter," I said. "It's an emergency."

"You look like shit."

"I know. I slept in the woods."

Peter looked at me with tired eyes. He seemed exhausted. He shook his head slowly, and started muttering quickly at me, staring at the pavement beneath our feet. "I'm just getting off duty right now, but I think I have to take you in. The special agents from the FBI have been all over me. Nice guys, but man do they have it hot for you. You're in serious shit. You ran through the fucking Porter Square tunnel? What were you thinking? I think I'm going to have to place you under arrest. I'm sorry."

I'd been afraid he was going to say something like that. But it didn't even matter. It didn't matter what he thought about me, or even what happened to me. I couldn't keep running forever. I just had to tell him about Matthew. "Fine, that's fine," I said breathlessly. "You can take me in, I don't care, but you just need to listen to me first. I think there's about to be another murder. Or maybe it's already happened by now. I don't know. I know there's not much time."

"Tell me about it," said Peter, quickly back to business.

I described my dream, and gave him the full details of my previous dream so that he would have a reference point. I was really amazed at how easily Peter believed my story. He didn't even arrest me. He told me that a story like the one I'd just told was something we were better off exploring outside of the structures of the police department. I wasn't sure where Matthew lived, but luckily Peter had some of his case files in his car. Matthew lived in Cambridge, less than ten minutes away. Within moments we were in his car on the way to Matthew Wiley's house.

Fifty Nine

7:22 A.M.

As we pulled up in front of his house, an unexpected sight stunned me. Steve Curtin was walking down the street, away from Matthew's house. It looked very much like he could have left through the front door moments before we arrived. It could have been something else entirely, but I couldn't imagine what else he would be doing walking past Matthew's house so early in the morning. I didn't say anything about it to Peter. There had to be some reasonable explanation why Steve was there. Steve was a nice guy. He couldn't possibly have anything to do with these murders.

Peter shut off the car engine and turned to me. "Listen," he said sternly. "You stay here. Don't move."

"What are you going to do?"

"I've been thinking, this thing is nuts. I saw a phone booth up the street, and I'm gonna call the police. This is way out of my jurisdiction. I don't even have my side arm. I definitely need some back up."

"Okay, but hurry," I said nervously.

"You stay here. Do you understand me?"

"Yes, of course."

"Under no circumstances are you to leave this car unless I tell you to."

"I understand. Jeesh."

"After I call the Cambridge police I'm going to go knock on the door. And you're still going to stay here."

I rolled my eyes and leaned back in my seat. Peter disappeared up the street and I sat staring at the house, wondering what was waiting inside. It certainly didn't seem like any demonic activity was going on. It was just a brick two-story apartment house, just like the brick two-story houses on either side of it. But I knew in my gut that something terrible was happening behind those doors, under the surface, between the lines.

And what did Steve Curtin have to do with all this? I decided that I really had to tell Peter I'd seen him. If he wasn't involved, he wouldn't have any problems. But if he was somehow mixed up in this, it wasn't right to withhold anything from Peter. Not now.

I eventually spotted Peter coming back up the street. He nodded to me without smiling, and walked up to Matthew's front door. He knocked. He knocked again. Nothing. I noticed him shuffling back and forth, wrestling with himself. I was sure that he wanted to go in, to kick in the door or something. He didn't, instead just walking back to me in the car.

"The Cambridge police are on the way. You can't stay here. I can't have you sitting in my car when they get here. That wouldn't be too smart for either of us."

I felt terrified. "What do you want me to do?" I didn't want to go back to running. I couldn't. Sitting in Peter's car had given me a sense of safety and peace, like everything was going to be okay. The idea of running around alone again gave me shivers.

"There's a Dunkin Donuts up the street just a little way. That's where I found the payphone. Go hang tight in there, and I'll meet you there once I know what's going on here."

So I went to Dunkin Donuts. As I sat sipping coffee, I realized that I'd still forgotten to tell Peter about seeing Steve Curtin.

Sixty

8:30 A.M. (Approx.)

I must have sat in Dunkin Donuts for at least an hour before Peter showed up. He looked exhausted and foul-tempered.

"You're probably going to cost me my job," he said, without even a hello.

His tone was chilling. "What's going on?" I asked, completely panicked. I knew the worst had to be true. I didn't even flinch at his next words.

"Your friend Matthew Wiley is dead. Shot in the head."

I couldn't speak. I hadn't known Matthew well, but I'd certainly known him better than I'd known the other two. This was all far too much for me. I was nauseous. Tears filled my eyes.

"And I had to lie for you... again," said Peter. "Said I'd received an anonymous tip- thought it was related to a case I was working on. But it doesn't all really add up. This isn't going to look good for me."

The image of Steve walking away from the house returned to me, and I knew I had to tell Peter. But I just couldn't bring myself to implicate Steve. He couldn't be involved.

"The second two murders were both gunshots," said Peter. He sat down heavily on the bench at the pink and gray plastic Dunkin Donuts table with me. "Totally different M. O. from the first murder. They might not even be related." He buried his head in his hands.

"They have to be, don't they?" I asked.

"I don't know, Alex. I just don't know anymore."

The Brotherhood of Light and Darkness

I'd never heard Peter sounding like this. I tried to be consoling. "You'll figure it out. We'll figure this thing out. I know we will." But I didn't sound very convincing. I was exhausted, crashing fast. I wasn't sure about anything anymore either.

"I'm gonna take you back to my place," said Peter. "Let you take a shower and get some rest. You really look like shit. Meantime, I've got some work to do. I've got a buddy on the job in Cambridge. I'm gonna see if I can get into that crime scene."

Sixty One

8:45 A.M.

Peter and Therese lived in a small, second-story, one bedroom apartment in East Arlington. The floors were entirely covered in yellowed linoleum. The whole place was six hundred square feet or less. I think it all might have been one room originally, with additional walls added to turn it into a tiny apartment.

Thankfully my sister Therese was out shopping or something when we got there. Talking to her was the last thing I wanted to do. I knew she'd just try to make me feel guilty about this whole thing and do her best to create problems. Peter gave me some clean towels, told me to rest up, and was quickly out the door.

I was very grateful for the shower and the bed. Once I'd scrubbed away the grime from my body, I took a nice long nap. It was a deep, comatose sleep. Thankfully, I don't think I dreamed at all.

2:30 PM

Peter woke me by shaking my shoulder. It took a long time for me rouse myself enough to remember where I was or what was going on.

"Come on, Alex," said Peter. "Wake up. I need to talk to you.

I forced my eyes open. The sun was shining right on me through the open blinds in the bedroom, and I squinted uncomfortably.

"Sorry, Alex," said Peter. "But we've got to talk. I got to look at some of Matthew's things."

Everything came rushing back to me. All the murders, Adin being a hallucination or something, my bizarre dreams, the insanity of it all. Peter kept talking to me, but at first I couldn't even follow what he was saying. I was trapped inside a bubble of my own racing thoughts and fears. Finally, I managed to focus on his words.

"And he also had a bunch of papers related to that Paul Mackey group you told me about- the Black Pullet Lodge. There was a bunch of correspondence between him and Mackey, rituals, membership rosters, instructions-"

"I'm sorry," I said groggily. "I wasn't following you. Did you just say that Matthew Wiley was involved with the Paul Mackey and the Black Pullet Lodge?"

"That's what it looks like," said Peter. "You might even be right about Mackey being a part of this."

I couldn't get my head around it. Was Matthew Wiley a spy for Mackey? He sure didn't seem like a spy. Or did he? Or was he spying on the Black Pullet Lodge for the A∴R∴T∴? This was all so strange. I didn't know what to think. But I hadn't known what to think for a while now. Then I remembered that Steve told me he'd been in the Black Pullet Lodge before he was in the A∴R∴T∴. And Steve was at Matthew's this morning!

"Peter. There's something I forgot to tell you. I saw someone from the A∴R∴T∴ this morning while we were at Matthew Wiley's."

"What? Who? Why didn't you tell me this before?" Peter's face tightened.

"I'm sorry. I was just so exhausted. I forgot."

"Who the hell did you see?"

"A guy named Steve Curtin," I said hesitantly. "But I- I don't think he could be involved in this. I don't know. I don't know anything for sure anymore."

After scowling at me silently for an inordinately long period of time Peter picked up a briefcase and opened it on the bed in front of me. He began rifling through a stack of papers. "I've got a file from the Feds," said Peter. "One of the special agents was a decent guy. Gave me some of their interview transcripts. I seem to remember seeing something from Steve Curtin. Yes, here it is. There's a red flag- a discrepancy in his interview. He said he was alone in his apartment at the time of the two murders... the first two murders. But when interviewed, two other people said he was with them at those times."

"Who are the other two?

"Uh, Lucy Grinder and Abraham Crane," said Peter, rifling papers. "At the time of the first murder, Abraham Crane stated that he and- huh, that's strange." Peter scanned through the documents several times.

"What?"

"Abraham Crane stated that he was with Steve Curtin and Matthew Wiley at the time of the first murder. Some sort of meditation retreat. What do you think that means?"

"I have no idea," I said. "What about Lucy Grinder?"

"She states that she was in her apartment with Steve Curtin at the time of the second murder."

I was confused. Why would Steve lie? Or were the other two lying? I didn't really know Lucy Grinder at all. I'd hardly spoken to her. But I did know one thing about her.

"Lucy Grinder lives at Abraham Crane's house," I said. "She rents an apartment upstairs in his house."

"This may be something."

"I know where Steve Curtin lives. I've been to his house," I said. "Maybe we should go talk to him."

"Alex," said Peter, immediately taking on a scolding tone. "This is now a police matter. You just stay here and rest. I can't be carting you around. You're in enough shit as it is. How would I explain it?"

"Look," I said. "I don't think Steve is a murderer. I really don't."

"Even if that's true-"

"I can help! I know I can! He won't talk to you, I know it, but maybe he'll talk to me if I'm there."

"I'm pretty sure I know how to make him talk."

"I'm his friend. I can get him to tell the truth."

"No way."

"Look," I said, sternly. "I thought you said you wanted to solve this thing. You asked me for my help and I'm trying to give it to you. But every time I try to help you try to stop me. Well, no more." Peter started to open his mouth but I just kept going, raising my voice until I was practically yelling. "If you want to spend the next few weeks talking to Steve's fucking lawyers, go ahead. Just go and try to get something out of him on your own. I wish you all the fucking luck in the world. But if you want to get to the bottom of this, close this case, maybe today, then take me with you because I know he'll talk to me. He's my fucking friend. He'll talk to me and he sure as hell won't fucking talk to you. We occultists don't trust cops. I guarantee it." It felt good to finally let myself fully speak my mind.

Peter looked at me like he was seeing me for the first time. I could tell I'd somehow broken through a wall, that he was actually now considering me on a fully human level. I knew that I'd won. Peter was going to let me come. He frowned, rolled his eyes and shook his head. "I think you're definitely going to cost me my job."

Sixty Two

We arrived at Steve's house. Peter parked right out front, and we stayed in the car a few minutes, watching. There was movement inside, a shadow on the curtain hanging behind the front door.

"Looks like someone's home," said Peter. He opened the car door and got out. I followed behind him as he walked up to the front door and rang the doorbell. A few seconds later Steve appeared at the door. He only opened it a crack.

"Hello?" said Steve cautiously as he stared at Peter. He didn't seem to notice me. His eyes seemed hollow, rimmed with red. He looked exhausted.

"I'm Detective Peter Ippolito with the Arlington Police Department. Could I have a few words with you?"

"I've already talked to the FBI," said Steve. He sounded apprehensive. He hardly looked like himself at all.

"Yeah, well we have a few more questions for you," said Peter.

Steve turned his eyes to me for the first time. He looked stunned, then relieved. "Alex?" He smiled at me weakly, clearly confused.

"Steve, this is my brother-in-law Peter," I said.

"Detective Peter Ippolito," said Peter, reflexively pulling out his badge and showing it to Steve.

"It's okay Steve," I said. "Honest. We just need to talk to you for a few minutes. Thing is, Steve, I saw you this morning at Matthew's house."

With that, the last remnants of Steve's façade cracked apart. He buried his head in his hands and began to sob loudly. "I don't know how this all happened," he said. "None of this was supposed to-" Steve kept his head in his hands and wept silently for several seconds. "It all just went crazy!"

"Let's all go inside," said Peter, his tone soft and soothing. "Relax and talk this over." Peter took hold of Steve gently by the shoulder and led him into the front hallway. I was surprised to see that Peter took control of the situation so calmly and efficiently. Perhaps he was more capable than I'd given him credit for. I followed, closing the door behind us. Steve's apartment was in total disarray. Two suitcases sat in the hallway, partially packed.

"Going somewhere?" asked Peter. He sounded fairly casual, but I could hear the slight hint of accusation underneath.

Steve looked up at Peter, wild-eyed. Tears flowed freely down his face. "If I talk to you, you've got to protect me."

Peter eyed him calmly. "That depends on what you have to say."

"No!" shouted Steve. He backed away from Peter like a caged animal, wiping the stream of tears from his cheeks. "I'm not saying shit unless you promise that I'm going to be protected! And that you're not going to try to prosecute me for shit! Because I didn't fucking do anything!" Steve leaned against the wall in his front hall, again burying his head in his hands. "I had nothing to do with any of it. I swear!" He moaned painfully, sobbing through his fingers.

"I believe you," I said, walking over to him. Peter eyed me fiercely, agitated. I could tell he really wanted me to stay the hell out of it. But I couldn't do that. I softly touched Steve's shoulder. "We just need you to help us figure this thing out."

"There's nothing to figure out," said Steve between his fingers. "Abe Crane is a fucking psychopath!" He flopped down onto the floor, continuing to weep. I sat down beside him.

"Are you saying that Abraham Crane is responsible for these murders?" Peter asked briskly.

"I'm not fucking saying anything," spat Steve. "Not until you tell me I'm going to be protected!"

"You'll protect him," I said. "Won't you Peter?"

Peter's face looked hard at first, but he eventually sighed. "Of course."

Steve looked up at him, his eyes red and swollen. "And you're not going to try to pin anything on me?" His voice was shaky.

"Not if you didn't do anything."

"Okay, well, it's hard to- well- I guess I just need to say it," said Steve. "My parents don't know- I'm not out to my parents at all. I don't want my parents to know anything about this."

"Don't worry Steve," I said.

"Okay, well- Abe was my boyfriend. At least I thought he was my boyfriend. I was so in love with him." Steve started to weep loudly again. "I really thought he loved me too." Steve continued to sob for quite some time without saying another word.

I looked up at Peter. He shrugged. We watched Steve silently weep for quite some time. His chest heaved unevenly, like a dying animal.

Finally he cleared his throat and started speaking again. "It was all so great at first. He taught me so much about sex magick. He was so wise- seemed so wise, anyway. He got me to quit the Black Pullet Lodge and join the A∴R∴T∴. God, I should have known!" Steve was now shouting. "Why didn't I see? I was so stupid!"

"What didn't you see?" I asked.

"That he was just using me," said Steve. "He was just trying to mess with Paul Mackey."

"How so?" asked Peter.

"They're both fucking drug dealers- In a major fucking way. Of course Abe is a lot bigger than Mackey- A hell of a lot bigger. But Mackey was constantly stealing customers, suppliers. I think Abe was only ever interested in me because he thought I might be able to help him figure out how Mackey was doing it. But I didn't know shit! I'm just a gay magician! A stupid, naïve, gay magician!" Steve sobbed some more.

"So, was Edward Bailey involved in this drug ring?" asked Peter.

"Yes, of course," spat Steve. "Jesus! Do you people know anything? Ed was one of Abe's little pushers. But I didn't know that at first either. We all started doing magick together. I thought it was just magick. And sex. But it was always really about the drugs. I know that now. I can see it so clearly now. We did a lot of demonic stuff. Black stuff- for power and money. It got fucking scary sometimes. When Abe's around those fucking demons are real- like you can see them- they can touch you. I was amazed by his power. He was a god to me." Steve wiped away more tears.

"So what happened?" I asked.

"Ed got fucking greedy. Said his stepmother was trying to contest his dad's will. To get him cut off. He said he needed more money out of Abe. Abe said no and..." Steve choked, unable to continue.

"And what?" demanded Peter.

"And Ed said he'd go to the cops if Abe didn't pay him. So-" Steve could barely speak through his sobs. "So Abe said he was going to destroy him with a demon- And he did! He fucking did it! He fucking destroyed him! I was there!"

"Are you trying to say that a demon killed Ed Bailey?" said Peter, clearly not quite believing him anymore.

Steve nodded his head, shivering. "Yes! Well, no, not exactly. We did a ritual, a ritual with Ed Bailey. Right in his house. He thought it was for him, but it was to kill him. We did a bunch of drugs, gave Ed even more." Steve closed his eyes, grimacing. "I fucked him. I fucked him to kill him. For Abe. Abe made me do it. I didn't completely understand what we were doing."

Peter eyed Steve in disgust and confusion. I didn't really know what to think either.

"Matthew was there, and Abe," said Steve.

"Matthew was involved in the drug dealing?" I asked.

"Yes," said Steve. "They both fucked him too. They chanted. They directed the energy. It wasn't my fault. I didn't think it could work, you know? But I told Ed to go crazy with protective symbols. And he did it too, on himself, all over the place, just to be sure he'd be safe. I hoped he'd be safe. I didn't want it to

279

work!" Steve threw himself forward, resting his head on the hardwood floor like he was trying to cool a burning fever. "I didn't think it would work," said Steve between sobs.

"What happened?" I said, desperately wanting to know what Steve was talking about.

"Just as I climaxed the doorbell rang. Ed freaked out. We didn't banish. We didn't finish. The doorbell interrupted us. We all went and hid in the bathroom. Ed answered the door. It was his stepmother. She got all freaked out by the symbols all over him, all over his apartment. She called him a Satanist- said he was putting the memory of his father to shame. She was fucking possessed! The demon had her! I know it! We all knew it! She was possessed by the demon and the demon tore Ed to pieces. We were right in the bathroom, heard it all, saw some of it. Ed started shouting at her. Just incoherent shit. He was pretty fucked up on drugs, fucked up from the ritual. There was a ritual dagger on the floor. That's how she started. But then she just fucking tore him to pieces with her bare hands. She was fucking possessed! And it was my fault as much as anyone's." Steve cried out in anguish. "I fucked him and he died!"

Peter and I looked at each other. I don't think either of us knew what to say or do.

Steve looked up at me, his eyes burning red like smoldering coals. "And Abe just smiled. He fucking smiled through the whole thing. I know I should have said something, done something, but I still loved him. I loved him so much. He was a god to me!"

"Where does Jeremy McClosky fit into all this?" asked Peter.

"He was dealing for Abe. Just on a small scale. To friends and what not."

Peter scowled. "Is everyone in the A∴R∴T∴ a drug dealer?"

"No. Abe, Jeremy, Matthew, Ed, I think that's it as far as I know locally. Abe didn't really even deal anything. He just arranged it all. But Abe has dealers all over the country. Mostly A∴R∴T∴ people from other temples."

"So who killed Jeremy?" I asked.

"Abe. But I only found that out yesterday. I'm not a part of this. I'm just the boyfriend."

"How did you find this out?" asked Peter.

"Abe told me, but I mean, I already knew, I guess, but I didn't want to know. You know? It was all just too much. But now I know for sure. He told me yesterday, and he told me he was going to kill Matthew. He said they'd become liabilities. I tried to stop it. To tell Matthew- something, but I was too late." Steve lost it again. He sobbed loudly.

"So you are stating that Abraham Crane is responsible for the murders of Jeremy McClosky and Matthew Wiley," said Peter. "He physically killed them. No demons or rituals involved?"

Steve nodded weakly.

"I'm going to need a written statement from you," said Peter. "You're going to have to come down to the station."

Steve nodded again.

Peter walked over to Steve and reached out a hand to him. "Let's go," he said. "This is my collar. I want this done now. I still don't know how I'm going to explain this all to my Captain."

"Hold on," said Steve. "There's more."

"Let's talk about it on the way."

Sixty Three

4:05 P.M.

We started back toward the Arlington police station in Peter's car. I sat in the back seat while Steve sat in the passenger seat next to Peter. For several minutes Steve fidgeted quietly in his seat, looking like he was struggling with something.

"What's wrong Steve?" I finally asked.

"It's just- well, I think Damian Webster might really be in danger," he said.

"Who's Damian Webster?" asked Peter.

"He's the head of the local A∴R∴T∴ group," I said.

"So what's he got to do with this?" asked Peter.

"Abe used Damian's gun to kill Matthew and Jeremy."

Peter pulled the car to the side of the road. "You've got my attention."

"I don't understand," I said. "I saw that gun at Damian's after Jeremy was killed."

Peter looked at me in irritation, but didn't say anything. It was perfectly obvious that I should have told Peter about that gun long ago, but it was now way past quibbling over my poor judgment.

"He put it back," said Steve. "But then he stole it again. I saw it. And he told me that Damian and I were the last two loose ends. He told me that today. Just before you got there. I mean I don't think he was saying he was going to kill me, but I don't know."

"Why didn't you tell me all this before?" asked Peter.

"I tried to," said Steve.

"Where is Abraham Crane now?"

"I think he was at home when he called me."

"Take me there immediately."

Sixty Four

6:35 PM

It was just starting to get dark when we arrived at Abraham Crane's. He lived in a large Victorian in Concord. Peter got out of the car with Steve and I following closely behind him. Peter knocked on the door loudly. No answer. Peter sighed heavily.

"I know where there's a key," said Steve. He walked to the side of the house, reached down, and turned over a false stone. He quickly pulled out a house key.

Peter shook his head. "I don't think I can go in there without probable cause, and I better call for back up anyway."

"Isn't what I've already told you enough probable cause?" asked Steve.

"I don't want to screw up this arrest. I can't screw this up. Not now."

"I'm allowed in this house," said Steve. "I practically live here. So, I can invite you in, right?"

Peter frowned, but he let Steve open the door. Peter took out his pistol and held it at his side, freeing the safety. We stepped inside.

"You two stay here," said Peter, and he started cautiously through the house.

The whole house had a grandfatherly feel. Paintings of wilderness scenes adorned the walls, and the furniture seemed ancient. The worn hardwood floors were covered with moldering Turkish rugs. I really wondered what Steve could possibly see in this old man. We both just stood there silently, frozen.

I could hear Peter creaking through the far rooms of the first floor. The place seemed very gloomy and foreboding in the twilight. No lights were on in the house.

As I looked around the living room it felt like the shadows were moving, as if they were somehow alive. I started to have a very creepy feeling in my stomach.

"This place is dangerous," said Steve quietly. "I've seen demons here." As he said that I saw a large shadowy shape move along the far wall, as if on cue.

"I think I just saw one," I whispered.

"It's not safe for us here."

I backed up against a wall, feeling very scared. As soon as my back touched the wall I felt a hand grip my arm. I thought it was Steve at first, but I looked over at him and both of his hands were in his pockets. I looked down at my arm in terror, but there was nothing there. The sensation vanished. My heart nearly burst out of my chest. It was getting darker, and in the darkness I saw shadows swarming.

There was suddenly a loud 'pop,' and muffled shouting.

"I think that was a gunshot," said Steve. The shadows swirled angrily all around us.

"What should we do?" I asked.

There were two more gunshots, and more muffled shouting.

"I've got to get out of here." Steve tried to head for the door, but he couldn't seem to move. I tried to run too, but I also found myself glued to the floor. I suddenly felt like I was dreaming. It was almost exactly the same sensation I'd experienced in my dreams. I just couldn't motivate my body to move. My muscles turned to jelly and my legs were in quicksand.

Several more gunshots rang out, and Peter hurdled into the room, gun in one hand, gripping his side with the other. His fingers were soaked in dark fluid.

"Crane is here," said Peter, choking. "Fucking shot me. I need fucking back up. I can't believe I let you talk me into just walking in here. Where's the god damn phone?"

Steve mutely pointed to a table in the distance. Peter stumbled toward the phone, then toppled over with a grunt. He struggled back up to his knees.

"I think something just fucking pushed me." Peter looked all around him. I could see the shadows swarming. Peter's eyes narrowed in pain and he gripped his side. "Fuck! I've never felt anything worse than this."

I tried to walk over to him, but I was hurled to the floor myself. Steve crumpled limply to the floor and buried his head in his hands. Peter reached up for the phone, but he never got his hand on it. Another loud 'pop' rang out and Peter doubled over onto the floor. Crane stood in the doorway, Damian's pistol in hand. Peter lay crumpled on the floor, unconscious, maybe dead for all I knew.

Crane eyed me menacingly. "You are really a pain in my neck," he said, turning the pistol on me. "So glad I won't have to deal with you anymore." And with that he pulled the trigger. But there was just an empty 'click.' I guess there were no more bullets in the gun. Crane looked down at the gun in irritation and tossed it away.

My heart started beating again. I looked over at Peter. His gun was lying on the floor next to him. It was only a few feet away from me.

I'd never even held a gun in my hand before, but I knew that I had to get my hands on it before Crane did. I tried to lunge for it, but I again found myself unable to move. I fell to the floor.

Abraham Crane laughed at me. It was a hard, wheezy, slow laugh. His utter contempt for me was absolute. Crane started moving toward Peter's gun himself. It was then that I noticed he was wounded too. He was limping as he walked toward me, his leg bleeding copiously at the thigh. He had to move right past me in order to get his hands on the gun, so I reached out and grabbed hold of his ankle. I pulled him down to the ground with me. He was stronger and more energetic than he looked for a man of his age. He punched me hard in the face, causing me to lose my grip on his ankle. He started for his feet, but I managed to get hold of his ankle again. I punched him as hard as I could in the thigh, right at his wound. He screamed and buckled over, then grabbed hold of me roughly. I tried to fight him off, but I found I could hardly move my arms. He got his hands around my throat and started choking me. I couldn't move at all. I felt the blood trapped in my head, a painful pressure in my jaw and sinuses. I couldn't breathe. I couldn't get him off of me. I felt faint, like I was starting to lose consciousness.

And then there was a gunshot. Abraham Crane fell on top of me with a moan, coughing and choking. I looked up and saw Steve standing over us with Peter's gun in his hand. He dropped the gun onto the floor and fell to his knees, weeping.

Abe soon stopped choking and sputtering. He didn't seem to be breathing at all. The room was silent, other than the sound of Steve's quiet sobs.

Sixty Five

8 PM

The police arrived, along with the fire department and an ambulance. Then the FBI arrived. Steve and I spent the rest of the night and into the morning detailing our story to an endless stream of interrogators. We must have told our story a half dozen times apiece before we were finally allowed to go home.

I managed to squeeze a bit of information out of Peter's boss before I left. Peter was at the hospital, in critical condition. No one was really sure if he was going to make it. Abraham Crane was also still alive, for the time being at least, also in critical care.

Ed Bailey's stepmother was picked up. She demanded a lawyer immediately and was refusing to talk.

☾ Monday, October 7, 1996

10:15 A.M.

When I finally arrived back at my house my mother held me tight for an inordinately long period of time. I let her hug me for as long as she wanted. She made me eat a whole plate full of fish sticks, even though I told her I wasn't feeling very hungry. But I never enjoyed fish sticks more than I did at that moment. As soon as I left the table I went upstairs and quickly dropped gratefully into sleep.

I stood before the black and white checkered stairs. I felt sure I could get to the top. I knew that I could make it to the portal of stars. I strode each stair confidently to the top. But as I reached the portal I hesitated. Before me stood a gateway into the unknown. My feet were right on the edge of an unfathomable infinity of stars. All I had to do was step through. But I somehow felt unsure.

"Alex," said the familiar voice of Adin Stone beside me. "It's time." He smiled at me warmly. "You're ready to go through this gate. It's time."

"What's on the other side?" I asked.

"The next step," said Adin, and with that he pushed me through the portal.

I found myself rushing in all directions, expanding and exploding all at once, splitting into thousands or even millions of pieces. I was flying at unbelievable speed, my consciousness spreading through solar systems, galaxies, toward infinity. I felt like everything was suddenly making sense to me in a much more real and powerful way than I could ever properly describe. The precise mathematical order and magnitude of the universe was literally a part of myself. I experienced the evolution of stars and planets within me. They were my thoughts, my cells, my neurons. The entire cosmos was within me.

But with my greater understanding of the cosmos came a rapid disintegration of everything that I considered my individual self. With an increased knowledge of the universal came an awareness of the lesser importance of the personal. I was becoming the universe, and I was becoming something beyond the universe. Alexander Sebastian was a speck, a molecule of water in an infinite ocean. I was expanding, shrinking, disintegrating, growing, and whirling all at once. I lost all sense of myself. I was everywhere, encompassing every particle in the universe, and I was also nowhere. I soon lost myself completely in a void of blackness.

When I awoke, I found myself lying in an alien landscape. It almost felt like I was on the moon. A pale, lavender sky loomed above me, starless and thick, like a velvet blanket. Empty hills and valleys stretched out before. I noticed that the gray landscape was shimmering softly, as if made up entirely of tiny diamonds.

Adin sat in front of me with his legs crossed and his arms folded in his lap. He grinned at me warmly. "Congratulations," he said.

"What did I just experience?"

"A taste of the totality of yourself. You've experienced the first glimpse of the true cosmic scope of your consciousness."

"It felt like I was going to pieces."

"Eventually you will come to a greater understanding of this state," said Adin. "But for now you have mastered the astral plane enough that you are beginning to experience the next stage in the teachings of the brotherhood, the next level of the interior order."

Everything that had happened in the last few weeks suddenly returned to my mind. I couldn't put it all together into a sensible image. "How does this all relate to the murders?" I asked. "What does this brotherhood have to do with all this?"

"I'm not entirely certain," said Adin. He sighed heavily, shaking his head. "But if what I darkly dare to guess is true, then this is just the beginning of something. All that we can do is continue forward. Unusual things are beginning to stir, and I feel more certain than ever that the A∴R∴T∴ will play a critical role in things to come. I can't say anymore."

"Why has this all happened to me?"

Adin smiled. "You have been working at this for many lives. You and I have known each other for quite a long while. You will come to remember more and more over time."

"I need to ask you another question," I said. "But please don't take this as rude."

"Sure," said Adin. "You can ask me anything."

"Why haven't you helped me more? I mean you're supposed to be helping me, right? You're some sort of teacher?"

"Yes, but there are very strict limits on our interactions. I cannot give you the answers to anything. I cannot solve your problems. I can only help you to deal with your challenges yourself."

"Are you going to continue talking to me?"

"Of course," said Adin, with a smile. "As much as I can. For as long as you wish to continue this journey."

"What is this journey?" I asked. "Where am I supposed to be going?"

"You are on the path to inner wisdom. You have taken the first steps toward self-knowledge in the interior order for this lifetime. In time you must take more initiations in the outer too. You have begun to walk a path with the A∴R∴T∴, and now you will have to complete it."

I'd have to think seriously about that one. My adventure in the A∴R∴T∴ had been a bit much so far. I began to feel a strange sensation I'd felt only once before. I was aware of myself, sitting here with Adin Stone, but I was also aware that I was lying in my bed at home. Adin smiled and winked at me. Both he and the dream landscape swiftly dissolved, as I felt myself falling back into my body completely. And just like that, I was once again alone in the darkness of my bedroom.

Sixty Six

Friday, October 11, 1996

12:36 P.M.

Almost a week passed after my final encounter with Abraham Crane. I didn't hear anything more about the situation.
Peter was still in the hospital, and though he was now apparently in stable condition, I felt a bit awkward going to visit him.
Especially just to find out what was going on with the murders.
Even my mother hadn't been to visit. Therese called several
times and kept us up to date.

I hadn't heard from Adin Stone at all either. I hadn't even
had any more strange dreams. I felt like my life was finally
getting back to normal. But I have to admit that I really missed
my magical adventure. I couldn't just go back to my old life.
Something in me had changed. I somehow knew that things
were going to keep transforming, and that soon I was going to
have to make a lot of changes in every aspect of my life.

But for now I was back working at the videostore. I was by
myself in the store; it was Melissa's lunch hour. There weren't
even any customers. I was completely alone, leaning wearily on
the counter. I felt stifled in this store. I couldn't imagine devoting
any more of my life to this boring job. But I really didn't have
any other plans for my future. Then, right in the middle of my
existential ruminations, the front door opened and someone very
unexpected walked in.

It was Paul Mackey. He lumbered through the doorway,
wheezing heavily. He looked at me and smiled painfully,

making his way toward the counter. Sweat poured down his face, and his shirt was soaking wet with perspiration.

"Jackie has the car, so I had to walk here. Quite a work out," said Mackey, puffing and gasping. "I was hoping I'd find you. Ninety-three, brother Sebastian."

"Hello," I said, not bothering to return his Thelemic greeting. I couldn't imagine why he'd want to talk to me. But I was sure that whatever it was, it would be unpleasant.

Mackey spent what seemed an inordinate length of time trying to catch his breath, coughing and sputtering quietly. But he finally got to the point. "So I heard that they've made some arrests on those recent homicides." He said it casually, but I could tell that he was trying to impress me.

I was very surprised, in spite of myself. "How did you hear that?"

"I've still got some friends on the job here in Arlington," said Mackey with a wide smile. He seemed very pleased with himself. As if having special connections somehow made him all the more important. "I guess that slime ball Crane broke down and confessed everything almost immediately. They read him Steve Curtin's statement and he just fell apart." Mackey chuckled in a dismissive gurgle. I guess he didn't think much of Crane. "Apparently Mrs. Bailey is still refusing to cooperate with the police. She's got some pretty noisy lawyers on her team. But she'll be going away for a long time. She didn't even bother to get rid of her bloody clothes. They found them in a hamper in the back of her garage!" Mackey laughed loudly, a phlegmy, wheezing cackle.

"Who told you all this?" I asked, still shocked that he seemed to have so much inside information.

"A few old friends," said Mackey. He shrugged casually. "A. P. D. owed me a favor anyway. I'm the one who gave them the tip that this thing was all about the A∴R∴T∴."

"You're the one who tipped them?"

"Of course!" Mackey chuckled again. He looked mildly embarrassed for me that I hadn't figured that out. "I was well aware of exactly what was going on the whole time. My dear friend Matthew was very helpful in keeping me informed."

Mackey sighed and looked down at the floor. He seemed genuinely troubled. "I'm going to miss Matthew."

I felt annoyed. "If you knew what was going on the whole time, why didn't you just tell the police everything?"

"Sebastian, I have my own interests to protect." Mackey shook his head, rolling his eyes as if I was very stupid. "Everything had to be uncovered in such a way that my activities wouldn't be exposed. Everything has really worked out perfectly, other than Matthew of course." He sighed again, and took a few slow breaths. He then smiled quite cheerfully. "But my business is really thriving already. I must thank you."

"No need," I said flatly.

"It was touch and go for a while though. I was very concerned when I saw you waving around those symbols from the crime scene. At first I thought I should try to get rid of you. But then I realized it was smarter to just help you to help me."

"You helped me?" I couldn't believe he was saying that. I was sure he was trying to sabotage me at every turn.

"Of course I helped you! I got Matthew to rush your paperwork so that you'd be initiated into the A∴R∴T∴ right away."

I couldn't believe it. Matthew told me I had a benefactor, but I never could have imagined it was Mackey. I was absolutely stunned. "I thought you told me to stay away from the A∴R∴T∴?"

"I did," said Mackey with an ugly smirk. "But I was sure my words would just make you all the more curious. I've been helping you at every step. I even lent you my favorite familiar spirit to help you unravel the secrets. Dear sweet Astaroth. I hope you've gotten along well. I will need her back at some point."

"I don't even know what to say," I managed to get out with a great deal of struggle.

"That reminds me," said Mackey. "I wanted to ask you a favor."

Ah, now he was getting to the real point of his visit. I knew he wanted something from me. "Yes?"

"I don't seem to have anyone left in the A∴R∴T∴ who can keep me aware of what's going on." Mackey smiled. "Do you think you might be willing to chat like this with me every once in a while, just to let me know what everyone's doing?"

"You want me to spy on the A∴R∴T∴?" I asked in amazement.

"No, no, gods no. I just like to keep track of the comings and goings."

"I don't know," I said, feeling sure I'd never do anything like that for Mackey.

"I could make it worth your while," said Mackey. He looked at me intensely. His gray eyes were fierce.

"You want to pay me?" I asked, feeling completely overwhelmed by this whole conversation.

"Certainly, if that's what it takes," he said with a chuckle.

"I'll have to think about that. I don't know if I'm even going to continue with the A∴R∴T∴."

"Well, you probably shouldn't," said Mackey very seriously. "They really are a terrible bunch. But if you do stay with the A∴R∴T∴ I'd love it if you'd keep me up to date."

"I'll let you know," I said, hoping that would be the end of it.

"Oh good," said Mackey. "I'm so glad that we're friends."

With that, Mackey said goodbye and departed. As soon as he walked out the door, I sincerely hoped it was the last time that I'd ever see him. But I felt sure that it wasn't. Adin Stone had clearly underestimated Paul Mackey. Whether or not Mackey was a great magical adept was still very doubtful, but he was certainly a very capable manipulator, trying to maintain a well-developed information network.

As soon as my shift at the store ended, I hurried home as fast as possible. The moment I walked in my door I rushed to the front closet and threw open the door. There it was, still sitting in the back of the closet just where I'd thrown it. The envelope with the talisman hadn't moved an inch. Adin and I hadn't gotten rid of it at all. The whole experience was just another dream. How many of my experiences in the last few weeks had just been dreams? I really wondered if this magical world would ever make any sense to me.

Printed in the United States
113855LV00005B/212/A

9 780615 156835